THE TRAGEDY OF OLI RICKER

RICKER

THE RICKER DUOLOGY
BOOK ONE

PHILLIP SNYDER

LIVING TOME
PUBLISHING

Book Cover by EAH Creative

1st print edition, second printing 2025

ISBN: 979-8999559821

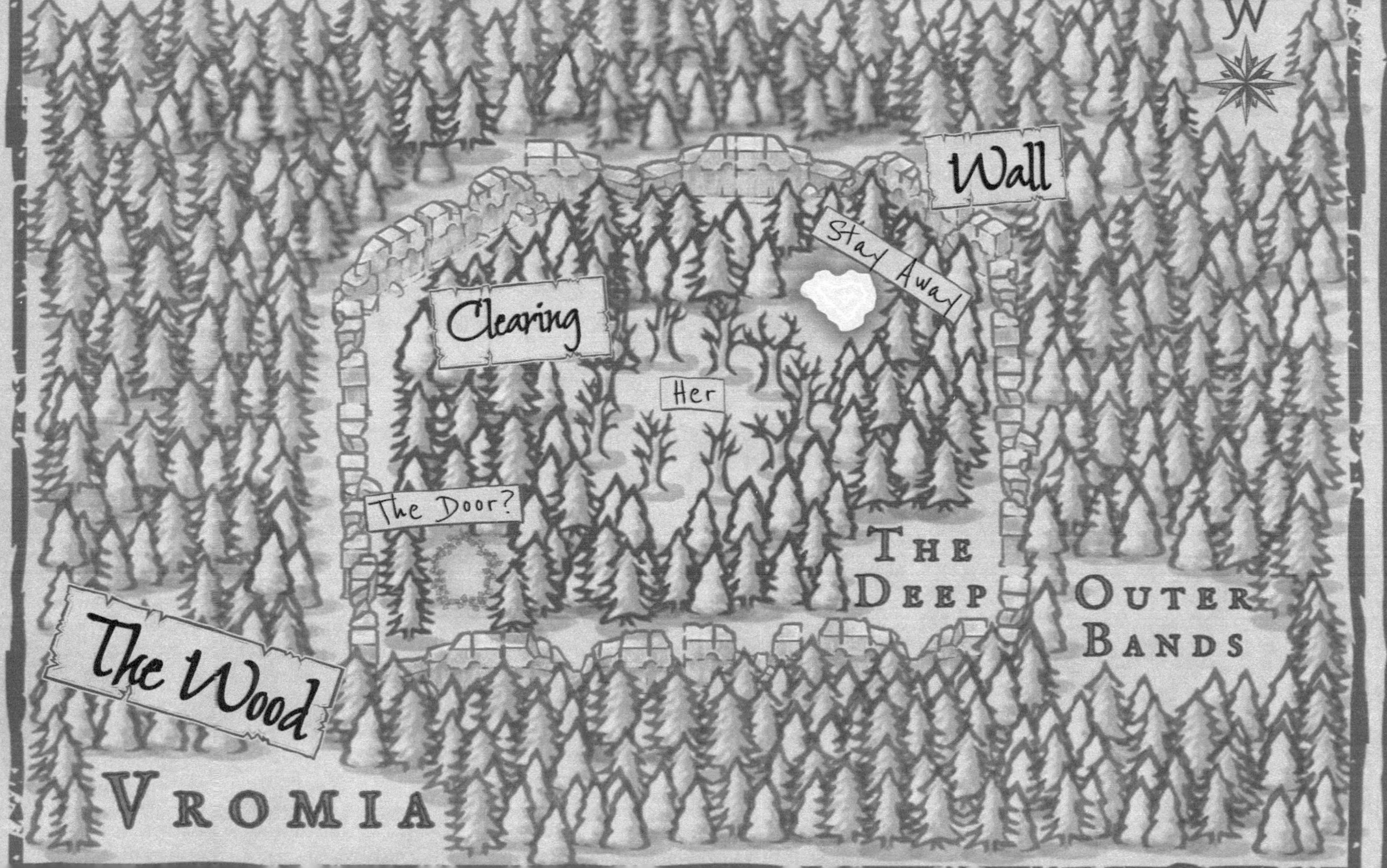
W
Wall
Stay Away
Clearing
Her
The Door?
The Deep
Outer Bands
The Wood
Vromia

To all those whose imaginations have yet to be baptized, may your journey be quickened.

PROLOGUE

THE SISTER

L ayla Ricker chewed her lower lip and prayed her father wasn't dead. Barefoot, she bounced on her toes as dying grass scratched at her calves, her fingers twisting strands of her hair until they knotted like thread in a broken spindle. Spanning the horizon in each direction was a wall of trees, leaves shivering in the bitter wind. Thunder rolled along in the distance and goosebumps ran up Layla's arm. Like a blanket, she wrapped her arms about herself to fend off the cold and fear.

It should be too late in fall for storms.

She hated it here, on the Wood's edge. The sight of the forest made her stomach clench in dread. Maybe it was the knotty trunks, or the way all the shadows beneath the canopy looked like knives, but whatever it was, Layla stayed at least a dozen leaps away from the treeline and muttered more prayers, this time grudgingly including Oli, her brother.

Oli and their father had been gone into the Wood longer than ever before, having left Watchful the morning of the previous day. Right now, the sky was full of darkening clouds, but Layla thought it might be a bit past midday. That meant it had been a full day, a night, and a half a day again since they'd left. Pa had never been in the Wood all night long before. In fact, as far as Layla knew, no one else had either. Mama said it was "too dangerous and too stupid" to do. But yesterday, Pa had marched off with Oli and a dozen other hunters and their dogs, the largest pack hunt anyone had ever seen. He wasn't planning on coming back until breakfast the next day. Which would have been breakfast today.

They were late, and late wasn't good.

Layla turned around, trying to spend her energy somehow. The land sloped gently upward for a dozen bow shots or so: busy farmland coloring the world in yellows and browns. Eventually the gentle slope turned to a sharp cliff face, at the top of which Layla could see houses of wood and stone sitting stoically on top of the hill. If she looked at it just right, she could make it look as if the houses were rising high into the sky. Her house was one of them, and Layla squinted to see if she could spot Mama through the kitchen window. Mama would be watching the forest's edge too. She was too stubborn to come down here, but Layla knew she'd be watching all the same. She always grew more stubborn when she was worried.

And the two of them wouldn't be the only ones watching. The whole town would have their eye on the treeline, though it surprised Layla she was the only one watching this close. She knew the Wood was scary and all, but shouldn't there be other daughters, other mamas, all waiting around for them to come back? There were plenty of fieldhands who kept stopping, leaning on their tools and wagging fingers towards the Wood while they talked to one another. But that was about it.

A twig snapped, and Layla spun back around, her breath quickening as she searched the trees. She didn't know if they'd emerge from here *exactly*, but Pa said she had good instincts, so Layla figured she'd guess right. She swallowed spit that pooled beneath her tongue. Why did her throat feel dry if her mouth kept making so much spit?

"C'mon," she mumbled.

Nothing happened.

The breeze kept blowing, making her legs shiver beneath her dress. She could smell the rain coming now, could feel pressure on her temples that told her it was going to be a bad one. Not just rain, but "one hell of a damnable storm", as Pa would say. But it was too late in the season for storms.

"C'mon," Layla said again, her words hardly audible. Her nose began to run with snot, and she wiped it with the back of her hand. "Come back."

Another twig snapped.

Layla turned to the right, certain now that's where the noise had come from. She stepped towards the sound and heard another snapping, then the rustling of tree branches. She ran towards the sound, getting closer to the Wood than she'd like, but for a moment she didn't care. There was sound, *life*, from within the Wood. And nothing, *nothing*, ever emerged from the Wood except the hunters that went inside.

Which meant that if she was hearing a noise—

A blur of motion burst from behind a large patch of brush beneath a white oak. It was all flailing limbs and flying cloak, but Layla could recognize her older brother anywhere. Fifteen and gangly, with curly black hair to match her own, though with skin a few shades darker, like Mama's. He tore from the Wood's edge with a cry, falling in a rolling heap to the grass, gasping for breath as Layla ran over.

"Oy! Ya all right?" It was stupid to ask. Before she saw it, Layla could smell the blood, the sweat, the piss. Even she knew those smells all mixed together was bad. Oli lay on his back, chest arching as he tried to suck in breath. His cloak was torn, his chest and legs and face all splattered with blood, and his bow was missing.

And he was alone.

Layla stood there, frozen as Oli writhed for another moment, gulping air as if he'd been drowning. And then, when air had filled his lungs, his eyes burst open to the sky above and he screamed.

And Layla screamed too.

It wasn't long until a crowd formed around Oli and Layla, a mass of bodies squirming like maggots on the outer edges of Layla's tear-blurred vision. They were the field hands, mostly, but others were coming now too, and Layla prayed Mama would be one of them. Oli thrashed about, crying out with wide eyes that couldn't seem to see her. Layla fell to her knees, close enough she could feel the warmth of his skin. But what could she do? Her hands opened, closed, opened again. Helpless to do anything but watch and fear and cry.

"Out of my way!" It wasn't Mama's voice, but an old man's, cackly with age and impatience. "Move. Now!"

Evanvalt was a priest of the Order of *Deōs*, with skin which may have once been light and fair but had grown leathery and spotted from years beneath the sun. He smelled so strongly of garlic and sweat that Layla involuntarily leaned away as he burst through the crowd and knelt frantically on the other side of Oli.

"Get back!" Oli cried, worming himself away from the priest and into Layla, staining her dress with blood.

"What happened?" Evanvalt said, his hands reaching forward and probing along Oli's head and chest before Oli could protest further, his knobby fingers coming away red.

Layla knew she should stop crying and tell Evanvalt whatever would help him save her brother, but tears only flowed faster from her eyes, her chest stuttering as she tried to catch her breath.

"Poor lad came skitterin' outta there," a woman said, finger pointing toward the Wood. "Been manic ever since. Ain't much else to tell."

Evanvalt grunted, and wispy strands of white hair fell around his ears. He muttered to himself, eyes half closed, "*Erkooda, feelia, ambalia . . . Yeolasi*. This is bad."

Bad. The word thudded in Layla's mind, and every time she sucked in a desperate breath between tears she could hear it repeated over and over again.

"Get back," Oli said again, but it was weak, and Evanvalt paid no heed.

Layla was vaguely aware of the world shifting around her, people squawking and moving. But it was all she could do to stay upright, the fingers of her hands entangled in her brother's hair, though she wasn't sure when that had happened.

"Oliver!" *Mama.* Layla opened her eyes and watched as her mother flung herself on the ground above Oli's head, tears matching Layla's own flowing over her cheeks. But her eyes were firm, fixed on Oli even through the tears.

"Oliver, what happened? Where's your father?"

Oli screamed. It was loud and bloodcurdling, his back arching as if the very question had brought him unfathomable pain.

"What happened, Priest?" Her voice demanded answers of the priest, but her eyes stayed fixed on her son.

"Your husband happened," Evanvalt growled. "He got the *Stražar* riled up and—"

"To my son!" Mama snapped, looking up and eyes flashing dangerously at the priest for a heartbeat before turning back to Oli.

Evanvalt shook his head. "Many things, Orelda. Bear claws are the worst of it, I think. But his mind has been rattled too, and the vines have leached his blood . . ."

"Can you . . ." Mama stopped, biting her lip hard enough to draw her own blood. Oli grabbed her wrist, pulling her downward toward him. She put her forehead to his, her tears falling into Oli's eyes, the blood from her lip falling into his hair.

Can you save him? That's what Mama wanted to ask. It's what Layla wanted to ask. But Layla couldn't say the words, couldn't stop crying long enough to catch her breath.

Evanvalt looked at Layla, his eyes twin black dots holding her dirty reflection. Those eyes had always made Layla want to squirm, to crawl inside of herself. They were the eyes of a priest: holy and sacred, pronouncing judgment every time they fell on her.

"I can save his body," Evanvalt said, speaking to Layla as if she'd asked the question. "But Deōs alone can save the mind."

Thunder rolled and Oli screamed again, his breath billowing out with such force that Mama's hair rustled with it.

"Demons," someone said.

"Not *Viemones*," Evanvalt said, standing. "Thanks be to the Maker, no Viemones. I'll stabilize him here, but we'll need to get him indoors soon. You," he pointed at a thickset man with soil-stained trousers. "Fetch a long blanket and bring it here. Everyone else, back away. I need room."

Layla hadn't thought he'd meant *her*, but Mama scooped her up and dragged her backward along the grass. "Let 'im work," she said into Layla's ear. "Only the Maker can save 'im now."

Evanvalt stood above Oli and breathed in deep, his hands moving to his sides like tools at the ready. Below him, Oli jerked about on the ground, though Layla wasn't sure if it was in pain or horror. A fresh wind of energy surged through him and his screams roared so loud Layla wanted to hold her fists to her ears, but she clung to her mother instead. And then, slowly, words rolled from the priest's mouth as his hands rose upward, fingers moving in complex patterns in the air above Oli. "*Elmes itkavo Deōs dioforce Nema elmes mi en vroma . . .*"

It began to rain. A pitter-patter of icy drops, like a hundred little warning bells. A few of the watchers scattered then, yet most stayed. Layla and Mama didn't move, their eyes locked on Oli. Evanvalt never faltered, just continued to pour out words whose meaning Layla couldn't fathom. The rain picked up, becoming a steady sheet of water blanketing them, but unable to smother the priest's chant.

Oli wasn't screaming anymore, and he wasn't writhing about either. He looked like he'd fallen asleep, his chest rising and falling, eyes closed and mouth open to the rain. Evanvalt kept going, fingers dancing as if he sewed a complicated stitch to mend a bad tear in a tunic sleeve. The priest kept his eyes closed, but Layla could see them twitch when he said certain words, as if this holy power caused him pain.

The rain came sideways now, and Layla shivered beneath the onslaught when a shadow moved across her, bringing with it the scent of death strong enough to cover the smell of garlic and holiness. She looked up to see Anej standing beside her, one hand stroking his long red beard and the other holding the bowl of a pipe overflowing with rainwater. He was a *velk*, which might as well just be called "a giant". Twice as large as Papa with his head as high as ceiling rafters and eyes Layla tried never to look at, the velk scared her. Mama held her tighter, but neither of them moved away, and eventually Layla turned back to Oli.

Where is Papa?

The thought snuck into Layla's mind, unbidden. She knew the answer even as her mind asked the question. How often had she been told to stay away from the Wood? Told it was dangerous, that the world inside was cursed and could kill? Every time her father had gone inside, he risked his life. And when he'd begun bringing Oli, he'd been risking his son's life as well.

Evanvalt stopped. It was sudden: one moment his arms and lips were both wagging, the next his shoulders went slack as if exhaustion had yanked them back down. Above the wind and rain, he called out, "Where's that blanket?" Men shuffled about, but no blanket materialized.

Anej stepped forward and Evanvalt gave him a sour look.

"Oy, if it's all the same to you, Priest . . ." Anej said.

Evanvalt looked to Orelda, who gave a stiff nod. "Gently, Velk," Evanvalt warned. "*Very* gently."

Anej gave a nod and placed his pipe between his lips, then knelt and scooped Oli into his arms with exaggerated caution. When he turned, Oli looked the size of a babe against the giant's chest. Mama stepped forward, hands coming up to caress her son's face.

"Priest," she said, placing her forehead against Oli's. The rain watered down the dried blood now so it ran in streams off Oli's body. "Tell me."

"He'll live," Evanvalt said, gesturing for Anej to get moving.

Mama's next breath was heavy and ragged as Anej carefully pulled away from her, starting toward the hill. "How do you know? Are you sure?"

"I've stopped the bleeding, inside and out," Evanvalt said, walking alongside the velk, his voice getting louder as the rain continued to pick up. Layla could hardly hear. "But I've told you, I can do nothing for his mind."

Orelda walked beside the priest, Layla following as if dragged by an invisible line. The rain had turned the ground to mud, and their boots *squished*, leaving deep prints with each step. Except for Anej, his boots still managed to *thud* down, splashing water and mud up to Layla's waist and leaving craters that quickly filled with rainwater.

"What do ya mean about his mind?" Mama demanded. "Don't toy with me now—tell me plainly."

The priest stayed silent for a long time as they trudged uphill, heads down against the battering rain. To Layla, it felt like they were mourning, as if this were a funeral procession happening beneath the tears of God. Lightning flashed and thunder rolled over them a handful of heartbeats later.

"His mind," Evanvalt said, hand waving in the air as if searching out the right words. "I could . . . feel its brokenness. It won't easily mend, Orelda. He'll need prayer. Peace."

"What do we do? How . . . how do we heal 'im? Tell me! The Maker . . . he *must* do something!"

"Get him into the temple," Evanvalt said, slowing his steps and turning to Mama. He ran a hand over his head, pulling back wet wisps of hair. "I'll write a letter recommending him to the abbey in Arason, if you'd like."

"He'd never—"

"Or I can work with the magistrate to apprentice him to one of the trades. Just, for the Maker's sake, Orelda, keep the boy out of that damn Wood."

PART ONE

CHAPTER
ONE

ELEVEN YEARS LATER

A shiver ran up Oli's spine as he crept along the forest floor. Orange and brown leaves rained to the ground around him, knocked free by the squirming vines above. His boots crinkled leaves and crunched small sticks, but it was his growling stomach he feared would give him away. A few paces ahead of him, his hound crouched low and silent, his reddish-brown sides gently heaving, his breath misting in the early winter air.

Although Oli couldn't see the hound's muzzle, Tuck's steady tail meant his eyes had trained on something Oli hadn't yet seen. Squinting, Oli tried to discern what had the dog on edge. His eyes scanned the crevices of rotting tree trunks and the shadows of the thick underbrush, but he saw nothing. Everything was barren, quiet. The sun was high and plenty of light illuminated the world around them, a benefit of the trees shedding their leaves in preparation for winter. And still Oli couldn't make out whatever had made Tuck's ears stand straight up.

Oli's eyes flickered back to Tuck, whose haunches slowly rose and muscles tensed.

He was about to pounce.

Trusting that Tuck's nose knew better than Oli's own eyes, Oli set his footing and lifted his yew bow, fidgeting with the arrow's fletching until he got it just right. Carefully, Oli extended his arm and pulled the bowstring back, still unsure of his target. Oli watched the forest ahead, keeping Tuck on the edge of his vision.

And then he waited.

In the stillness of the moment, the sounds of the Wood gently permeated Oli's mind. Birds chattered from above, twigs snapped in the distance, rodents rustled leaves behind him, distant howls echoed from the far northeast. It was equal parts beauty and terror to be inside something so alive.

Breathe, Oli thought, feeling a muscle in his arm twitch with the strain of holding the bow taut. He silently cursed his picky hound, who always waited until—

Tuck sprung forward, barking and yapping as his paws slipped on loose soil and fallen leaves. But in a blink his paws found purchase and then his barks were echoing off tree boughs as he raced towards a hollow stump twenty paces away. He became a blur, a furious storm of fur and teeth and spittle.

Oli didn't try to think. If he had, then this moment, and his food, would be gone for good. His body simply reacted, years of memory tweaking his movements based on the still images his mind collected with every pound of his heart.

Something with grayish fur moved to the right of the stump and Oli's arms jerked toward it, letting the arrow loose. Relief flooded his muscles, and he released the breath he'd been holding. Even before Tuck's barking quieted, Oli knew he had gotten whatever it was. He could *feel* the arrow hitting its mark, as if part of his soul had gone with it. In the end, he wasn't surprised when Tuck brought back a plump rabbit with an arrow sticking out of its red-stained fur.

"Good boy," Oli said, keeping his voice quiet as he scratched behind the hound's ear. Then he repeated his words, but this time in a language Tuck understood, *"Dolbrye."*

Tuck panted, tongue lolling from his saliva drenched mouth, and watched as Oli removed the arrow and placed the dead rabbit in the empty leather sack on his hip. Blood had dripped on the ground at his feet and gently soaked into the soil until it had disappeared, gone as if it had never existed. An ever-present reminder that the Wood was not his friend. It was a maw, attempting to suck in all life.

Oli led Tuck away a dozen paces from where they'd been standing, sending the brown vines above retreating to the perch they'd been descending from. Oli shivered again, twisting about, checking all around him. If he didn't keep moving, then the Wood would find a way to trap him. It was as much a hunter as he was.

And just as much alive, too.

"This ain't enough, old boy," Oli said, thinking about his mother and sister as he patted the near empty bag. There had been one too many scarce meals lately, with nothing more than small shreds of rabbit in a salty broth. But he and Tuck had been stalking the Wood for hours already, and this was the largest thing they'd seen yet.

Oli's eyes drifted to the east. Deeper in the Wood there would be more game and bigger animals. It was also as good as a death sentence to make a habit of going too far. Might as well pick a fight with the magistrate and his men, at least their spear points would make for a less painful end. Oli sighed, then gave the dog a gentle nudge west, doing his best to keep up as Tuck bounded away.

Tensing his voice, Oli called out to Tuck, *"Diomok."*

It was a command, from the Language of the Wild, the language passed down from one Stražar to another, generation after generation. It meant, *home.*

The village of Watchful sat upon a large hill a few good bow shots from the treeline of the Wood. The hill gently rose up on its south-eastern edge, a winding dirt road like a muddy vein of life running through to the top where three massive homes stood tall, guardians of the township catching the light of the setting sun. The three towering mansions on top stood more tall than wide, made of clean-cut stone darkened with age and covered with vines which wrapped themselves around doorways and windowsills. Vines that didn't try to strangle people of their own accord. Normal vines, Oli supposed. The other three sides of the hill were rocky, with the north-western side being a sheer cliff so tall an arrow shot from below may not have been able to reach the top. Below the hilltop mansions stood modest buildings made of wood and looking far more weathered, though they had to be half as old. Smoke rose from the chimneys: gray swirls rising above the homes like incense, while the fires within fought off the dry cold. Oli cupped his hands to his mouth, letting the warmth of his breath bring color back into his palms. He almost longed to be back among the trees where the wind didn't pierce his skin so easily.

Almost.

Oli made his way south through wheat and potato farmland, eyeing the fieldhands as he went. More than once, he had "grazed" the edges of the field, and he may find himself doing that again this year. But his mother abhorred stealing more than starving, and so Oli kept on without stopping. They occasionally passed alongside thick fences looking as if they intended to keep out an invading army, behind which Oli and Tuck could hear the baying of sheep and bleating of goats, loud and pathetic. Each of the animals would be tied up and penned, their lives spent caged up in the shadow of the Wood and its Call.

Once, Tuck would've run about and barked at the fence and bothered the fieldhands. Now, many years into his life, he puttered alongside Oli, tongue lolling and tail wagging. Even as long as he'd been around though, Tuck still drew glances from everyone within eyeshot. He was the only free animal in all Watchful proper, every-thing else had been caged up and behind walls to keep them from bolting off into the Wood. The Woodsmen, traditionally called the

Stražar, bred the hounds to resist the Call. But Oli was the only woodsman who still lived in town. The rest were hermits, coming into town to either trade or drink. That made Tuck an oddity, the only four-legged creature running about freely for miles at least.

Oli made his way to a lone building east of the Russett's barn where, for most of the year, it was downwind from the rest of town. Modest, though sturdily built, the home of the tanner was something of a mystery to the eyes. It was a building that, when seen from a distance, appeared *off*. The doors felt wrong in proportion to the roofline, the windows too long, too thin. It wasn't until someone got close to those double-sized doors and windows that they'd realize this home was out of scale, built for a velk.

No smoke rose from the chimney, nor was there movement from inside the open windows. Instead, all the life was outside on the grassy lawn. Animal skins hung on drying racks, a low fire slowly dried meat into jerky, and animal bones lay piled in a bucket nearby. There, standing upon a patch of dirt, something like a man stood—if you took a man and spread him out twice as wide and nearly twice as high. Anej was a velk, a giant from the mountains in the east, beyond the Wood. His arms were as thick as felled trees, and his back wide enough to shoulder a boulder. Wherever he stepped his boots left an impression as large as one of Oli's own strides.

"And there ya are," Anej's gruff voice called out to Oli, his knife working deftly to cut through a deer's hide. His hands and wrists were soaked in deep red blood that complimented the massive mane of orange-red hair covering his head and face. The velk had tamed his beard into a braid so large Oli could've used it as a blanket, but the hair down his neck flew about freely in the wind.

"Oy," Oli called back. Tuck dashed forward, yipping and panting around Anej, passing along his own greeting.

"Bring something in, have you?" Anej said, eyes flashing to the sack over Oli's shoulder. "I've got jerky for you to take as well. Fresh cuts too."

Oli gave Anej space as he worked, dropping his leather bag on a scarlet stained table, then looked over to meet Anej's sidelong glance. The giant's eyes were a story of themselves, with one a deep and unnatural blue, while the other looked . . . broken: a shattered black iris on the otherwise white eye like splattered ink on a canvas. And yet, despite logic, the velk could see well from either of his eyes, as if he were unaware he should be half-blind.

"Aye, I've brought in a little game. Nothing like that beauty there though. Who bagged it?" Oli said, eyeing the doe Anej worked on and not failing to be impressed at the deftness of the velk's hands. It wasn't natural, the way the giant moved more nimbly than Oli despite having hands twice the size.

"Don't ask questions you already know the answer to. It ain't pleasant for either of us," Anej said, carefully peeling back the pelt from the muscle and bone.

"Don't be like that," Oli said. "Come on, out with it."

Anej shrugged, not pausing his work. "Larz brought it in this morning. Only now gettin' to it though."

"I don't believe it," Oli shook his head. "That incompetent oaf didn't bag no beast like that, ain't no way. He couldn't stick an arrow into a stump at five paces."

"Told you not to ask."

Oli snorted. "Well, next time lie to me."

There weren't many like Oli and Larz any longer. They were the Stražar, and they had become a dying breed. Some of the old tales, of the kind everyone still shared and no one believed, tell of a time in which everyone who lived in Watchful walked the forest floor, knew the Language of the Wild, and heard the Call of the Wood. Now though, there were less than a dozen of the hunters left, and those were fading fast. Most, like Oli, kept to the outskirts of the Wood where the game was scarce but the terrors were fewer.

Only there ain't game like this in the outskirts, Oli thought, eyeing the doe and imagining the pounds of jerky that would come from it. *Not anymore, at least.* Oli walked over as Anej turned the doe about, pulling with firm but careful tugs to separate the pelt from the rest of the corpse.

"I haven't even seen something like this in the outskirts in a few months at least, not since the potato harvest this summer. Where's Larz finding these?" Oli said.

Anej stopped then, rolling his shoulders which cracked and popped. With a sigh he looked out at the Wood, his black-shattered eye moving slowly along the treeline. The view was unobstructed by the grasslands between Anej's cabin and the forest's edge, and the treeline could be seen spanning the entire horizon. "Larz says he went deeper."

Oli snorted. "So he didn't tell you where he really found her? Figures, the selfish prick."

Anej kept silent as he went back to pulling the pelt free from the rest of the doe, placing it quickly over a drying rack. Then he stepped over to a wooden bowl large enough to bathe a child and rinsed his hands free of blood.

"Don't know 'bout that," Anej said finally. "But I think there's some truth to it. He'd have to go further east if that's where the game is, aye? Beyond the Wall, I'd think."

Oli scratched his beard and looked away to avoid the giant's gaze. Anej shrugged and stepped inside his home, his boots creaking on wooden floorboards so loudly it almost drowned out the sound of Tuck sloshing water from a bowl Anej kept beneath one of the tables for him.

Oli tried not to think about what Anej had said, about Larz going further east. His imagination betrayed him though, and he couldn't help but see that dreaded wall in his mind, beyond which lay both horrors and food. The Wall was the barrier separating a dangerous world from a truly terrifying one. It had been over eleven years since Oli had seen it last, a blur of stone as he fled the Wood, leaving his father and a dozen others behind.

His own fault, Oli thought, his eyes having drifted off to the distant treeline. *He got his own self killed.*

From here, where the hill began to rise, Oli could see over the nearer trees. He thought he could see where the treetops turned from brown to green, though his mind might have been playing tricks on him. Beyond the Wall, the Wood did not change with the seasons. All year round the leaves were green, the air warm. But whatever dark magic kept the world unchanged also twisted the beasts. They grew bigger there, thicker of fat and muscle. Aggressive. Hungry.

Anej reappeared a moment later, a small bundle of jerky wrapped tight with twine in his hand. "Here's your portion from the last haul. It ain't bad but . . ." Anej trailed off.

"But," Oli said, taking the offered bundle. "It's not enough."

Anej shrugged. "Might be best if you brought back somethin' like her." He gestured to the doe's pelt, stretched out to dry. "Like as not, you may best have a word with Larz, eh?" The velk looked upward, bushy eyebrows arching. Then he sniffed in the air. "I'd gamble on a heavy and long winter if I were you, Woodsman. And you've a few mouths to feed, so you'll need more than a brace of hares if you want enough pelts to trade and meat to eat. We'll have merchants any week now, with stores enough to see you through."

"Aye, if I have enough to sell that is," Oli said, shifting about uncomfortably. He tread this same line of thinking day after day. "And if I do go into the Deep, and if some horror in there takes me and gives my blood over to the soil, then who'll feed my sister and ma?"

"Best not to die then, I'd think."

CHAPTER
TWO

L éonie Baudelaire, Princess of Trevelar, stood upon the roadside with her hands firmly on her hips. A dozen curses threatened to erupt from her tongue, but they remained held back by a lifetime of tutoring in the brutal arts of courtly etiquette. And so she settled on nothing more than a scowl.

Her carriage wheel had broken.

A solid wood spoke had somehow snapped in half, making this the twelfth delay on a long and cursed journey. All about her a whirl of attendees flittered like mosquitoes: maids trying to make her comfortable, guards setting up a perimeter around the caravan, and a dozen others aimlessly looking at the broken wheel and discussing at length what to do about it.

"M'lady," a voice said from beside Léonie. "A word?"

Léonie turned at the sound of Amandine's voice, giving the aging courtier a glare which would have withered a lesser woman.

"Speak," Léonie snapped.

Amandine's perpetual frown deepened, and Léonie wondered if her tutor would give her a tongue lashing then and there, but mercifully Amandine simply raised her chin and said primly in her thick, courtly accent, "Night is coming upon us, I think. This . . ." she waved at the wagon and the gaggle of people all about, " . . . situation will not be solved before dark. As head of this expedition, you may be wise to give orders for the servants to set up our camp."

Léonie nearly growled. Through gritted teeth she said, "We are hardly an afternoon's ride away from *Spectare*. We are this close, no?" Léonie held up two fingers so tightly together the slight tremor in her hand made them touch.

Amandine showed no reaction. Even after weeks of hard travel, the woman remained as calm and poised as if standing in the ballroom of a galleria. Her lightly lined face had not aged a day, though Léonie was certain this trip had robbed herself of whatever youth she had possessed before they began.

It wasn't fair.

Amandine stared at Léonie, her expression both chiding the princess and yet communicating a profound respect. Respect paid, Léonie knew, to her title and not herself.

"Bah!" Léonie threw up her hands and turned away from her broken carriage and the insufferable woman. She needed room to breathe, room to *think*. There was precious little space in her life on even the best of days, but traveling made it worse. Even as she walked away, guards flanked her on every side: four ever-present walls made of man and steel. They had broken down near the top of a small hill, with plenty of sightlines and not a tree or bush for miles. She doubted any assassins or enemies lurked about, and yet her guards suffocated her with their presence nonetheless.

She would have preferred her enemy right in front of her, sword in hand, rather than a thousand trifles pestering and nagging her unto death. *Our kingdom burns and we are plagued by broken carriages.*

The grassy meadow on the hilltop stood knee high and alive with little insects and wildflowers. Perhaps *too many* little insects. The pests appeared to be everywhere, and Léonie suspected she knew why. It had been miles since she had seen a bird in the sky or any critter scurry along the ground. And where the predators were vacant the prey flourished. Over the last day of travel it had become an impulse for Léonie to see what was missing from the world, which appeared to be anything that flew in the air or scurried along the ground, and was larger than a mud beetle. It confirmed her suspicions, justified her mission, and gave her a glimmer of hope. Though, it did also give her pause regarding the caravan's own horses. What would happen to them?

"M'lady," a gruff voice said from behind.

Léonie startled, not realizing how lost in her thoughts she was, or how far she had walked. She twisted about, realizing she had gone two hundred paces from the rest of the caravan and had begun climbing the next hill. A long trail of wagons, carriages, and horse-mounted troops stretched out before her, and from their direction marched Captain Thibault. The perimeter of guards parted to let him pass. As always, the captain's hand rested on his sword pommel. He looked every part the future general as he approached her: his beard neatly trimmed and his eyes focused. Hardly in his mid-thirties, the Court rumored him to be quite the rising star.

"Yes?" Léonie said, rolling her shoulders back and lifting her chin. It was all she could do to appear regal.

"If I may, I thought I would offer to escort m'lady for a time. I think it prudent to discuss the nature of our plans for the evening." He bowed as he spoke, his chainmail clinking.

"Our plans are to get ourselves to the town of *Spectare* and within walking distance of *Vromia* as soon as possible. That is something we could accomplish tonight, no?"

The captain met her eyes, his dark brows furrowing on his pale face. "M'lady, it is perhaps more . . . prudent for us to establish camp before nightfall. Our animals are skittish and your carriage—"

"Leave it." Léonie snapped.

"M'lady?"

Léonie stepped toward the captain, her accent thickening as her anger rose. "You remember why we are on this journey, no?"

"Of course, Your Highness, I merely—"

"And you remember that my lands are ravaged and my people are *dying*, no?"

"Yes, Your Highness, I—"

"Then you shall have no qualms about leaving the carriage where it lies. It means nothing to me, and it should mean nothing to you. Understand?"

Thibault looked more than a little annoyed, but he breathed in deep and kept his calm. "M'lady, it is not only the carriage. Night is not the safest time for our caravan to travel. There are Yelmes about. Our rangers spotted them again, some leagues west of here. If we weren't certain before, we can be now: they follow us."

Léonie turned her back to the captain, her eyes squinting in the direction of the treeline they had escaped that morning. "Dark Ones? On our trails this far from Turris Regis?"

"Yes, Your Highness. If we break for camp we can set up a perimeter and—"

"Get us to *Spectare* as quickly as you can, Captain, and we shall have a far better position to defend ourselves."

The captain's mouth twitched, but he gave a curt nod. "I'll have your carriage emptied and left beside the road, m'lady."

Léonie waved a hand dismissively. "Ensure my books are not left, Captain, nor my sword. I shall have more need of those than of my wagon, I am sure."

"Yes, m'lady." With a bow, the captain strode off back toward the caravan, calling out orders as he did.

Léonie sighed. They had brought twenty wagons and carriages, dozens of soldiers, cooks, maids, and servants . . . for what? She cursed herself for having let Amandine come along. The woman understood nothing about travel for war, for urgency.

Father needs a weapon. It was a thought Léonie had had a thousand times over. *He needs a weapon and I shall deliver it even if I have to cross Yeolasi's river. But he needs it* now.

Léonie put her hands back on her hips and looked up towards the darkening sky, her imagination conjuring an image of the temple back home. There would be parishioners there, lighting incense and praying beneath the watchful eyes of the priests. Prayers and incense would be ever-present in the temple now, a never ceasing parade of the weak and frightened living in the shadow of the end of the world.

"Tell me," she said curtly to the clouds, "Whose side are you on?"

The clouds returned no answer. After a moment, she trudged back towards the others, wondering if Deōs still heard prayers.

CHAPTER

THREE

As the sun made its way down toward the horizon, Oli and Tuck stalked up the dusty lane in Watchful proper. Oli's mind whirled like the dust storms of summer, his dirt-stained fingers fidgeting with the bag of dried meat. The old velk was right, and Oli knew it. He didn't have enough pelts and meat stored up for the winter, and things were already scarce. If he didn't do something soon, there wouldn't be enough to go around when the snow began.

People passed by, trying not to trip over Tuck who dashed about through the street, narrowly avoiding more than one hastily thrown kick. Oli couldn't say how many people lived in Watchful exactly, but perhaps a hundred and a half, maybe two. It was a busy place with folks running around and making a commotion about this or that. To Oli, it formed a comfortable sort of loud. All around him, the people he'd known his whole life did what they'd done for as long as anyone could remember. Their hands created the thrumming sounds of *doing*: milk was turned to cheese, holes in boots and skirts were mended, wood was carved, bread was baked, iron was beaten and shaped, all in an interconnected web of noise, sights, and smells.

It was all familiar, including the side-eyed stares thrown Oli's

way. Most didn't take too well to the Stražar or their hounds. The
Call drew all the animals into the Wood, which meant few souls born
and raised in Watchful had seen any beasts, wild or domesticated.
About the only way to see something with four legs was to work one
of the ranches. But the cattle there became so crazed, living under
the sound of the Call, that they were dangerous in the extreme. The
sounds of their frantic bleating and mooing were like the cries of
children in the night, and if the breeze blew westward to carry the
noise up the hill, there'd be a whole host of restless sleepers.

So most treated Oli and Tuck with a tolerated suspicion.
Tolerated because traders came yearly for, above all, the pelts from
the Wood. They were, Oli was told, finer than anything else the
traders could get their hands on throughout Trevelar. Which made
the Stražar valuable enough to keep around, even if it was at arm's
length.

Oli stopped at a small cottage with solid walls and a roof which
hadn't leaked in weeks. It also hadn't rained in weeks, so Oli's
painstaking work with pitch and shingle likely wouldn't be tested
until the first snow. The window shutters were closed and smoke
gently ascended from the chimney. Without so much as slowing his
pace, Oli pushed open the door and stepped inside as the reddish-
brown blur that was Tuck, shoved past his feet, nearly toppling him.

"Oy, gonna kill me, dog!"

"Oy," a female voice called out from inside, "Close the door won't
ya! Lettin' in a draft."

Oli kicked the door shut, then pried off his boots and socks before
he could be called out for dragging dirt and mud inside. He sighed as
his feet touched the warm floorboards, smoothed from years of
Ricker feet, and stained with a million tiny memories.

Though the outside was as plain as the homes to its left and
right, the inside of the Ricker home was a testament to Watchful's
propensity to draw to itself those who didn't belong anywhere else.
All one large room with two lofts to either side, the cottage was a
flurry of colored rugs, animal heads mounted to the walls, and

rough-hewn shelves filled with knick-knacks and totems from all about the world: not only the kingdom of Trevelar, but from the Bada Republic to the north, and Velik to the east.

At the fireplace, tending carefully to a stew smelling of vegetables and earthy herbs, was a woman twice Oli's age and from whom he took his looks, including his darker skin and lanky form.

Orelda didn't turn as she said, "And how is my favorite son today, eh?"

Oli snorted. "Midland to south, I'd say. This chill is comin' on quick, and I can't seem to nab anything bigger than a stuffed rat."

When Orelda turned, her thick braided hair bobbed above the open stew, her hand still twirling the ladle around the pot. "Aye, but look at ya. Back home, alive, and without a scratch on that beautiful face of yours. That's enough for today, Oliver."

Oli shuffled about, putting away his things and letting his body and mind settle into the patterns of home. "And tomorrow and the next day? It's not enough, and ya know it. Anej mentioned traders will be here soon. If I don't—"

"That old oaf of a giant don't know nothin'," she said, waving a hand dismissively as she turned back to the stew. "Before he stumbled on into town we did just fine, me and your father. Even in lean years, we made it. Just be cautious and stick to the Wood's edges and we'll be fine."

Oli fell into a creaky chair at the table beside the fire. From there he could see the firelight in his mother's eyes and the cracking of her dried lips. He sighed, not wanting to argue but knowing there was more to be said. Instead, he watched his mother for a moment. She was beautiful, and still of marrying age. It was a mystery she hadn't found another husband after Oli's father had died, and perhaps someone with a bit more coin, too. To Oli, it made her stronger, as if her singleness stood as an act of defiance. A way to say to Watchful, to the world, that she had power on her own. She was strong on her own.

"I might not be stayin' on the Wood's edge for long," Oli said, voice growing quiet. "There's no game, Ma. And, like it or not, you and Pa never had a winter without a deer hide or two."

His mother stayed quiet for a long time, with nothing but the small crackling of logs and Tuck's loud panting from the corner breaking up the silence. She had a way of setting her jaw, lips creasing downward, which made Oli unsure if she were ready to fight or admit the hard truth.

"Well," she said after a time, "ya ain't gotta go it alone. Before ya do somethin' rash like that, I could—"

"No."

"No?"

"Oy. *No.* Ya ain't goin' in there."

"Before you were born, your father and I—"

"You've told me, and I don't care," Oli leaned forward wiping his hand in the air as if he could swipe away her words. "Pa's judgment wasn't ever the best, or he wouldn't—" Oli cut off the words before they could go further, but he'd said enough.

Orelda's cheeks flushed and her lips drew to a line. She released a sharp breath through her nose a moment later, nostrils flaring like a boar about to charge.

Oli coughed, his own cheeks growing warm. "Ma ... I—"

"Oy, I know it. Ya didn't mean it, did ya?"

Oli sat back, biting the inside of his cheek.

"'Course ya didn't. Yet here we are, you spittin' judgment at the very man you're the spittin' image of, all the way down to how ya throw them words about."

"Ma, really, I'm sorry, I—"

"Hush."

Oli had enough sense to listen, and his shoulders slumped as he breathed out, forehead dropping into the palm of his hand. He felt too tired for the sparring. Too tired, too hungry.

"Well, we can talk about that later," Orelda said with a wave of her ladle. Drips of stew splashed along the wooden floorboards, peeking Tuck's interest. "You're stressed about money, eh? Well, your sister has been busy of late, maybe this winter each of us can do our part."

Oli perked up. "It's settled then, she'll be workin' for Mister Yigguns?"

"Don't know if it's settled yet, we'll find out soon. If the rumors be true, they'll be payin' a sight more than that pittance ol' Thatcher sees fit to have me scramble for. I swear if he mumbles one more thing 'bout 'the responsibility of good indebted folk' I'll strangle his hide myself."

"It'll end one day. Won't be long now. Just . . . what? Another winter, then—"

"Then I'll be free of that toad of a man and his beckoning. I mean, the nerve of him to be takin' advantage of a distressed widow when—"

The door opened, and a thin framed figure slid inside and kicked the door shut as both Oli and Orelda called out, "Shut the door!"

"I know it already! Can't ya give half a moment?" Oli's little sister, a woman of nineteen now, dropped the hood of her cloak and kicked off her boots, her eyes hard and her mouth turned down into a scowl. Her cheekbones were high like their mother's, but her bright brown eyes and wide ears were their father's.

Orelda kept turning the stew, her face unchanged as she saw her daughter, but Oli noticed a subtle droop in her shoulders as if she already knew what was to come.

"Well," Orelda said, turning back to the pot. "Tell us, Layla, how'd it go?"

"How'd it go?" Layla slapped a bare foot against the plank floorboards. "I'll tell ya 'how'd it go'. That slimy, no-good, dirt-eating, mud-licking, son of a roach is screwin' me over!"

"Mister Yigguns?" Oli asked, cocking his head to the side.

"What?" Layla asked, looking at him, her full head of curly hair bobbing around her face and falling into her eyes. "How stupid are ya? No, not Mister Yigguns, but that sick little Windsun Tote. He's makin' darn sure ain't no one be hirin' me, and I'm 'bout ready to get my fingers around his slimy little throat and—"

"Enough," Orelda warned, eyeing her daughter. "Won't do no good makin' no death threats 'round here."

Oli looked at his mother and raised an eyebrow, her own threats lingering in his mind.

"Well," Layla continued, "If we don't do somethin' it'll be us whose graves get dug this winter. We can't be livin' without no coin and—"

"Oh stop it, child," Orelda said, standing straight up to reach for bowls on one of the shelves. "Ain't no graves being dug this winter. We'll be fine."

"Well, from your lips to the clouds, Mama, but don't be blamin' me if I ain't sharin' your faith." Layla said, shaking her head and kneeling down to pet Tuck who'd come to her, belly up for scratches.

"And Deōs hears, I'm sure," Orelda said, scooping stew into bowls.

Oli scratched his beard, head cocked in confusion. "I don't think I'm understandin' at all. You sayin' Windsun doesn't want you working?"

"Aye, he wants to take me for a tumble in the sheets instead," Layla said in a huff.

"Layla," Orelda chided, placing steaming bowls of stew on the table.

"It's true, Mama!" Layla pulled a chair free from the table, falling into it.

"So," Oli said, the word coming out slow and long. He had a strange nagging in the back of his mind, similar to the feeling of following a game trail and waiting to be ambushed by Maker-knows-what. "Windsun don't want you to work 'cause he wants you to ah . . . well . . ."

Layla sighed, rolling her eyes looking ready to curse the Maker for having to deal with a brother so thick. "Windsun wants to *marry* me, Oli. He's asked me so many times that half the town thinks we're already rollin' 'bout in the hayloft."

Orelda tutted in frustration as she sat, but Oli kept going before she could cut in. "Windsun is Gregor's boy, eh?"

"Aye," Layla said, grabbing her spoon and greedily taking bites. "Ain't a boy no more, though."

Oli paused. The Tote family lived in the nicest of the mansions on the top of the hill, called the Warden. Gregor Tote was the Magistrate, tasked with collecting taxes and overseeing the town guard, small as it was. Around Watchful, the Totes generally had their way, and to their credit they didn't often push too far. They kept an odd sort of peace between the Hilltoppers and the rest of Watchful.

"So he's tryin' to starve ya out? Keep ya from work 'til you finally go on and marry him?"

"Aye, that's the thick of it."

"But, I mean . . . *you?*" Oli quirked an eyebrow.

Layla's eyes flicked with flame that was, probably, a reflection of the fire light. Her reddened cheeks weren't a trick of light though. She leaned forward, jabbing a finger at her chest. "Aye, *me*. Ya think that's so crazy, Oliver Ricker? Do ya? I ain't the only one here who sees it, eh? Just 'cause you off frolickin' in your fancy forest out there dancin' with wolves or whatever don't mean your sister ain't growin' on up and turnin' them boys' heads and—"

"Woah, now," Oli said, but Layla only grew louder.

"Some of them boys now wanna tie the ole' knot, but—"

"All I was tryin' to—"

"Enough," Orelda wielded her spoon like a spear, pointing its stew laden tip at each of her children. Her voice was sharp, her eyes sharper, and both Oli and Layla closed their mouths. Orelda sighed a moment later, leaning back and dabbing the sides of her mouth with a small cloth. "Layla's probably right. Windsun got his eyes on your sister a few months back and ain't lettin' it go. Even come knockin' round here more than once. He knows things are tight, Oli. Probably thinks if your sister can't work she'll say 'yes' to his fancies. The Totes ain't hurtin' for no coin, that's for sure."

"He's treatin' me like a backroom whore," Layla said, and Oli thought he caught as much shame as anger in her last word.

"Well, I'll be . . ." Oli said, leaning back and running a hand through his hair. "Didn't think none of those Hilltoppers would think twice 'bout one of us. Seems . . . well . . ."

Orelda shrugged. "Windsun's the youngest of the Tote boys. His brothers married respectable types already, and two even left Watchful to do it. I don't think nobody's got their eyes on Windsun much. He can probably be with whoever he chooses, I think."

"And he wants what he wants," Layla said. "Even if he got me, which he *won't*, then he'd probably drop me like a gnawed bone when he was done. I ain't no fool, there's no weddin' at the end of whatever he wants, not really. And I ain't the first one he'd done this to either. Same story with Priss down the way. Maybelle too. Promises, promises, promises, then he's bored and moved on."

At the word "bone" Tuck whimpered a bit, and Oli grabbed a bit of meat from the stew and dropped it on the ground for him. "And there ain't no work in the fields?" he asked.

Layla shrugged. "I'll ask again, but there's already too many workers and not enough harvest. And before anyone asks, I've been askin' about work up and down the hill. Ain't much about, and Windsun has put a word about town, and ain't nobody wanting to pick no fight with the magistrate, especially before winter."

Oli nodded again, his mind racing as he leaned forward and began to slowly eat his stew. Inside, emotions stirred up in him, but he kept his expression flat. He conjured up an image of Windsun in his mind, trying to remember the last time he'd seen him. It had been awhile, Oli was spending more and more time in the Wood, and less around town. Quietly, though, he promised himself he'd make time to find Windsun soon enough.

"Oy," Orelda snapped, hand gently slapping Oli's own. "*No.*"

"What?" Oli said, leaning back.

"You keep your fists to yourself, Oliver. I see what your mind is thinkin' and you can't fix this problem by breakin' a nose. We'll wait it out. Windsun will give up soon enough, I'm sure."

Oli spread his arms out to the side. "Oy, I wouldn't think of it, Ma."

Layla snorted. "Well, either you were thinkin' 'bout knocking Windsun flat, or you were thinkin' 'bout puttin' an arrow through his eye." She looked distant. "And ya know, I'm fine with either, if ya ask me."

"*Layla*," Orelda said, exasperated.

But Layla only shrugged.

CHAPTER

FOUR

Layla chewed her lip as she watched Oli leave, a breeze slipping into the Ricker home before the door closed. Orelda pointedly didn't watch. Even as Tuck pawed the closed door and whimpered, she kept her eyes firmly on the fire as if the burning wood had something to say.

She hated Oli leaving, which made Layla hate Oli leaving.

"I'll clean up," Layla said, rising with a sigh.

Orelda blinked and looked at her daughter. "Oy, I can do it."

Layla didn't bother to reply, just grabbed the bowls and spoons and carried them to the water bucket beside the fire. A brown and orange stained rag hung on a small hook mortared into the stones around the hearth. Layla took it, dipped it into the murky water, and began wiping off the spoons one by one. There was little stew on anything, the Ricker family having been careful to lick every drop away, but Deōs says all dishware, clothes, and even bodies were to be cleansed by water regularly. That's what the Order taught, anyway. Though, sometimes Layla wondered if the Maker cared about such things. Was it possible a divine being could consider the mundane to be holy?

She turned and asked her mother.

Orelda looked at her, one eyebrow raised. "I suppose he might. Who knows what Deōs really thinks."

"Well if it is, I'm not sure I wanna be all that holy."

"Mmm," Orelda smiled. "We should get Evanvalt to clean our dishes then. Pretty sure he thinks he's holy enough for us all."

"Let 'im," Layla said, tossing the rag back onto its hook and then leaning against the mantle near the fire. The heat felt good on her cheeks and hands, and she knew the fire wouldn't burn for too much longer. They didn't have the wood to spare to keep the flames high through the night. "Or maybe Oli should do it, eh? Wasn't he supposed to be sent off to an abbey or something?"

"Oli would have made a terrible priest."

Layla snorted. "I don't know, he's crotchety enough to be one of them."

"And what do you know of 'them'? You ain't never met one, other than Evanvalt."

"Have you met any others?"

"Oy, of course. Before Evanvalt there was Piyon who was, if you can believe it, even more ancient."

"Than Evanvalt? How?"

Orelda shrugged, the corner of her lips twitching in a faint smile. "Not sure they ever die. Just become more wrinkled."

Layla shook her head and then stepped toward the bed she shared with her mother, sitting on its edge. "And what was this Piyon like?"

Orelda thought, her finger and thumb rising to scratch at her chin the way Oli did when he was thoughtful. "Crotchety."

Layla laughed, the sound ringing itself loose from her gut. "I told ya, Oli would fit right in."

Orelda smiled. "No . . . I don't think so."

"And why not? I could see him growing into one of them wrinkly old hermits. And besides, he keeps to himself so much he'll probably stay celibate too."

"Maker, help me."

"Well then," Layla said, leaning forward. "Why wouldn't our little Oli make a good priest, eh? I could see it."

When her mother looked up, Layla saw clearly the lines around her eyes, deep with a lifelong mixture of laughter and sadness. "Oli is many things, Layla. But a priest is not one. He just isn't . . . I don't know . . . content."

"Content?"

"Piyon, Evanvalt, they're both content. They have what they have, and they're fine with it."

"Sustained off garlic and prayers."

"Whatever sustains them, they're pleased enough with it. They don't really *want* anything." Orelda gestured with her hands, casting shadows on her chest that looked eerily like claws.

"But Oli . . ." Layla began.

"Your brother wants *everything*."

"That ain't fair, Mama. I mean, he worries that any day now the whole world will be scorched like the last Epoch War, and if we don't have enough jerky sittin' in our cold box we'll all collapse into dust. But other than that, he seems fine."

"He's anything but fine."

"He's *fine*, Mama. And we'll be fine too."

Orelda stood and walked toward the bookcase near the door. She reached out a long finger, brushing the spines of each of the books in turn. "Your father wanted everything too. It's where Oli gets it. He would pour over these books, looking for . . . somethin'," she shrugged. "And when he'd thought he'd found it, he went for it with all he had."

Layla said nothing. Her mother never talked of her late husband. Sometimes it felt like she pretended the first nine years of Layla's life had never happened, as though Layla and Oli had never had a father at all.

Orelda continued. "He was . . . hungry. Never satisfied. I liked it, at first. When he came to town everyone feared him, a learned man who wanted to become a Stražar of all things." Orelda shook her head. "A Stražar . . . the Hunters of the Wood. Your father was *obsessed*. Followed them around until finally he just up and became one.

"He could read, *read!* And yet he wanted to learn the Wood." Orelda dropped her finger back to her side. "I didn't push gettin' Oli into the Temple. Maybe I should've, but he didn't want to go and your brother is thick in the head when he wants to be. And, well, those priests would've taught Oli his letters."

"Sounds wonderful," Layla said, scanning the books on the shelves. They had taunted her, tortured her, all her life. Existing so closer to her, holding secrets upon secrets, without a single living Ricker who could read them.

"Maybe, but I figured if he learned his letters and all, then eventually..."

"He'd read these books, and then find whatever Pa had."

Orelda nodded. "Then I'd lose him too. *We'd* lose him." Orelda looked down, her eyes heavy and dark. "We'd lose him to whatever mad thoughts took your father. The same obsession is there, lurking inside that boy. He's his father's son."

"Why didn't ya just get rid of the books? Ulian would probably buy 'em, or one of the Hilltoppers."

Orelda twisted a finger through the braid of her hair. "Because I'm a fool, that's why. Now I'm goin' off to bed, and you might as well too. I've a busy day tomorrow."

"Aye. I'll be off to Rossetta's in the mornin'. Hopin' she'll have work for me."

"Just keep your distance from the Wood."

"Mother, please."

"I'm just sayin'. Good practice to give reminders, I always say."

"I've never, ever, heard you utter those words."

"Nonsense," Orelda said, walking toward Layla and pulling off her dress. "Now toss me my night dress, eh? I'm freezin'."

CHAPTER
FIVE

Watchful had two taverns and neither was particularly worthy of a song. The Downwind sat nearer to the bottom of the hill and was frequented by the strange and poor. The door hung cockeyed, the thin glass windowpanes glowed with a dirty-yellow light, and the smell of sweat and beer wafted out to greet Oli as he walked toward it.

The other tavern was within spitting distance of the mansions at the top of the hill. Oli had never been inside.

He shoved the door of the Downwind open against the will of its rusty hinges, and kicked the heel of his boot against the doorframe, so as to leave a little dirt outside. The taproom should have been spacious, but tables and chairs crowded it so much that even when it was busy, the place felt dead. Oli grunted as he squeezed and shimmied himself around nicked tables and irritated field hands murmuring over half-filled mugs, trying to make his way towards the bar.

Off to the side, a healthy fire burned inside a brick hearth, but only hot enough to warm half the room. Lanterns hung from chains looped around the rafters, drifting to and fro as the breeze from the door hit them, scattering shadows over tables, card games, and dirty faces.

Familiar faces, most of them. Familiar, but not friendly. No one called Oli's name nor smiled up at him as he made his slow trod through the tavern. As usual, Oli only lowered his hood and kept moving. He might have been born in Watchful, but he was of the Wood. That fact alone bought him distance, and stories of his father didn't help either.

But Oli wasn't here for beer or games. He wanted to find Larz and see where he'd found a doe, but the aged Stražar hadn't shown yet. Oli kept moving toward the bar anyway, trying to focus on the creaking floorboard beneath his boots instead of the wave of silence following him whenever he passed crowded tables. Larz would appear eventually. He'd crave an audience, someone he could cajole into listening to his stories, as overblown as they were. There was a better chance of sky-fire raining down and wiping them all out than for Larz to miss the chance to brag about a hunt, even if his only audience hadn't the slightest idea what he went on about. No one liked the Stražar, but at least Larz gave them all something to talk about.

Oli leaned on the bartop and eyed the bartender. Ulian was an odd character, even by his own race's standards. He was average height for a *maeifa*, which meant he stood as tall as Oli's waist. Like most of his race, he was stocky, with broad shoulders and a thick gut. His head and face were mostly clean shaven, except for an exotic looking mustache hanging in braids down to his chest. On his thick nose rested a pair of spectacles, and in his hands a thick volume with a gray-green cover. He muttered as he read, elbows on the bartop. He'd had the floor behind the bar raised so he always met his human customers in the eye.

Neither his stature nor his avid reading was unique for a maeifa, though. They were a people found, more often than not, in the universities all throughout the kingdoms of La'Azurus, or so Oli had been told. What *was* odd was Ulian being *here*, not only in Watchful, but as the owner and bartender of the town's less prosperous tavern. When he'd shown up six years earlier everyone had expected him to take a job tutoring Hilltopper children with the other handful of his race living in Watchful. Instead, he'd bought this place from Ol' Tiskman for no small sum of money, and then he just hadn't left. People had grumbled at first, but when Ulian began playing about with different brews of ale, everyone grew content. Tiskman's swill had been like piss and been made only from dirtwheat, but this maeifa knew how to brew ales from fruits and potatoes that went down smooth and easy.

Oli rapped a knuckle on the bar a few handspans away from Ulian, but had no success in drawing his attention from his reading. Again Oli knocked, and still nothing. He cleared his throat, then banged on the counter and called out, "Oy, Ule!"

"Huh? Oy, I see you, Master Oli, one moment." Ulian threw up a finger and continued reading. Oli grunted and shook his head. A moment later, the book slapped closed. "Fascinating, absolutely fascinating. The impact which the meteorological conditions have on the response of fauna and flora in a region heavily influenced by maiyea is, well, fascinating."

Oli shrugged, "I'm just lookin' for ale."

Ulian's brow furrowed. "Well, of course, Master Oli. I made a fresh batch of that hiwaya-grape you like so much. Been three full moons now it's been sittin', so I broke it out this morning. Real, real, good stuff."

Oli placed a small copper chit on the bartop, the blurry visage of an old king staring back at him. He groaned inwardly as that little king disappeared into Ulian's apron pocket a moment later, swapping it for a mug of frothing ale.

"Oy," Oli said, raising the ale in thanks and fighting off sour thoughts. He told himself he wasn't drinking away one of the last chits they had, though he *was* drinking, and that *was* one of the last chits they had. He had to talk to Larz, and this was the only place Oli knew the man would show. Still, even the Downwind had standards, and no one sat for free. Besides, one chit wouldn't keep them alive through the winter. They needed more. A whole deer-hide more.

"And?" Ulian asked, leaning forward, his spectacles sliding down the bridge of his nose.

"It's good," Oli said, wiping his mouth against the back of his sleeve. The hiwaya-berries added a tang which danced in tension with the bitter hops.

"That's good. Very good." Ulian nodded in one of his absent ways that told Oli he could've said the drink tasted like dungwater and Ule wouldn't have noticed. "You know, I was reading the other night about some of the stories told of our fantastical little forest out there," Ulian waved in the general direction of the Wood. "Tales for children, mostly, but well, I wondered if I couldn't get a bit of your time, one evening. An ale on me, for a few stories of your own, eh?"

With every word Oli's face grew hot. He'd been down this road before with Ulian, and he had no intention of going again. "The Wood is there for ya. With stories enough to share if you'd like. Feel free to go to it and ask all you want."

Ulian's smile never slipped, and the light twinkle in his eye made Oli want to punch him. The bartender had a way of handling every rush of anger or emotion in the Downwind with the same, resolute, smile. It was infuriating. "Oy, I thought you'd say that, but I've been reading lately and I've come across something that may interest you. Perhaps we could trade tidbits of knowledge?"

Oli stood up straight and shook his head in frustration. "There's nothin' in them books I need, Ule. I'm sure Larz will run his mouth enough for us all, ask *him*."

"Oh, I have," Ulian said eagerly, removing his spectacles to clean them on his apron. "He's been very helpful. Still, sometimes I can't help thinking that Master Larz . . . well . . ."

"Lies?"

"I was going to say 'has an alternate understanding of truth'."

Oli snorted. "I've known Larz a long time. Rest assured, he lies. In fact, I was hopin' to find that liar here tonight. You seen him?"

"No," Ulian said. "Not this evening, but he finds his way in often. But Master Oli, I was hoping we could continue this conversation about your experiences within the confines of—"

"Well, if ya see him, let him know I'd like a word, eh?"

Oli turned and made his way towards the taproom's hearth where a pair of wooden chairs soaked up the fire's light and heat. Oli sank into one, resting the mug on his knee, and breathing out a heavy sigh. His eyes watched the dancing and crackling tongues of fire, and for a long time, he was quiet.

A little more than an hour later, Larz stalked into the Downwind. The taproom had filled out even more, and someone had even taken to playing the flute, the notes sailing along the rafters and above the drawl of banging mugs and ruckus voices. And yet, above it all, Oli made out Larz's gruff growl for beer at the bar.

Oli turned to see Larz's smile fade as Ulian whispered in his ear, pointing to Oli. Begrudgingly, the old woodsman nodded, and wound his way through a gaggle of women, tables, and a newly arrived serving boy before he found his way to the chair beside Oli's.

Larz sighed as he sat, shifted uncomfortably, then took a long pull of the pint he held in his hand.

"Oy, Ulian the Prat says you wanted to talk." Larz's voice was a deep rasp, making him sound both angry and out of breath. Though, for all Oli knew, both were true. Larz's face was a ravaged thing. His left eye, the one facing Oli, was covered with a leather patch beneath which protruded long, aged, scars. The cheeks beneath his scraggly beard were pockmarked and his nose was bulbous from too many breaks. Against all odds, this man had spent thirty winters hunting and killing within the treeline and still had his life. It should have made him a legend. Instead, he was universally despised, even amongst the few Stražar still living.

"Aye," Oli said, straightening up. "We need to talk."

Larz chuckled, his lip curling into a smile that deepened the lines of his scars. "*You* need to talk. How 'bout I listen and we'll see how this goes, eh?" Larz never turned towards Oli, only pulled his cloak in a bit tighter and sat back more relaxed. "Come on, out with it."

Oli leaned forward, keeping his voice low. "You nabbed a doe today, big one. There ain't been thick deer in the Outer Bands for near a year. Was it a fluke, or do ya know somethin' I oughta?"

Larz turned so his eye could look Oli up and down. His breath stank like rotten whisky, his fingernails black and yellow from years of fingering cheap tobacco. "I ain't never killed nothin' off no fluke, *boy*. That doe came down 'cause I *made* it. Tracked it, stalked it, downed it, just like that, see?"

"Anej says you made your way deeper in. That true? You goin' past the Wall?"

"Well, that ol' velk can't keep his trap shut, but he don't tell no tales, that's for sure. I told him true, I went deeper." He shifted, sipping from the tankard.

"Past the Wall?" Oli asked, voice strained.

Larz was silent as he leaned back and turned towards the fire. He took a long pull from his mug, then said, "Aye, past the Wall, little Ricker. And what's it to ya?" Oli sat back and cursed, but Larz continued on, "Like ya said already, ain't no real game anymore about the outskirts. The Wood . . ." Larz stopped and sighed, looking about to see if anyone sat within earshot. When he started again, his rasp of a voice was a notch quieter. "The Wood is callin' louder now, bringin' the beasts closer to its heart. Hard to say, but . . . somethin' ain't right. Don't tell me you ain't notice it too."

"The hells you mean it's callin' louder?"

Larz shook his head. "How are you a Stražar and you can't feel it? The Call is louder than a woman pushin' out a babe. Everything is running on in deeper, past the Wall."

In a way, Oli understood exactly what Larz meant, but unlike the older man, Oli hadn't felt anything shift in the Wood. The idea that Larz felt something he couldn't, made Oli's skin crawl. Assuming

Larz told the truth, anyway. But change or no change, it was impossible not to notice how barren the Outer Bands had become.

Larz leaned back and took another swig of his ale. "Still, whatever it is, it don't matter now, does it? All that matters is we best be pullin' in meat and furs in plenty before them Westerners come on in for trade or it'll be a scarce winter. So yeah, ol' Larz has been crossin' over the Wall and into the Wood proper once again. Been too long, if you ask me."

"Too long?" Oli sat forward. It took everything Oli had to keep his voice low so wandering ears wouldn't hear. "Forever ain't long enough, Larz. We'd agreed, we'd all agreed, not beyond the Wall. Not no more. Not after last time."

Larz snorted. "I ain't agreed to nothin'. And besides, it's been what? Seven winters now?"

"Eleven," Oli said, voice flat. "And you damn well know it."

"Eleven," Larz said, voice drifting. "He'd have been nearly thirty then."

Oli said nothing. He knew the "he" Larz was talking about, and Oli had no intention of going there. Oli had lost a father eleven years ago, Larz a son.

Slowly, Larz stood, swaying on his feet. He looked down and Oli could see his reflection in Larz's eye. "When your pa died he took near everyone with him. Maybe it took a few years for us to figure it out, but we ain't a group no more. We're on our own, each of us. Whatever pact we had, that's gone just like your old man, and good riddance to both."

"Goin' beyond the Wall is dangerous, Larz."

"Starvin' is too, understand? Look, I ain't got nothin' to hide or to explain. I went past the Wall, and I'll be goin' again, and if you wanna eat through the winter then you'll be goin' too." Larz turned to step away, but paused.

Oli looked up, watching the man's mouth twitch. Hate lingered behind that one eye, but Oli knew it wasn't hate for him. To Larz, Oli was the living embodiment of Roi Ricker, the man who'd convinced

Larz's son to venture off towards the Wood's heart in search of power. Instead, Larz's son had died like everyone else. Or, almost everyone else.

Oli had survived.

"Best to kill those memories," Larz said. "They'll eat ya alive, and they'll do it just as good as the beasts."

Larz walked off, leaving Oli in the chair by the fire, his body still and his eyes fixed on the flames. The old Stražar could say what he wanted, believe what he wanted. Oli knew the truth though. Memories couldn't die.

CHAPTER

SIX

L ady Amandine's carriage was both smaller and yet somehow more sophisticated than Léonie's own. On one end of the carriage, the elder woman looked solemnly out the window towards the dark horizon, her eyes standing out against her ebony skin like jade rocks. On the other end of the carriage, their knees practically touching, Léonie held up a small lantern beside a piece of parchment pinned flat onto a wooden board so she could read it one-handed in the dark.

The two of them had been this way for half an hour, the monotony only broken when Léonie occasionally asked Amandine to hold her lantern so she could switch parchments. It likely would have stayed that way, except Amandine happened to look down at her former pupil and catch a stray word on the page.

"Oh my. Léonie, what are you reading? Is that *Fae?*"

Léonie raised her eyes to meet Amandine's. "Oh, I see you still know *De Le Terre* when you see it."

Amandine tutted quietly. "Stories for the children, girl. Have I not taught you that much at least? You embarrass me."

"Was it not you who once told me children hold in their hearts more truth than all the libraries throughout Trevelar? Perhaps their stories hold something as well."

"Hmph. You take my words too far. Clearly, I did not mean for you to go trampling off in search of magical items the moment you had enough liberty to do so."

"Ah, now you will say the maiyea is also not real? That shall put you on shaky ground with your refined theology, no? Though I hear some in the Order have been moving in this direction. Or *were*, I suppose."

Amandine stayed silent for a long time. Léonie, for her part, had returned to her reading and scribbling the occasional note. When Amandine spoke again, it startled Léonie, forcing her quill across her page in an ugly streak.

"I say only that I wish magic were not real, and that more and more I believe those powers are not intended for us to meddle with."

Léonie brushed aside a strand of hair, hoping she did not smudge ink along her forehead. "Our priests meddle in magic every day, Amandine. Many of us would not still be walking this earth without their healing prowess."

"That is different," Amandine snapped. "It is not maiyea, it is prayer."

"It is semantics," Léonie said, but with a small sadness weighing down her words. "Perhaps I too wish maiyea could have stayed right where it was: in stories for children and on the lips of those we thought unwell."

"Unwell? You mean those we ridiculed, no?" Amandine said, bitterness soaking each word. "Those we called 'doom sayers' and 'heretics' now have proved to be prophets, and us fools. They were right when they said the land of Kātsracha was breaking forth. They were right when they said the boots of the Dark Ones would—" Amandine stopped speaking, her jaw tightening.

"Would 'scorch the very dirt beneath our feet', I believe." Outside the carriage wheels grated and jostled along the rock-strewn path, the metal chains and buckles hitching the horses rattled, and the muffled voices of guards could be heard. There were no bird calls though, and even the crickets were silent. Or absent. "I did not believe any of them either, not until Worchestern burned. Even then, well, it was not until I met the power with my own blade—saw the magic with my own eyes— that I believed."

Léonie's hand gently touched the scar along the inside of her left forearm: a dull gray against her pale skin, stretching from wrist to elbow. She had recovered well, thanks in large part to the priests and their "prayers". Now the wound was of no more consequence than her vanity. Well, her vanity and her nightmares. Oh, how often she had woken in the middle of the night, forehead soaked in sweat and her scar burning like a hot iron.

"Well," Amandine said after a long silence. "Perhaps meeting heresy with heresy is unwise."

Léonie laughed, though Amandine's words were not truly funny. Having this argument again, after weeks of committed travel, was ridiculous at best. She was thinking about her retort for Amandine when the carriage began to slow. "Shall we march down this path again?"

"Léonie, hear reason," Amandine's eyes searched Léonie's. "The priests *alone* have been ordained to wield power."

"You mean prayer."

"I mean *power*, in all its forms, including prayer. What you seek is not only forbidden—"

"Nothing is forbidden the crown."

"—but is also dangerous beyond all comprehension."

"Which is why we must have it *now*, before more of Trevelar falls to death and destruction. We need that which is 'dangerous'."

"We need only the mercies of the Maker who—"

"Bah," Léonie snapped, waving a hand to silence Amandine. "Where was Deōs when you were besieged within the walls of Worchestern? I would not be on this quest if he had deemed to intervene when—" Léonie's body swayed as the carriage came to a stop.

"If we stopped and yet have not arrived then it is possible I shall have Captain Thibault strung up by his—"

"*Léonie*," Amandine chided. "You are a lady."

Léonie snorted. "And yet I am still familiar with male anatomy. Are you not?"

The duchess's eyes narrowed. "More and more you distance yourself from the girl I remember."

That girl had not yet spilled blood, Léonie thought. Before she could say anything, however, three quick raps on the carriage door interrupted them. Léonie tried not to notice the way Amandine tensed at the sound, the tips of her fingers shaking as she interlocked them together. The duchess had her own scars, her own nightmares.

The knocking sounded again. Léonie leaned forward to see down from the window. The carriage stood high off the ground in the style which had become so popular, and Léonie nearly had to stick her head out the window to see the guard.

"Yes?" Léonie asked, eyeing the guard standing there so intently his mustache quivered beneath her stare.

"M'lady," he said. "We've arrived."

Arrived. Léonie let the word fill her for a long moment, moving it about in her thoughts and savoring it. She could have cried with joy. For weeks they had traveled, fleeing the capital in a frenzy after long weeks of planning and convincing and . . . she steadied herself. "Good. Have the captain take us in and find us rooms."

The guard bowed and then marched off.

As he left, Léonie leaned back, satisfaction and relief breaking through into a smile which reached her eyes. "Finally. We sleep within the walls of *Spectare* tonight."

Amandine cocked an eyebrow and frowned as the carriage began to move again. She worked hard to keep her breathing calm, controlled. A simple knock and Léonie could tell Amadine had been sent back to a dark place. "I think we shall not find walls in any settlement so far from the heart of our kingdom, Your Highness. Even beds for the night may be much to ask."

Léonie paused, thinking back to the news of the forces of Kātsracha, the Yelmes, on their trail. She had been hoping for defenses for her and her people when they arrived. Watchtowers, low walls, anything.

That is tomorrow's problem, Léonie told herself, forcing down the rising pressure in her chest. "It does not concern me," she said, feeling the untruth of those words. "If the maps are correct, then *Spectare* is but a short walk from *Vromia*. We have arrived, Lady Amandine, are you not glad for it?"

Amandine raised her chin slightly, eyes turned to the window. Darkness had settled outside, but it was easy enough to make out the small orange lights of fires burning inside meager homes. "I am not glad, m'lady. I am cautious. There is much we do not know of this place and this people. I have heard it said the people of Watchful worship the *Vromia,* offering it human sacrifice, even."

"Bah, foolish tales, I'm sure." Léonie said. The homes were becoming quickly less scattered, closer to one another. All was quiet, and Léonie wondered how late into the night it was. "What was that name you used? Is it what the commoners call this place?"

"Watchful, I believe. The peasants changed it from *Spectare* some time ago, usurping the former magistrate as well. That was eighty years ago, no? All the outlying towns and villages back then were 'throwing off their regal chains', as they say."

Léonie hardly listened now, Amandine's words fading in her mind as soon as they hit her ears. Instead, her eyes locked upon the images of homes passing by as her lips practiced the word "Watchful" soundlessly.

What is it you all watch for, I wonder.

CHAPTER
SEVEN

Oli sat on the hillside just behind his family's home. It was well into the night now, and both stars and a south-rising moon lit the sky. The clouds of the day had moved into the west, carried along by the wind. A few paces away, cradled amongst the tall autumn grass, Tuck snored, his sides rising and falling rhythmically. The night's chill raised goosebumps along Oli's arms and the back of his neck. But the world lay quiet, and so it was worth suffering the cold.

From where he sat, Oli could see the tops of the outer homes, including the wooden shingles of Anej's cabin and the long planks that sloped along the half dozen barns filled with restless cattle. Beyond those, past where the hill turned to grasslands, the treeline of the Wood loomed: a long shadow below the horizon, stretching out for miles. Beyond it, the Nevihta Mountains consumed the horizon, their snowy peaks gleaming in the moonlight.

Oli held a small needle connected to a forearm's length of black thread, carefully working to mend a tear in his cloak. It was cathartic, piercing the fabric with the needle's point then pulling it back and watching the edges squeeze tight.

"Oy," said a quiet voice, startling Oli from his thoughts and making the needle slip.

Oli muttered a curse, then looked up to see Layla, wrapped in one of their few blankets, making her way around the house towards him. She moved in near silence, hardly disturbing the moon-soaked grass.

"Oy," Oli said, turning his eyes to a now bleeding thumb.

Layla pushed aside the curls of her hair and sat beside him, looking out towards the eastern horizon. The way her forehead creased as she squinted towards the mountains reminded Oli of their father. Wonder came so naturally to her, as though she existed always on the edge of being awed.

Oli wiped his bloody thumb on the grass nearby. "It's late, eh?"

"Aye," Layla nodded. "I like it. Might be the most beautiful time, I think. Moon's startin' to dip, not a cloud up there. Best time for prayin'."

Oli snorted, looking back to the fabric as he worked the needle again.

Layla eyed him, and Oli thought she'd pick up one of her lectures, but she only shook her head. "So, I'll be off to talking with ol' Rossetta tomorrow. Gonna see if she ain't have work for me."

"Didn't think her garden needs tendin' weeks before snowfall."

"It won't." Layla shrugged. "But she knows me. Maybe she'll want help with somethin' or other. Heard she bought a whole heap of milk, probably for cheese curdlin'. Maybe she'll need help with that. Or . . . I dunno. Chopping firewood, maybe? She must need help with something, she's getting pretty old now."

"Aye, she is."

Tuck rolled over in his sleep and gave a quiet *yip*, then continued snoring. Oli paused his sewing and looked him over. "*Palmaditze chiazspiatz.*"

Layla leaned forward, looking from Oli and then to Tuck. "What does that mean? Palmo chee . . . what'd ya say?"

Oli smirked. "'*Palmaditze chiazspiatz*'. They're the words of the Wood."

"I know that, ya dignugget. I wanna know what they *mean*."

Oli kept his eyes down as he finished the last stitch. "It ain't nothin'. Just words, is all."

"Oy, just words." Layla crossed her arms and then fell back into the grass, eyes on the stars. "If Pa was around, he'd tell me."

Oli felt the words rattling out of his mouth before his thoughts could catch up. "Well, he ain't, so let it go."

For the briefest of moments, Oli saw it. A reflection of light at the corner of Layla's eye, the briefest hint of a tear, then she sat up with a sigh, turning her head so Oli couldn't see. Guilt and anger boiled and mixed in his gut, but Oli pressed his lips together as he tried to think about the torn fabric. The problem was what the problem always was: Oli's hands and mouth moved far faster than he could think. "Layla, I'm—"

She spun toward him. "I ain't askin' ya to take me into the Wood or nothin', but give me *somethin'*. Teach me the words, at least."

"Why? What do you need to know Woodspeak for?"

"I don't, I—"

"Then why? Why not leave it alone? Move on. Be glad ya ain't gotta deal with it all and just . . . just—"

"Just what? Get some borin' job pickin' vegetables or sweepin' floors?"

"That's good work, Layla. Mama's been doin' it a long time now."

Layla clicked her tongue and looked away, fingers clenched. And then, a heartbeat later, she whipped her head back around. "You and I both know where she wants to be."

Oli looked to the Wood in the distance, teeth pressing into his bottom lip, but Layla pushed on.

"But good for her, eh? Stuck inside earning a slave's wage payin' off Pa's debts. You'll have to get over the fact that maybe I ain't all that excited 'bout it. Maybe I want somethin' else."

"Fine. Do somethin' else. Just not in there," Oli jabbed a finger east. A gentle fog settled over the Wood now, making it look more and more like the forest of horrors it was.

"I told ya, I ain't talkin' 'bout that. I get it, alright? I just wanna . . . learn."

"Learn? 'Bout what."

"About *it!*" Layla shoved her hands out, pointing to the Wood. "All of it."

"*Why?* You ain't gotta worry 'bout it."

"That ain't the point, Oli, it's just—"

"Then what is the point?" Oli's voice rose right along with his frustration. "I've been in there every gods-forsaken day for, what, ten years? More? I've got so many scars that if Anej flayed me, my skin wouldn't even make a good rug. I don't sleep without nightmares, can't walk 'round without stares, and for what? Our bellies are still grumblin', ain't they? I'm doin' my best to keep you clothed, fed, and away from that place, and now ya want to *learn* about it?"

Layla flinched. Something about the way her jaw clenched or her chin dropped, made Oli warm with satisfaction.

"Pa loved it," Layla said. "The Wood, I mean."

Oli's shoulders slumped and any satisfaction he'd felt seeped away like water on cracked earth. Even finishing up the stitch, which usually gave him a quiet sense of joy, felt dull and pointless. Silence settled between the siblings. No sound emanated from the house behind them, which meant their mother was either asleep or listening. Probably listening.

"Aye," Oli said after a long moment. "Pa loved it."

"That's about all I know 'bout him, you know. Can't remember much else."

Oli closed his eyes, and forced down a groan.

Layla leaned forward, looking to the distant Wood. "I'm gonna learn 'bout it, Oli. With or without ya. I ain't tryin' to be stubborn, but it's about the only way I'm gonna learn 'bout him."

Oli looked up to the sky and cursed. He was too tired for this. If his father were here, Layla wouldn't be crying, wouldn't feel . . . Oli didn't know exactly what she felt. Alone? Lost? He understood those pretty well. "'Remember in your dreams.'"

"Huh?"

"It's what the words mean. *Palmaditze chiazspiatz*. Means, 'Remember in your dreams.' Or, somethin' close, anyway."

Layla looked her brother square in the eyes, wrinkled her nose, and said, "That don't make a lick of sense."

"Ya asked," Oli said with a shrug. "There's your answer."

Layla leaned forward, looking about as eager as a child at Noonfest. "What's he supposed to remember?"

Oli shrugged. "Everything."

"That is the dumbest thing I've heard."

"Little about the Wood makes any sense."

Layla smiled wide. She mouthed the words, and Oli thought he could see her playing them out over and over again in her head. She'd practice them when he wasn't around, and in a few days time they'd roll off her tongue as smooth as butter on hot bread. She'd sound like their father, which was what Oli feared the most. Everything she did, Layla did it the way Roi Ricker had done. She'd have been his spitting image, if he'd had the chance to train her in the Wood.

"Thank you," she whispered. Then she lay back down, eyes up to the stars but mind already somewhere else. "For everything."

Oli shook his head. "I wouldn't thank me yet. I ain't bringin' home nothin' much lately. It'll be a tight winter, and, well, I'm sorry."

Layla hit him.

She was quick, rising up enough to reach Oli's head with the back of her hand.

"Oy!" Oli hissed.

"Oh no ya don't. Don't you dare apologize for me havin' to earn my own keep. I don't intend to be a lazy clod my whole life, eh? And I ain't be needin' your pity. We'll be fine this winter. Always are.

Besides, there's got to be work 'round here that don't involve me spreadin' me legs to someone further up the hill."

Oli shrugged. "This'll be your what? Nineteenth winter? Lots of other lady folk are married by now. Mama was."

"Aye," Layla snapped. "Find me a good man and I won't wait. 'Til then, I plan on earnin' my keep."

Oli shifted, setting the cloak aside. "Ain't just money, ya know."

"Huh?"

"With Windsun, I mean. If ya did marry him, money wouldn't be the only part."

"What do ya mean?"

"Think 'bout it: he could go 'round and tell everyone else what to do, even Mister Yigguns. If ya married him, well—" Oli saw the blow comin' this time, and leaned aside so Layla's backhanded swing went wide.

Layla stood up, jabbing her finger in Oli's face. "Don't ya say it, Oliver Ricker. Don't. Ya. Say. It."

Oli shook his head. "Just thinkin' that a bit of that kinda power might be nice is all."

Layla snorted and folded her arms. "*Power*, whatever that means. Ain't never met anyone with it who wasn't more than a bit twisted."

"You only ever met the Totes."

"Like I said."

"So you could do it different, maybe. Marry Windsun, then, I don't know, do some good for this place. Some good for Ma, for sure."

Layla kept silent and Oli thought she may actually be considering. He took the moment to slide his thread and needle into the small pouch on his hip.

"I think," Layla said, words seeping out slow and thoughtful. "If I married Windsun so I could have 'power', or whatever, then I'd be someone who shouldn't have it anyway."

Oli shrugged. The next few minutes dragged on in silence. The air grew colder. Layla scooted next to Oli, and he placed his cloak over her. Eventually, she let out a wide yawn.

"It's late, Oli. We best get sleep. I gotta earn a few chits tomorrow."

"Oy." Oli stood, then turned and pulled Layla to her feet. "And I'll be back tomorrow with something big. We'll be alright this winter. Promise."

"Something big? What do ya mean to do?"

He tried to smile, but his attempt only made Layla's frown deepen. "Hunt."

Before she could reply, Oli turned and gave a small whistle. Tuck opened one tired eye, turning it lazily towards Oli. Layla leaned down, patting her knees invitingly toward him. "C'mon, boy." Tuck stretched, got onto his paws, yawned widely, then trotted over to Layla who began scratching him behind his ears. Then, in her best imitation of Oli, Layla looked at Tuck and said, "*Palmodi chiapat.*"

Tuck cocked his head and panted, still staring at Layla.

"*Palmaditze chiazspiatz.*" Oli said the words slowly, letting Layla listen and catch on. She repeated them, and Oli nodded.

"I still don't get it," she said. "What do you want him to remember?"

"Me. Us."

Layla snorted. "Like he's gonna forget." Oli said nothing, and Layla turned to him, one hand still scratching Tuck. "Wait, really?"

Oli nodded toward the Wood. "The Call is strong, and Tuck follows me into it each day. Eventually it *will* win out. Those words, they're like my own Call. They keep him here, ours, for now. But eventually—"

"He'll go mad," Layla said, looking down at Tuck with fresh eyes. "Like all the cattle."

"I wouldn't let him go that far."

Layla paused, eyes moving from Oli to Tuck, and back. "Is that what happened to Pa and the others? Did they go crazy?"

Oli looked away, teeth grinding involuntarily as his imagination dragged old memories up from the dark. He looked to the Wood, the sky, the road, anywhere to find a distraction. And, in the rare appearance of a miracle, he found one. "Oy, ya see that?" Oli said, pointing. At the bottom of the hill where a line of moving shadow seemed to emerge from the dark. He squinted. "Wagons, I think. The merchants."

Layla stood beside him, squinting. "How in the Deep did ya see that?"

"Odd they ain't got no lanterns."

Layla shrugged. "Moon is bright enough."

"Maybe." He thought of the moon's cycles, counting days. This wasn't right. The few merchants who traveled into Watchful throughout the year were—if nothing else—consistent. The first of the wagons shouldn't be arriving until just after the first snowfall, a week or more away. "Ain't right though. They're early, and coming by night." Oli could feel his heart quicken. He had nothing to sell and now no more time to prepare. They only stayed a week—no more, no less—then they were gone, and their money with them.

Layla grabbed Oli's shoulder and squeezed. "Oy, they're here now. By night and early and all that. Best not to worry. There'll be time enough to gawk when they're settled in the mornin'."

Oli followed Layla into their home, mind unsettled. The traders would only be here so long, and if Oli couldn't sell them a few good pelts, then there'd be no redemption for their winter.

Which meant his time was up, and his options scarce.

CHAPTER
EIGHT

Léonie's sword flashed with color, its dirty blade catching the light of the momentary blasts of lightning shattering the world around her. Only the lightning moved, appearing and then disappearing with a bone-crushing *crack*. The soldiers around her were all frozen in time: some with shields and spears raised, dozens of others in the last throes of death. The sashes and surcoats which should have been the Baudelaire orange had become drenched in blood.

But there were not only human bodies frozen around her.

Her retinue of guards was nowhere to be seen. Gone was the human fortress protecting her day and night and gone was the safety of Turris Regis. She stood alone on the battlefield outside Worchestern, the burning city giving them all enough light to see by.

Light enough to see the Yelmes warrior before her. Its eyes blazed yellow, its mouth opened in a war cry. In one hand he held a black blade crackling with invisible energy, the other he had raised to the sky. With that raised hand he would call down a judgement only Deōs should be able to bring. He could wield lightning.

The Yelmes was a young boy, and yet not a boy at all. Human, and yet unrecognizable as human.

Léonie wanted to scream, to thrust her sword out or to run away, to do anything but stand there with her eyes fixed on this beast of a thing, this monstrosity of an almost-human. This being that would devour her with fire from the skies—the *skies*! That domain the Order said was Deōs's alone, violated by these beings from Kātsracha.

They weren't supposed to be real.

Then the boy moved, slowly, as if he were forcing himself through whatever hold this dream had on time. His free hand moved slowly downward, pointing towards Léonie. This had happened before, every night since Worchestern. Léonie did everything she could to step forward, to bring her raised sword down, but she was fixed in time. Immovable.

The Yelmes's fingers crackled with blue energy and then the sound of his scream rose over the violent sounds of battle. Then there white light and searing pain consumed her, and Léonie screamed.

CHAPTER
NINE

L ayla shuffled her feet, kicking up dirt on the street. A rusty gate hung partway open, beyond it a wooden building with white paint that had either faded or flaked off so now it looked sickly and pale. Above the dark-wood door hung an insignia: a large circle with a smaller circle inside it, and inside that a triangle around which were little squiggles like light or lightning.

The Order of Deōs.

The sun hadn't fully risen, its light only now beginning to stretch over the edge of the world, and yet Layla was certain Evanvalt would be awake. The smoke rising from the chimney smelled of rose and myrrh, which meant the old priest was in the middle of morning prayer. Any other day, Layla would've thought it rude to interrupt, but today she slipped through the gate and up the rocky path.

A metal knocker hung dead center on the door, speckled like pox with copper-colored rust. Layla blew warm air into her palms, then lifted the knocker. The hinge let out a small squeal as metal scraped metal, then Layla made three, quick, raps. As the sound of the last knock echoed away, Layla blew more air into her palms and bounced on her toes. She hated the way the cold made her feel. It wasn't the chill, exactly, but the vulnerability of it. No inch of her skin was safe from its bite, and once the snow started falling it would be worse. The cold reminded her she was frail in the face of the world, hopeless if not for the heat of a fire and the warmth of blankets and clothes.

She looked around while she waited, noticing for the first time small pots of herbs off to the side below the shuttered windows. Well, perhaps they had once been herbs, though now they had withered to leafless twigs, standing tall and barren amid tubs of chalky dirt. Layla was still staring at them when the door opened.

"Yes?" Evanvalt smelled of garlic. It was always the first thing Layla noticed, and she could never figure out why. Did the man bathed in the cloves each night? But beyond the smell, he looked like anyone else in Watchful. His skin was spotted with age and as tough as leather, his head was shaved, but white hairs grew sparsely on his cheeks and chin: wispy and long. His white robes, stained and dirty, were all that marked him as a priest. Well, that and the demanding tone of his voice.

"Priest Evanvalt." Layla bowed her head slightly. "Good morning."

"It is almost morning," the priest said, his eyes roaming beyond Layla. "Public prayer begins in an hour, if you would like to return then." He shifted from foot to foot, his fingers drumming along the door frame.

A pit of nerves grew in Layla's stomach. She couldn't decide if coming here had been wise or not. "Well, I'd like to come, it's just I'll need to be off to find work soon and—"

"Work," the priest said, dragging the word out slow and steady. "Work is good, though sometimes I wonder if our hands toil more than they need. Maybe if more people took an ounce of time to ask Deōs for favor and blessing then the weeds wouldn't grow so voracious, the cows would give their milk freely, and our shoes wouldn't wear themselves so thin."

Layla opened her mouth to ask what, then, the cobbler would do, but shut it a moment later. She'd only ever spoken to the priest a handful of times, and she already regretted her choice to make it a handful and one.

"Never mind, child," Evanvalt said with a huff. He stepped back and opened the door wide, warm air rushing over Layla. "Just come in before a draft can follow you. Come on now."

Layla hustled inside, squeezing past Evanvalt and trying not to gag. Did garlic even grow in Watchful? Where did he get so much? But she quickly forgot the smell as her face began to thaw, the tension around her eyes and cheeks easing. Behind her, the door closed with a *thud* and the priest shuffled past her.

The Sanctuary wasn't large, and Layla hadn't been there often enough to think of it as familiar. A hearth sat in one corner, an envious amount of wood stacked beside it. Dozen long benches filled the center of the room, all pointing in the direction of a small dais around which incense burned. It occurred to Layla that it may be the incense Evanvalt burned which gave him the scent of garlic, though she couldn't be certain. Honestly, she couldn't smell the incense over the smell of the man himself.

"I don't have much in the way of food," Evanvalt said. "It's been a hard year and there have been too few alms for the poor. Still, there is a sack of beans and a tater or two in the back. If you give me a moment I—"

"Oh no," Layla said, holding a hand up to stop the priest. "I ain't here for food. My brother would throw one hell of a fit if I brought handouts back home."

Evanvalt stopped, one eyebrow raised. He looked strangely gentle in this space. Perhaps it was the light of the candles and the fire casting a myriad of shadows over him that softened his features, or maybe the incense smoke simply eased the old man's tension. She thought being alone with him would scare her, but she found it the opposite. "Pride has been the destruction of many, Layla. I beg you not to join them."

Layla's heart paused when the priest spoke her name. It unnerved her, making her feel exposed, as if the eyes of the divine were on her. The word reached for her like the cold outside, touching everything. Deōs seeing her through the eyes of his servant. Was that how it worked? Was Evanvalt God's spy?

The priest shrugged. "If not food, then what is it I can do for you? Prayers? Intercession? Confession?"

Layla's mouth went dry. She should have been expecting the question, of course, but now that it had been asked, she didn't know what to say. Truthfully, she hadn't meant to come here at all. It had been a whim, a small detour on the way to Mad Rosey's. Evanvalt stayed quiet as Layla floundered, his eyes narrowed, but not harsh. It would have been easier if he'd snapped at her, told her to spit out whatever she needed to say. Instead, he stood a few paces away, and waited.

"It's my brother, Oli," Layla began, the words finding their way out. "Well, my mother don't think he's alright. And I think maybe—I don't know—that maybe she's right, you know? And things ain't been easy for him, and us too, and . . ." She sat on one of the hard benches, words rushing out and blending together. "He left this morning for the Wood, like always I guess, but it don't feel like always. And what is always anyways?"

Evanvalt stepped toward the fire, and his voice echoed off the walls when he spoke. "It's been hard for the Stražar, yes? Harder than normal, I mean."

"He says there ain't been much to hunt. Just small game."

"And even that is growing scarce, yes?"

"That's what he says, anyway."

Evanvalt took another step toward the hearth. Like many buildings in Watchful, the Sanctuary was constructed with a combination of wood and stone. One wall was a motley collection of gray stone while the wall across from it was built from large slats that let tiny rays of light through. As Evanvalt leaned against the mantle, his shadow stretched out wide behind him like a black tear through the center of the room.

"I have felt it. The change, I mean."

Layla cocked her head. "Felt what?"

"The disturbance. The shift in the Wood. It is a time of upheaval, though I do not know why. It is as if the Wood senses something. As if it grows afraid."

"I don't understand. You sound like one of the Stražar," Layla said, looking around as if she'd see a bow hanging on a wall. "Like you know somethin' about the Wood."

Evanvalt snorted. "I'm certainly no hunter, but there are those of us in the Order who understand such things. There is a reason it is me assigned to this Maker-forsaken stretch of country. Not just anyone can be trusted here. This task is delicate, and requires . . . perception."

"That don't make no sense."

Evanvalt turned back to her, eyebrows furrowed together. "Life has a way of making no sense, until suddenly, when you least expect it, it makes all the sense in the world. Unfortunately for us, the experience of revelation is often unpleasant. Perhaps I spoke too freely. I had assumed your father had shared more with you, but I stand corrected."

Father. The word made the warmth in the room sink down between the floorboards. "What should my Pa have told me?"

"I never said he *should* have told you anything."

"Oy, don't play those word games. Just tell me what you ain't tellin' me."

The priest shook his head, and the shadow behind him shuddered. "Not today. Though," he lifted up a finger, silencing Layla's oncoming objection. "I will consider in prayer what I should and should not share with you. I, for one, will seek the wisdom of Deŏs, as should you. But come, you did not end up on this doorstep just for cryptic messages. You came looking for help for your brother, yes? You fear for him?"

Layla ground her teeth, frustration and fear all wrapped up in her chest. "I'm afraid he's off to do somethin' more than a bit stupid. He's gettin' desperate."

"Desperate. Aren't we all? What truly marks a man is what he is desperate for. You know, I tried to convince Oliver to join the Order, years ago."

"He hates that name. Only Ma can call him that."

"He refused. He was desperate to get back into the Wood. He had to take care of you and your mother, he said."

"And he's done it."

"Yes, he has. As best he can."

Silence stretched out through the room. The shadow behind Evanvalt grew smaller as the fire in the hearth shrunk slightly. "Your brother has a good heart, Layla. Troubled, yes. Sorely troubled, in fact. But good in most of the ways which count."

"Can you help him?" The words were hardly above a whisper.

"No."

A cold tear seeped out of Layla's eye, tickling her cheek and resting on the edge of her lip. She let the saltiness of it sit there, her body still.

Evanvalt sighed. "There is food here if you need it. And you can spend time in prayer as long as you would like. The Maker is the only one who—"

But Layla didn't hear what else the priest had to say, she was already slamming the door shut on his words, cutting them clean through.

CHAPTER
TEN

Oli hadn't slept.

Every time he closed his eyes he saw the dust of the merchants' caravan as they left Watchful, and an empty Ricker home. Eventually, he'd given up trying, pushed aside his patchwork blanket and welcomed the frigid air. He'd left well before light, he and Tuck making their way into the Wood in the earliest hours of morning when the air was so cold it stiffened his joints and numbed his nose.

That was hours ago. Now the world was dimly lit with early morning light and Oli was nearing the end of the Outer Bands.

The Wood was a wild thing, but there was the faintest sense of order to it. It was something like a circular lake, the edges of which were shallow and more tame. But as one goes further out into the water, eventually the sand beneath their feet drops off, sudden and sharp. There, the dangerous creatures swim and look for something to devour.

In the Wood, the shallow stretch of tame forest was called the Outer Bands. Tame for the Stražar, anyway. Beyond the Outer Bands was what the Stražar called the Deep, and Oli had avoided it since his father's death. He'd been playing in the shallow end of the water for years, but today he was forcing himself to swim.

Between the Outer Bands and the Deep was a miles long wall made of the same stone as the Hilltoppers' homes: massive white bricks as wide as a man's arm span. The Stražar referred to it—rather predictably—as "the Wall", and it had often served as the marker between where one did and did not go.

Oli stood there now.

"Been a while," Oli said, keeping his voice low. Tuck yipped beside him. There was a stretch of barren ground about a dozen yards long between the treeline of the Outer Bands and the Wall, and that stretch had always made Oli nervous. After the cover of the trees, stepping into the sunlight felt dangerous and vulnerable. As he stepped forward, Oli couldn't help but look over his shoulder a half dozen times, checking to see if any vines or beasts were stretching themselves out to grab at him.

There was nothing, though, which only made Oli feel as if the Wood was urging him forward.

The Wall was old, hundreds of years at least. If Oli's father was to be believed, it was as old as the forest itself. Oli wasn't sure he believed that, but something about the stones reeked of another time and place. They were too clean cut, too large, too *precise*. Nothing Oli saw in Watchful was like that, even the mansions up top didn't feel the same.

It didn't matter now though, many of those bricks lay on the ground, knocked free sometime in the last hundred years. Now they lay in small craters or rubble filled stacks on the ground, yellowed grass and weeds sticking up between the cracks. Every fallen brick Oli had ever seen lay on the *outside* of the Wall, toward the Outer Bands, as if something inside the Deep were trying to break free. That bothered Oli, and it always had. If the Call drew beasts *inward*, why would the Wall be crumpling *outward*?

Perhaps one day, long ago, the Wall would have done an excellent job in keeping people out of the Deep, but that hadn't been the case in Oli's lifetime. Instead, the crumpled sections of bricks formed a staircase up to where one could simply drop to the other side.

Through the gap in the Wall, Oli caught his first sight of the Deep in more than a decade. Vivid green leaves dangled from every available branch, standing in stark contrast to the browns and oranges of autumn behind him. It stood in defiance to the natural order of the world, a frozen moment in time refusing to budge any further onwards. It was the same as Oli saw it every night, whenever his eyes closed and memories became nightmares. He could feel sweat breaking out on the back of his neck, his heart picking up its pace and making his breaths sharp and jagged.

"Maybe we should go back," Oli said, kneeling down and scratching Tuck behind the ears.

Tuck wagged his tail and yipped, stepping towards the Deep. Oli wouldn't turn back now, and they both knew it. The traders would leave within the week. They came for what little Watchful had to trade, and they'd be wanting meat and pelts from the Wood. They always did, and they'd pay good coin for it.

Think of warm blankets on cold nights. Think of food over the fire.

With a sigh, Oli stood. His knees quivered, but he clenched his teeth and forced them still. He shook his hands and rolled his shoulders, working out the cold beginning to settle into his joints. Then he stepped up onto the first of the rubble, and paused.

Beneath the thin sole of his boot, Oli could *feel* the stone. Not the outside coarseness of the rock, but something deeper, as if the rock were trying to say something, to cry out. Oli swallowed, his heart pounding. This had happened before, years ago.

Everything in the Wood had a name, everything had a language. Everything was alive in the realest sense of the word. Once, long ago, the Stražar were less hunters and more namers. Speakers. Those who communed with the Wood. They had formed the Language of the Wild. And in this language they had spoken with all the beings of the Wood. But, over time, the Wood had become dangerous and as the Stražar died, so did much of the Language.

Oli lowered his hand, placing the tips of his fingers on the rock's surface. Whatever it wanted to say, whatever primal call was inside it, was either too muffled or Oli was too deaf. It was like a distant moaning in his ear, a pained, vague noise. Oli swallowed, then looked around. Tuck was beside him, sniffing at the stone.

"*Tviarka*," Oli said, the word coming to him slowly. "That's its name, I think. Isn't that what Pa had called it?"

Tuck only sniffed about.

Oli stood. "What difference does it make anyway?" His father had believed understanding the Language was essential to surviving in the Wood, but Oli had watched him die, and the words he'd been screaming in those last moments hadn't helped him at all. "C'mon, boy."

A few steps later, Oli was straddling the lowest point of the Wall he could find, looking out over the Deep: a world out of time. Rocks shifted as Tuck struggled up beside him, panting.

"We'll regret this, likely as not."

Tuck snorted, then nuzzled the back of Oli's knee, urging him forward. And with a small leap, Oli dropped into the Deep.

CHAPTER
ELEVEN

Léonie rubbed her sore eyes as she stared through the dew-covered window of the small study, watching the fingers of orange light rise from the east and stretch over the plains to the north. She imagined Kātsracha troops on those plains: a blanket of black armor leaving burning grasslands in their wake.

She was on the third floor of the largest home in Watchful, which said little for the town. Still, the home was on the precipice of the large hill Watchful resided on, and the view was breathtaking: miles and miles of rolling downs and farmland in all shades of orange, yellow, and brown. They were the colors of resistance, the world fighting the final moments before winter.

She turned away from the window with a stifled yawn.

The study was the antithesis to the view outside: dull and forgettable. It was small, hardly twenty feet in each direction, and filled with thick oak shelves roughly hewn and covered in books of the unremarkable kind. The shelves had become so blanketed in dust Léonie wondered if the inhabitants of the home were even literate. Metal framed lanterns hung from the ceiling at various heights, most low enough Léonie's fingertips could touch them. The candles inside burned low, pointless now sunlight trickled into the room, chasing the faint glow of candlelight away.

Captain Thibault stood across the room, his feet shoulder-width apart and hands clasped behind him. His curly hair and neat beard made him look out of place beside the old, chipped wood of the study's only door. He was the portrait of a man of court and war, trapped in this house's peasant frame. Still, he seemed un-bothered by it all, the deepening bags beneath his eyes the only sign of wear.

Léonie absently rested a hand on the scar along her forearm, her fingertips caressing the raised skin. Did she have bags beneath her own eyes? She had not checked her mirror yet today, and she did not look forward to the experience. Last night had been as rough as the one before, and the one before that.

If Thibault was out of place in this backcountry home, then Lady Amandine was an alien in a strange land indeed. She sat erect in the chair across from the large desk, likely where the commoners sat when attempting to plead with the town's magistrate. The duchess had a way of sitting on the chair's edge, as if attempting to touch as little of the wood and cushions as possible in case she may catch an infection. And yet, even sitting so far forward, she managed to be perfectly still. She was a statue of courtly perfection: no hair of hers was out of place, her makeup was applied in such a way as to compliment her lines of age, and even the wrinkles of her dress presented themselves as intentionally designed ruffles. Lady Amandine was twice Léonie's age, had refused sleep the night before, and was still far more in control and composed than Léonie.

"So," Léonie said, struggling not to rub her temples and disrupt what little semblance of propriety her hair still had. "What is it you are trying so desperately to say, Captain? Perhaps now would be the time to speak plainly."

Thibault shifted on his feet. "Princess, it is as I told you before we left Turris Regis: our current location lacks the defensibility to withstand a direct confrontation with the Yelmes forces. When the enemy reaches us—"

"We shall die . . . no?" Léonie searched the captain's eyes, praying she would find in him some level of contradiction. Thibault said nothing, only shifted his eyes downwards.

Lady Amandine coughed politely, pulling Léonie's gaze toward her. "Duchess?"

Amandine smiled, though only enough to let the smallest of lines show at the edge of her mouth. "Your Highness, perhaps it would be best if we began to take steps to inform the residents of the coming danger. The people of this township should be made aware and given the chance to flee. They are citizens of your father's kingdom, after all."

Léonie stepped over to the desk, pulling free the large chair sitting behind it. *I have maids for this*, she thought sourly as the chair's wooden feet scraped against the floorboards. Maids who were too preoccupied with thoroughly cleaning her newly acquired bedchambers, unloading her luggage, preparing her breakfast, and drawing a bath. And so she sat, scooting the chair up to the cluttered desktop on her own.

When she was settled, she said, "It is not so simple, I am afraid. I doubt little more than rumors have made their way this far through the kingdom with the trade caravans on hold. We would cause hysteria if we told them what was to come. Demons from legend besieging the kingdom and now on their own doorstep? I see no good it would do."

"No good? Your Highness, it would give them time to *leave*."

"And where should they go?" Léonie flung an open hand toward the window, gesturing to the vast expanse beyond. "Days before the first snow, homeless, with demons roaming the countryside? I think not, Lady Amandine. I am sorry, but this is not Worchestern, and not all the lessons learned there will apply here."

Amandine leaned back slowly, mouth closing to a thin line and her eyes narrowing on the princess. Léonie had, it seemed, gone too far. Again. A small knock on the study's door saved them both. Léonie raised a questioning eyebrow as Thibault opened the door a crack, the hinges giving an annoying squeal, and peered into the hall.

He turned to Léonie a moment later. "Your Highness, with permission, Corporal Tâl is reporting in."

"Bring her," Léonie said, leaning forward with elbows firm on the table, the fingers of each hand entwining together.

Léonie could only remember speaking with Tâl once or twice before. In many respects, she looked like any other of the King's Spear, the division of scouts and rangers sworn to the crown: she wore a travel-worn cloak of midnight blue, the hood obscuring her features. Beneath the cloak, her shirt, trousers, and boots, were all caked in dirt and worn with much use. A short sword dangled from her hip, an unstrung bow hung alongside a quiver on her back.

As Tâl stepped into the room, she tossed back her hood and dropped to one knee, head bowed low.

"Report," Léonie said.

The woman stood, lifting her head and looking directly at the princess. She was almond skinned with dark eyes shaped in a subtle slant, giving her a look of intense focus. Her neck was thin, and the way she carried herself *too* graceful, as if she floated through the room while everyone else was weighed down. Léonie wondered if it was her mother or her father that was of the Badaui, the seafaring people to the far east. Tâl had the telltale features: a subtly thinner frame, an aura of grace. It had likely given her a thin edge in the King's Spear.

"Your Highness," Tâl said, each word precisely. "I bear news about our pursuers. Their advance party shall emerge from the Southfern Forest later today if they have not already."

"How many?" Thibault asked, one hand absently scratching his chin.

"A hundred strong, give or take a dozen." Léonie sucked in a breath. "If they continue traveling as they are, we believe they'll arrive in two days' time. Three, if they collect themselves and approach with caution."

"Two days," Thibault said, shaking his head. "Two days and the Yelmes will be here and looking to put you to the sword, Your Highness. We cannot stay."

Amandine looked from Tâl to Thibault. "There is much we do not know, Captain. Why do the soldiers of Kātsracha pursue us? How did they come to discover our expedition? We are not even certain they are aware of the princess' presence here. Perhaps they have come looking for the same cursed artifact we have?"

Thibault shifted. "You are correct, of course. However, we must assume the worst. We cannot allow the princess to stay and fall into enemy hands."

Léonie gave a snort which drew a frown from Amandine. *I do not intend to stay here at all,* she thought, but aloud she said, "Tell me, Captain, what is it you propose? Fight and die out in the open? Flee towards the mountains in the east and seek shelter with the remnant of the Velk?" Léonie jabbed a finger at the top of the desk. "No, this means only that we have two days to do what we came here to do. If we obtain the power we seek then no horde, big or small, shall stand in our way. They will simply be the first to fall in our campaign to purge this kingdom from these viemones and send them back to the gates of Yeolasi."

"My lady, you can still be sent to safety while a contingent is sent into—"

Another knock at the door cut him off.

Léonie thanked the Maker for the moment of relief. She did not have the patience today to deal with the captain's protests, well meaning or not. She waved dismissively at Thibault. "Go, Captain, this conversation is over. Do what you can to make the town defensible. We will not flee. Our fate is now intertwined with this sad lot."

Léonie watched Thibault's lips thin, but he bowed low, then opened the door to reveal two men who contrasted one another in every way. One was old and red-faced, with a thick gut and a furrowed brow, but beside him was a younger man with handsome features and a carefully manicured mustache.

Amandine stood as Thibault slid out, nodding to the men at the door. "Welcome," Amandine said, voice sweetening. "Magistrate Tote, is it not?" Léonie raised an eyebrow at the duchess, suspecting she had arranged this meeting, if not the timing.

The red-faced magistrate appeared ready to explode as he stepped into the study. "If you mean the rightful owner of this home, then yes."

Amandine didn't flinch. "I understand you feel displaced, Magistrate, but do come and sit. Perhaps you shall learn enough to put your agitation at ease, yes? Besides, it is not every day one gets the honor of hosting the daughter of the King, is it?"

Tote hesitated. Léonie could imagine the irritation he felt: being invited into a room of his own home would be humiliating. Oh, how Léonie had felt like that before, her father and brother not so subtly reminding her of her place. Still, the Magistrate stepped into the room. Amandine gestured for them to bow, waiting in her patient way as they fumbled through a laughably shallow imitation of court courtesy. If her father were here he would have had the two of them whipped. They sat, the fat one causing his chair to squeal. They smelled of sweat and cheap perfumes and she wanted them gone already.

The door stayed open and two guards filed in, flanking each side of the doorway, their faces unreadable. Corporal Tâl hadn't left with the captain, but faded into the corner, her hood back on and casting her face into shadow. It was ridiculous, in a way: three soldiers to guard two men who had most certainly already been checked for anything near a weapon. Beside her, leaning against the drawers of the desk, was her own sword, *Balam Eoduun*. It had been a gift from the Badaui embassy years before, and a constant companion since. Léonie could have dispatched both of these with her own sword, but such was not enough of a shield for a princess.

Protections upon protections.

Amandine remained standing near the door, and all eyes settled on Léonie, whose hands were once again folded together before her.

She eyed Magistrate Tote, ignoring the younger man entirely. She waited, and was a little disappointed when it took but a few short heartbeats before he began to squirm.

Eventually the tension forced words from his mouth, water gurgling from a kettle. "My lady, it is——"

"Your Highness," Amandine interrupted from behind. When he turned to her, causing his chair to squeak and squeal again, she repeated, "Commoners should refer to the Princess of Trevelar as 'Your Highness'."

He looked from Amandine to Léonie, sputtering, "C-c-commoner? M'lady, how *dare* you? I am the magistrate of this community, and the proper resident of *this home*. How dare you call me a——"

"Silence." Léonie snapped, and he complied instantly. *At least he knows how to play the dog.* "We have not the time for this. I have not arrived for the purpose of confiscating your home. There are things at work that you cannot fathom, and like it or not, you and your residence shall be of service to me for as long as I need. This is your rightful duty to the crown, of course. You are loyal to the crown, are you not?"

Tote's eyes widened. "Of course! Your Majesty, the Tote family has——"

"Good," Léonie said dryly, both her and Amandine ignoring his use of "Your Majesty" which should have been reserved for her father. It was an attempt, at least, and perhaps soon it would be appropriate. "I would hate to have to erect a gallows in such a lovely town." Léonie let those words dangle for a brief moment. "Now, to business. We have two days, perhaps three, to send an expedition into the *Vromia* and return with a . . . weapon. Are you familiar with what I speak?"

Tote swallowed, and Léonie thought she could see an image of a gallows in his eyes. Or perhaps that was fear. "Familiar? No, Your Majesty, I——"

Léonie scoffed. "And you say you are not a commoner? Do you

not recognize the old tongue when you hear it? The *Vromia*, it is 'the ground which lives', yes?"

Tote looked blank, mouth slightly open, eyes dancing around in search of an answer. Beside him, the young man's eyes narrowed. "You mean the Wood, Your Highness?"

Léonie raised an eyebrow. "That name is rather base, I think . . . but yes, that is what I mean."

"The Wood?" Tote said, managing to look somehow even more confused. "There's nothin' in there but critters and ghosts, eh? Did you say you're sending in an expedition? Nonsense. People don't survive a day past the treeline."

Léonie nodded slowly. "I have read that the *Vromia* is dangerous. Alive with something like a mind of its own. It is why I have come. At the center of your Wood lies that which gives it all its power. A weapon, and one I mean to wield. And you shall help me." Léonie was unsure why Amandine had summoned the magistrate, but she would not squander the moment. Everything and everyone before her was there for one reason: to get her to that weapon.

Tote teased out a hasty laugh. "Me? Your Highness, I haven't the slightest wish to die in the Wood. Besides, I have responsibilities, and this isn't even—"

Léonie ground her teeth. "I do not expect *you* to go, Magistrate. From you I need only information. The finest leathers and furs come from this little stretch of the kingdom, no? One would imagine your huntsmen are both skilled and familiar with the dangers of the *Vromia*."

The younger man leaned forward, cutting the magistrate off before any more words fumbled out of his mouth. "You mean the Stražar?"

"Stražar . . ." Léonie said the word slowly. It was an odd word, out of place and time. Léonie was familiar with most of the languages of La'Azurus, but this one she could not seem to place. Amandine caught her eye, and Léonie got the sense the older woman was equally at a loss.

The magistrate waved a hand, "He's my youngest, Your Highness, forgive him, he—"

Léonie glared Tote into silence, then turned back to the younger man. "What do you speak of?"

The man coughed then glanced at the magistrate. Léonie suspected they were father and son, though the resemblance was not strong. "The Stražar are hunters, Your Highness. Woodsmen. They're the only ones who can go into the Wood and come back, and they go daily. But there aren't many of them left and most don't live in town. They're strange, Your Highness."

"Strange?"

"Not normal."

"I am aware of the word's meaning. Strange in what way?"

He flinched, sitting up straighter. "Well, they walk about in these cloaks, smelly and dirty all the time. Half the time they won't look you in the eye, and I swear they twitch whenever you even breathe near them. And sometimes you'd swear they weren't there at all, then they are. People call them wraiths, ghosts. They mumble to themselves when they think no one's looking, and a whole cart load of other things. They're just . . . strange."

Léonie pondered his words, her fingers drumming silently on the desk. "What is your name?"

"Windsun," he said, flashing a toothy smile which was both wide, and yet confined, not working its way up to his eyes.

"Well, you seem useful at least. You shall deliver a message to these hunters. Tell them to come dine with me this evening at supper. It is urgent, Windsun, very urgent. Do you understand?"

He nodded.

Léonie looked up, beckoning Tâl over with the wave of her hand. "Corporal, take a pair of guards and escort young Windsun here. Ensure he does not disappoint me."

At the wave of Léonie's hand, Windsun stood, looking unsure of himself. He bowed awkwardly, following Tâl's far more graceful example, and then they withdrew, leaving only Léonie, Amandine, and a nervous looking magistrate. In the following silence, Amandine stepped forward and took the seat beside Tote, confidence and calm exuding from her the way warm sunlight drifted in from the window.

Tote fidgeted, stammering out, "Well, it seems you have whatever it is you need. If there wasn't anything else—"

Léonie lifted a hand, and he stopped. Amandine met her gaze and gave a stiff nod, as though she knew what it was Léonie was thinking. *Oh, Deōs, may I not regret this.*

Léonie looked back to Tote, noticing for the first time how tired and bloodshot the man's eyes were. "What do you know of the Mienracha?"

"Mienracha? Oh, you mean the Yelmes, eh? The dark souls trapped in Kātsracha." Tote looked towards the bookshelves. Léonie, for her part, was impressed he knew the traditional name for their enemy. Perhaps he had read a few of his books after all. "Children's stories. Stuff of legends and nightmares. Nonsense, if you ask me. 'Tales of the Fae', my father would've said."

Léonie and Amandine glanced at one another. Perhaps they would have said something similar, months ago. Now, Léonie could not help but see the glimmer of fire in Amandine's eyes, as if Worchestern was alight all over again. *She is right,* Léonie thought, her stomach souring. *I should tell him. Should give them the chance to flee, to escape.*

But to do so would be to invite a form of unpredictability and chaos. What would these commoners do? Flee en masse? Grab axes and pitchforks and fight? Turn on her?

Amandine leaned forward, urging Léonie on.

"Please understand," Léonie said, releasing a heavy breath, "what I am about to tell you will sound far-fetched."

Magistrate Tote left the office with a pale face an hour later.

"There will be panic now," Léonie said, pacing slowly alongside the bookshelves, reading spine after spine. The candles had burned themselves out, as if they knew they were no longer needed now since sunlight flowed through the room.

Amandine stood, rolling her shoulders. "You have done what is right, Your Highness."

Léonie snorted. "I'll leave for the *Vromia* in the morning. Will you contain whatever mob the peasants form?"

"If needed, Captain Thibault and I can mitigate any hindrance caused by the commoners. The point is, now they shall at least have a *choice*, my lady. They shall face the darkness on their terms."

"They will flee, and when they do they shall be cut down like cattle in the field," Léonie reached out a pale hand and pulled free the ivory spine of *Sir L'aon's Catalogue of Velik Burial Sites*. She gently brushed away the layer of dust and opened to the first page. Without looking up, her voice hardly more than a drifting breeze, she said. "Their blood shall be on my hands."

The duchess said nothing.

CHAPTER

TWELVE

Oli crouched low beside Tuck, his bow ready, eyes roaming. The world here was alive in a way that made the Outer Bands feel dull. Lizards skittered across the brown and white bark of giant birch trees, squirrels leapt from branches, birds sung and fluttered about. The forest floor was a latticework of writhing vines and shifting shrubs, a maze of living snares.

"Let's get in and out, eh?" Oli said, more to himself than to Tuck who was wagging his tail in anticipation. With a shaky breath, Oli firmed up his voice, preparing to use the Language. "*Niasti*."

Hunt.

Tuck's body twitched and his snout rose up to sniff the air. A moment later, he was off and Oli was trailing behind, an arrow at the ready. Tuck picked his routes through the tree dense forest, avoiding roots, odd-looking fallen branches, and anything else which made the hound's nose flare or ears twitch. They gave a wide berth to the vines sprawling down from trees, intertwined like webs spun by some massive, twisted spider. Oli checked Tuck's paths incessantly, sometimes calling him back to take a route further around a large tree or unnerving brush.

There was so much motion.

Something was always moving: hares dashed back to their burrows, squirrels skittered up trees with acorn treasures, snakes slithered beneath leaves, toads croaked, birds sang, and even the trees stretched themselves out towards Oli. Their movements were slow, but Oli knew to look for them, noticing roots stretching higher, branches dipping lower, and the green moss on the trees' bark shifting. It could have been paranoia, a decade of nightmares haunting him, but he gave the trees plenty of distance anyway.

"C'mon boy," Oli said, annoyed at the way his voice quivered as he nudged Tuck away from another trail of rabbit droppings. "We need somethin' bigger." *Much bigger.*

They'd been traveling mostly in zigzags, Oli shooing Tuck away from scent after scent the moment he realized it was small game. But it was the game Tuck had grown used to, what he was trained to find.

Oli cursed as realization hit him. Tuck didn't know *how* to look for anything else, or at least he didn't know he was supposed to be parsing out the scent of something larger from all the barrage of smells he was getting. Oli needed a word, a command in the Language to give Tuck something to grab onto.

But he couldn't remember.

"Find a deer, boy," Oli said, still running to keep up with Tuck's frantic pace. The dog was following another scent now, and from the droppings Oli was seeing, it may be a fox. But he wasn't here for a fox.

Oli started going through the Language, looking at everything around him and working to name it, praying that just naming things would bring the word to his mind. Tree root . . . *korain*. The lizard . . . *yiasht*. The robin . . . *scermuha*. Oli's mind raced, picking up speed as the words came quicker and quicker. A pair of spiders, one black and one pale white, their webs intertwined: *ciar biabuke* and *ulmciar biabuke*. The fox Tuck was tracking would be *lishka* and a deer would be—

"Loviti jyuiam!"

It was like striking flint to dried kindling.

Tuck didn't hesitate or falter. The words sunk in with force, and he lurched off eastward. Oli trailed behind, hustling to keep up. Less than five minutes later, Tuck slowed and Oli saw the tracks. Large impressions in deep soil. A print like two ovals beside one another, each with a fine point at the end. And they were as long as Oli's hand, meaning the buck would be . . . what? Larger than what Larz had nabbed, for sure. Tuck must have caught the scent before but had ignored it. Maybe there were deer in the Outer Bands after all, and Tuck hadn't known to look for them.

The thought soured Oli's stomach, but it didn't matter now. If Tuck had slowed, that meant they were close. *Very* close. It meant maybe they'd leave with enough meat and pelts to sell and buy blankets and clothes and food and—Oli shook his head. He needed to focus.

They had entered a stretch of forest whose trees were old and massive, but the underbrush was more scarce. Water trickled in a creek in the distance, sunlight poured through the leaf laden canopy, birds swooping through the light's rays. Oli and Tuck kept themselves low, creeping along in the shadow of an oak, Oli peering ahead.

And then there it was, as simple as that.

The antler was visible first, twelve bone-white points bobbing gently up and down as the buck grazed, its snout working at something on the ground. Most of the deer was hidden behind a large willow whose branches dipped and swayed near to the ground.

"Good boy," Oli breathed, hardly even a whisper. He placed a knee to dirt, giving himself a solid foundation, then raised his bow and drew back the string. He took a deep breath, gently pushing the air from his body, a command rolling out with it. *"Zibich."*

Kill.

Tuck launched forward, sprinting for the rear of the oak behind the buck. As he rounded the tree he let out a bark and, predictably, the deer sprang forward, revealing himself for a split second.

He was gorgeous. Beautiful white spots along his flank, easily a third larger than anything Oli had ever seen before. Oli's muscles moved of their own accord: his arms twitched, aiming slightly up and to the right as he let the string go.

In a heartbeat, the buck jumped, the arrow flew, and then the deer had disappeared behind another tree.

"We got 'im," Oli said, breaking into a grin. He'd seen the arrow fly true, finding its home somewhere near the animal's lungs. And he could *feel* it: the part of him that went with each arrow. He could already see the fresh blankets he'd buy, could smell the carrots and potatoes, could feel the coins in his hand. Tuck would track it easily enough, and then—

Oli had gone to stand, but his knee was still planted firmly to the ground, held fast. Panicked, he looked down and saw a vine as thick as three fingers wrapping tight around his leg and working up towards his hip. Horror choked the breath from his lungs as effectively as if the vine squeezed around his throat. The vine pulsed, purple liquid moving beneath the green flesh. Sharp thorns budded along the vine's length, piercing his pants and calves, pulling blood free so it could drink.

It moved quickly now that it was on him, but Oli stared, frozen.

The vine was creeping upward, thorns pushing into Oli's thigh and drawing thin lines of blood which spilled out in a pool onto Oli's pants before being sucked into the vine, slurped up like the last bit of stew.

Dark memories filled the world around Oli and that vine. There was fog, the barking of dogs, hissing of snakes. He could hear his father yelling for him to fight, but Oli only watched, listened. Those screams rang through the forest now like they had then. His father's voice, but not only his father's. Jem, Kalerina, Umon, Prague, and others. Broken and bloody, he'd watched as beasts and vines had consumed them all, dragging every drop of their blood to the soil.

It'll take me. I'm dead too, I'm dead too, I'm—

Oli saw the knife sheathed at his hip, about to be engulfed by the vine. There were older memories too, and they whispered in his mind and, more importantly, his muscles. He could remember feeling that same blade cut into vines like this before, his father looking over him, instructing him, his large hand covering Oli's smaller one, sawing it back and forth.

Oli snapped the blade from its sheath and brought it down—point first—to where the vine slithered up from the forest floor, pinning the vine there and cutting off its advance. Then Oli twisted the blade, quickly moving it to a slicing motion. Purple liquid, thicker than blood but with the same copper smell, poured from the incision. Moments later, the vine was cut clean through. The part of the vine still on the ground writhed, but what was wrapped around Oli's leg was limp and lifeless.

Dropping his bow, Oli used both his hands to peel back the dead vines from around his calf and thigh, his eyes drifting to the points of blood on the tips of the thorns. His blood. The sound of rustling leaves behind him sent shivers up his spine, but he didn't look. He snapped up his bow and rolled forward, away from the sound, relief making him heady. Sweat ran into his eyes, and he wiped it away as he twisted to see if the vines followed, imagining them slithering after him like a brood of vipers. Two of them hung from a tree above where he'd been, tips now stretched out lazily toward him.

"Idiot," Oli snapped through gritted teeth. He knew better. He wasn't in the Outer Bands anymore, he wouldn't get the opportunity to stop, to think. Here, you keep moving or you die.

Oli ran to where he'd seen the buck last, then took off in the direction it had run, eyes peeled for blood and tracks. He found both in abundance, especially Tuck's familiar line of prints in the muddy soil. He followed the trail as fast as he could, one eye always roaming for danger.

It wasn't long before he heard the sound of Tuck's barking. A moment later, Oli burst into a small clearing where the buck lay beside a small creek, Tuck's front paws on its side: claiming it. Oli's arrow was stuck halfway into the deer's chest, blood pooling around it. Vines stretched downward from all the trees encircling the clearing, drawn to the dead and dying.

Oli bounded over, yanking his arrow from the beast and dumping it back into his quiver, blood and all. The buck twitched, one eye locked on Oli, shaking and quivering in pain. Oli's knife was still covered in the purple life-blood of the vines when he ran it through the buck, ending its suffering. He didn't bother to clean the blade before sheathing it, the sounds of shifting leaves rushing him along.

He wanted out, now.

Oli heaved the buck over his shoulders, the animal's blood warming his back as it soaked his cloak and tunic. He would have to scrub for hours to get the smell out, though the stain would be permanent. The weight on his shoulders was heavy, but not quite as much as a full grown man. He'd be hard pressed to run, but he would move quick enough. He had no choice. Oli stepped back, boots squishing dirt made muddy by the passing stream.

There was a moment where Oli wondered if he could carry the deer all the way home. He was tired already, from the running, the nerves, but then one thought cut through all the others: *Move or die.* It was that simple. He needed food, he needed the pelt, and he needed to keep moving. Either he pushed through, or he died.

"Take us home, boy," Oli said, stumbling away from the descending vines. It only took him two paces to realize Tuck hadn't responded.

Oli turned, the imbalanced weight of the deer almost toppling him. Tuck was a few paces away, edging away from Oli, eyes east and tail still. His paws moved slowly, but deliberately. His whole body aimed eastward, towards something, somewhere, in the distance. The Call.

"Tuck," Oli called, voice firm. Tuck didn't even look his way, nor did his ears twitch in recognition. Oli's stomach sank and his throat went dry. Nightmares of this moment, the moment when Tuck gave into the Call, had haunted him night after night, but he wasn't ready for it now. Not now, not ever.

"Tuck," Oli said again. "*Palmaditze.*"

Tuck faltered, his ears twitched and his head cocked to the side, though he still didn't look back. Oli firmed his voice, adding steel to the edge of each word. "*Palmaditze! Preezt!*"

Come.

He threw the words out like a chain, wanting to capture Tuck and pull him back from whatever darkness the Wood was calling him towards. It was at the last word that Tuck shook his head and turned. He trotted over to Oli, tongue lolling as if nothing at all had happened.

"Don't act all innocent," Oli said. "Nearly killed me with fright. Now, take us home. *Diomok.*"

Tuck yipped then dashed westward, Oli trailing behind. Vines retracted back up into the trees, their prey now gone.

Oli was moving too slow, and he knew it.

The buck's weight made it impossible for anything more than a fervent walk, which would have been bad even if he hadn't been leaving a trail of blood behind him. But with the scent of blood running down his back and to the forest floor, he might as well have been screaming for the Wood to come devour him whole. The critters scattered at his passing, getting as far away as they could, sensing what was coming. This was the Wood, and even the roaches knew what fresh blood would bring.

But the vines writhed in pleasure, descending eagerly upon the pools of blood.

Just get over the Wall.

If he could, then they'd be safe enough. As far as he knew, none of the beasts in the Deep ever left. If he and Tuck could cross back into the Outer Bands they'd be fine. The Wood would be eager there too, but it wasn't the same and he could handle that. Oli thought about putting the buck down and doing something to stop the flow of blood, but stopping would be asking the vines to snare him.

Keep movin'.

And then Oli heard the howling.

His mind screamed in terror and he moved faster, picking up his pace to a painful and awkward jog: the best he could manage. The blood poured out faster and Oli nearly collapsed as the weight of the jostling deer increased with his pace. Any playfulness in Tuck was gone now, the dog moving faster through the winding maze of trees.

Another howl, closer this time. It was a twisted, gurgling sound which drew goosebumps along Oli's arms. He had to force himself not to look and see if a wolf pack was bearing down on him. Wolf howls traveled far, and a wolf half a mile away could sound as if it were merely at arm's length. He might have plenty of time . . . though he doubted it.

The path Tuck was carving for him seemed complicated now, dragged out. Wide twists and turns that felt more reckless than just barging straight westward. Every extra step was more time, and all that to avoid the *possibility* of a trap or unsafe terrain. But behind him was the certainty of a fight.

Oli charged forward, choosing the fastest way over tree roots, through piles of leaves, and even over squirming vines. He ignored the path Tuck carved for him, and moved faster as another howl ripped into his eardrums. He ran with all he had, praying whatever gods actually existed would find a scrap of mercy and let him make it to the Wall. He prayed his lungs would hold out, that the wolves were further away than they sounded.

He prayed he would live.

Then the toe of Oli's boot hooked onto an outstretched tree root, and he fell. The ground rushed up to meet him, the buck's weight driving his head down hard, and the world shattered into a thousand splinters of light.

THIRTEEN

There was no breath in Oli's lungs, no sound in his ears. He was on the ground, working to recall how he'd gotten there. His back and neck were wet with something warm, pleasant in the cool of the day. Slowly, pieces of recent memory seeped in. Scenes playing back in his mind. Tuck running in front of him, himself leaping from the Wall into the Deep. Why would he do that? It was foolish, stupid. What would be the point of hunting for food you'd be too dead to eat? He remembered the vines, and the most amazing deer he'd—

Oli's eyes shot open and he inhaled air. He put his palms to the ground and pushed upward: shivering from sweat and blood as he looked around him, parsing reality from dream and memory. Tuck was growling and clawing at something on the ground, the guttural sounds he made savage and wild.

"Tuck," Oli stood, voice choking on fear. Had he gone wild? Listened to the Call? Then, Oli saw the vine beneath the hound's teeth: a vine that had been slithering toward Oli's arm. *Thank the Maker.* Tuck was protecting him. Oli stumbled to his knees, yanked his knife free, and shoved Tuck aside so he could slice through the vine. Tuck had gotten halfway through with teeth and claws, and Oli made quick work of the rest.

"Good boy," Oli said, voice hoarse. He pulled Tuck to him, scratching behind his ear and inhaling the scent of him. Tuck's muzzle was scratched and bloodied from the thorns, and Oli had to force away feelings of guilt.

Around them, leaves rustled and crows cried, and Tuck began to twist about barking at everything and nothing. When Oli stood, his head swam as it tried to drink in the colors and sounds. And then the howling started up again.

The wolves.

No.

The buck lay a few paces away, two large vines already engulfing it. Oli scrambled forward, and lashed out, cutting them clean through. "Go! *Diomok*!" Oli screamed to Tuck, fumbling his knife into his sheath. He grabbed the buck and lifted it over his shoulders, trying to stay on his feet. He tasted his own blood and could feel the stream of it flowing down from his nose, which wasn't good.

Later, he thought. *That's a problem for later.*

Dirty, bloody, and tired, Oli picked up his bow as another howl split the air. It was louder now, which meant closer. A lot closer. Whether a second or a minute, he'd been out too long. Outwardly he grit his teeth, but inwardly he screamed, willing himself on. One step, then another, and another, and another. On Oli went, moving as best he could. Tuck was a red blur out in front, constantly running ahead and then doubling back for Oli, not used to the slow trod, unsure how to act with wolves bearing down on them.

Out of the corner of his eye, Oli saw them: three dark-gray wraiths bursting from the pits of Damnation and bounding after them.

"Tuck!" Oli yelled. He stood tall, letting the buck drop from his back. He couldn't outrun them now. Escape wasn't an option anymore, Oli had seen long ago what happened when you tried to outrun wolves. "*Sastavi!*"

Stop.

Tuck skidded to a stop, dashing back to Oli who was already nocking an arrow. The three wolves didn't slow. They were already within bow range, their legs a flurry as they zig-zagged amongst the trees. Tuck stood between Oli and their enemy, his bark loud and fierce, his body tensed.

Oli twisted, looking all around him, wanting to be sure he and Tuck weren't being surrounded, but he saw nothing except the slow creeping of vines down the trees nearby. He cursed and turned back to the wolves, raising his bow and trying not to think about the encroaching vines.

He couldn't outrun the wolves, and he couldn't stay there for long. Whatever happened, he'd need to end it fast.

"Calm down," he growled as he wrestled the bow to center in on the closest wolf. His breath was frantic and his arm shook with fear, two things which would mean a sure miss.

Tuck had stopped barking and crouched lower, body shaking with fear and anticipation.

"*Mneir*," Oli said, firming his voice as best he could.

Calm. It was a word for him as well as Tuck, and he felt his body giving way to a semblance of peace. His hands shook a little less, at least.

Oli tried to remember the word for "wolf", but he found nothing in his memory, though even if he could remember, it would hardly matter. The wolves would have to remember their own name for there to be any power in the words, and Oli doubted they would. Whatever was within them that was "wolf" was long gone, and Roi Ricker was the only one Oli ever knew who understood why. And he was long gone too.

The largest of the beasts dodged behind an oak at least two paces wide, disappearing for a blink of an eye. Oli turned, aimed his arrow to the side of the tree the wolf would emerge from, then loosed. The arrow flew through the air and . . . hit nothing.

Oli paused, then the wolf bounded out from behind the opposite side than Oli had anticipated, the same side he had come from. It bore down on Oli impossibly fast, covering the distance in eye blinks. But Oli's muscles worked faster, snatching an arrow from his quiver, nocking it, and letting it fly when the wolf was near arm's reach. The beast lowered its head and the arrow instead found the fatty flesh of the wolf's back, near its hind quarters.

The wolf made a sound like a cry and a yip all at once, as Oli dropped his bow and pulled his knife free. And then the wolf was on him, crashing into his chest with battering ram force, head still down. Oli flew backward and rolled along the ground, coming to his feet in one motion, knife ready. From the corner of his eye, he watched Tuck clawing and biting and thrashing about with the other two wolves.

Oli's wolf rolled away and rose to its paws, lunging immediately. Oli jumped back as the wolf bit, dodging once, twice, and then, when the wolf was about to launch itself a third time, Oli attacked. He reared forward, grabbing the wolf by its ear and violently yanking it to the side to expose its neck, jamming his knife downward. The wolf twisted and avoided a direct stab, but Oli's blade still cut open a wide gash along its neck. The wolf reared back clawing at Oli's arm, but Oli's hand was locked firmly on its ear, and so he was pulled forward into the beast.

Oli's attack was frantic and random, his knife pushing through fur and into muscles over and over again, making a handful of shallow slices wherever he could reach. He yelled, pouring his anger and fear into words of savage nothingness. He held the wolf close, refusing to let it gain distance or leverage: keeping it where his knife could reach. The wolf, unable to bite with Oli holding its ear and pulling back its head, clawed at Oli with its forepaws, scraping at his thighs, chest, and bicep. It hurt each time, but the claws couldn't get enough purchase to do any real damage, so Oli kept jabbing his blade up and down until the wolf's body stilled.

Oli stumbled to his feet, standing over the wolf, his hands, chest, and legs covered in blood. The wolf's eyes were vacant, void of the fire and hunger that had stared him down moments before. Hands shaking, eyes wide, Oli breathed in a ragged breath . . . and then the sounds of fighting wormed into his ears.

Tuck.

Oli left the buck and ran toward his hound, who was still tumbling on the ground with one of the wolves, his jaws around the beast's throat. The other wolf dashed in and out of the fight, working to get its own jaws around Tuck's head. Oli caught the wolf unaware: coming up from behind and thrusting his knife deep into its eye before it could do so much as twist or bark. The second wolf, the one Tuck's own jaw was about, went down just as easily: Oli jabbed the blade into its back over and over, making a mess of its pelt until it went limp in Tuck's grasp.

"Oh no!" Oli said, throwing the wolf's body to the side so he could get a good look at Tuck.

Blood was everywhere, and Oli couldn't tell what was from Tuck's wounds and what was from the wolves. His fingers prodded around the amber fur, pressing in gently where he thought the blood was darker than the rest. Tuck whimpered and swatted at Oli, who ignored him, hands moving quick. When Oli touched a spot near his belly, Tuck squealed in pain, his eyes filling with tears.

That was bad.

"Oy, you're a real pain, ain't ya?" Oli said, looking around as if help would materialize. None did. "I'll have to carry ya. Alright? It'll be alright. You'll see."

Oli grabbed his bow and flung it over his back near his quiver. Then he carefully lifted Tuck, tutting and shushing in what he wanted to be a reassuring voice, but he sounded manic even to his own ears. Then Oli turned, eyeing the buck on the ground a few paces away, and the wolf he'd stabbed in the eye. Already a large vine had squirmed atop of the buck, but the wolf corpse was free and clear. When was the last time someone had brought back a wolf pelt? There'd be coin for something so rare, and a lot of it. He thought of Layla, of his mother, of winter nights and hungry bellies.

Tuck whined in his arms.

He couldn't think of a way he could carry both it and Tuck. Maybe if he had time, but the Wood never gave time. If he stayed, what else would emerge? It was a pelt or a dog. Food or starvation.

"I got ya," Oli said quietly, closing his eyes and turning his back to the buck, the wolf, and so much more. And then he said it again, and again, and again. Over and over, as he moved through the Deep in the direction of the Wall separating him from the Outer Bands, and eventually to the hillside of Watchful. "I got ya."

CHAPTER
FOURTEEN

Léonie had little interest in meeting the priest. Still, she had less interest in listening to Amandine prattle on incessantly. "When one plans to knock on the doors of Damnation," the duchess had said, "should they not at least seek He who has the keys?"

And so Léonie stood at the door of what appeared to be a bundle of driftwood assembled into an imitation of four walls, her shawl held tight around her neck to ward off both the chill of the wind and the eerie feeling this wretched town gave her. For the third time, she checked the sigil above the door. This simply could *not* be the town's Sanctuary. She hardly considered herself pious, her brother Bastion had always been the holy one, but even she understood the disgrace it was to have the Order of Deōs housed in a ramshackle hut. *The Magistrate will need to go.*

"My lady," Thibault leaned close to her ear, though his attention was firmly on the street behind them. "It may be best if we move inside."

Léonie gave a quick glance over her shoulder, letting her eyes graze over the two dozen other pairs staring back at her. Predictably, a crowd had formed. She could not hear any one thing being said, of course, but a crowd had its own kind of language, its own way of communicating and making its intent known. A lifetime in the public eye, and she had grown rather good at listening to the language of crowds. This particular bit of rabble was not dangerous. Or, not yet. There was confusion and fear mixed in with awe. *Is that really the princess? Here? It can't be*, and so on.

"Princess?"

Léonie sighed, checked the sigil one last time. "On with it, Captain, lest I have to stand an evening of tireless bickering from the duchess."

Thibault, his nose red from the cold, opened the Sanctuary door. He stepped in quickly, announcing Léonie as he went. "Arise for the Princess of Trevelar, Jewel of Turris Regis, and daughter of the High King: Princess Léonie Baudelaire."

At the last, the captain stepped aside and bowed, clearing the way for Léonie. She cringed as she stepped from cobblestone side-walk to creaky floorboards, each dirtied with traffic and age. The room (for Léonie refused to think of it as a Sanctuary) was cramped, a feeling made worse by the small benches crowding most of the floor. To the side, the hearth burned high enough Léonie felt compelled to unwrap her shawl lest sweat break out along her neck. An elderly priest stoked the fire, his knobby hands shaking as they worked a long iron poker. He turned toward her, bowing so she stared at the top of his wrinkled head.

A bow is something, at least, Léonie thought.

Priests were, to Léonie's utter annoyance, not required to observe the formalities of Court. There was a pretense of being above the muck and mire of state politics, the Order divorced from the fetters of mortal life. They did not need to bow, or pay taxes, nor sow or reap in the fields. Supposedly, they need not pay head to any authority but Deōs.

But it was all a sham, like those illusions they called "miracles". Léonie's father enjoyed their privilege about as much as Léonie did, though he had chosen to keep the peace. He had little choice, for it was within the rights of the High Priest to revoke the Maker's favor from the Baudelaire name and create a vacuum of power at the top of the Trevlarian court. Likewise, the king could stem the flow of gold from the crown's treasury to the Order, creating paupers of priests.

Each had a knife to the other's throat, the way God ordained.

Religion and politics, Léonie thought with a sneer.

"Have I displeased you already, Princess?"

Léonie blinked, focusing again on the priest whose brow was furrowed as if inspecting a suspicious ailment. "Not yet," she said. "And let us hope you do not plan to."

The priest snorted. "If I were much for plans I wouldn't have wound up *here* of all places. I would be teaching at one of the coastal abbeys in the north."

"Discontent is unbecoming from someone wearing the white." She stepped further into the room, away from the heat of the fire. "Will you not have to pray prayers of repentance lest you be unable to intercede for the people of this town?"

"If God were going to shy away from a bickering old man, he would have done it by now. Besides, this town hardly cares if it is interceded for." He waved his hand around the empty room. "You have interrupted the noonday gathering, though it would seem our pious patrons do not mind."

Léonie considered the priest. She had known dozens of them throughout her life: tutors mostly, educating her on Trevlarian history and the importance of maintaining her virtue. They were stuffy, old men, every one of them. White-robed skeletons with desire tugging at the corners of their eyes, wanting the power which came with nearness to the crown. This priest was old and stuffy as well, but his eyes appeared indifferent, apathetic.

"I have been taught that Deōs demands his subjects to be content, whatever their lot in life. Yet you stand here longing for a comfortable abbey."

"The opposite of contentment isn't complaining, Your Highness."

"Then what is?"

"Hunger."

Something about the way he said the word, the way he drew out the last syllable, made Léonie's face flush. She felt like a child again, a tutor calling out a fatal error. "And you hunger for what then? A comfortable abbey with the smell of saltwater upon the air?"

He chuckled. "Rest assured, Princess, I am content. More or less, anyways. Only occasionally do I dwell upon my sorry lot in life, and even then it is but a brief foray into depression and self-flagellation. Nothing to be concerned about. But please, you have not come to listen to the mutterings of an old man. In fact, please forgive my frankness, but I can't imagine why you've come at all."

"To this town or to your Sanctuary?"

"Yes."

Léonie said nothing as she turned her attention upward. The rafters were visible above, thin strips of daylight slipping through the roof slats. Candles burned near the dais, illuminating a small plate of half-eaten bread and cheese.

"Forgive me," the priest said when he saw where her gaze lay. "Your guards only notified me minutes before your arrival. I was eating lunch."

"In the Sanctuary?"

"Do you think God will mind?"

"A touch disrespectful, no?"

"Hmm. Deōs grew the wheat for flour, blessed the cows with milk, and then curdled it for cheese. After all of that, I doubt he would begrudge his servant a meal in his presence."

Léonie waved a hand dismissively. This was already an utter waste of time, and she turned to leave. And then, sudden and unbidden, a thought crossed her mind. She looked to the priest. "Nothing will touch it."

"Your Highness?"

"The food," Léonie was looking around again, this time her eyes searching for clues. "Nothing will touch your food."

"Uh, well . . ." His eyes furrowed for a brief moment, then realization dawned. "Ah, you mean pests. A problem elsewhere, certainly. They say that, in Turris Regis, even your mice have mice and your fleas have fleas. But no, not here. On this edge of the world, our scraps are safe from all but time. There is little in the way of pests, which is a rather wonderful silver lining, I suppose."

And that was when Léonie noticed it, or rather realized what was missing. In the corners and above in the rafters, there were no cobwebs. "Even the spiders have been lured into the *Vromia*, then?"

The priest nodded. "A million little miracles keep our ecology alive. Somehow flowers bloom and seed spreads without all the insects, birds, or rodents. Scholars have occasionally arrived to study this stretch of mystery, though perhaps the foremost scholar is also our local bartender, if you can imagine it."

Léonie could not.

"What was your name?"

"Evanvalt, Your Highness."

"And which sect do you come to Watchful from, Priest Evanvalt? Which abbey oversees the souls of those this far from the heart of our kingdom?"

Evanvalt was quiet for a time, giving up poking at the fire to simply stare. When he turned to Léonie, his face was red from heat. "The Arason Abbey has been charged by the Order to oversee the protection of Watchful."

Arason. Léonie rolled the name around in her mind. It tasted familiar, known, but she found it hard to place. "It is an old sect, is it not?"

"Very old, Your Highness."

"Yes," Léonie nodded, it was coming back to her now. "Heretical, no? You were brandished traitors during the Cleansing. For opposition to the war with Velik, I believe."

"*I* was not branded a traitor, as it was a touch before even I was born." Evanvalt frowned. "But what you say is true. The monks of Arason did not condone the war."

"It was more than that. Rather recently, in fact, I read Father

Pionoche was burned alive for harboring enemy soldiers. The monastery was a field hospital for the enemy."

Evanvalt twitched. "Our monastery has stood as a refuge for *all*. Velk lay beside Trevlarian soldiers on our infirmary beds."

"That is aiding the enemy. During a time of war, no less."

"I would like to remind Your Highness that the monastery was . . . purged, and established anew decades years ago."

"Oh, do calm down. I am not threatening to throw *you* into the flames. Unless, of course, you have wounded Yelmes resting in your infirmary."

Evanvalt snorted. "I would prefer you not jest about the flames."

"If only I were jesting. Kātsracha has opened its maw again. Demons roam our land and your *God* seems to have little to say." Léonie dropped her hand to her side, wishing her blade hung there. She hated talking about the Yelmes without steel nearby to ward off the memories.

The priest said nothing, only looked at her, eyes searching her face as if trying to detect a lie. Eventually he turned and trudged up toward the small plate at the front of the room.

"Your brethren tore their robes when they heard the news," Léonie said, eyes narrowing on the priest's back. "You hardly seem surprised."

"Those in Terris Regis ripped their splendid finery, did they? I'd have paid to see that. But no, I can't say I'm all that surprised. Nor am I caught off guard by this turn of events. Our sect has been preparing for this day for many long years," Evanvalt raised his voice so Léonie could hear him over his shoulder. "It would be more troubling if I were surprised."

Léonie faltered. "Do you mean to say you *knew* the Yelmes would return?"

"I mean to say that the head of our order tended to Velik wounded centuries ago because *he* believed Kātsracha would burst forth once more. But before he died, Father Pionoche charged the monks and priests of Arason to stay vigilant, and we have."

"Vigilant for the return of demons?"

"I'm not certain the demons have ever left, Your Highness. But for the return of the Yelmes, we have watched." Evanvalt sat down and lifted a wedge of bread and tore it between his bony fingers.

"The Land of Darkness is far to the west," Léonie spat. "It is little wonder you have missed the signs. More warning would have been appreciated, even from heretics."

Evanvalt raised an eyebrow. "Who said we have missed the signs? We saw them. *I* saw them. Letters were written, messengers sent. The High Priest was too stubborn to listen. Elatus would have had to admit his position was not as comfortable as he would have liked."

Léonie stepped forward. "How could you have known? How could *anyone* have known?"

"One need only learn the signs, Your Highness. If you hear the bell toll, you can be sure someone stands below tugging at the rope. If the fishing rod bends, something surely is caught on the line. Two things need only to be connected for the signs to become clear."

Léonie's head spun and she leaned a hand against one of the nearby pews. "Speak plainly, priest. My patience runs thin these days."

Evanvalt spread his hands wide. "I suspect I know why you are here, Princess Léonie. You seek what lies inside the Wood, yes?"

Léonie stared at him. She said nothing, could say nothing. How could this decrepit old man, priest or no, know so much?

"The power inside the *Vromia* is contained, but only barely. After a thousand years it has nearly worn its fetters down. My sect has sensed this, and they dispatched me here to watch and wait."

"And why you? What could you possibly do against such power?"

"Do? Very little. I am simply gifted at seeing connections. It is my sad lot in life. And the Ancient One is tied to Kātsracha, a deep link formed long ago when Trevelar was but a budding collection of villages warring over half-dug wells. The nearer this power has come to breaking free of its chains the more tumultuous the Yelmes must be growing."

Léonie sat down, though a part of her mind knew it would take her maids all afternoon to get the dust and dirt from the butt of her gown. "Then you know what I seek. *Whom* I seek."

Evanvalt nodded. "Though, to be sure, I expected to see the Yelmes at our foothills instead of the crown. With that in mind, this is a rather fond surprise."

"The Yelmes are not far behind."

The priest's shoulders slumped visibly. "Well then, I suppose I have another letter to write to my brethren."

"Letters," Léonie waved her hand. "All anyone wants to do is send letters, demand support, and talk their way out of the end of our kingdom."

Evanvalt pulled free more of his bread and said nothing.

"I am here because I plan on *doing*. The power contained in the *Vromia* will be mine, and with it I will do what was done a thousand years ago in the last Epoch war. I will open up the ground and have it swallow the Yelmes whole, filling the earth with blood until my kingdom is safe once more. I will not stand by and send letters or talk any longer."

"I sympathize with your plight, surely, and I'm prone to agreement. However, it does beg a certain question. Why are you here now, speaking with *me*?"

Léonie stood, waving a hand in annoyance. "Duchess Amandine of Worchestern advised I come and receive the Maker's blessing. Foolishness, of course, but less foolish than listening to the woman send barbs my way all evening."

"She is a wise woman, then, this Duchess of Worchestern."

"She seems to think so." Léonie turned for the door.

"Surely she knew I would refuse."

"Excuse me?" Léonie stopped and turned back around. "Refuse the crown?"

"Refuse to bless your endeavor, at least. It is more than foolish, Your Highness. It is heresy."

"And this coming from a heretic?"

"My sect was cleansed."

"Cleansed and then quarantined off into the farthest reaches of the kingdom."

"Entrusted with guarding the Order's greatest secret."

"Staradovna."

Evanvalt bowed his head, his voice low. "If you were not of the crown, I would not be permitted to let you live."

Léonie coughed out a laugh, though Thibault moved forward and drew his sword.

"Peace, Captain," Léonie said, though she did not order him to sheath his weapon. "So this is how such a wild thing has been left to flourish in our kingdom with nothing but rumors making their way to the capitol. The Order has a heretical sect of spies and assassins, yes?"

"Most of our work is in misdirection," the priest said, raising his hands to the side, palms up. "But we are careful about the caravans allowed through, the travelers and scholars permitted in . . . or out."

"All to keep the secrets of the *Vromia* contained?"

"To keep fools from attempting to take it for themselves."

Léonie glared at the priest. "Do you think me a fool?"

Evanvalt chewed on his next words, his jaw working left and right. "You are of royal blood. I am bound to not interfere with your plans, for the High Priest has deemed your family appointed by Deōs to rule this kingdom. But I beg of you not to attempt to enter the Wood. Stay here and defend this place from the Yelmes who would also seek this power. I shall send for reinforcements from my Order, and together it shall be possible to hold this line."

"*Hold the line,*" Léonie said, her lips and voice sneering. "You expect so little of me? How many thousands will die elsewhere in the kingdom while we sit here trying to hold this line? All while your secret power lays dormant and within reach? No, I refuse passivity and weakness. I am a Baudelaire. I will enter the *Vromia* and I will tame whatever power is within for my purposes. That is my will, and I shall have it done."

Evanvalt rose to his feet, but Léonie did not wait to hear any more. She turned and marched through the Sanctuary's poorly hung door, slamming it behind her hard enough for the whole building to shudder.

CHAPTER
FIFTEEN

Oli emerged from the Wood, walking with equal parts determination and fatigue. Tuck's breathing was steady, but the strips of cloth Oli had wrapped around him were stained red. It was impossible to know how bad the bleeding was without removing the makeshift bandages entirely, and he didn't dare do that. Oli was in a rough state too: breathing hard, mouth dry, and cheeks soaked with blood-mixed tears. Once he'd gotten past the Wall, he'd stopped to rip up his cloak into bandages for Tuck, and he'd taken a moment to look himself over. He was like a rag doll that'd gotten into a fight with a pair of knives. A gash near his bicep looked particularly bloody, and he'd tried to wrap it as best he could.

Exhausted and sore, his thighs and arms bleeding, Oli cursed himself for ever having gone beyond the Wall. He should've doubled down and settled for the small game in the Outer Bands, and just muddled through the winter as best he could. Instead he'd gone ahead and gotten Tuck maimed, maybe killed, and where did that leave him?

He was still crying as he left the Wood, snot dripping onto his upper lip. To his shame, Oli wasn't crying for Tuck. Even if Tuck survived, it'd be weeks or more before he'd hunt again, and what would Oli do in the meantime? It was near impossible to bring in enough game with Tuck sniffing it out, but without him? Oli wouldn't catch much. He could navigate the Wood without Tuck, but slowly, and not while also tracking game. Larz had been the only one Oli knew who'd figured out how to hunt alone, but he also didn't have anyone else to care for.

But not Oli. His mother and sister depended on him, they *needed* him. His mother earned hardly enough to pay off the debts she'd been left with after her husband's death, it was Oli's responsibility to keep food on the table, and he'd failed. If this winter had spelled disaster before, now the first flurries of snow would most certainly herald at least one grave in the Ricker home.

Anej saw him coming, his Velk eyes keen enough to make out Oli before Oli would have ever spotted the giant. By the time he arrived, Anej was ready with a pitcher of water and clean cloth.

"I'm a tanner," Anej said as soon as Oli was within earshot. "Don't be expecting miracles."

Oli nodded, gingerly laying Tuck down on the same wooden table Anej had skinned the deer the day before. The sun was just beginning its descent below the hill to the west, the mansions on the hilltop haloed in orange light. The two worked side by side, man and giant, racing against the looming dark. They removed the bandages and cleaned Tuck's wounds with water from Anej's well. With the blood cleaned from the fur, they could make out a pair of jagged slices along the belly: each a finger long and a fingernail deep. Tuck whimpered, and gave a weak growl.

"It ain't good," Anej said. "Best sew 'em up and quick."

"He'll live?"

"Not if we don't sew him up."

Oli nodded numbly as Anej disappeared into his cabin, emerging a moment later with a small sewing kit not unlike Oli's own. Oli nearly offered to do the work himself, but a quick glance down at his own bloody hands told him he was still shaking far too much.

"Best hold him still," Anej said. "Don't think he'll like this much."

It was terrible work. Oli struggled to keep Tuck pinned to the table as he barked and moaned. Anej's needle was a blur, moving in and out of Tuck's skin, pulling the wound closed with quick tugs of the thread. The velk's fingers moved deftly, poking and pulling on the needle with such precision Oli wondered if Anej's mother was a seamstress back wherever he'd grown up.

If velks had mothers, that is. Or seamstresses.

But the way blood leaked from the wounds in small spurts was a firm reminder that this was his friend, and not some piece of cloth being stitched up. Eventually, Tuck stopped shaking and growling, his body too weak for anything except pitiful whimpering. Anej placed a small stack of clean cloth over the wounds when he was finished, then tied it down with twine.

Then Anej gently lifted Tuck and began carrying him towards the cottage. "Best let him rest for a time before you make your way up the hill. He's asleep, and waking him would be a fool's work." Anej paused, narrowing his eyes at Oli. "First though, you grab that bucket and cloth and go out back. Draw water and clean up. This is the tanner's house, not the trash pile."

Oli nodded and grabbed the bucket and the least bloodied cloth.

The well was a simple thing: stones stacked around a hole in the ground, a large rope coiled beside it, ready to be tied about the bucket's handle. Oli had left the tattered remains of his cloak near the Wall, and now he stripped what remained of his clothes, groaning as he pulled his shirt and trousers away from the wounds on his arms and legs. Naked, he worked at removing the dried blood from his skin, carefully taking stock of himself as he went. His thighs, stomach, and chest were a mess of shallow cuts, but they'd heal up well enough. His bicep had taken most of the beating: purple bruising blossoming around a short, and jagged gash. Oli cursed as he cleaned it, flinching at his own touch. He should have been cold, naked and with the wind nipping at him. But all he could feel was the pain in his arm. Otherwise, thoughts of Tuck had him unfeeling.

Anej cursed as well, stomping out from around the house toward him. "Oy, how'd you get the pup all the way back there with an arm like that?" Oli didn't answer and Anej didn't press the point. Instead, the tanner produced a small jar of ointment and clean linen, then gestured for Oli to hold out his arm. The smell of honey and turmeric wafted from the jar when it opened, leaving Oli lightheaded and the world slowly shifting.

"Steady now," Anej said, holding Oli as he began to sway. Anej worked with the same deft and intentional movements as he had with Tuck, and in moments a small bit of ointment filled Oli's cuts, and a strip of linen was wrapped about his arm.

"Now get dressed and come in. Stew should be ready."

Oli sat beside the hearth in the only chair Anej owned that was sized for mere humans, his belly content, if not full. He held a mug of warm ale in both hands, Tuck asleep beside the hearth near his feet.

He's alive, Oli thought for the dozenth time. Relief came with the thought, but was quickly replaced with regret when he considered the wasted wolf pelts left for the Wood to devour. And then there would be the relief of knowing Tuck was alive, and then the image of the wolf pelt, and the cycle would repeat.

But in the end, Tuck *was* alive. For now, at least. But he wasn't healed yet, and nothing was guaranteed.

Anej sat beside Oli, his bulk resting on a chair made of thick cedar beams and large strips of animal hide. In the velk's mouth was a pipe of pale briar wood which puffed smoke to the rafters. His eyes watched the flames, reflecting their light back out into the world.

Oli had never been in Anej's home before, and it felt oddly comfortable. Well made, with stone walls and thick wooden rafters holding up a sturdy roof. Animal hides were everywhere: a massive bear pelt was the rug beneath Oli's feet, and the pelts of foxes and wolves had been sewn together to make blankets that draped over a bed large enough to sleep a family of six. On the walls hung pelts the color of black and ivory, beasts Oli couldn't place. In the dead of winter, Anej's cabin may be one of the warmest places in Watchful, with all the furs to hold in the heat and keep out the cold.

But what truly kept drawing Oli's eyes, more than the trophy heads on the wall or the massive bed in the corner, were the spear and shield laid against the side of the hearth. The shield was perhaps as tall as Oli was, and the spear was far taller, its shaft as thick as Oli's fist and the spearhead as long as his forearm. It was a truly inhuman thing, an object that made it all the clearer Anej was from another land entirely. Another world, as far as Oli was concerned. With a weapon like that, the velk could skewer a fully grown bear in one thrust. What would it have been like, Oli wondered, to have fought against such giants back at the start of the Second Era? The war with Velik was heralded as a great Trevlarian victory, but it seemed an impossibility humans like Oli could ever have stood against the Velk for one battle, let alone win a war.

"I'm grateful, Anej," Oli said, or tried to say. It came out a hoarse whisper off a parched tongue. Oli took another swig of ale, then repeated. "I'm grateful to ya."

Anej answered by leaning back and blowing a ring of smoke up into the vaulted ceiling. "The Deep, eh?"

Oli nodded.

"Alone, I suppose," Anej said, shaking his head. "Your pa would be proud, but that's 'bout the only good that'll come of it."

Oli bristled. "Squirrel jerky and rabbit fur don't get much coin. I need somethin' them merchants would buy. I was less than a mile or so past the Wall when Tuck caught a whiff of a deer worthy of your walls." Oli gestured with one hand at the animals trophies hanging about. "If I'd been faster . . ." Oli trailed off.

Anej's eyes furrowed. "It's hard times for you folk. Dangerous too, and gettin' all the more dangerous."

Oli turned, looking the velk over. How old was he? The giants didn't age like normal men, but Oli figured the tinges of gray in his matted beard meant he wasn't young. The look in his eyes, the way they were hard in the center and soft about the edges, he must be getting old.

"You know something I don't?"

Anej chuckled. "Maybe a thing or two, but probably less. No, I don't know anything, but do I suspect some things. And I hear things from people who *think* they know."

"Larz."

Anej nodded. "Larz, aye. But more than him. All you Stražar come to me. The Wood is more dangerous today than yesterday, and will be more dangerous tomorrow." He took a long puff from his pipe, then blew the smoke gruffly out through his nostrils. "Something's brewin'."

Oli scratched his chin. "You wasn't always a tanner."

Anej nodded, slow and steady. "That's right."

Oli pointed to the large shield and spear. "Were ya a fighter then?"

"Over the mountains, we're all fighters."

Oli grunted. Everyone in Watchful grew up in the shadow of the Nevihta Mountains knowing the other side of those peaks was Velik, the home of the giants. A whole kingdom of people like Anej. "So why'd you come here? Why be a tanner?"

Anej turned to Oli, lips firm around his pipe. Oli met his gaze, and felt the familiar twisting inside at the sight of his shattered iris. There was a story there, but Oli figured he'd always be too afraid to ask.

"I was called," Anej said after a moment. "Like the rest of us."

Oli said nothing. *I was called.* "Called" was a Stražar word, laced with meaning for those of the Wood. But Anej wasn't of the Stražar, yet he understood the Wood as though he were one.

Oli leaned forward. "Well, I best get Tuck home and get him settled. If I leave now, might even get to the merchant stalls 'fore they close up. See what it is they brought with 'em."

Anej laughed humorlessly. "Aye, I wouldn't be expecting to find no merchants up the hill, if that's what you're thinking."

"I saw 'em drivin' on up in the dead of night. You tellin' me I saw ghosts?"

"Aye, you saw something comin' on up the hill. I saw 'em too, mind. But they ain't no merchants. Ghosts may be more like it, seein' as the last time Trevlarian royalty come on through here it was a bloodbath. Don't suppose nobody remembers that though."

"Royalty?"

"Aye," Anej said. "You heard right. Princess Léonie Baudelaire, daughter of the king, rode into ol' *Spectare* last night and has been causing quite the ruckus. Ulian said she's done confiscated every room in his inn, as well as the Penny's rooms and Tote's entire mansion, if you can believe that."

Oli couldn't believe it, and he said so.

"Well, believe it or not, there's finally something stranger here than even the Wood and all its happenings." Anej leaned in close towards Oli, tapping the stem of his pipe on his bearded cheek. "Mark my words, Woodsman, this won't end well. Folk about here don't remember it now, but us folk across the mountain do. When the eyes of the King fall upon *Vromia* then that is a bad omen indeed. History is like a wheel, going about over an endless road."

Spectare, Oli thought. *Vromia*. His father had used words like those, and Oli had thought they had died with the man. To hear Anej use them, and to hear the giant talk about princesses and old wars, made him dizzy all over again. "Let me get Tuck home, then we'll both sleep and in the morning this nightmare will be over."

"I figured you'd know by now, runnin' away don't make the nightmare end." Anej turned towards the fire in the mantle. "Just keeps the dream goin'. And besides, if you move the pup he might not—'' A pounding on the door cut Anej's words short.

Anej stood, looking at Oli, as if he might know who was knocking, but Oli only shrugged.

"What in the depths?" Anej muttered to himself, putting the pipe back between his lips, the bowl of which still trailed smoke. In two strides Anej had made it to the door, and swung it open.

"Aye," Anej growled. "Who might you be?" With Anej's bulk looming in the doorway, Oli couldn't see who was on the other side, nor could he hear anything other than the velk's own rumbling, baritone, replies. "And what has that got to do with me?" Anej said, puffs of smoke billowing up above his head.

There was a muffled reply, and Oli thought it might be a man's voice. Something about the whole interaction made his ears burn and sweat bead on his neck, though he didn't know why. Oli spared a glance at Tuck, then stood and turned toward the door, hand moving to the hilt of his knife.

"Aye, I know him." Anej said.

More muffled talk, followed by silence.

Anej was shuffling his feet, and Oli watched as one of the giant's hands slipped behind his back, gently lifting up his shirt to reveal a blade sheathed there. It was probably a small dagger in the giant's hands, though to a man it would have been a short sword.

Oli moved toward the door in about four strides of his own.

"Oy," he said, putting a hand on Anej's arm and nudging him aside. "What is it?"

Anej let the handle of the blade go, then turned to the side so Oli could see the newcomers.

The sun was casting the colors of twilight on the eastern mountains, pinks and oranges splayed out on distant peaks brilliant enough to be painted and framed inside one of the homes up the hill. But Oli didn't see the beauty of those distant mountains, for in front of him was a familiar looking man with a pretentious caterpillar of a mustache and black hair curled in tight loops. Behind him stood two men in chainmail and travel-stained orange surcoats, their eyes narrowed on Anej and their hands held fast to the pommels of the swords. A few paces to the side was a hooded figure whose face Oli couldn't make out, though he saw the unstrung bow at their back.

"There he is," the younger man said to the soldiers behind him. Then, to Anej, he growled. "You just said he wasn't here."

Anej cocked an eyebrow. "Don't recall sayin' anything of the sort. All I said is I know him."

The soldiers exchanged looks, and the younger man looked ready to object, but Oli cut in. "Oy, you're Windsun? The Tote boy?"

Windsun looked back at Oli, face screwed up in either insult or disgust. "Obviously. And I'm here on important business from the crown."

Oli hardly listened, his mind racing through his conversation with his sister. It was only last night, but last night felt a long way off now. If he remembered right, this was the man harassing Layla, and he'd come to Anej's home looking for *him*. Oli's eyes darted to the men behind Windsun, eyeing their strange colors. He couldn't think if he'd ever seen orange fabric like that before, and especially not so travel worn. "And these," Oli pointed to the men behind Windsun, "are your guards?"

Windsun turned about, looking uncomfortable. "Uh . . . no. These are men from the guard of the Royal Princess. This is why I've come, you see—"

Oli stopped listening, though Windsun's mouth kept moving a moment longer. What Oli saw in front of him was a barrier, an obstacle, stopping his sister from honest wages and the freedom to move about Watchful without being harassed. He saw danger, a threat.

A beast.

Oli crossed the threshold of the home in one stride and then he was in front of Windsun in one more. In the same motion, his good arm shot out, fist balled, cracking against Windsun's eye. Windsun dropped to the ground with a cry that wasn't quite loud enough to drown out the sound of swords sliding from scabbards. Oli spared a glance at the soldiers, expecting them to spring toward him, but they didn't. Instead, they took cautious steps back, their blades resting in front of them defensively.

And they weren't looking at Oli, they were looking *behind* him.

Oli turned, but Anej was doing nothing other than chuckling, leaning back against his door frame and blowing a particularly large puff of smoke up into the air. Oli looked back to Windsun, stepping above him as he writhed, hand over his face as he slung out curses haphazardly.

"What in La'Azurus?" Windsun yelled, looking at Oli through his one good eye. The other eye he covered with one hand while he backed himself up along the ground toward the soldiers. "Why would you—"

"Oy! How 'bout ya keep yourself away from my sister, eh?" Oli snapped.

Windsun froze, mouth agape. "How dare you—"

Oli lurched forward, grabbing Windsun's shirt collar and jerking him up with one hand while the other yanked the knife from its sheath, lifting it to Windsun's throat. Part of Oli's brain acknowledged the pain shooting through his arm, but it was easy enough to ignore with Windsun's lip quivering before him. The soldiers still held their positions, but their eyes were no longer on Anej. They looked at Oli now, wary and . . . frightened?

Oli imagined what he must look like to them: his clothes caked with dried blood, his arm bandaged, a stench reeking off of him that even he noticed. Even his blade was still marred in wolf's blood.

He looked like an animal. A beast.

Windsun's breath came in ragged gasps, hot against Oli's face. Oli's voice was hoarse. "If Layla don't get decent work by tomorrow's eve, it won't be my fist, but my blade in that eye next time. Ya hear me?"

Windsun said nothing, though his eye widened and his face paled. Oli gave him a quick jerk, rattling him out of shock. "Leave my sister alone. And ya best go back to Yigguns and let 'im know he should be hirin' her for work. Now, nod your head if ya hearin' me."

Windsun nodded frantically.

"Good, good. Now get goin', best not waste time." Oli dropped Windsun to the ground, and he skittered backwards, standing up when he was a few paces away, never looking away from Oli who was looking toward the soldiers now. They weren't a threat though, and seemed not to care about Windsun at all. They had returned their stares to Anej, likely the only one they saw as a threat.

But where was . . . Then Oli saw him: the cloaked man. Except, it wasn't a man, but a woman. She'd dropped the hood of her cloak, her dark hair falling in uneven lumps around her shoulders. Her hands were clad in fingerless gloves, held out before her as if to calm Oli down, taming a wild beast.

"Out with it," Oli said, shoving his blade back into its sheath. Windsun had gone now, running back up the hill with fretful glances back towards Oli. "I'm too tired for games, if ya can't tell."

The woman lowered her hands, then gestured to the guards who, after a long pause, sheathed their swords. She was pretty, her skin olive and feminine, but marked with subtle scars and calluses on her fingers which served as a testament she knew how to use the bow slung over her back. She was Badaui, if only in part. It was the way she moved that was the giveaway: careful and brisk all at the same time, her arms and legs totally controlled. Oli felt a burst of self consciousness as she stepped toward him, and he placed his hands on his hips, unsure what else to do with them.

"Are you Oli Ricker?"

"Aye. Who's asking?"

"I am Tâl, ranger in service to King Baudelaire, on assignment from his daughter, Princess Léonie Baudelaire. She has, as I understand it, invited you to dinner."

"I—" Oli had nearly told her to screw off when the meaning of Tâl's words sank in. Instead, he mumbled a dumbstruck, "What?"

Tâl smiled. "It's best to say 'yes' and then come along. We'll need to get you new clothes and we should be quick about it. The princess isn't one to keep waiting, and supper will be served soon, if it hasn't been already."

"New clothes?" Oli looked down at his bandaged arm, his ripped pants, blood stained shirt.

"Aye." Tâl said, stepping forward and giving Oli a cautious sniff. "Shame we haven't the time for a bath too. It'll be alright though. The princess ain't the squeamish type."

The princess . . . Oli's mind was more than numb, it had gone totally blank. There was no reference point for it to work from, no understanding to grab onto and make sense of the woman's words.

"Go on," Anej called out, stepping back inside his home. "Tuck will be safe with me. Ya best be goin'. Royals have a way of hangin' them people who say 'no'." And then he shut the door, the *thump* of it like thunder.

Tâl looked at the closed door and gave a nod of approval, then turned and began marching up towards Watchful proper.

"Oy," Oli said, jogging until he was walking alongside her. "I don't understand. Why does the Prin—" Oli stopped, unable to say the word. "Why does she wanna see me?"

Tâl didn't look his way, but Oli watched her lips purse, as if she were trying out different replies in her mind. "It isn't *you*, exactly. She ordered Windsun to bring her the local huntsmen. Stražar? Is that what you call yourselves?" Oli nodded. "I spent the whole day following that *sigmil* around, and you're the only one we found."

They walked in silence then, Oli's mind trying to catch up to their feet. By the time they were in the town proper, the sky was dark and the only light on the street spilt from the Downwind's windows and open doorway, the sound of clanging mugs and chatter spilling out along with it. Beyond the tavern, the whole of Watchful was bustling, even in the sun's absence. Where normally there would be quiet streets in the wake of sunset, now there were wheelbarrows of dirt or picked crops being moved about, handcarts with boxes being wheeled this way or that, pairs of folk of all kinds standing in doorways and alleyways conspiring, and soldiers . . . so many soldiers stomping about in rattling chainmail, barking orders to one another and each looking insufferably important. Most wore the same strange orange as the soldiers, though Oli caught sight of hooded figures like Tâl who moved in the shadows and away from the torchlit streets.

Soon they passed the Ricker home, and Oli breathed out a prayer of thanks that neither his mother nor Layla peeked outside. Trying to explain whatever was happening to him right now would've been too much. It was all too much already, and there was a small mercy in each step that put his home further behind.

"Strange, isn't it?" Tâl said, glancing at him.

"Which thing?"

"That we didn't find anyone else. Just you. Most people aren't sure where the others live, and what homes we did find were empty."

Oli snorted. "Aye, I ain't surprised." He was the only one of the Stražar living in town. All the others lived as hermits in cottages or shacks up and down the treeline, miles away. Larz was in town often enough, but he wouldn't drag himself in for ale until later in the evening. "Wouldn't have done ya no good, anyways, if you'd found 'em all. Most wouldn't have come."

Lanterns hung on makeshift poles, giving light to everyone working on the street. Oli had never seen so much of the town lit up by firelight before, and he wasn't sure how he felt about it. Wood and oil were precious here, but it was being spent in surplus now.

Tâl leaned closer, her face reflecting the orange glow of those new lights. "So why are you coming then?"

"Too tired to argue, I guess."

They walked in silence the rest of the way. Wooden constructions faded into the nicer stone and brick work of the homes further up the hill. The dirt path turned to cobblestone, the presence of soldiers doubled, and Oli watched in shock as dozens worked hard to construct a form of low wall in the middle of the street.

"A chokepoint," Tâl said as they passed.

"A what?"

"Brings your enemies to a narrow place so you can fight them in smaller groups. It makes superior numbers more manageable."

Oli stared at Tâl. "What in Yeolasi you talkin' about?"

"I would no longer be so quick to speak the name of Damnation. It strikes too close to home."

Oli spat to the side. "I don't understand anything no more."

"It'll be quite the dinner," Tâl said with a frown. "For what it's worth, I'm sorry."

Oli shook his head. His head hurt, and he rubbed his forehead. Tuck nearly dead, royalty instead of merchants, a dinner invitation from the princess, all on the heels of nearly becoming wolf food. And didn't his arm hurt? Oli prodded his bicep with a finger, sending a stab of pain through him. Ironically, it made him feel better, more grounded. *This day needs to end.*

At the top of the hill, the ground leveled out, but the number of torches increased, their light dimming the stars above. Only three homes stood at the hill's top, though "home" was hardly the right word. They were small castles of stonework far beyond anything the tradesmen of Watchful could have dreamed up. Their windowsills had curved, soft edges, and the windows themselves had been made of clear, thick glass. The doors were dark timber, carved with ancient runes Ulian had shown more than a little interest in. Around each home stood walls of stone, eight paces high and topped with iron stakes, and the gates were guarded with the only armed and armored men and women in the town. Or, they usually were.

Tonight though, they were far more than just "guarded", the whole place was under occupation. The three homes all centered around one main courtyard which had become an encampment. A bony woman sharpened swords at a grinding wheel, her eyes intense. Pots of food hung above fires spread all about, each one tended by a single cook who walked from pot to pot with a spoon as long as his forearm and an apron covered in motley stains. Supply wagons filled with people rummaging through crates lined the courtyard, their wheels wedged with rocks and their harnesses horseless.

Bet they're havin' a terrible time of it with their horses, Oli thought. The merchants had to rent stalls in the barns at the foot of the hill, where their steeds would usually start to go crazy from the Call until the merchants paid a small fee for the beasts to be drugged. The courtyard was a mad flurry of activity and Oli slowed his pace to take it all in, eyes darting about trying to make sense of it. One of the soldiers trailing Oli gave him a nudge with a large hand.

"Get on," the man muttered.

Oli obliged, catching up to Tâl, who was winding her way through the throng of people, making for the northern mansion. They passed through the gate to find Windsun near the door, talking with a tall and well armored man with shoulder length hair and a beard as pristinely trimmed as Windsun's mustache. The man was uninterested in Windsun, who was growing red faced as he talked. When Tâl stepped into the courtyard the man turned from Windsun entirely and made toward them.

"Found one?" he said to Tâl as he eyed Oli.

"Aye," Tâl said, turning and looking to Oli. "But only one. Did a number on Windsun, though you heard. Something about his sister."

The man ran his gloved hand over his beard. He looked ready to say something, but Windsun barged forward, finger jabbing at Oli. "That's him, Captain, that's the man!"

The captain sighed, and looked at Windsun coldly. "Take your backwater problems somewhere else, *Mister Tote*. I have neither the time nor the patience. You," he said, finger pointed to Oli's chest "Get cleaned up and get inside. The Princess is waiting, and that's rarely a good thing for anyone. Tâl, see it done." Then he turned and was immediately on to other things.

Tâl turned to Oli. "Come on, one of my men is about your size, I think. We'll see what we can do." Tâl marched off around the side of the home, Oli in tow, both of them leaving an angry and helpless Windsun stuttering near the front door.

CHAPTER

SIXTEEN

Layla stood on ol' Rossetta's front porch as the sound of her knocking faded away. The hem of her dress was muddied and her back and shoulders were sore. Sweat had matted her hair, and Layla did her best to comb the worst of it away from her eyes as the door creaked open, revealing a frazzle-eyed woman looking up at her.

"All done then?" Rossetta said in her quick clip, the smell of tobacco wafting into Layla's face with each word.

"Firewood stacked up just like ya asked." Layla jerked a thumb over her shoulder towards the wide lawn behind her, if you could call it that. Rosetta, known by most as "Mad Rosey", had built her cottage a couple miles south of Watchful. Her "lawn", as Rosetta called it, was a wide stretch of land in front of her home she kept more or less well tended. To one side of the lawn Rosetta had tamed a patch of wildflowers, near her steps sat rows of disturbed earth where vegetables had recently been harvested, and in the back were a handful of hiwaya trees currently barren of leaves.

"Oy, good girl." Rossetta flashed a toothy smile. "Come back tomorrow and I'll send ya into the Wood to fetch me more."

Layla snorted. "My brother would light up faster than dried pistil weed dunked in oil and tossed in a bonfire." She stopped, eyes growing a touch wide as Rosetta's words found root. "Wait, ya go into the Wood?"

"Well, it's that or freeze to death. How else ya thinkin' I got all that firewood?"

"Well, I dunno. Ain't it . . ." Layla paused, leaning forward and searching Rosey's face for a telltale sign of someone leading her on. "Isn't it dangerous?"

"Everything's dangerous, girl, especially out here. But I ain't one of them hunters, mind ya. Don't go beyond the treeline, really," Rosetta waved a hand back and forth as she spoke. "I more *change* the treeline, if ya catch my meaning."

Layla didn't.

Rosetta sighed. "I only cut down whatever's on the edge, girl. Bunch of us do it. Everyone else buys from us." She shrugged as her eyes turned toward the Wood, just a few hundred paces away and well in view. Rossetta's eyes usually bore a ring of wrinkles about them, which Layla assumed was from all the suspicious squinting, but as she looked to the treeline those wrinkles softened, becoming more shallow and gentle. Wistful.

Rosey shrugged. "Ain't that dangerous, really. I even like it, ya know? I can feel that tingle somedays, the one you get when your boot crosses whatever invisible line the place has. You get me?"

Layla shook her head. "I ain't never been inside."

Rosetta sighed and shook her head. "Well, no matter. I was pullin' ya leg anyway. Splittin' the wood and stackin' it was plenty for me, and I'm mighty grateful to ya."

"Ain't no problem, and I can come back tomorrow if there's more work."

The small woman's lips flattened out, going straight and thin. "That probably ain't for the best. In fact," she pulled out three copper chits, dropping them into Layla's hand. "Best not to mention this to anyone, eh?"

Best not mention this to anyone. Layla ground her teeth, face flushing. "Oy, Windsun seen you too then?"

"Not yet, but I heard enough. And I suspect he'll be here soon, 'specially if he hears 'bout this. Which he won't." Rosey narrowed her eyes.

Layla's nostrils flared. "Nah, he won't."

"Good. I should've turned ya away before, but your Pa . . . he was good people. Good to me. Good to a lot of us. Owed him a thing or two."

Layla's chest burned hot and she felt like she couldn't breathe. Her fingers clenched against the chits in her hand until her palms hurt, and she couldn't make up her mind whether she should turn and walk away or punch Rosey square in the mouth. "Well," she managed, "I'm sure Roi Ricker would be mighty proud of ya. Real hero, Rosey."

Rosey stepped back, eyes darting to the side. "Well, I, uh—"

Layla turned and marched off, boots thudding on the wooden boards of the porch for a step before crunching on dry dirt. She could feel Rosey's eyes on her back. Layla should have kept walking, just left and let that be that.

Instead, she veered toward the firewood, neatly stacked. There was an especially nice log in the bottom corner: thick, dry, and knot filled. She kicked it out, hard and swift, so it skidded away as the whole stack tumbled down. Layla stepped over the crumpled logs, grabbed the one she had wanted, and walked away.

There was no path or road back towards Watchful, so Layla marched her own trail north through tall brown grass sticking out defiantly from the winter soil. A harsh wind had cooled the heat in Layla's muscles built up from splitting wood and burning bridges. With nothing else for it, she pulled her jacket tighter, held the firewood closer, and tried to ignore the wind and the splinters. The wind had a mind of its own though, and the moment the jacket was tighter the air whipped around and blew up her dress, grabbing at her thighs with icy fingers.

Gonna make Oli sew me a pair of trousers so warm and so hideous both the cold and Windsun will stay away.

With nothing else to guide her, Layla kept her eyes on the hill about a mile away. Chimney smoke trailed about in dozens of places, and Layla longed to be at the base of any one of those smokey pillars. The Wood was off to her right a hundred paces or so, looming and large. Or, at least it had been. When Layla looked towards it again she noticed how close it was now: a stone's throw away at most. When had it gotten so close? She'd kept her eyes on the hill, her thoughts on the cold, and now she was uncomfortably close to the only place in all of Trevelar off limits to her.

Oy, off limits according to Oli, she thought. Rosey hadn't thought it all that dangerous though, and Layla felt a sudden surge of certainty that if Mad Rosey could handle the Wood then she could too. *If I wanted to, anyway.*

She just didn't want to.

Still, she let herself veer closer, thinking maybe she'd walk along the treeline for a time. Her father would have liked that. It would be like walking with him. Besides, why did Oli get any say over where she could and couldn't go? Neither him, nor Windsun, nor anyone else should be telling her what to do.

The sun was disappearing behind the western horizon when Layla came close enough to the treeline to reach out and touch the bark of a particularly barren oak. She didn't, of course, but it felt good to be close enough. Layla had stopped walking now, taking a moment to look around, to get a sense of the world here on the edge of Wood. It was dark. The trees, even shed of their leaves, let precious little light inside, and with the sun setting it made it all the worse. If she threw the firewood now, it would disappear into the black maw long before it landed. That didn't frighten her though as nothing around seemed dangerous. Mysterious, yes, but not *dangerous*. She wanted to step in and know what was back beyond the trees. And why shouldn't she? Nothing gave her the sense she'd die a gruesome death like Oli told her she would.

The ground was strange and beautiful as well, covered in orange and brown leaves like a plush rug beckoning her to fall down into its soft embrace. Her muscles felt sore and her eyes drooped with fatigue, and that soft dirt promised her a night beneath the stars. A night alone, without worry and without nagging. There'd be no Windsun here, no Oli or Mama—only her and the night sky.

And her father. He was here too. Or, something about him was. It was in the air, the same smell always in his clothes when she'd cuddled into his lap. During those first few months of grief, Layla would sleep with her mother, the two of them curled up together, one of her father's spare cloaks between them. The scent of it was here, just inside the Wood.

That meant Layla's father was here, too, in a way.

The wind blew harder on her back, pushing her onto her toes and nudging her to step into the midst of the trees.

If Oli Ricker hadn't been her brother, she would have done it, too.

It's the Call. Layla recognized it only because she knew to look for it. Promises of comfort and peace telling her to take one step forward, then everything would be fine. The power of the Wood conspiring to get her to step further in, to go forward and not stop.

It might as well have been Windsun beckoning her in, considering how hollow those promises were.

And at the thought of Windsun, whatever grasp of a spell was on her broke, and Layla stepped back, gasping for air. She hadn't been breathing. Why hadn't she been breathing? Stumbling a few more steps back, frantic and hurried, she fell to her butt and dropped the firewood.

"Deōs help me," she whispered between gasps, shaking herself back to reality. Tears left icy trails on her cheeks and she shivered from the cold and the fear. She'd nearly done it, had almost stepped in and chased a ghost of her father. Before morning, she would've been dead, of that she was sure.

Layla sat there a long time in the shadow of the Wood before she was able to stand to her feet and run back to Watchful.

CHAPTER
SEVENTEEN

Léonie second guessed her choice of wardrobe. Traveling in a caravan that (in theory rather than practice) was designed for haste meant Léonie had little in the way of fashion variety. Still, of the three dinner dresses she had brought along, she wondered if she had chosen correctly. In an attempt to appear dignified and regal, she had gone with a black dress embroidered with the royal orange fabric and adorned with solid gold thread. It was a ravishing piece, but in the garish dining room in which she now sat, with its chipping gold embroidered door frame and obnoxious chandelier in need of polish, she looked like another decor piece struggling to fit in.

Perhaps I should have gone with something travel-stained, something which says, "I am not from here. I am only passing through." She imagined vaguely what that would have looked like instead. She would have stayed with something black, of course, perhaps one of her—

"Your Highness."

Léonie looked up from the tabletop where her fingers drummed lightly, raising an eyebrow at Lady Amandine who sat in the space to her left. The woman looked to be posing for a portrait. Even the dull lighting of the chandelier only made her more refined and mysterious. Sometimes, Léonie felt as if the whole of Creation was trying to bend itself to Amandine's will.

Lady Amandine bristled when Léonie only stared her down, then sighed. "It would appear our company will be delayed. As the princess, it is well within decorum for you to allow yourself to dine in the meantime."

That is the closest she shall ever come to admitting she is hungry. Well, Léonie was hungry too, so she could hardly blame her. Had she eaten breakfast? She thought she had, but she could not be sure.

Léonie sat up a little straighter and rolled her shoulders. "I am far more famished for answers than food, Lady Amandine. But since the former will not arrive anytime soon, let us eat." Léonie looked at a maid girl who stood by the set of large double doors, her hands clasped before her, fingers interlocked and fidgety. With a wave from Léonie's hand, the girl bowed low, then scurried out of the room.

The duchess sipped wine from a goblet as hideous as the wall tapestry behind her. *No,* Léonie considered, *perhaps the tapestry is worse. Was that a dragon? A toad?*

Lady Amandine read her thoughts. "It is all rather Selirian, I think."

"That would explain a great deal," Léonie said with a frown, eyes still fixed on the tapestry. "Though I think even Queen Selia would be offended to see how misshapen her influence has become. I do not recall burgundy fabric intended to accent redwoods," Léonie held up one end of the red tasseled table runner.

"Well, misshapen intentions and ideologies are all the rage these days, no?"

Léonie's eyes flicked to the duchess and narrowed. Amandine, for her part, was casually turning away from Léonie and towards the set of doors the maid had gone through. Her words had been precise: vague enough to technically not be accusatory, but under context to make her feelings about Léonie rather clear. Léonie wondered if she had talked with the priest, then decided she most certainly had.

"Well, if you take such issue with—"

A knock sounded, filling the room with its dull *thunk, thunk, thunk*. Léonie gave an irritated sigh, then nodded to the guards posted on either side of the door. One leaned over and opened the door a crack, conversing with whoever was outside. A moment later he turned and announced, "Ranger Tâl is requesting entry, Your Highness. She brings with her Oli of Watchful, a local huntsman."

"They may enter."

With a nod, the guard pulled the door open wide.

Two figures stepped into the dining room. The first was Tâl, who dropped to a knee and bowed her head the moment she saw the princess. The second was, at first glance, another one of the king's rangers and, if not for the guard's announcement, Léonie may have dismissed him as one. He was dressed in the ranger garb and shifted his weight from foot to foot in a way Léonie had grown accustomed to seeing among scouts and the like. Yet he was without armaments and clearly lacked any understanding of decorum.

Lady Amandine's voice rang out loud and clear, sharp even. "Commoners *bow* before their princess."

The man looked at Amandine and raised an eyebrow. Then, with a shrug, he knelt next to Tâl.

Léonie almost laughed aloud. *Kneeling* was for those within the royal service, for those who would die for the crown. Commoners bowed instead, bending at the waist to demonstrate their submission. Amandine clicked her tongue and shook her head, but before she could correct the man, Léonie raised her hand to stop her.

"Rise, the both of you. Oli, was it? Thank you for coming. Dinner shall be served shortly. Come, sit. Corporal, you are dismissed."

Oli felt lightheaded and awkward. Tâl had made him clean his hands with a purple-hued bar of soap, and the lavender scent filled his nostrils. His new boots had too much wiggle room for his toes and the tunic and cloak they'd given him hung stiff. His knife had been left behind with his bloody rags, and he felt he might as well have been naked because of it.

Now, after all that, he stood in a room that was far too bright and far too big and far too ornate for it to belong in Watchful. The table stretched out before him was longer than his home was wide, and every inch of wall was covered with paintings, tapestries, or decorations, and every one of them could've been sold to feed his family for a month. It was beautiful, frightening, and disgusting all at once.

And then there was the princess.

After seeing her, the rest of the room faded away into a dull visual clutter. Oli hardly noticed the guards flanking him or the grouchy hag scolding him or even the rest of the furnishings. For one instant, Oli felt as if her presence was like the Call, something too beautiful and unknowable to be real, and therefore impossible to look away. Her black dress was the night sky, the pale skin of her neck and cheeks, the moon. She met his eyes with such confidence, such assurance, Oli could only assume she'd never known anything but power.

She gestured to the seat beside her.

That gesture, that simple beckoning forth, clicked something in Oli's mind. He braced himself, steeling his mind and forcing himself to look away. *Palmaditze*, he reminded himself the way he would Tuck. It took a dozen of Oli's racing heartbeats before he could force himself to move toward the seat beside the princess. She was seated at the head of the table, and she'd indicated the seat to her right, which felt important in a way Oli didn't understand. Floorboards creaked beneath his weight as he made his way towards the princess on shaky legs.

Léonie eyed the woodsman carefully as he sat. His face was calm; lips turned into a frown that appeared so natural, Léonie assumed it was a permanent fixture. His beard was scruffy, unkempt, and Léonie noticed subtle cuts and scars all about his cheeks, eyes, ears, hands, and wrists . . . nearly every visible inch of skin was marred. More than a few looked fresh, and she could see one tunic sleeve puffing out, a sign there was a bandage beneath. It was not an unfamiliar sight; she had grown up around soldiers and guardsmen, but it told her much about him.

A warrior of sorts, Léonie mused. *And one who can meet my eyes.* In fact, he was still doing it, eyes locked on hers, neither of them willing to break away. That meant he was either brave, or he had not the slightest clue he danced with a grave offense.

"You are one of the . . . oh, what did that boy call it?"

Amandine cleared her throat, and Léonie looked away from Oli and towards the woman on instinct, cursing herself the moment she did. Had she just lost some small power play with this man?

"One of the Stražar, I believe, Your Highness."

"Ah, yes," Léonie said, looking back at Oli. "You are one of the Stražar, yes?"

"Aye," Oli said, rubbing his chin.

Léonie waited a moment longer for Oli to say something else. *Anything* else. But he was silent, comfortable even with Léonie and Amandine's expectant eyes on him. After a moment Léonie said, "I received a report early today from the ranger who brought you here. She said there are few of you Stražar around. So few, in fact, she had expressed doubts about finding any of your kind at all."

Oli nodded, giving a soft grunt.

Is this *what we must work with?* Léonie had worked with brighter scullions. "Perhaps you can tell us more about yourself and the other Stražar? Why are there so few of you, for starters?"

The woodsman's eyes roamed about the table as if looking for a lost thought, and she began to wonder if he was capable of speech in any extended form when he gave a small cough, then shrugged. "Just not many about, is all. Wood is a dangerous place, some of us don't live long. Ones who do live off aways. Don't come into town much."

Léonie leaned forward, trying to meet Oli's eyes again, though they were wandering about now. She had enough dealings with court intrigue to tell when someone was an open book and when a person's thoughts would be locked and hidden away. The latter was usually true, and that was what she sensed now. She settled into familiar territory.

There was a small rap on the door.

"Ah," Amandine said with a faint smile. "That would be the food."

Oli sat still, his heart pounding in his chest and his tongue swollen and moist in anticipation. He'd smelled the cooking meat when he'd first entered this place, but watching the platter placed gingerly on the table before him made him doubt reality itself.

Delusional, he thought numbly. *Took a harder beating than I thought.* He gingerly touched his bicep and felt the sudden stab of pain from the bruising. No, he wasn't dreaming. This was real, somehow. Food, and a plethora of it: Roasted lamb—raised in one of the pens near the bottom of the hill—covered in dark gravy, carrots soaked in honey, rolls gleaming with glaze, potatoes on a bed of onions and garlic . . . Oli's stomach rolled and he couldn't decide if he'd devour it all for longing or vomit at the sight. It was all so fantastic and so *wrong.* His mother and sister were three bowshots away with nothing more than soup filled with broth and beans.

"Please," the princess said, her arm sweeping across the table to take it all in. "Eat whatever you would like."

Oli's plate was before him; a silver disc polished to the point of reflecting his own ragged features. He looked like an animal beside the princess, hardly civilized at all with his scraggly beard that still had bits of dirt and dried blood speckled in it. And yet, he was still a man, if a haggard one. He had principles.

A kindly looking girl placed a filled plate before the princess, then bowed and stepped away. Oli cleared his throat and gave a small nod to the food. "Thanks, but I ain't hungry."

The princess leaned to the side, elbow resting on the side of her chair. "You lie." The words were frank, a statement from a woman fully assured she knew the truth. The blunt accusation sounded odd when mixed with her heavy accent. She spoke with such flourish that everything sounded *more* than it needed to be, as if her words were as dressed up as her body.

Oli nodded. "Aye."

"Do you think I would try to poison you, Woodsman? I assure you, this food is safe. See?" She skewered a small piece of lamb from her plate with her fork, then carefully put it in her mouth as if to say, *Watch me, savage, and see how to eat.*

Oli shook his head. "Ain't that. Just somethin' wrong about fillin' my belly when people I care about are hungry. Some things just ain't right, eh?" As carefully as he could, Oli pushed the plate away, hoping no one saw his trembling fingers.

Léonie nodded, but Oli saw the way her lips twitched in something like frustration, or distaste. Either way, Léonie dabbed her lips with a soft napkin, then pushed her own plate away.

"There is honor in that, if perhaps foolishness also. Well, I shall join you in fasting this meal, and my maid will ensure you leave tonight with the remainder of the food." The princess snapped her fingers and the young woman stepped forward, bowed, then removed the food from the table. "Now, if we are bypassing supper, we should bypass pleasantries as well. Let us discuss why I brought you here."

Léonie hardly cared as her plate was removed from her. The one bite of veal she had eaten made it clear her chef was unable to create a true meal with the inferior quality of what he had been given. The duchess, apparently, had different feelings. Despite her usual disposition towards diplomacy, Léonie noticed Amandine continued eating, waving the maid away when she came to retrieve her meal the way she had already taken Léonie's. The woman's discomfort made Léonie smile inwardly, though outwardly she ensured all her attention stayed on the woodsman, who was growing more and more a conundrum to her.

She had meant her words about honor and foolishness. In fact, she was tempted into a larger conversation about Illian economics as compared to the Crown's policy on free trade but restrained herself. She doubted Oli's thoughts were so sophisticated, and it was not the time.

Oli was watching the food leave, longing playing itself out in the creases of his eyes, though his face stayed otherwise stoic. Léonie made a small commitment to herself that she would break him: make him flinch, make him show his weaknesses.

"So why *did* you bring me here?" Oli asked, shifting in his seat.

"Because I need to go into the Wood, and I need a guide."

Oli froze. It was subtle. He had not been moving much before, but Léonie caught the signs: eyes stopped their moving, chest halted its rising and falling, fingers gripped around his chair. And then, in the matter of two or three heartbeats, he was nodding carefully along, seemingly unbothered.

You are good at this game, it seems. It was talent wasted on a commoner, though. She knew more than one noble who would still be alive if they had been able to control themselves so rigidly.

"Oy," Oli said. "And why are you goin' in there?"

You know already, do you not? "Because we—" she glanced at Amandine, sighed. "Because *I* believe that within the depths of the *Vromia*, what you call the 'Wood', is the key to our kingdom's many problems."

Oli squinted at that. "What problems?"

"Have you heard of Kātsracha?"

Oli nodded but said nothing.

"Good. Well, I shall not bore you with our kingdom's rich history then, hm? I can let Lady Amandine do that another time. Instead, let me say simply that the Land Without Light is active once again, and the Yelmes have invaded from the west. The Armies of the Shattered Land batter and pillage our towns, our cities, just as they did long ago. In fact, a band of a hundred or more have come east—following me, I presume."

The woodsman stared at her, his expression blank, disbelieving. He opened his mouth to speak, then closed it. Opened it again, then closed it.

"We were as shocked as you," Léonie said. "Or perhaps more so. I was raised to believe the tales of Dark Ones were more metaphor than truth. Tales of the Fae, they said." Léonie did not look towards Amandine, but she could almost hear the woman grinding her teeth. "But it is true. What had become myth after an epoch is now reality once more. And we have been found . . . unprepared."

Oli met Léonie's eyes. "Why should I believe ya?"

Amandine sucked in a breath, and before Léonie could say a word the duchess leaned forward and said, "How *dare* you? Do you question the Princess of Trevelar?"

Oli looked casually at the older woman. "It's a bit of a tall tale. Monsters from legend on their way to our little stretch of the world. Don't seem likely, is all."

Léonie nodded and put out a hand to silence Amandine's oncoming reproach. It was not the time for the older woman's outbursts. Besides, Léonie loved how clearly Oli rankled Amandine. She may keep the commoner around for that alone.

"I appreciate your skepticism, but I speak the truth. Months ago, I was in the capital when we received frantic reports of the armies of Kātsracha pouring forth from the west. By the time we mustered our troops and rode to meet them, they had already surrounded the great city of Worchestern, Lady Amandine's home." Léonie gestured to Amandine, who looked away. "We fought hard but . . ." Léonie lifted her forearm, letting Oli's eyes take in the scar there. He had noticed it already, she was sure; she never bothered to hide it. "The

Yelmes have power, a magic of sorts that imbues their weapons, their bodies. They slay three of our soldiers for every one of theirs." Her hand was shaking slightly, and she looked at it as if it did not belong to her, before placing it carefully on the table, pressing it down hard enough to still it. "Worchestern is in ashes now, and the rest of Trevelar will follow if something is not done."

"And so, you've come here . . ." Oli's voice trailed off, his eyes flickering over Léonie's face, her scar.

Léonie leaned forward, voice quiet, letting her intensity push each word out past her lips. "I believe within the depths of the *Vromia* is an ancient power, a power that once pushed back the forces of Kātsracha in the last epoch. I want that power, Oli. I want to save our kingdom."

Oli could have wretched. He knew what she wanted. He'd seen it before, and the thought made him sick. He sat as still as he could, focusing on his breathing, palms sweating. The world around the princess blurred.

You're fine, Oli thought to himself. *You're fine.*

He was looking at the floor now, taking in the grain of the hardwood. *Where's Tuck?* He wanted to see him, pet his fur, hear his breathing, and know he was fine, Oli was fine, everything was fine. But Tuck was back in Anej's cabin, half-dead from their escapade into the Deep. Things were not fine.

And now the princess wanted to go deeper, further. Oli knew where, he knew *exactly* where she wanted to go. He could take her, but he wouldn't, couldn't. He'd been there before, seen *it* before. Watched his father die there before. They all died, and he'd watched them. Seen them. Stood there, slack jawed, as—

"Oli?"

He blinked. The princess came into focus again, her eyes narrow. She'd been calling him, hadn't she?

"Oy."

Princess Léonie gently put her elbows on the table, letting her fingers fold together until her arms formed a triangle before her. "You know where I need to go. You know what it is I want."

If it had been a question, Oli would have denied it. But it wasn't, and he didn't.

Léonie nodded, Oli's silence as good as his agreement. "You will take me there."

"No."

The princess leaned back, as if slapped. Her cheeks and neck reddened, and her mouth worked silently, looking for words, but it was Lady Amandine who spoke.

"You are afraid, are you not?" The words weren't angry, weren't an accusation. Oli heard . . . concern? When he looked at her, he saw her eyes were soft, working hard to repress tears. This woman was a conundrum. One moment ready to flay Oli alive with her words, the next moment ready to weep before him.

Still, something about the softness of her eyes, her voice, made the dam in Oli shudder. It didn't break, but it cracked a little. "Aye, I'm scared. I know what she wants," he looked at the princess. "What *you* want. I've been to the deepest part of the Wood, where the trees have all died and the beasts aren't natural. More than ten winters ago my—my father took us there. Me and others, a dozen. Stražar, all of us. We knew the Wood, but we hadn't been that far, that deep. He talked about power, about magic. He knew things."

"What things?" Amandine said, drawing his eyes back to her. She leaned forward, brow furrowed.

"He was learned, ya know. Knew his letters. Had books. He wasn't from here, wasn't born to the Wood like me. He came looking for something. For *someone*." Oli turned and saw Léonie leaning forward, her lips mouthing a word Oli knew by heart. A word he hadn't spoken aloud in a long, long time. "Staradovna."

Léonie's eyes widened, eager and hungry. "Did you find her?"

Whatever spell had come over him, that had loosened his lips when the duchess had called out his fear, was broken at the sight of her longing. He saw his father behind her, the same drive which had killed him. Oli said nothing, only met those eyes with a blank stare, working quickly to rebuild whatever wall Lady Amandine had begun to tear down in him.

But he didn't need to say anything, for Amandine said it for him. "He died, did he not? Your father, I mean."

Oli kept silent, eyes still on the princess. Her hunger made her seem like a ghost. The pale skin that had drawn Oli's eyes like a moth to flame now repulsed him.

"And those he brought with you?" Amandine was still speaking.

Oli looked at the older woman, but this time he didn't let her soft look break him. He met her kindness with a cold stare, hoping it would ward her off.

Amandine nodded as if his silence told her everything she needed to know. And it did, Oli supposed. "You alone escaped. You said it had been ten years?" She looked at Léonie, taking a deep breath and setting her shoulders before speaking. "He was only a boy when he saw his father killed searching for this same twisted power. If you have mercy, Your Highness, you will leave him out of this."

Oli turned back to the princess, keeping his eyes on hers. *Will you have mercy?* Oli wondered. *Will you leave me out of this?*

He knows. The thought consumed her. This was far more than she had hoped for. Before her sat a man who knew the way to Staradovna, who could lead her there. And Lady Amandine thought she could leave this woodsman out of this?

"You will take me there, Woodsman," Léonie said once more.

"No."

They held one another's gaze, and Léonie watched as her guards near the door prepared themselves. They would beat him, if she asked. But what would that gain her? He would be useless then. She could take his family hostage. Did he have family? He said he had people he "cared about", and so she could threaten them. But Oli's eyes were cold, hard. He was a killer, whether he knew it or not. She had been around many of them, men and women who could take life. *She* was one, was she not? And she wanted this man to lead her into a dangerous, unfamiliar place. If she threatened his family, he may slit her throat at the first opportunity. Threatening him was, she decided, a poor tactic for now. At best, he would try to kill her in the *Vromia*. At worst, he would succeed.

No, this was not the time for the rod, but the carrot.

Léonie nodded. "I see you are a determined man, and that has my appreciation. Lady Amandine is wise as well, and I would like nothing else but to do as she asks and leave you out of this. But there are far too many lives at stake. That power you have seen, that power which did such harm to you, we must turn it against the Yelmes or everyone we love, everyone you care for, will burn beneath the wrath of monsters. I have seen what they can do, Oli. But *you* can help me save countless people, including the ones whom you love."

Oli's eyes shifted. *Good. Let that sink in.* Léonie waited for a heartbeat, then continued. "But those who serve the crown should be rewarded, no? And this task I am asking you to perform is one of great personal trial. It is worthy, I think, of great reward." One of Oli's eyebrows twitched upwards. *There it is.* "On behalf of the Crown, I charge you to bring me to Staradovna, and in exchange I will give you five hundred gold nūmuns."

There, Léonie thought, watching Oli's eyes go wide. *He could buy the whole of this village with that.* Amandine sucked in a breath, predictably, reinforcing the grandeur of the offer.

"I—" Oli started, but then stopped. Had she gone *too* high? Could he even imagine so much? The woodsman coughed, looking away.

Léonie pressed in. "All you need to do is bring me there. You need not confront her, need not relive your past. Just *bring me to her*. Do that, and you shall have enough money to live as you would like until you are old. You could move away from here, taking your loved ones to live in the lap of luxury in Cheretone or Southfern. You could travel, see the Badaui Republic, visit Turris Regis and see your kingdom's capital."

She had him, and she knew it. He fidgeted, licking his lips and looking away. The story of this man's life played itself in his disconcerted look. He merely needed to do this one thing, and then all his problems would vanish.

"Oy," Oli said after a moment. He cleared his throat, looked away and took a deep breath. "Aye, I'll take ya. But only to the edge of the Clearing. I ain't goin' no further."

"The Clearing?"

"Aye. Deep in the Wood, near the heart of it all, there's a circle of dead land. Nothin' grows, nothin' lives. That's where she is, right in the center of all that. We call it the Clearing."

Léonie nodded. "We are in accord. You will lead me to this Clearing tomorrow. Once done, the crown will reward you—"

"Now."

"What?" Léonie blinked.

"I want the gold now. Or some of it, at least."

Léonie said nothing, only cast her withering gaze on the woodsman and let it do its work. Except, the man did not flinch. He held her gaze, cool and steady. She had been in negotiations before, of course, but not with a commoner. The idea grated her. *Insulted* her. Bargaining with the Crown was—

"Of course," Amandine said. "It will be a dangerous mission, and you have loved ones to consider. An offering of good faith would be polite and would ensure that even if you do not return those you leave behind will be taken care of."

Witch, Léonie thought, wanting to scream. She had never intended to pay the man. It was a problem she had intended to postpone until later, praying that by some ill fortune she would not have the need. How much gold did Léonie even have with her? Certainly not five hundred gold nūmuns.

Léonie cleared her throat. "Of course, the lady speaks on behalf of the Crown. *One* gold nŭmun will be provided to you this evening, and you can entrust it to whomever you would like. I can spare no more until the power is within my possession. And I shall send a guard with you this evening to ensure your safety until morning." *And to make sure you do not sneak off with my gold.* Before Oli could object, Léonie snapped her fingers, bringing the maid to her side. In a moment she had given the girl instructions, and the girl left.

Léonie stood. "Now, I think it best we all get rest. In the morning, an hour or so before dawn, you will meet me and my people in the courtyard outside."

Oli stood, then left without a bow or even another word. His eyes glazed over, distant.

Silence stretched itself out over the dining room in the woodsman's absence, the echo of the closing door fading. Léonie clenched her hands into fists and turned to the duchess. "You just cost the Crown a gold nŭmun, Lady Amandine. A dozen soldiers could be armed, trained, and paid for a year with that kind of money."

Lady Amandine cocked an eyebrow. "I am sorry, Your Highness. It appeared you had offered *five hundred* of those same nŭmuns on behalf of the Crown. Unless, of course, you were lying to one of your subjects while representing your father."

Léonie's fingernails bit into her palms, teeth grinding in the back of her mouth.

Amandine stood, gently flattening the ruffles of her dress. "I have been your confidante since you were a child, Your Highness. I am here with you now, not because of my love for your task, but for my love for *you*. You are my Princess, and by the Maker's grace I pray you will one day be my Queen." Amandine breathed in deep, the braids of her dark hair gently rising and shifting on her shoulders. "But until such a time, I will hold you to account for your words and deeds. That way, *if* you ever sit on the throne, then perhaps you will be worthy of it."

There was silence once again, and then the gentle *clap-tap, clap-tap* of Amandine's shoes as she walked around the table, past the guards, and out of the room. Before the door closed for a second time, Léonie waved away her guards, dismissing them so she could be well and truly alone.

For an hour or more, Léonie sat in that garish dining room alone. If someone had looked in, they would have seen the princess leaning against the arm of her chair, her chin resting on her closed fist, eyes distant. For Léonie had gone into the confines of her mind, in a place like an art gallery. A place painstakingly constructed in her imagination by a young girl whose circumstances meant she never knew solitude.

On the walls of this internal place, she walked by tapestries, paintings, and sculptures. Her body sat fixed beside the fire in the dining room of the Tote estate, while in the depths of her mind she walked by pieces of art on display for her and her alone. Each detail emerged from memories: moments in time she had frozen and saved for this silence, for this time of aloneness. She made her way through childhood memories of rope swings and carefully tuned harps, to adolescent ones of court intrigue and potential suitors. She walked briskly by the most recent ones: a statue of a screaming Yelmes soldier, the edges of her mouth alight in literal fire, lightning crackling from her blade. A painting of her father, standing before his throne, frozen in anger as he yelled, ordering Léonie to stay in the city.

She had left that night, under the cover of darkness.

Eventually, she turned into a compact room with speckled-gray stone walls and rows of framed canvas leaning upon one another. Here her memories lay dormant, awaiting the time in which she could study each one, choosing those to be burned and cataloging the rest.

Carefully, she pulled free one of the canvas-memories near the front of the row. A portrait of the magistrate stared up at her, encased in a nicked and splintery oak frame. It portrayed him sitting in the study, cheeks flushed red, eyes bulging. He cared for Watchful, Léonie realized. Oh, he cared for himself more, surely. Still, there was something in the way he dressed, in the pathetic comb of his hair . . . he hadn't adopted the fashions of the Trevlarian elite. At first Léonie had thought of him as a simple commoner, too far from civilization to know what counted as fashion. But more was going on. Magistrate Tote had wealth, and he had traveled—evidenced by the small figurines and trinkets on the study shelves. He *chose* to ignore the fashion of nobility.

Every magistrate, mayor, or lord of every city, town, or village Léonie had visited in Trevelar had always tried to imitate the fashions of those above them in station, with varying levels of success. But not this man. He dressed like one from here, if nicer. He spoke like a commoner and dressed something like one: he *cared* for this place.

Léonie walked on, looking at paintings of Thibault, of Tâl, of Amandine. She paused, remembering the sunset from that morning, the painting on the wall of her mind nearly as breathtaking as the real thing. After returning home, she would paint the scene and move this portrait from the wall of her mind to the wall of her bedchamber.

Léonie moved on until she stood before a painting of Oli. The painting had emerged from the first instant she had seen him, Tâl kneeling beside him and out of focus. He was not a handsome man: his eyes and cheeks too sunken, his teeth too yellowed, his body too scarred. Still, even in that first moment, Léonie could see the strength of him: his determination born of a combination of stupidity and courage.

Stupidity and courage.

She could use that, wield that. Léonie smiled.

CHAPTER
EIGHTEEN

The Watchful Layla returned to didn't feel at all like the Watchful she'd left that morning.

There were strangers about, and not the kind she'd expected. Where she anticipated merchants, she saw strange men and women in chainmail and travel stained boots marching in groups of two and three, calling orders to one another and cursing anyone in their way. Spears and swords were everywhere, and Layla's skin crawled at the sight of them.

Her friends and neighbors eyed the newcomers with the same suspicion she did, but all of them seemed caught up in the same flurry of activity. By the light of dozens of torches, they hustled about carrying boxes, buckets, and timbers of wood, dumping them in large piles at bowshot distances up Watchful's street. There, soldiers with intent looks sifted through the piles. It was manic: a cacophony of noise and confusion which made the Downwind seem serene on even its rowdiest nights.

Layla plowed on through, head down and firewood in hand. She'd gone back for it once she'd calmed down, the need not to waste greater than her initial fear. No one paid her much mind, except to curse mindlessly at her when she got in the way. More than once, she'd nearly been bludgeoned or impaled by someone hurrying downhill with a box in their arms or stack of wooden boards on their shoulders. Layla considered stepping into the Downwind to ask Ulian what was going on and to get out of the barrage of noise and bodies, but crossing the street to the tavern felt like far too much trouble. And besides, Layla felt an urge to know her mother and Oli were safe. So she kept to the side of the street and worked her way up the hill.

When she had gotten to within a stone's throw away from her home, she stopped. Firelight poured forth from the cracks in the window slats, illuminating two figures who stood by the front door. There wasn't much about them Layla could make out: they wore cloaks and had the cowls low. One loomed large, with a gloved hand holding a smoldering pipe. When they put the pipe to their lips, the glow of the bowl illuminated bushy eyebrows and a thick beard. The other cloaked figure seemed a touch thinner and stood unmoving.

They both faced Layla.

"Come here, girl," the one with the pipe called, beckoning her forward with his free hand.

Layla didn't move. She looked about, praying there was another "girl" around. There wasn't.

The man stepped forward. "C'mon, get over here. We don't bite."

Layla was fairly certain that if someone needed to say that, it probably wasn't true. Her feet stayed planted where they were. She could turn and run, but she wasn't sure where she'd go. And if Oli and Ma were inside, then did they need her help? *Could* she help?

The second cloaked figure lifted their hands and dropped their cowl, revealing a woman's face with tightly braided red hair falling over one shoulder. Her eyes were hard, her chin scarred, and she looked more annoyed than dangerous. That was, until, she put her hands on her hips, pushing her cloak back to reveal the pommel of a sword. She opened her mouth to speak just as the door to the home opened behind her, Oli stepping out into the dark street.

"Layla, that you?"

"Oy!" Layla called back, raising a shaking hand.

Oli waved her over. "Get on in here, Ma's worried sick."

Layla stepped forward, eyes on the cloaked figures. "We got visitors," she said.

"They're here for me. Should be alright."

"'Course they are," Layla said, doing her best to squeeze by the man and woman while also staying an arm's length away. "Explains everything."

"Is that firewood?"

"Shut up."

A moment later, orange light and warm air washed over Layla, the door closing behind her with a squeal of hinges. Her mother sat with eyes locked on a large bag spread on the table, her mouth slightly ajar. The whole home smelled of meat, spices, and something burning. It only took a moment to realize what the latter was: black smoke rising from the stew pot over the hearth.

"Aw, hells," Layla said, tossing off her boots, dropping the log, and running over to the fire. The stew was boiling over, the lid dancing as brown liquid poured over the pot's edges and onto the flames below. She grabbed a pair of cooking linens and used them to remove the pot from the heat, setting it on a flat stone beside the fire. She grabbed the ladle, stirring the stew and scraping burnt beans from the pan's bottom to salvage what she could.

"No, no, don't you be worryin' 'bout it," Layla said, back hunched. "I'll take care of it. No need to thank me."

No one did. No one said anything. Biting her lip to keep from lashing out, she grabbed bowls and scooped out three portions of the burnt stew, then turned.

Oli and Orelda were looking at each other, jaws tight. The bag hadn't moved from the table, but from this angle Layla could see inside it. It was full of food, all dropped together into one messy mash that made Layla's mouth water and stomach growl. Bread, carrots, potatoes, lamb . . . all of it sitting on *their table*. And what were Oli and mother doing but staring at one another, eyes locked in a battle of wills which Layla hadn't the slightest understanding of.

"Oy," she said, but no one looked her way. With a huff, she stomped her foot on the floor. "Oy! What's the matter with ya? And what's with all the food?"

Her words shattered whatever ice had been forming in the room between the two of them. Oli turned away with the shake of his head, but Orelda rolled her own shoulders back and picked up her chin. "Good to see ya, dear," she said, turning to Layla. "Your brother brought it home, and from the queen, no less."

"Queen?" Layla turned towards Oli so quick stew splattered on the floor. "Ain't she dead?"

"She means the princess," Oli said with a shrug. "It's been a long—"

"Maker help us!" Layla cried out, stepping towards Oli, eyes wide. "What happened to your arm? And wait, what are ya wearin'?" He looked like he'd been recruited into whatever cult the two outside belonged, his own shabby cloak in a tattered pile near the door. After one day away from town, Layla thought Mad Rosey might be the only sane one. Oli opened his mouth to answer, but Layla jabbed her finger in the direction of his chair and snapped. "Sit, now."

He spread his arms wide in exasperation, but sat anyway. Layla dropped the bowls of stew at their places on the table then sorted out the mess of food from the bag onto the last of their dishware. As for the soggy canvas bag, she tossed it atop of Oli's tattered clothes, trying to ignore the blood-red stains on his cloak. Then she plopped herself down at the table between Oli and mother.

"First, we eat," Orelda said. "Then we can talk."

"Maker be blessed," Layla said, nodding. "We have a feast."

Oli shook his head, picking up a hunk of lamb from his plate. "Don't think Deōs has got nothin' to do with this one."

Layla waited for their mother to argue, to chide her son for blasphemy and to bless the Maker for the food. But she only leaned forward and picked up a roll. Her eyes roamed over it in a mixture of awe and suspicion. But Layla was too hungry to stare. She bit down on a chunk of sauce-covered potato, giggling with a heady joy that warmed her belly and blurred her vision.

"Oy," Layla said, when the dishes were away and the extra food stored in old jars. "Where's Tuck?"

Oli grunted as he used the back of his hand to wipe away sauce from the corner of his mouth. "He's safe with Anej. He's . . . healin'."

"Healin'? What happened to 'im?"

"I didn't do nothin'." Oli leaned forward, hands pulling at his hair. "Been a hell of a day, and he got the worst of it."

Layla folded her arms. "Best start talkin' then."

Oli stayed quiet for a long time, eyes locked on the table. Then, with a foul curse, he sat up. "Fine. You ain't gonna like it, though."

Oli recalled his day and Layla hardly believed a word of it. The Wall, the deer, the wolves . . . it all sounded fanciful and distant. But when Oli talked of Tuck, Layla knew every word rang true. Oli Ricker rarely cried, but his red eyes told her he'd done enough of it tonight. When he muttered about punching Windsun, though, Layla stopped him and made him say it again, louder.

"Oy, I hit 'im, alright? Ain't nothin' to worry 'bout, though. He won't mess with you no more. Made sure of that."

Their mother groaned, but Layla sat back with her mouth agape. Oli only continued on, pushing past the story of Windsun as though it weren't monumental. He'd *hit* the magistrate's son. That was either the greatest or worst thing Oli had ever done. Layla just couldn't fathom which.

"Well, anyways," Oli continued with a shrug. "The princess had me brought to her, and that's where I came from. Dinner."

"With the princess?"

"Aye."

"Of Trevelar."

"Aye."

"*The* princess."

"Do we only have one?"

Before Layla could retort, her mother leaned forward. "Oli, you said she knew about Staradovna? About the Wood?"

Layla glanced at her mother, frowning. Oli hadn't said a word about that, which meant this wasn't the first she'd heard of it. Clearly they hadn't waited for Layla to return before they started talking, so once again Layla had walked into a conversation between the two of them which she wasn't a part of. Like a child intruding on the adults' conversation.

"Well . . . I . . ." Oli shifted uncomfortably, glancing at Layla.

Of course, can't talk in front of the child, can we? They wouldn't lie, but that didn't mean he'd tell her everything. If he could, he'd keep her in the dark to "protect" her, keep her safe.

"Whose Stara . . . doma?" Layla asked, eyes moving from Oli to Orelda, and back.

Silence.

Layla leaned back, crossing her arms. "Ya'll didn't go deaf suddenly, did ya?"

Orelda coughed. "Stara*dovna*. She was a woman some believe pushed the Dark Ones back to Damnation, all them years ago in the Great War."

"I thought it was Deōs who did that," Layla said. "That's how them stories go, anyway. The Maker sent the earthquakes, the lightnin', all that." Layla could still recall priests from the Order traveling through and sitting in the square up the hill. They were always men and always old, but they were good storytellers. Layla thought back, reciting what she remembered, " . . . *and in the seventh year of the war, Deōs opened the ground wide and allowed the Depths of Yeolasi to swallow the armies of the Kātsracha whole, ending the Epoch War.*"

Orelda shrugged. "Your father believed that, in a way. Just thought the earthquakes and lightning was coming from a person: this Staradovna."

"Father?" Layla's heart skipped. She hadn't expected this to turn to her father.

"Aye, that's what he thought," Oli said, fingers playing with his beard, eyes locked on Orelda. "But he didn't think it was something to go talkin' about."

"He'd have told her," Orelda said, voice harsh. "When she was older, he'd have told her."

Oli clenched his jaw but said nothing.

"Well, right then," Layla said, drawing the words out so her mind could work. "So Pa thought the Maker used this lady to beat the Yelmes. Why does it matter?"

"'Cause the princess thinks the same," Orelda said. "That's why she's here."

Layla shook her head. "Nope, that doesn't help a bit. Why would she be *here*? What does this Saradoma—"

"Staradovna."

"Sure. What does she have to do with *us*?"

The question swirled in the air like smoke between them, and Layla crossed her arms and sat back. Nearly any conversation around Roi Ricker made Oli and their mother squirm. Usually, Layla let it go, but not tonight. Tonight, there was food and soldiers and a princess, and a sense that all Yeolasi was breaking out.

Oli groaned, looking as though he wanted to throw their table across the room. "It matters 'cause Pa thought Staradovna was in the Wood. The Call, the strange beasts, the power of the place—he thought it was *her*." Oli's finger jerked to the shelves and the dozen old leather-bound volumes there. "These books and scrolls are all just garbage that brought him here, fillin' his head with nonsense. It's why he came to Watchful at all, why he became a Stražar. All of it was for *her*. It's why he died, the bastard!" Oli stood, pacing and clenching his fist, eyes roaming anywhere but towards Layla and their mother.

Orelda nodded, and Layla saw the faint whisper of tears in her mother's eyes. "He's right," she said, voice just a hush. "Your father talked about her for years. *Years.* He would search the Wood, mapping it, learning 'bout it, writing 'bout it, until finally he thought he understood it. He'd found the Wood's heart, the place Staradovna called home."

"Oh," was all Layla could say. She knew where this would lead, but she didn't have the courage to say it.

Oli kept going. "And so he took me and those stupid enough to follow 'im and dragged us through the Wood and into the Deep . . . half of us died just tryin' to get there. The rest . . ." Oli shook his head, and Layla saw light glisten off a wet trail down his cheek.

"And now," Orelda said. "The Princess of Trevelar is here looking for the same thing your father was. And she is makin' your brother . . ." Orelda's voice trailed off, eyes blinking away her own tears.

But she didn't need to say it, Layla understood well enough. "And she's makin' Oli take her."

Oli snorted. "No one *makes* me do nothin'."

"But you're goin', aren't you?"

Oli turned and splayed his fingers out flat on the wall, as though he wanted to push the whole house down. No one said a word for a long time, the crackle of the fire and the muffled noise of workers outside filling the space.

When Oli did speak, his voice echoed off the wall before him. "I don't think I got a choice."

"Will she, you know . . . kill ya?" Layla's voice faltered.

Oli shrugged. "I think she'd hang me if I said 'no', but that ain't it. Or, that ain't all of it, anyway."

"Then what?" Orelda said, her voice thick and heady. "Then why go back?"

"'Cause she says the Yelmes are back, if you can believe it. It's why she wants to go *there*. And worse, she says they're comin' here, to Watchful."

The world swam, and Layla had to fight to keep upright. "Monsters? Here?"

"They were followin' her."

"So, all them soldiers outside, and everyone workin', it's 'cause—"

"They're gettin' ready for an attack, I guess. She says if she don't get to Staradovna that everything here won't last. Everyone . . ." Oli moved his hand through the air as if wiping the whole town away in his mind.

Orelda closed her eyes and bit her lip, her hand shaking against her chest. "So if you don't help the princess, then—"

"Watchful burns . . . and us with it."

And that was it. What argument could be made now? Her brother would go to the place of his nightmares, where he had watched their father die, because if he didn't then they would all die anyway.

But for Layla, there existed a "before" and an "after" in her life, and it all centered around the death of her father. In the "before", there had been times of laughter and smiling and joy. Her mother had been younger, in a sense deeper than just time, and Oli had still been a boy. The "after" meant more than just the loss of those things, but the onset of dark days and hungry nights listening to Oli fight demons in his sleep.

Now, would there be another "before" and "after"? Would it be worse this time?

"You don't need to go alone, Oli," Orelda said in a voice hardly more than a whisper.

"Not now, ma," Layla said, but her protests were blown away by the force of Oli's own.

"Don't you dare do this." Oli turned from the wall, jabbing his finger at Orelda. "I've been through too much today."

Orelda eyed her son as she stood. "Oy, you have been, I'll give ya that. But you ain't the only one." Her words felt solid enough to touch, spoken with a careful finality that only Orelda Ricker had mastered. "Don't forget that I stepped past the treeline before you were born. Walked beneath those boughs while you were in my womb, do you understand? It ain't just Roi Ricker who made you a Stražar."

Oli said no words, but Layla could hear the grinding of his teeth.

Their mother spoke again, words slow and deliberate. "All I'm sayin' is ya don't gotta go alone."

Oli shook his head. "Yes, I do. If I don't go alone then there ain't no point in goin' at all."

"Your life is more than just takin' care of us."

"No, it ain't."

Layla sighed. Orelda and Oli were done now, Layla could feel it. They'd both mope off to their corners, and neither would say another word for the night. Monsters may be coming, but it still annoyed Layla no one would ask her about her day, or listen to her story of Mad Rosey, or laugh with her about the log she'd taken. Her eyes drifted to the fire, popping rather nicely, filled with good looking logs which hadn't been there that morning. The princess had probably sent Oli back with firewood too, which meant her own log wasn't needed.

"Well, I made a few chits today," Layla said into the thickening silence, forcing something like a smile onto her face.

Orelda nodded, her bloodshot eyes looking everywhere and nowhere.

"Oh, right," Oli said. "There's this." He rummaged into a pocket and removed a large gold coin, throwing it on the table where it clinked and rattled about before coming to a halt before Orelda. She leaned forward, color draining from her face. Layla's eyes tracked from her mother to the coin and back, waiting for an explanation or revelation to dawn on her.

"Is that—" Orelda started.

"A gold nũmun," Oli nodded. "If the princess ain't lyin', she said she'd give me five hundred of 'em if I take her into the Deep. This is a down payment."

Layla stared at the piece of metal before her. It was smooth around the edges and about as wide as her palm. The face of a woman she didn't recognize had been etched into the clean gold. The edges were engraved in words that, to Layla, were nothing more than squiggles.

A gold nūmun.

She'd never seen one before, hardly heard of one. It was worth, what? Ten gold pieces? That sounded right, and each gold piece was worth five silver nūmuns, and those were each ten silver pieces . . . Layla's mind tried to follow that trail down to copper nūmun, then copper coins. One copper coin broke down into the smallest Trevlarian currency, and the only one Layla had ever held: copper chits. She had never been good with numbers, and Layla's mind couldn't grasp the worth of the gold piece before her. She knew the three chits she'd made today would buy a loaf of bread, and if she had ten of them she'd have the value of one copper coin. What Oli had just thrown on the table could feed them for, what? A year? Ten years? Twenty?

"How is any of this possible?" Layla said, leaning back, dumb-founded.

Oli laughed, the sound dark and humorless. "Like I said, been a hell of a day."

CHAPTER

NINETEEN

Layla fell into the fitful sleep that comes when the body is exhausted but the brain cannot be slowed. Her mind conjured up dreams and nightmares of four-legged things bustling about in the shadows of trees whose branches leaned down and plucked at her hair. She had an ax in her hands, but her arms couldn't move to swing it and defend herself. She wanted out. Out of the forest, out of her dream, out of her life.

She was awake enough to know what she wanted but not enough to *do* anything. A limbo of semi-consciousness and fear: paralysis.

The four-legged things had six legs now, and they moved from the shadows into the light—their mouths were dagger-like mandibles stretched out toward her ankles and knees. Certain they'd eat her, she wanted to scream as they scrambled all about her with violent speed.

And then they were on her, legs on her chest, her ribs, pulling and shoving and—

"Layla, wake up. Wake up!"

Layla pulled her eyes open, pushing at the blurry form above her. "Stop it. Get off of—"

"Shh, no, don't say a word. Quiet." Her mother's voice, the sound of it like cold water on her face.

Layla's heart still pounded in her ears. Though she could see her mother's firelit face come into focus, the shadows in the corner of her house seemed to squirm and crawl with whatever nightmare creatures had been atop her in her dream. Bits of straw poked out from the thin mattress, scratching at Layla's elbow as she sat up.

Orelda leaned close, stroking her daughter's hair and leading her mind away from the nightmare.

"Listen," Orelda said.

"What?" Layla's mouth stuck together, parched. She needed water.

"I'm leavin'."

Leaving? Layla sat up further, pushing Orelda's arm away. "What?"

"I'm leavin', dear," she said, leaning back and visibly swallowing. "Your brother just left to go meet the princess and, well, I'm goin' too."

Layla rubbed at her eyes and looked her mother over, her mind working to catch up. Her mother looked different than Layla had ever seen her: dressed in boots and pants, her dead husband's spare tunic tightened around her waist with an old belt, and the strap of a quiver over her shoulder.

"I—" Layla couldn't breathe, couldn't quite think. "What?" She stood uneasily on her feet, the cold from the floor pushing its way through her socks. "That's crazy, Mama. You ain't goin' nowhere. You can't go." Layla put a hand out toward the door as if to cover it, to stop her.

"I'm so sorry," she covered her mouth with her hand, her eyes crying. "But I have to see, Layla. I have to know."

"Know what? You can't just march off into the Wood, you'll—"

die. But Layla couldn't say the word aloud, couldn't speak it over her mother like a curse. "Oli will throw a fit."

"Your brother may need me. I wasn't there before and look what happened. Oli *needs* me. And there won't be another chance. This is it."

"Mama, this is crazy." Layla blinked, tears blurring the world the way sleep had moments before.

Orelda reached out, but Layla pulled back. "This is our only chance," Orelda said again, quieter this time.

"Chance for what?"

"To see *him*. Your father. To be, I don't know, close to him again."

Layla shook her head, biting hard on her lip to keep it from quivering. *Our.* Orelda had said "our". She would let Layla come, if she asked. She wasn't going to stop her, not like Oli. They could go into the Wood together. They wouldn't be alone, but with each other.

"He's not there." Layla wiped away tears from her cheek, annoyed they were there at all.

Orelda bit her lip and looked away. Shadows cloaked her eyes. "I'll be back, okay?"

And before Layla could say another word, her mother pushed past her and left. When the door creaked shut behind her, only shadows filled her place. Layla didn't move. She stood there as the fire cackled low, the fading heat on her calves and ankles. In time, the fire died too. And when the last hisses and pops of the flame had died away, the remaining silence was deafening.

CHAPTER

TWENTY

The Woodsman was late.

Léonie paced back and forth, her boots upsetting the frost clinging to the dead grass. The treeline loomed less than forty yards behind her, foreboding in the early morning darkness. Thick shadows danced beneath the boughs, and Léonie shivered whenever she looked in their direction. The sight of those dark tree limbs made the chainmail she wore feel like a childhood blanket. Her fingers drummed along the teardrop pommel of her sword, her gloved fingertips feeling out the dents and grooves in the metal. Once it had been inlaid with gold, but little remained now.

"He will come, Your Highness," Tâl said. The woman was like the trees, her only movement the gentle billowing of her cloak in the wind.

"You know him so well already?"

"I only mean we can trust Singer and Fjord, Your Highness."

Léonie snorted. They had been standing here for a quarter of an hour already: Léonie and her complement of The King's Spear. Well, all of them except Singer and Fjord, who had been assigned to ensure Oli's presence this morning. Tâl stood closest to Léonie, but behind her stood two others, each cloaked and wraithlike, bows already in hand. Victer was a skinny, older man, the gray hairs along his arms visible whenever he drew back his bow. Collin was his opposite: young and thick in his arms and chest.

Léonie kept her eyes on the way they had come, following the winding road back toward Watchful. From here she could see the captain's handiwork: skeleton-like barriers up the main thruway, smaller barricades along the town's perimeter. At this distance, it looked ragged and disordered, but from up close it had looked worse. Léonie had done all she could to keep her expression blank as she had marched past walls made of old kegs, tables, broom handles, and a few tankards thrown on top for good measure.

"They're dead men," Léonie muttered.

"M'lady?"

Léonie did not reply but looked beyond the town to the rolling hills to the west. Hidden in one of the valleys between those hilltops was a small army that would crash through the captain's defenses like a child wading through a sandcastle. It would be quick, one-sided.

"I should have sent them away." Léonie sniffed, the cold making her nose run. Tâl said nothing, but Léonie could hear the crunch of her boot as she stepped forward. "It should have been the first thing I did. Packed them all up and sent them north, towards Cheretone."

And still, Tâl said nothing.

"Instead, they will fight and die on that little hill of theirs. Cursing my name, in all likelihood. I brought this down on them."

"We will not fail, Your Highness."

Léonie turned. Tâl's face was all shadow above her nose. She almost commanded the woman to remove the hood so she could see into her eyes, see if she meant what she said. Was there the same certainty in her gaze as in her tone? But Léonie did not really want to know. She liked the words and the sliver of reassurance they gave. She dared not ruin it.

"Perhaps. Though I doubt it will matter if we do not leave soon."

Tâl smiled faintly, her lips only just visible in starlight. She raised a gloved hand and pointed.

Three cloaked figures came at a jog, each of them looking the part of the King's Spear. Léonie recognized Fjord's wide shoulders, and Singer's red hair, lightly bobbing as she went. Which meant that between them, shoulders hunched and tense, stalked Oli Ricker.

"You're late," she snapped as they neared. Singer and Fjord bowed, apologies gushing out like vomit.

Oli spit to one side. "Ya said the courtyard."

Léonie narrowed her eyes. "I said an hour before dawn—"

"*In the courtyard*. I ain't deaf. We were in the courtyard. That captain of yours had to set us straight."

"I said no such thing," Léonie stepped forward, finger pointed towards Oli's nose. "And you shall remember who you are speaking with."

Oli raised an eyebrow. "Whatever. Doesn't matter now, eh? We best get goin'." He marched towards the Wood's edge rolling his shoulders and looking around at the rangers gathered there.

"Keep up," Oli said, and then he jogged into the Wood.

In her youth, Léonie had often vacationed to a mountain-fed lake to the west of the capital. The surface was always like calm glass, still and unmoving from a distance. But whenever she would first dive into the water—freshly melted from the mountain—the chill of it would rip the air from her lungs and bring back stark memories of winter.

The Wood was the same: calm and eerie on the outside, but once Léonie stepped onto the soft soil beneath the trees, the world around her erupted in noise and color.

Bird songs were the loudest of the cacophony: sweet and high, they sang their morning songs on every branch in the canopy above. Though she had not seen or heard them moments before, now black jays and swine tips swooped so low she could have reached her palm upward and caught one mid-flight. Dragonflies and mosquitoes buzzed, the former chasing the latter as fat, web-footed squirrels looked on from where they clung to the sides of tree trunks. The bittersweet scent of jasmine hanging in the air brought Léonie back to the window of her childhood bedroom. The memory came on so vividly she could almost see out across the rooftops of Turris Regis, the sunlight blazing off the golden domes of the Order's sanctuaries. Her rangers shifted around her, dropping their hoods and twisting left and right, caught up in the same violent rapture.

It was wrong the way the world came to life simply by stepping beneath the boughs of the trees, as if an invisible threshold separated this place from the rest of the world. Sights, sounds, and smells burst into existence with nothing more than a step. And the wrongness of it gave it beauty, the strangeness made it breathtaking. Léonie was swimming through the currents of magic and mystery, her body and mind spinning about to consume it all.

She inhaled, wanting to suck in this moment, committing everything she could to memory. She would paint it later. She would bring the birds alive by blurring their wings, layer the trees with grays and browns and have the white jasmine flowers contrasting the oranges and reds of the leaves on the ground. Oli would be centered in the frame, the anchor of the moment. Hate him or not, Léonie could not help but watch the way he stepped carefully ahead, bow in hand and shoulders hunched forward. He appeared both tense and at ease all at the same time, a warrior in battle stance, a journeyman exploring familiar, dangerous ground.

Oli turned his head, his eyes meeting hers, his brow furrowed. He was too serious to be in a place so rich with beauty and wonder. Should he not be happy? Joyful, even, for a man who daily descended into such paradise? Music ran beneath the soil, something so royal and divine Léonie knew she alone could hear it and understand. It begged her deeper, urged her onward. She would find what she sought in this forest. This place *wanted* her here; it needed her to go on, eastward.

Oli tilted his head and called, loud and clear, "*Palmaditze!*"

And then the vibrant colors fled, faded to dull browns and oranges. The jasmine seemed like an odor, and Léonie's skin crawled as she took in the beasts around her anew. The squirrel looked famished, his hungry eyes lingering on her. The birds swooped too low, and Léonie ducked as she stumbled forward. Whatever music Léonie had been hearing fled, the notes shattered to silence. And Oli . . . he was *far* ahead, much further than she had thought.

He cupped one hand near his mouth and called, "I told ya to keep up."

Blood warmed Léonie's cheeks. "Keep going," she said, as much to herself as to the rangers around her, who all shook their heads and blinked as if emerging from some group coma. Or, no, that wasn't right. Tâl alone had stayed clear-eyed, her hand on Léonie's elbow, concern etched into the lines of her forehead.

"M'lady?"

Léonie shook her head and brushed away Tâl's hand. What had the Woodsman said? *Palmaditze?* Was that magic?

"Your Highness, are you alright? I was calling you, but . . ."

But I could not hear you. That was a frightening, teeth-grinding, thought. "It is this place," Léonie said. "It is enchanted."

Victer grunted. "Well, I wouldn't mind turning about already."

The Woodsman, for that was what Léonie had decided to call him, never slowed. His long strides moved him through the forest as if he both feared it and owned it all at once. Each step declared him confident and bold, and yet always he cast furtive glances over his shoulder.

"What was that?" Léonie hissed when she had caught up to him, reaching forward and yanking Oli around. "What happened to us?"

"The Wood's a dangerous place. Figured you knew. Ya seemed smart and all."

He moved to step away, but she grabbed his shoulder again. "What happened to us? Or what *would* have happened—"

"You'd have died. Now, c'mon. We keep movin'. It's the first rule of the Wood."

Léonie nearly screamed as she marched after him, hand flexing around the handle of her sword. "You never mentioned any rules."

"You didn't ask," Oli said, picking up his pace.

Fjord stepped closer to Léonie, lowering his voice. "Your Highness, I can restrain him if you would—"

"No," Léonie waved her hand, as if swatting something away from her face. "I have questions, Woodsman."

Oli didn't even turn, just shook his head. "We never stop movin'. Wanna talk? Fine, but do it while we walk."

Léonie picked up her pace. "Is there anything else we should know, or will you tell us after this place has already sent us to the grave?"

"There ain't many rules, but ya best learn the ones there are. And the first one is the most important. Keep movin'."

"And the second?" Léonie asked, grinding the words out as she stepped over a tree root. Or, *almost*, stepped over a tree root. The toe of her boot caught the root's edge sending Léonie stumbling forward, her body landing in a pile of leaves and loose soil.

"Watch your step," Oli said, turning with a frown. "That's the second. Now come on, best be gettin' up, and quick."

She would kill him. She was sure of it now. She might have pondered mercy for the infractions so far. Perhaps only a beating, then she would let him keep the nũmun for his efforts. Now, when this was said and done, she would erect gallows and string him up.

She sat on the ground still, Singer and Tâl standing nearby her, trying to find a way of offering to help her up while pretending not to see her in this pathetic state.

"Oy," Oli called again, from further away. "Up."

How dare he command *her*? Heat rushed through her cheeks and ears, her vision blurred. How dare he think that he, *of all people in*

Trevelar, could speak to her in such a way? She bawled her fists, her jaw hurting now from grinding her teeth.

"Get up!" Oli called, voice angry. He walked back towards her, his lips set and eyes narrow.

Léonie twisted about on the ground. "How dare you speak to me like this? I am the princess of this kingdom, and—"

Oli moved too fast to follow, and Léonie saw only still images: him raising his bow, the jerking of his arms, then she heard rather than saw the hissing of an arrow. Her mind reeled around one thought: *he is going to kill me*. It made both no sense, and yet all the sense in the world. Get her out here into the Wood, where no one but her small guard defended her, and then—

Léonie's eyes involuntarily snapped toward the arrow as it slammed into the ground beside her. He had missed. Léonie breathed out a sigh of relief in one breath, then a command with the second. "Seize him."

Victer moved first, unsheathing his blade and stepping forward.

But Tâl raised a hand, calling out, "Wait!"

Victer faltered, sword still held in Oli's direction even as he turned to Tâl, following her as she reached down and grabbed the shaft of the arrow.

"Your Highness, look." Tâl raised it up for Léonie to see.

Skewered to the arrowhead like a fish on a line was a monstrous snake, its tail still jerking around in awkward, unnatural, spasms. The size of it stunned Léonie: its body thicker than her fist, and the top so heavy it bent the long arrow shaft as Tâl hefted it. Its scales blended in with the leaves on the ground impossibly well. The back end of the creature, which still shifted on the ground, appeared to *change*, its coloring shifting so it always matched the ground beneath it. If it had been a painting, there would have been no difference in the brush strokes between the snake and the leaf-laden forest floor.

Magic.

"Oy." Oli marched towards them, shoving Victer's sword away

with his bow. He held up one finger and said, "First rule: *keep moving.* The Wood don't care that you're a princess."

Oli snatched the arrow from Tâl's hand, ripping it free from the snake's head, and readying it on his bow once more. Blood dripped from the tip, landing on Léonie's boot and leaving a red streak. Oli turned and marched away, past Tâl, Singer, Fjord, Collin, and Victer, who still held his blade awkwardly at his side.

Léonie stood then, hands brushing away leaves and dirt feverishly in case more deadly creatures lingered within them. If snakes of this place could disappear into the ground, what about the spiders? Wild monkeys? Would a leopard or cougar appear from thin air and rip them limb from limb?

Fjord coughed, his breath misting. "I bloody hate this place," he said, removing an arrow from his own quiver and nocking it on his bowstring.

"A wonderful little hell-hole we found," Singer muttered, nocking her own arrow.

Léonie stomped after the Woodsman, the rangers falling in around her and the dying snake writhing behind.

CHAPTER

TWENTY-ONE

Oli felt exposed. Naked. His back and neck burned, and no matter how he shifted his cloak he couldn't shake the feeling of being watched. And the cloak felt all wrong. His boots fit all wrong, too. And his shirt and belt . . . everything was off, twisted about like helplessly tangled thread.

He felt like an interloper now, an intruder into the Wood. A foreigner followed by foreigners.

This place was supposed to be for him and Tuck, and no one else. Dangerous and strange, yes, but still *theirs*. And now he led a group of city-dwelling snobs who didn't understand the first thing about this place, and he did it without Tuck.

In the Wood, there was peaceful clarity tied to understanding its danger. Things had always been clear, the rules understood: keep moving or die, stay away from the trees and vines, watch for large clumps or piles of leaves, don't drink the water, and don't eat the fruit. And don't ever go into the Deep.

But he'd broken that last rule, and somehow fate had strung his stupid mistake into a whole string of impossibilities. Now he drug around the princess and her lackeys through this holy ground for *money*.

He wanted to retch.

Oli forced himself to remember the hunger pains, the worn clothes his mother wore, the dwindling firewood. He didn't do this for money; he did it for his mother, for Layla, and for the life they could buy when this ended. He just had to get this done and get out.

If the princess saw any of the tension in Oli's face or shoulders, she ignored it. She walked beside Oli, peppering him with questions. Her eyes never left him, and Oli felt a confusing mix of irritation, fear, and longing. It became harder to focus than he would have liked, especially when sometimes she got close enough he could feel the faint brush of her breath on his cheek.

"Away from that," Oli snapped, using his bow to point to a small pile of leaves the red-haired ranger was about to step in. The woman paused, then backed away, going around the spot in a wide arc.

"Tell me," the princess was saying. "How did you break the enchantment when we first stepped into the Wood? Do you possess magic?"

Oli laughed. "No."

Léonie kept quiet as they passed beneath a branch, twitching vines dangling from it. They were still in the Outer Bands, so if they kept up the quick walk they shouldn't have to worry about the vines for now. But Oli wanted to run, to become a blur to everything that would otherwise kill him. He could run all day in the Wood, but he doubted it would be the same for everyone else. They'd be running once they got past the Wall, so Oli decided to let them save what energy they had.

"You spoke a word," Léonie continued. "When you said it, I came back to myself. It was like a dream, and then—"

"It's the Call. The Wood's way of makin' you easy prey. You'd have started walkin' deeper in without knowing."

"Deeper?"

"Aye, deeper. Would've led ya into a viper pit or bear den or somethin' just as nasty."

Léonie had her own sort of Call. It was hard not to sneak furtive glances, catch glimpses of the dimple on her cheek, the narrowing of her eyes. But it wasn't an attraction, he told himself. Just curiosity. The trouble he had breathing must just be the perfume she wore.

"But it does not have any sway on you, this Call?"

"Not for a long time."

"Why not?"

Oli said nothing. He felt tempted to keep up the banter, to hear more words spoken in her thick accent. But he had limits. Boundaries.

Léonie looked back briefly, then said, "Tâl also seemed unaffected."

And that *was* odd. Oli had noticed it too, but he wasn't sure what to make of it. His father had talked of people who didn't hear the Call, but Oli hadn't met any of them and his father hadn't explained more. "Strange," Oli muttered.

Léonie sighed, becoming utterly interested in the Wood around them, looking everywhere but at him. She breathed deep, grinding her jaw like a fighter bracing themselves.

She began slowly. "Back there, with the snake . . ."

Twelve Hells, Oli thought, throat going dry. The last thing he wanted was the princess trying to thank him or apologize or something else equally suffocatingly awkward. Whatever she had in mind to say, he wanted none of it.

"So, there's a war," Oli cut in.

"Yes," she said, drawing the word out.

"So, how's that going?" Oli shifted to the side, giving a low-hanging willow a wide arc.

Léonie pursed her lips. "Not well. The armies of Kātsracha have taken Worchestern, our western-most Sentinel city."

"Sentinel city?"

"Do you learn nothing this far from civilization?"

"We learn to stay upright," Oli said, glancing at Léonie's dirt covered trousers.

She scowled, scrunching up her brow. Oli thought he could see his head on a pike reflected in her eyes. "The Sentinel cities are a network of large fortifications throughout Trevelar which form the core of our kingdom's defenses. Any incoming army would, eventually, have to deal with these cities and the large battalions stationed there. Worchestern is—was—outside the mountain pass that leads to the Land of Darkness. Our primary defense on the western side of the kingdom."

"And there's no hope of takin' it back?"

Léonie's voice grew quiet. "There is nothing to retake."

Oli had little context for cities and war, but there he sensed reverence to her words that made him figure it was pretty bad. "And you were there? At Worchestern?"

"I was, as was my brother, Prince Bastien. We fought the forces of Kātsracha in the fields outside the city." She touched her forearm. "We had hoped to clamp down on the enemy like a vice, pressing them between our forces and the great walls of Worchestern. That is not what happened."

"Why not?"

Léonie shifted as she walked, pulling her hand away from the scar beneath her sleeve to clutch her sword handle. No one else wore armor, and her chainmail *clinked* ever so lightly as they walked. "When we pressed into the enemy, they destroyed the walls of the city. It should not have been possible. Built of black stone, twelve yards thick and impossibly high. Those walls were an engineering marvel, built a thousand years ago and over four lifetimes. And they tore them down."

Oli scratched his chin, thinking of the Wall a few miles away.

"Is that like, what, ten paces?"

"What?"

"Twelve yards. How many paces is that?"

Léonie looked around as if pleading for help. "I have not the slightest—"

"Fifteen," Fjord chipped in. "'Bout fifteen paces, I'd say."

"Well," Oli said, spitting to the side. "That's a thick wall, eh? How in creation did they manage to break it?"

"Magic. I have little understanding of how it works, of course. That would be heresy, but somehow the Yelmes could conjure up a . . . a . . ." Léonie's hands moved in front of her, closing in together and separating wide. "An explosion unlike any you could imagine."

"Like, fire and oil?"

"Yes, but more."

Tâl spoke up from behind, "It was as if a grain silo filled with oil went up in flames."

Léonie nodded. "The sound of it was deafening, as though God himself were ripping open the skies."

These were all just words to Oli. He tried to imagine thunder, oil burning, large walls, but he could summon nothing more than vague images. He had no way of knowing if anything the princess said was real or not. Could just be fae tales and lies. Though, to be fair, Oli couldn't come up with a good reason why Léonie would lie.

Léonie continued, "When I left Turris Regis to come here, the Yelmes had established themselves in the ashen ruin of Worchestern, reinforcements pouring out from Kātsracha to join them. In effect, they have made their position a permanent one."

"Won't the king lead an attack or something?"

Léonie laughed. "You mean, will he ride in and save the kingdom like some children's story? No, I think not. He would not have much of a unified army to do it with anyway."

Oli looked at her, "Oy?"

"Politics," Léonie said the word like spitting out poison. "We are still a fractured kingdom. Many lords and ladies were there with me at Worchestern. They saw what the enemy could do, and so they fled to their cities, hiding behind their own walls. If the king were to try and muster them all . . . well, it would be interesting to see, I think.

Some would follow, but others would pretend they never received the command at all. No, Trevelar is doomed unless a power is unearthed to match that of the Yelmes. We have time—even a powerful army cannot conquer a kingdom overnight. This war may drag on for a year or two, slowed down by snow and the logistics of moving an army. But the end is inevitable unless—"

"Unless you find a magical weapon? Then you can ride in and save the day?"

Léonie frowned. "It sounds like a children's story, yes?"

"Pretty sure it *is* a children's story."

"Perhaps it is. And yet, it is our only hope."

"Maker help us," Oli muttered.

"Indeed."

"Where's Collin?" Tâl said. Oli turned to her as she said to Victer, "I said, where's Collin?"

"He was here a moment ago," Victer said, shrugging. "Am I his keeper?"

Singer readied her bow. "He was bringing up the rear."

Oli counted the rangers. There were only four: Singer, Fjord, Victer, and Tâl. Oli had figured out Collin was the young one, though he was gone now and Oli knew he wouldn't be the last. He turned back around and picked up his pace. "Keep movin'."

"No," Tâl said, shaking her head and stepping in front of Oli. She set her jaw, dark eyes meeting his own. The early morning sun had risen higher, and the branches cast shadows in scattered patterns along the woman's neck and cheeks. "We stop and find him."

Oli pushed past her. "If he's lost, he's lost."

The princess stayed beside Oli, and the rest followed close, worker bees behind the queen. Tâl alone slowed her pace, twisting between the group and the stretch of the Wood they'd come from. "Where is he?" Tâl called after him.

"Dead," Oli called back. He didn't know for sure, but it was probably true. Whatever had happened, give Tâl hope enough for her to run off would be a bad—

"I'm going to find him," Tâl said, turning and running back the way they came. Oli watched her go, contemplating trying to stop her.

Léonie shook her head. "She will find him. Lead on, Woodsman."

"She'll die."

"Unlikely. Each of the rangers in the King's Spear is highly trained."

Tâl had already disappeared into the Wood. "She's fast, I'll give her that. If she's cautious, she'll live. If she's reckless, she'll just die faster."

"You seem very concerned about my soldiers."

"You sound unconcerned."

"They have a duty, and there is honor in letting them fulfill that duty."

Oli snorted.

"You disagree?" Léonie cast him a sideways look, eyebrow arched.

Oli glared back. Maybe she had no soul. Maybe whatever crown she wore back in her palace sucked out whatever would have made her human. He thought about saying as much, but instead muttered, "We best keep movin'."

TWENTY-TWO

They had left the gold nūmun.

Layla twirled the large, round coin between her fingers, slurping stew and munching on meat and bread from the night before. After a little while she was, for the second time in as many days, full. Her body was a wreck of mixed emotions, a blur of contradictions. Her belly filled with stew that she'd slurped through lips so cracked from the cold they bled. Her ears rang and her head pounded like she'd spent the previous day downing mugs in the Downwind, though her throat felt as if she hadn't had a drink in days.

No noise stemmed from inside the home. No stirring, no snoring, no pattering of paws on the floorboard. Even the crackling of the fire was gone, along with the heat. The Ricker house was silent, all except the hissing wind and the chatter of thoughts in Layla's head. How could thoughts be so loud?

The only noise to keep her company was the faint sounds drifting in from outside. Muffled, but present: the rumble of voices, the rattling of cart wheels, the thudding of a hundred boot steps. But those were out *there*, and they gave Layla little comfort. She would have thought the gold in her hand would have been comforting, but it only made her colder.

A gold nūmun. *Freedom*, Layla thought. *That's what this is, ain't it?*

She could go anywhere she wanted, could pack up her things and leave before this supposed attack. Go north, see Cheretone and then on to Demare. Names she'd only heard about, dreamed about, but now they were places she could *go*. For the first time in her life, she had options. She could travel, see the Sister Mountains, and pay one of the maeifa to teach her to read. *To read!*

She had to leave, to pack up and start out—to go and not look back. The roads weren't an option, of course. Even when monsters of legend weren't on the horizon, it was dangerous to be a lone girl on the road. But she could stay off the main road, cross the countryside and sleep beneath the stars. There was a monastery only a week's march away, she thought. The priests had visited Watchful, spinning tales of Deōs and of Trevelar's past. They'd take her in for the winter, then after the snow thawed, she could move on. Maybe see the whole of La'Azurus.

Layla stood, looking toward her boots tucked beneath the cot, their laces visible in a streak of dust-filled sunlight.

"I should go." She said the words aloud, her throat so dry she coughed. Then she said the words again, trying them out as if breathing them into the air could make them real. "I should go."

And she should, shouldn't she? What kept her here?

Her mother and brother had left her. They were gone and, if time had taught her anything, they wouldn't be coming back. They would probably die in the Wood, but even if they did return to Watchful, could Layla stand to see how wrecked they would be? When Oli had returned from that last god-forsaken errand with their father, he'd come back broken. Layla couldn't see that again, and she couldn't watch it happen to her mother. And besides, if the Yelmes *had* returned and if they *were* going to attack Watchful, then wouldn't she just die here? She wanted nothing to do with a war, let alone one with the monsters from the west.

All she had to do was leave.

But leaving felt so final.

Orelda and Oli Ricker weren't dead yet. Or maybe they were, and Layla didn't know it. It tortured her, having her family be both alive and dead in her own mind. If she left, would she be only acknowledging what already was, or giving up on the only family she had left? Her grandparents had died long before she was born, her mother had no siblings, and her father wasn't from Watchful. Layla had no one except her mother and brother.

But they'd *left*.

Layla squeezed the coin in her palm so hard it hurt, squinting her eyes to keep back tears. Whatever this moment was, it wasn't the time to cry. She needed to make a decision. Do something, anything.

A bang at the door shook Layla from her reverie, and she dropped the gold coin. It tumbled to the floor and settled with the visage of the woman's face looking up at Layla with a disappointed stare.

"Deōs help me," Layla muttered as she stood, legs shaking from both the cold and the shock.

The pounding came at the door again, this time accompanied by a male voice calling out, "Layla, are you in there? Are you alright?"

Layla closed her eyes and muttered a curse. The voice was too familiar. She grabbed the nūmun from the ground, dropped it into her pocket, then glanced up towards the ceiling. "You have got to be joking."

No answer came from the rafters, only more knocking from the door. "Layla! I know you're in there. I heard something. What was that? Are you alright?"

She sighed and straightened her dress, running her fingers quickly through her hair as she stepped towards the door. She thought about reaching for a knife but today was probably a bad day to stab someone. She had enough problems.

She slid back the rusty locking bolt, then flung open the front door swift enough the hinges hardly had enough time to let out their customary scream. And there he was: Windsun Tote. He stood before her, fist ready to bang on wood, mouth halfway open to call out her name again. His face, normally so carefully manicured and presentable, looked as if it had played the part of an anvil for the smithy. One eye had swollen shut, rings of black and blue forming around it. His cheek and lip looked inflamed: red and lumpy.

"Oy," Layla said with a nod. "You've talked with my brother then?"

Windsun stepped back. "Yes, well . . . he isn't here, is he?" He winced as he spoke, as if certain words forced his mouth into painful positions.

"Don't think that's any of your business, eh? Now, tell me what it is ya want so you can be off."

Windsun worked his jaw the way he did when frustration nagged him, which made him wince again, then curse. "I've come to get you. We're all leaving, and you should be coming too." Layla caught whiffs of thyme on his breath, as if he'd been trying to freshen up before seeing her.

She laughed. "What are you talkin' 'bout? I ain't goin' nowhere with—"

"*Everyone* is leaving." To prove his point, Windsun stepped aside and gestured to the street. He wasn't joking. Most of the town had crowded into one, tangled line that streamed down that hill at a shuffle. Hand carts were filled with children and bags, people shoved and yelled, and every face she saw looked angry and afraid.

"What?" was all Layla could think to say.

"My father's orders. We're making for the south."

"South? What's south?"

"Anteron. Father sent a runner on ahead to let them know we're coming. Winter comes later to the south, so if we hurry we may beat the snowfall."

"But . . ."

"We spotted the Yelmes."

Layla met his eyes. He'd said the words seriously, deliberately.

Somehow, Layla understood that *he'd* spotted the Yelmes. From the top of the hill they could see for miles, so the Hilltoppers would've been the first to see them.

And that meant they were real. Actual monsters from legend stalked the hills near her home. The realization made her heart skip, and she put a hand towards the wall, breathing deep. She hadn't believed, not until this moment. Her *mind* had understood, but understanding and belief were not the same thing. Not until that moment had she actually *believed* demons were coming.

"How long?" she asked, voice fading to a whisper.

"What?"

Layla swallowed. "How long until . . . you know."

Windsun ran his hand through his hair. "How should I know? How should anyone know? Hours? Days? It doesn't matter because we won't be here. Pack your things and come on."

Immediately, irritation replaced all of Layla's fears. "Oy, you don't tell me what to do, Windsun Tote. If I wanna leave, I'll do it *without you.*"

"Don't be a fool." Windsun stepped forward, pushing past Layla into the home.

Layla's jaw dropped, her face burning. He was in her home. *Her. Home.* "Get out!" she said, finger extended to the street.

Windsun shook his head as he looked around, eyes fixing on a large satchel hanging from a rusty hook. It was decorative and had been there for as long as Layla could remember. One of the knick-knacks from her father's travels adorning the Ricker cottage. And then Windsun grabbed it and began indiscriminately stuffing clothes and sheets into it while shaking his head. "I will not"—he picked up the shirt—"leave you"—he shoved the shirt into the bag — "to die."

"Get out!" Layla said again, mind frantic. Her head grew light and her feet heavy.

Windsun stomped his foot and turned toward her, bruised face scrunched and angry. "Why do you put me off? You belong with me! I'm trying to *save* you."

He shouted the words and Layla stepped back, hip touching the bookcase. "Get out," she said again, voice quieter this time.

Windsun dropped the bag, keeping his eyes locked firmly on her. He stepped forward, shaking his head. "No."

Layla swallowed, moving one hand onto the bookcase, fingers feeling about for something, anything, but she found only pieces of parchment and old books. Windsun stepped toward her again, looking away to peer out into the street. His eyes narrowed on something, then he leaned over and grabbed the handle of the door, slamming it closed.

And Layla's mind went blank.

This was bad. She *knew* this was bad.

"Why won't you let me save you?" The words slid from Windsun's lips like oil, quiet and dangerous. Layla said nothing, mouth opening and closing. "You're leaving, Layla. *With me.*"

And then he slid the bolt of the door closed. The ringing of metal as the latch caught and locked was like the shattering of glass. She couldn't breathe.

"You need to see that I am trying to help you. I am here for you." He stepped within arm's reach, his chest dominating her vision. "I didn't need to come. I could have let you stay here, could let you burn at the hands of monsters. But I came to save you, and what do you do?" Windsun slammed his fist on the door, his voice rising over the banging of wood. "You push me away!"

"Get out," Layla hardly said the words in her mind, let alone out loud. They were a whisper.

"Get out? Is that all you can say?" Windsun reached out toward her shoulder, his hand suddenly seeming like the mandible of the creature from her nightmare.

Layla shoved herself away from the bookcase, slapping Windsun's hand away. "Just get out, Windsun. Now. Or—"

"Or what?"

"My brother—" Layla backed into the kitchen table so hard it toppled over, and she fell right alongside the dirty plate and fork she'd left there. She rolled to her butt, scooting backward as Windsun walked closer.

"Your brother is in the Wood on a fool's errand," Windsun shook his head and stepped forward, kneeling down towards her, reaching his hand out, every finger seeming ready to devour her.

Layla kicked.

She didn't think, just brought her knee up to her chest and slammed her heel into Windsun's face as hard as she could. He toppled backward, screaming and flailing, curses flowing like blood from his lips. Layla scrambled to her feet, rushing toward the fireplace and the small clay jar beside it that held the half-dozen kitchen utensils the Ricker family owned.

"Witch!" Windsun cried, his boots pounding on the floor behind Layla. "Maker help you, I'll—"

Layla reached out and grabbed a worn wooden handle sticking up from the clay jar. When she spun, the jar flew from the shelf and shattered on the ground, but her hand held fast to the handle of a long cooking knife.

Windsun moved fast, his face a blur of spittle and blood as he reached out his hand towards her. That hand filled her vision, and she swung the knife, feeling it catch and land between his fingers, slicing down toward his palm. Blood, then screaming, then Windsun's body crashed into her. Out of control, he yelled and writhed in pain. His shoulder hit Layla's chest, slamming her back into the stone of the fireplace and knocking the breath from her lungs. They fell into the warm embers of the fireplace, soot and ash exploding beneath their writhing bodies. Layla tried to push Windsun off, but he only pushed her harder into the ground. She caught a glimpse of his eyes, bloodshot to the point of inhuman. She felt his hand on her chest.

She went to swing her knife again, but her hand was empty. The knife had dropped from her hand in the fall. She felt around on the floor, trying to track down the wooden handle again, but Windsun thrashed about as he tried to control his pain and anger. He tried to get to his knees while keeping her pinned to the ground, the weight of him suffocating on her chest. Soot shot into the air, but though it filled her lungs it didn't drown out the scent of thyme.

Layla pushed at his chest, shoulders, and head, but he ignored her. She squirmed but couldn't get him off. Breathing became harder as she drowned beneath his weight and anger. Her back lit up in pain, her chest compressed, her mouth tried and failed to suck in air.

And then his eyes locked onto her again, staring death and possession into her. She decided she didn't need a knife, and so she lashed her hand out and stabbed her fingers into those eyes hard enough to draw blood. Windsun screamed and reared back off her.

She could breathe again. She made to stand, but before she could, the door of the home cracked and shattered open, light pouring in.

"What's going on?" A soldier stood in the doorway, the royal orange tunic like sunrise. The door's latch was bent, the wood of the door frame broken.

Hands shaking, *body* shaking, Layla scrambled to her feet, eyes moving between Windsun and this soldier. The newcomer was a man, maybe twice her age, his hand on the pommel of his sword. He looked from Layla to Windsun, then said, "Tote, is that you?"

Windsun looked up, face covered in sweat, soot, and blood. "Captain! Thank Deōs. The wench tried to kill me!"

The captain looked about the cottage, taking in the table, the sheets Windsun had scattered about in his mad dash to pack her bag. Then he looked Layla up and down. "You the Ricker girl?"

She swallowed spit, praying her fear would go down with it. It didn't. She met the captain's eyes as best she could, and stammered out, "Aye, I am. And whose askin'?"

The man let out a dark, low laugh. "Aye, you're his sister,

alright." To Windsun he said. "Get up, Tote. I don't have time for you."

Tears streamed from Windsun as he got to his knees, bloody hand clutched to his chest. "But she—"

The captain removed the sword from its sheath. It reminded her of Oli sliding an arrow from his quiver. It was a practiced, determined motion. Something done by a man who had used the blade before and knew what he was doing now. Windsun's voice cut off into a pained whimper.

"Do you know what the punishment is for rape?" The captain asked. Windsun said nothing. "It's death, Tote. And here, on the eve of battle, as the officer in command of this forsaken dung heap of a town, I have no courtly obligation to give you a trial. Do you understand me?"

Windsun stood, still hunched. He nodded twice, though it may have been mere twitching from pain. The captain took a step away from the door, moving himself between Layla and Windsun. "Then leave, before I reconsider."

Windsun fled out of the house, shouting for people to move as he turned up the hill. The captain shook his head, sheathing the sword. "Well, Miss Ricker," he said, twisting about and stepping back from Layla. His palms were open, an annoying and obnoxious way of making himself look less threatening. "If there is anything I can—"

"I'm fine," she snapped.

He paused, looking ready to say more, until he settled for scratching his chin. "Well then, good day, I suppose."

He turned, but Layla stepped forward, "Oy, ya didn't tell me whose askin'."

"Excuse me?"

"Who are ya?"

"Ah," he turned back and gave a small bow of his head. "Captain Ronald Thibault."

Layla ran her shaking hands down her skirt, smearing blood.

"And how'd ya know me, eh? Didn't think I was the type to have a soldier knockin' on my door."

Thibault looked at the open front door, which swayed back and forth slightly. "Mister Tote tried to get me involved in his feud with your brother yesterday. I understood something about unquenched love for a sister and . . ." the captain shrugged. "I deduced the rest when I entered."

"And you make a habit of bargin' into peoples' homes, breakin' latches and all?" Layla wrapped her arms around herself. Everything felt colder than before, and her shoulders shivered. And what was she doing? She should have been grateful, should have been thanking this man for saving her from Windsun. But she didn't *feel* thankful. She felt angry and scared, and she wanted to throw something. Hit something.

Thibault smiled, and Layla wanted to smack him. "I was looking for Tote and caught sight of him before he closed the door. I prayed he could convince his father to call off this stupid exodus before they get everyone killed. When I heard the clatter, I didn't bother to knock."

"Well," Layla said, and then said nothing else. Well . . . what? Thank you? Don't come into my house again? Please leave?

"Well, indeed. If you need nothing else, I'll be going."

He'd nearly gotten to the door when Layla burst out, "Can you tell me I won't die if I stay here?" She sucked in air, voice shaking. "Why shouldn't I leave?"

Thibault looked her in the eye, working his jaw thoughtfully. "Here, in this town, is a candle of hope, Miss Ricker. A fighting chance. On the roads and fields outside, there will be no survivors." He looked around the cottage and the trail of desperate destruction. "Go to the Downwind and get a blade, help us hold out until the princess returns. Until *your brother* returns."

"I don't want to fight. I just want to live. I just want to be safe and alone and . . ." Layla bit her tongue, blinking to force the tears backward.

"Me too. But war has come to Trevelar, Miss Ricker. It has come *here*, to your quiet stretch of earth. And I am sorry, truly. But if you want peace, if any of us want peace, then we had best be prepared to fight for it."

"That don't make no sense. Ya can't fight for peace."

Thibault smiled sadly. "None of it makes sense anymore."

And then he turned and walked away, and Layla was alone.

CHAPTER
TWENTY-THREE

"What's that?" asked Singer, pointing off to their left. "Did you see it?"

Oli slowed his pace and squinted, everyone else doing the same. Fjord coughed and Oli caught a whiff of tobacco. "Don't see a thing," he said.

Oli didn't either. He saw only a wide patch of leaf-barren birch trees, piles of leaves, and the ominous green twirl of vines around thick branches and boughs. If Tuck were here, Oli would be able to tell if there was something to worry about. But he wasn't, and Oli had only his excessive caution.

"Keep walkin'," he said, nodding to the east. Singer grunted her acknowledgement, but Oli didn't miss the way her eyes lingered and her shoulders turned northward.

"What did you see, Singer?" Léonie asked.

"I . . . I'm not sure, Your Highness. A shadow, maybe."

"The Wood will make you see things," Oli said. "Best to keep goin'."

"But—" Singer began, but Oli cut her off.

"It'll lure you along like a fish goin' for bait. Just keep on, alright?"

Léonie walked alongside Oli, her presence warm and strange. It was still hard to focus in those moments when he realized how near she was. Léonie Baudelaire was infuriating, cold, and heartless but she was also more—in ways Oli couldn't put words to.

She leaned forward, asking, "Your words, the ones you spoke to break our spell, are they of the same enchantment as the Call?"

Oli hunched as he passed beneath a low branch. "Just words."

"Words do not have power like that."

"They do if they're the right words."

"You are intolerable."

Oli sighed. The thing was, he liked the questions. His whole life he'd shirked away from the inquisition of anyone but his mother or another Stražar. Now he walked the Wood with someone other than Tuck. It felt uncomfortable, but also strangely pleasant. It had been like this, in a way, with his father. Except, then it had been Oli with the questions. Maybe, Oli thought, he would have liked bringing Layla in here.

"Look," Oli said, his words working their way out slowly. "My Pa would've said there are *true* words in the world. Words that have roots in the soul of a thing, in its truest form. Speak those words and you speak to its inner self."

Léonie squinted at Oli as if trying to discern if he was lying. "That sounds like maiyea."

"Ain't that what the priest calls magic?"

"Indeed. And it is heresy to practice such things."

"Oh? And I don't suppose it's heresy when a priest does it?"

"The Order would say priests do not perform magic, but *péramate*. Miracles."

"Is that what you plan on calling it when you take whatever power you find here? Call it a miracle and no one calls you a heretic?" Léonie said nothing, and by the tightening of her jaw Oli figured he was close enough to the truth. "A crown must be a nice shield."

"Perhaps now is a good time to learn to keep your mouth closed."

Oli ignored her. "What is maiyea anyway? Strike flint and get a spark. Put that spark beside tinder, get fire and smoke. Fire from practically nothing. Ain't that magic?"

"That is nature. Science. It is how the world was intended. There is a natural, observable, order to the world. Magic subverts nature and such order, changes the way things should be."

"That ain't true."

"That is the basis of scientific observation of the known world. Who are you to call it untrue?"

"Magic has to be natural."

"What?"

"You've *seen* magic, haven't ya?"

"And?"

"So, if Deōs or whoever *made* all this then he must've also made whatever you call 'magic'. And if they made it, then it's how it was supposed to be. And if that's how it was supposed to be then ..."

Victer laughed from behind them. "Ah, I get it. Then magic don't exist 'cause it ain't a subversion of the normal. It *is* the normal because it's how things was made." Victer's smile faded when Léonie gave him a withering look. "Apologies, Your Highness."

Léonie looked back to Oli, lips firmly in place. "Thank you for the demonstration of your philosophical prowess. Perhaps next time you could simply answer my questions."

"Depends on the question."

"Indeed."

Singer coughed, her voice shaking. "Your Highness, there's something out there."

"Just keep up," Oli said. "You're seein' things."

"How much further?" Léonie asked, her eyes roaming the trees around them.

"A while yet. Should be to the Wall soon, then a long jog through the Deep. Before nightfall we'll be there."

Léonie nodded then took a small swig of water. She paused afterward, eyes lingering on the waterskin in her hand. "Is there water in this Wood? A stream or spring, perhaps?"

"Oy, both," Oli said, but shook his head. "Best stay clear of 'em."

"I suppose they will try to kill us too?"

While Oli pondered a reply, a scream sounded out through the Wood, sending shivers down his bones. He turned, searching for Singer. He didn't see her, but Fjord and Victer were making their way quickly to a small hole dotting the forest floor behind them, its edges rough and leaf covered.

"Stay back!" Oli called, sprinting back towards them. They didn't listen, but approached the rim of the hole, leaning forward to peer in.

Fjord cursed and turned away, face pale.

Victer, to his credit, kept his eyes locked on the hole in the ground. "Singer! Can ya hear me? Singer, girl!"

Oli approached quickly, lowering his bow and looking over the edge. Singer was dead. Her body lay in a crumpled tangle about seven or eight paces down, but it wasn't the fall that had killed her. At the bottom of the pit, small as it was, squirmed a mass of thorny vines and writhing snakes.

"Back up," Oli said, grabbing Victer as the man leaned forward to call again, yanking him back. "Keep movin'. She's gone."

The princess had caught up, and Oli felt a sudden urge to stop her from looking over the edge, as if to protect her from the sight of it. He didn't, and the stoic look on her face when she turned from the pit told Oli she'd seen worse before.

"Keep moving," she muttered to herself, then turned to Oli, eyes hard. "Keep moving, yes? Any other rules we should know about? Perhaps something about piles of leaves covering up little death pits?"

Oli gestured to the Wood around him. "She shouldn't have been here. I've been keepin' us well away from spots like this. Listen, if ya wander off, you're dead. Simple as that." Oli paused and looked up. "We best keep movin'. Vines are takin' an interest."

"Vines?" Léonie looked up, following Oli's gaze with furrowed eyes. A heartbeat later, her eyes went wide. "They move?"

"Aye, and they do more than that. Now c'mon."

They hadn't gotten a hundred paces before they were stopped again.

"Somethin' behind us," Fjord said, voice trembling. When Oli turned he saw the broad man raising his bow, looking west. The sun cast golden streaks like strips across the man's back. There was nothing but trees.

"No one's there," Oli said. "Keep calling like that, though, and somethin' might just show up, which won't be good for any of us. Let's keep—"

"I see it too," Léonie said, cutting Oli off with the wave of her hand.

Oli seethed, tension and frustration building up in his bones like a boiling kettle. "Maker curse you all, I said we keep—"

A voice called back from the west. Far closer than it should have been for Oli not to have seen anyone. "Lower the bow, Fjord. It's me."

"Tâl," Léonie said. "Good."

Fjord eased the tension in his bow. "Good on ya. Is that Collin too?"

Oli could see her now, working her way carefully around the trees, sticking mostly to the shadows. Another figure trailed behind her, walking with care but without the same grace. Nor the same sort of cloak. Instead, they were wearing something old, tattered, and . . . familiar.

"Collin didn't make it."

Fjord spat to the side.

Victer stepped between the princess and Tâl, his bow raised. "Then who's with ya?"

Oli knew. He understood the moment he saw that cloak, his *father's* cloak. Only one person would be so stubborn, so reckless, and so foolish. Who else would *want* to go to the deepest parts of the Wood?

"No." Oli didn't mean to say the word aloud, but it came out anyway, a pained whimper. *She's supposed to be home.* He was doing this for her, wasn't he? For his mother and sister, so they could eat and be safe and live and thrive. All for them, all to keep them safe. And now *she* was *here*, and *here* was *not safe*. Here was death, so much death. "No."

Léonie turned, a small smile crossing her lips. Oli could punch her. Tâl and Orelda were close now, Oli's mother looking as determined as ever though her hair curled about her face in an unkempt mess and her trousers appeared ripped and dirty. In her hand was one of Father's old bows, and she shifted its weight awkwardly from hand to hand. The rangers seemed tense. Oli imagined they hadn't expected a visitor.

"Your Highness," Tâl said. "I present to you, Orelda Ricker. I found her following our trail."

The look in Léonie's eyes as she moved from Orelda to Oli made him shiver.

"Take her back," Oli said. "Take her back now, Tâl."

"Oli," Orelda said, holding out her hand and stepping forward, but the princess cut her words short.

"No," Léonie shook her head. "She wants to follow us, yes? I shall grant her what she wishes. She is now under my protection."

Oli spat. "Then I'll go back. You can find your own way."

Léonie jabbed at Oli, "You will take me where I want to go, Woodsman, or—"

"Or what?" Oli slapped her finger away. "You'll kill me? Without me you'll die."

Léonie shifted one foot back and pulled her sword free, the blade ringing as it emerged from its sheath. Oli stopped thinking. He drew his bow, aiming for the princess's eye while stepping backward, expecting the slashing of her blade.

But Léonie didn't aim her blade at Oli.

Léonie moved fast, her blade seeming to materialize with its tip at Orelda's throat. And then the princess leveled her eyes on Oli's. For a heartbeat, nothing happened. Oli's arrow pointed at Léonie. Léonie's sword at his mother's throat. Then Fjord and Victer nocked arrows, aiming them at Oli, while Tâl unsheathed her own blade, carefully holding it against the base of Orelda's spine.

And they all stayed still, Oli ready to kill the princess, the princess and Tâl ready to kill Orelda, and the others poised to kill Oli.

When Léonie spoke her voice did not falter. "You *will* take us the rest of the way, Woodsman, and your mother will come along to ensure you do."

Bile swirled in Oli's stomach. "What kinda princess are you? You'd kill her?"

"I am the kind of princess who sees a bigger picture," Léonie ground out each word between barred teeth. "The kind of princess who has seen *thousands* of Orelda Rickers burned already and is trying to save tens of thousands more. Can you even fathom so many people? Can your mind grasp the sheer *weight* of what we are doing here?" Each word became a hammer, beating in rhythm with the *thump thump thud* of Oli's pulse.

Léonie didn't stop. "I do not trust you. You are impulsive and shortsighted, ready to leave any one of us for dead. If you had the chance to leave us to die here in this forsaken place, you would, would you not?" Oli said nothing, but he could feel the perspiration on his forehead as he worked to keep the bow steady. Léonie only nodded. "And so, your mother will stay with us. My fate will be her fate. If I live, she lives. I must get to Staradovna, and I must return with the power to save Trevelar. Your mother's life is not worth the kingdom."

Oli glanced at his mother. She stood still, hands splayed to the side, eyes looking not down at the blade before her, but at her son. Her chest heaved in and out, and she rolled her shoulders back as if to try to avoid the blade's point on her back.

"You and your kingdom can be dragged down to Yeolasi, for all I care," Oli said. "I just want us left in peace."

"What peace will there be when the Yelmes burn down your homes and pillage your corpses? Think *bigger,* Oli."

"Thinkin' bigger just gets ya killed."

"What will it be, Oli?" Léonie leaned forward, the blade touching Orelda's throat now. "Tell me."

Oli worked his mouth but said nothing. It was impossible. If he dragged his mother deeper into the Wood, she'd die. He knew it, was certain of it. But what other choice did he have? To watch her stabbed through right here? *Might be a better end*, Oli thought. *An easier end. A quicker end.*

He'd seen how his father had died. It wasn't quick or easy. A sword would be better.

Something cold touched Oli's shoulder. It was a slow thing, smelling of earth and weeds and pressed oils. He knew what it was, and knew if he could feel it, it was already too late. They wouldn't be only at his shoulder, but his ankles too. Léonie's eyes went wide and the sword faltered at Orelda's neck.

They'd stopped moving for far, *far* too long.

"Damn it," Oli said.

And then the vines ripped him off his feet.

TWENTY-FOUR

Oli hit the leaf-strewn ground so hard the air popped from his lungs. He released the string of his bow as he fell, the arrow flying wildly into the branches above. For three heartbeats Oli lay on the flat of his back, watching the rays of sunlight weaving themselves between the treetops. His eyes traced the path of a dragonfly which whirred sporadically between leaves drifting on the breeze. The ground felt soft. Warm too. Everything in Oli's life was cold and demanding. He didn't want to get up.

What would really happen if he stayed here? He could lay unmoving and let all his problems work themselves out. His sister, his mother, and the princess could all fend for themselves. They could find their own food, their own sacred powers, and whatever else they needed without him. He was tired, so tired, and just wanted to—

Oli sucked in air involuntarily, as though he'd nearly been drowning. And with the air, flooded back all the fear and anger he'd had moments before. The Call had tried to grab hold of him and that only fueled his anger more.

He grabbed his knife as he twisted and squirmed in the vines' grasp. He wasn't going to let the Call take him, and he'd be damned if these vines would hold him down any longer. With every twist of his body, he could feel the resistance of the vines on his ankles and around both his shoulders. A particularly thorny one slithered in from the left towards Oli's face, but he couldn't think of it now. Cries of pain and fear surrounded him, but Oli couldn't think of them either.

The vines nearly had him held fast. He'd screwed up, let down his guard, and if he didn't stay focused now he'd be dead soon enough. Those vines would squeeze until his life popped from him like juice from a tomato.

Oli brought his knife up and sawed at the vine around his shoulder. He desperately tried not to think of how close his blade was to his neck, nor about the slight tingling beginning to grow in his feet as the blood flow slowed. Time moved impossibly, as if everything moved both too fast and too slow all at the same time. Beyond him the world moved in a blur, a cacophony of sound and motion so fast and loud he could make out none of it. But here, in this little world of blade sawing against vine, every single movement took an eternity. The fibers of the vine snapped as his blade worked, releasing small droplets of purplish-life blood. He could see his own blood sliding up the vine's thorns, pulled from his body the way children drink with reed straws. It became a race to see who could bleed the other first.

And then, with a final back and forth of his blade, the vine on Oli's shoulder snapped apart. Oli jerked upwards as the pressure he'd been fighting against suddenly disappeared. But he wasn't free yet.

He flipped the knife to his other hand, working to cut the vine on his other shoulder. He had turned away from the thorny vine working across the ground toward him. He had cut nearly halfway through the second vine when he felt the tingle of a vine on the back of his neck. Oli gritted his teeth and worked faster, leaning away from it as best he could.

The next vine snapped free and Oli jerked forward again, his still-moving blade cutting through his tunic and drawing blood. There was no time to care. He spun about and grabbed the vine trying to work itself around his neck. Thorns bit into his fingers, but Oli gritted his teeth and thrust his blade into its fleshy skin, scraping the blade awkwardly to the side, leaving the vine cut open and pouring its blood onto the ground. He chucked it aside.

Oli cut the vines from his ankles in short order, grateful for the rush of feeling back into his toes as he stood. When he looked around, the group was in chaos. The princess lay on the ground a dozen paces away, squirming and thrashing in the leaves as Tâl tried to get her blade in to chop the vines away. Fjord dangled upside down a few paces into the air, trying desperately to whack the vine at his ankle with his sword even as it dragged him higher. Victer looked uncertain as he aimed his arrow toward the vine holding Fjord, bow drawn back, arms shaking.

In fact, the only person who wasn't either trapped in vines or trying to help someone else get free was Orelda, who was sprinting towards Oli. Her left shirtsleeve had ripped in a dozen places, but otherwise she seemed fine.

"Are ya alright?" she called, grabbing for his shoulders and yanking off bits of dead vine.

"Aye." Oli brushed her hand away and grabbed his bow. "But what in the Twelve Hells are ya doin' here?" He nocked an arrow, pulled back the string, and let it go a heartbeat later. The arrow flew straight through the vine holding Fjord off the ground, and the man came tumbling down with a cry, Victer leaping backward out of the way.

"I had to come," Orelda said, following Oli as he marched towards the princess.

"Oy, did ya?" He neared the princess. Vines had wrapped themselves around her ankles, knees, chest, and arms. All the thrashing and yelling hadn't gotten her anywhere but more stuck. Her eyes didn't hold fear though, but anger. She looked pissed. *Real* pissed. So much so, Oli didn't want to get involved.

"Woodsman!" she screamed.

"Oy," he said.

"Get me out!"

Oli grunted. "Should probably let you die."

Tâl hacked away beside the princess, trying to chop away at the base of the vine wrapped around the princess's chest. She did her best to land each blow in the same place, as if to break open the vine the way she might chop up a felled tree. Oli could let Tâl go at it, getting nowhere while the crushing pressure of the vines sucked the princess's life away.

He could take Orelda and leave, right now, and never look back.

He planned to, had every intention of it, but when he turned towards his mother her eyes fixed on him. "Help her," she said.

"She'd have killed you."

"Help her anyway." Orelda reached up and placed her palm on Oli's cheek. "She's desperate, Oli, and don't we each do the dumbest of things when we're desperate. Go. Help her."

And then Orelda pulled her own knife free and made towards Victer as he tried to kick encroaching vines away from an unconscious looking Fjord.

Help her anyway.

Oli turned back to the princess. She was beautiful still, even covered in cuts, dirt, and nearly entombed in vines. But beautiful in the way a thinly frozen lake might be. The moment you step on it, get too close, you'll fall beneath the surface and die. Oli growled and shook his head, but stomped over and grabbed Tâl's hand as she reared back for another blow.

"Stop it." Oli pushed her aside and knelt beside Léonie. He brought out his blade and looked the princess in the eye. For one split second, he thought about sliding it right through her iris. Instead, he muttered, "Stop squirming," and got to work. Half a dozen careful slices later, the vine broke away.

"You cut it like rope," Tâl said, dropping on the other side of the princess, sawing away at the nearest vine.

"Sure," Oli said with a shrug. "Like magical death rope."

TWENTY-FIVE

L ayla stood in the center of the home which still bore the wreckage of her fight with Windsun. A pack rested at her feet, loaded with everything she would need for a journey northward: food, water, blankets, tinder, and kindling, along with every knife she could find. After everything with Windsun earlier, she wasn't going anywhere without near half a dozen knives within easy reach. Still, she didn't feel ready.

She danced the tips of her fingers along her lower lip, looking around the modest home. She hadn't bothered to right the table or chairs, hadn't seen the point. Soon she'd be gone, and she doubted she'd come back. Though, to be fair, she doubted a lot at the moment. She hadn't the slightest idea where she would go, but she figured it would be the opposite direction of Windsun. That captain could say all he wanted about a "fighting chance", but if there were demons and death coming their way, Layla wanted nothing to do with it.

"Ah." Layla's eyes locked on the bookshelf. With the door latch broken, she'd gone ahead and slid the whole thing in front of the door.

It was foolish, she knew it the moment she thought it. Still, she removed one of her father's old books, one with a green leather cover and gold inlay which had entranced her for hours growing up. She hadn't the slightest clue what it said, or what it was about. As a little girl, she'd pretend she could read, imagining her father showing her the words and bringing them to life. Before he died, her father had started teaching her letters and the sounds they made. It had been brief: an hour here or there when he wasn't too tired or too consumed in his maps. She remembered nothing but the feeling of freedom held in those moments.

Layla slid the book into her bag, then nodded to herself. "Nearly there." She looked down at her dress, considering, when a banging on the door shook the bookshelf so hard it would've toppled if she hadn't held it up.

"Who's there?" she called, pulling a knife free from her hip.

The pounding stopped, but the silence contained its own sort of fear. Layla started to imagine the door exploding inward, making way for a horde of nightmarish creatures to come screaming in. Or maybe it would be Windsun again. Instead, a thick voice, whose every word seemed to weigh a millstone, called back, "Oy, I've come about your pup." A pause. "Layla, lass, that you?"

Layla breathed out, her shoulders crumpling in relief. *Anej.* "Aye, it's me." She heaved against the side of the bookcase, wood scraping against wood. But once the bookcase slid past the doorframe the door creaked open on its own, revealing the tanner. He knelt so the sight of him could fit in the doorframe, his braided beard hanging low near the ground. In his arms he held a reddish-brown ball laying eerily still: Tuck.

"Thought I should bring him home." Anej placed Tuck gingerly into Layla's arms. Tuck was alive, she could feel the slow beat of his heart, and his eyes flickered open to look up at her.

"He doesn't look good."

"No, he don't," Anej said, nodding. He bent a tad lower so Layla could meet his eyes. Or see them, at least. Looking them straight on wasn't easy. "Your brother stumbled outta the Wood yesterday, near dead the two of 'em. But I'll be a two-horned black cat if them Stražar and their hounds don't hold on to life like bark on a tree."

Layla shrugged. She hadn't the slightest idea what a two-horned black cat was, though she imagined Tuck with black fur and horns, figuring that was close enough. She turned and carefully carried Tuck toward the fireplace. She'd need to get a flame going for him. He felt too cold. "Will he be alright?"

Anej stroked his beard. He looked awkward, squatting down to be seen through her doorway, but he didn't seem bothered by it. "If he had the chance, maybe. It'd be a long road though, and I ain't sure it'll matter."

"No, I guess not." Layla had forgotten about Tuck, nearly marching north without even considering the pup. Oli had *said* Tuck was with Anej, nearly dead, but Layla hadn't seen him. She'd forgotten.

She stood and stretched, then did her best to look straight at the velk. That wasn't an easy feat though, with his unnatural blue eye beside the strange milkiness and inkblot of the other. She looked away a moment later with a cough, her face warming. They were so *strange*, those eyes. Every time she saw them, she felt like she witnessed something private, like she'd walked in on Anej stripping down for washing.

"He ain't up for travel, eh?" she said.

"Travel?"

"Aye, travel."

"Where ya goin'?"

"Anywhere. Away. I don't wanna be here when . . ." How long until the Yelmes arrived? Days? Hours?

Anej shook his head and leaned his hand just inside the doorway. The whole home groaned. "Quickest way to get killed, if ya ask me."

"That's what the captain said."

"The captain?"

"Aye. Captain Tie-Bolt, or something like it. He's with the

princess. Says everyone who left is gonna . . . well, that they ain't gonna make it."

Anej said nothing. He looked sad, like someone had strung a weight about his neck and he'd been forced to remember everything bad that had ever happened. Layla began to right the chairs and table, wanting to busy her hands.

"Captain's right," Anej said. "They won't make it. The Yelmes ain't known for mercy. Women, children, it don't matter. If they want to, they can chase 'em and cut 'em down like stalks of wheat. It'll be quick though, which I suppose is a mercy."

Layla imagined Windsun's body cut down and left to rot. Hate him or not, she didn't want him dead. And then Anej's words settled in. *Women and children.* Layla could see them too: the Gorkin family with their little army of toddlers, Miss Winglet, the Fletcher twins . . . she didn't actually know who had left with the Totes but she could imagine. Layla bit her lip and shook the thought away. "And how do you know, anyway?" she asked. "Ya make it sound like you've run into them before."

Anej said nothing, and when Layla looked up she saw the velk watching her carefully. His breathing was loud, his nostrils flaring gently.

Layla laughed uncomfortably. "Ya can't tell me you've seen them before, right?"

Anej sighed. "Best thing to do now is to settle in for a fight. I don't want it, mind you, but fleeing won't do any good. And besides, we've won before, eh?"

"That was an epoch ago."

Anej nodded. "Then we'll see if the race of men can remember their courage."

He stood, his face disappearing beyond the door frame. Layla watched as he leaned forward, his hands taking something out of view which had been leaning against the side of the Ricker home. A spear and a shield. Layla caught her breath as Anej hefted them. The spear was as thick as the corner posts of her home, the shield a shade larger than the open door.

"And don't count your brother out just yet," Anej called, his voice muffled, dispersed throughout the whole home like the voice of Deōs rattling through the shingles.

And then he left, his boots pounding dirt as he made his way up the hill.

CHAPTER
TWENTY-SIX

Léonie rubbed at her neck, reassuring herself she was fine. Just fine. No vines had gotten around her throat, the Woodsman had seen to that. Still, Léonie could not help but imagine the way it would feel: the thorns pushed in like pinpricks, tugging and pulling as they squeezed the air from her lungs. She shivered. She had been terrified, truly terrified. She had nearly died, entombed in a coffin of living vines.

Maker help her, she *hated* this place.

Blade in hand, she twisted and turned every which way, waiting for the next strike. Paranoia. She recognized it for what it was. She wanted to move, to leave, to run west and never look back. But dying by the swords of the Yelmes was not any better than dying here. East was her only option. Staradovna and whatever power she held was the only conceivable way to save Trevelar. To save herself.

She started in what she thought might be an easterly direction. At least, it was the direction they had been going before they had been ambushed. She walked by Tâl and Victer, their eyes wide and hands shaking as they fell in line behind her. Fjord limped along, dazed. Victer doubled back and half-carried him on. The Ricker woman appeared fine, the way peasant women always were. Her face set, eyes hard. Léonie and Oli were in similar condition: clothes and skin dotted with a hundred pinpricks of blood, each leaving little red trails down skin and cloth.

There was a popular art style from Soreen involving poking thousands of holes into a canvas with various sizes of needles, then putting the canvas before a set of candles and a mirror. It created a sea of pinpoints through which the light could paint images of flowers, cityscapes, portraits, and more.

Oli and Léonie looked as if one of those canvasses had ended up in the hands of an amateur.

"You're off, then?" Oli asked as she passed.

Léonie faltered, memories from the moments before the vines washing over her. She was a fool.

"Am I to assume you will take us no further?" Léonie stood straighter, running a shaking hand down her jerkin as if fixing a dress.

Oli looked around, taking in her haggard rangers. "Will this get bloody if I don't?" His voice stayed as flat as a Badaui banker, but she did not miss the tension in his forearms, the shifting of his hip.

She would have liked nothing more than to teach him a lesson, but what would she gain? She needed to get to Staradovna quickly, before anything else could happen to stop her. And, if she were honest with herself, she felt too scared and tired to stay and argue, let alone have things get bloody.

Léonie opened her mouth to speak, but Orelda stepped forward with a huff. "Oh, for Maker's sake, if you two keep fightin' like children we'll all end up dead."

On reflex, Léonie raised a finger and stepped forward, but Orelda left no room for whatever she intended to say.

"This is how things will go. Oli, you're takin' us to Staradovna. No, don't you say a word, boy, you're already walkin' the line with me. You've got a sister back in Watchful who'll die if the princess here can't get the power she needs, so you'll get your act together, and you'll do it now. And you," Orelda whipped around, jabbing her own finger toward Léonie. "You point one more blade towards me or my boy and I swear on Deōs I'll whip your hide so raw you'll wish I left you to the Wood. I don't know much 'bout savin' a kingdom, but I do know you won't help things by stabbin' your own in the back, eh?"

And then she stormed off, shoving past Léonie as she went.

Léonie watched Orelda go, tightening her grip on her sword. When she turned back, Oli stared into her eyes.

"That settles it then," he said, his tone making it clear nothing was settled.

Léonie swallowed. She needed his help and wanted none of it. "You shall take us then, yes?"

"I'll take her," Oli pointed at his mother. "If anything happens to her though . . ."

"Then things get bloody."

Oli shrugged. "Better than waitin' for you to hang me when we're out of this, eh?"

Léonie said nothing.

Oli spat on the ground, then shook his head. "Whatever. We're off to the Wall. C'mon."

Tâl stepped forward, filling the space between Oli and Léonie. "Your Highness, are you alright?"

Alright? She was anything but *alright.* But she said nothing and pushed forward behind the Woodsman, afraid of what would happen if they lost him in this place.

When Léonie explained to Tâl what had happened with Singer, the ranger said nothing. Already, two rangers were dead and now Fjord hobbled, injured. Whatever divine support Léonie had been hoping for from Deōs, she witnessed none of it. Perhaps she had needed that priest's blessing after all. Or maybe she truly had become a heretic.

"This is it," Oli said, coming to a stop up ahead.

Léonie stepped up beside him. Her feet were sore, and much of her skin felt cold and dry. The shallow cuts along her arms and legs were now scabs pulling at her every time she moved. And yet, all those thoughts of pain and soreness vanished when Léonie looked at where they had arrived.

Before her lay a stretch of grass without trees, bright in the afternoon sun. Beyond that, perhaps twelve yards ahead of her, stood one of the strangest things she had ever seen. Even though Oli had told her what to expect, it felt odd to see something so civilized and ancient amid the wild. Built of white stones darkened with age, the wall had fallen into a strange form of disrepair. Many of the stones lay cracked on the grass before them, but those that still stood were incredibly daunting. Each stone was cut to shape perfectly, meaning that where two stones still stood, no gap existed between them. And the wall went on to her left and right for as far as she could see: miles and miles each way.

Léonie could get a sense of what this had been in its prime, of the impossibility of its construction. And that unnerved her because she had seen a similar construction before—the walls of Worchestern. Those had been taller and thicker, and made of a glossy black stone, but it seemed as if both the age and the form of construction had been the same.

It was, amongst other things, a reminder that Trevelar had been built upon epochs of other kingdoms. Most of those peoples had been lost to memory, with only these relics to herald back to any past at all. Had those people been crushed beneath the weight of a foe like the Yelmes? Is it why they did not exist today?

And yet, even more fascinating than the wall, was what lay *behind* it.

In Trevelar, and in the world as a whole, early winter reigned: cold air blew leaves from trees, leaving them bare. Leaves of orange and brown covered the ground except where snow had likely already begun falling in the far north. Grass rose in the plains around the kingdom, dry and yellow, months away from the rains which would bring back the vast array of lush greens. So whatever Léonie saw now could not be possible.

Life and vibrancy. Spring and summer. Just paces away.

Different shades of green leaves bloomed in the treetops, along with pinks, purples, and reds from treetop wildflowers. Everything looked wet and alive, as if a fresh rain had watered them an hour before. The wall rose too high for her to see much more, but Léonie could imagine.

"Maker, help us," Victer said, spitting to the side.

"It's real then," Léonie breathed. "The Timeless Depths."

Oli snorted. "It's real enough to get you killed, anyway. And we just call it the Deep."

Tâl's lips twitched in disgust. "The Wood, the Wall, the Deep . . . has no one told you Stražar that names have power? They *mean* things. Look at this," she gestured, hands and eyes trying to encompass the Wall down to where it disappeared on the dark horizon. "No people spent a lifetime constructing this and then called it 'the Wall'."

Oli walked alongside the large stones, his fingers reaching out and grazing them gently. Orelda stood beside him, whispering something Léonie could not hear.

"Peace, Tâl," Léonie said, as she walked toward a cracked stone, taking a closer look. "Do not expect too much from our guide." Vines moved lazily along the stretch of wall near her. Her skin crawled at the sight of them, and her hand rose up involuntarily toward her throat.

"Is he alright?" Fjord asked, pointing towards Oli who leaned on an intact portion of wall, his palm flat on the smooth stone, his head bowed. He looked ready to try and shove the section of stone over.

"Come, Woodsman," Léonie called. "It is time to go, I think."

Oli said nothing, only kept his hand firmly on the stone before him, lips moving without sound.

Léonie looked to Orelda. "Woman, what is he doing?"

Orelda shook her head. "Oy, Your Highness, I—"

And then Oli spoke, his voice deep and commanding. "*Tviarka pochúite. Pyosa.*" Each word shivered the air around them, energizing the air and making Léonie's hair stand on end.

"Gone mad," Victer said, backing up and holding his bow a little higher.

But Léonie did not think so. Those words he spoke were not familiar to her, and yet she felt like she should know them all the same. Not only because they were clearly of the same language he had spoken before, but it felt as though she had seen and heard this tongue in her distant memory. As if she had heard this language as a child, but forgotten all but the most distant whisper of it.

The last time the Woodsman had spoken in this tongue, the enchantment over each of them had been broken. Now, Léonie waited expectantly for magic to stir the air.

She was not disappointed.

The stone Oli touched began to shudder. The ramifications of his words rippled out along the wall in waves, like a stone hitting a pond. Rock shoved against rock, creating a low and terrible rumble lasting for a dozen seconds, then stopped. The following stillness hung heavy, weighed down by a mixture of understanding and confusion. They all knew something miraculous had happened, and yet the significance of it lay beyond them.

One thought thrummed through Léonie's mind, though. She knew that if a rock were given a language, then *that* was what it would sound like.

"Maker . . ." Tâl said, falling to her knees.

"This ain't good," Fjord muttered, running a hand through his hair. Victer nocked an arrow.

Orelda beamed, her hand rising to her mouth in either awe or pleasure. "It's been so long."

"The stoned moved," Victer said. "The whole wall moved. That ain't right."

"Maiyea," Léonie said, ashamed at the tremble in her voice. "It *is* magic."

Oli looked at Tâl, pointing a thumb at his chest. "We Stražar know the true names of things, or . . ." he looked about himself, as if searching for something. "Some of them, at least. And we use those names sparingly. So, aye, in the common tongue we just call things what they are. The Wall is a wall, the Wood a wood. You don't disrespect a thing by callin' it what it is."

Tâl shook her head, muttering, "Yidumetcha." A Baduai word Léonie recognized. *Namer.*

Oli ignored her then leapt atop a fallen rock, moving toward the Deep. "Once we're over there we'll be running the whole way. No stopping."

"Running?" Fjord said, glancing at his ankle.

Victer stepped near him and put a hand on his shoulder.

Orelda followed her son as he worked his way up to the top of the Wall, climbing from one fallen block to another. "You don't wanna be walkin' in the Deep. It's a bad way to die," she said, looking back at Fjord. "It'd be best to turn back now."

Fjord shook his head and looked to Léonie. "I can keep up, m'lady."

"You ain't got a choice," Oli called out, looking at his mother with a frown. "You'll just die on the way back if ya try it."

"Oli, he can't run," Orelda said.

"Then his blood is on her hands." Oli gestured to Léonie. "Now c'mon, we gotta go."

Léonie worked her jaw, looking from Fjord to Tâl, and considered what to do. Would the man die either way?

But Fjord spoke first. "I've been through worse, Your Highness. I'll keep up, you have my word."

And it was settled then. Not to honor the word of one of her soldiers was to dishonor them. Despite what the Woodsman said, Fjord's blood would be on his own head.

"Then follow," Léonie said, making for the crumpled portion of wall Oli and his mother climbed.

Near the top, Tâl said, "It'll be dark soon. How will we make camp?"

Oli stood on the top of the Wall, pointing downward. "The moon's always bright over here, and you'll see enough to take your next step. But they'll be no camp and no rest until we're back out of the Wood entirely. Our best hope is to keep goin' as fast as we can and pray we don't get noticed."

"Noticed by what?"

"The Wood."

"And if we are noticed?" Léonie asked, coming to stand beside Oli.

Oli shrugged. "Just kill whatever you see before it kills you."

"Can you not use your power? If the stones obey, then will not the vines and creatures?"

"No," Oli said, the word tinged with longing. "Maybe someone could've a long time ago, but nothin' over there remembers its name. I mean, look at them," Oli said, pointing to the vines writhing along the Wall. "Ain't supposed to act like that. Forgot their name, became somethin' else."

"Don't make any sense," Fjord muttered, still climbing. His head drenched with sweat, cheeks flushed red.

"Nothin' makes sense," Oli muttered.

Léonie hardly listened. She could not peel her eyes away from the thousands of flowers hugging the forest floor like a carpet of red and yellow. Butterflies and bees, blue jays, and sparrows, fluttered about like royal criers. The tree trunks appeared wide enough for doors to be carved into them, and many of their limbs grew as thick as small trees. Each looked ready to bear fruit by the hundreds, though their buds were still firmly closed.

It was a garden for a king, except Léonie knew well that even kings had to succumb to natural laws. This, then, was the garden of a god.

Is that what she is? Léonie wondered. *Is Staradovna a god?* If so, what did that mean for Léonie? Had she come to tame a god, to make a puppet of the divine? The idea constituted heresy, of course, and yet had Léonie ever seen the Order produce such wonder?

"Best keep up," Oli said. Then he dropped down into the Deep.

"'Cause if we don't keep up, we die," Fjord said as he scaled the last stone to stand beside the rest.

Léonie said nothing. Twice already she had nearly died, and it felt more dangerous as they entered the Timeless Depths. She was unsure she could keep up with the Woodsman, and certain he would leave her behind.

But not his mother. Léonie watched as Orelda slowly lowered herself down. *He will not leave her.* No matter what, Léonie only needed to stay with *her*. If she could do that, then she would find herself under Oli's protection as well.

"Come," Léonie said, avoiding Fjord's eyes. And then she, too, dropped into the Deep.

CHAPTER
TWENTY-SEVEN

Layla tapped her fingernails on the leather sheath of her sword. *Her* sword. She'd laid it out on the bartop in the Downwind after pushing aside a half dozen dirty mugs and a basket filled with breadcrumbs. The bar had never been this dirty, as far as Layla could remember. The boy hired as help had probably fled town with the others.

"The girl's in shock, she is," said the quartermaster behind her, muttering to someone she couldn't see.

Shock. That's what they'd said about her after her father died, what people had called the numbness which comes with being helpless. It was more than fear. She feared Windsun, but she could fight someone like him. But as she sat in the Downwind, she felt nothing but a deadening of emotion and a certainty she would die.

The empty streets of Watchful had convinced her. It was as if the vacantness of her home had stretched out over the whole hill. When the captain had told her to stay and fight, she'd been ready to leave anyway. But when Anej had said the same, it felt different. After her father died, the velk had come around now and then, never saying much, but being there nonetheless. She even had the strange feeling the tanner had kept Oli alive, somehow.

And now with Tuck back at home, she felt anchored in place. She had set the dog up with a small fire—food and water beside him. He had hardly stirred. She'd searched through her brother's things and found trousers he'd outgrown years before, but they were too long for her. After some quick work with sheers, they fit into her boots nicely. She tailored her working dress next, giving it a quick snipping to become a workable tunic, especially after she wrapped a belt around her midriff. Soon she would strap the sword's sheath to that belt, and then she'd look about as much like a soldier as she ever would.

Which was not saying much.

"Oy, Miss Ricker!" Ulian called from across the room, eyes wide behind his spectacles. He dropped the mugs he carried on the table before two sullen-looking farmhands (who also looked dumbly at their own swords) and then hurried over to her. Flushed and covered in a light sweat despite the growing chill inside the tavern, Ulian looked every bit the haggard innkeeper. He pointed at her, his smile wide. "Just who I was hoping to see."

Layla leaned onto the bar as Ulian jumped up the steps onto the platform behind the bar, bringing him eye level with her. "Busy?" Layla asked, nodding to the room behind her. About half the table and chairs usually occupying the bar had been piled up outside to help form the barriers up the road. Brooding men and women occupied the seats that were left, quiet except for low mutterings.

"Aye," Ulian nodded, raising bushy eyebrows. "Why, I tell you Miss Ricker the Downwind hasn't seen business like this in all my years as proprietor. I've read war is good for the economy, but this wasn't what I had envisioned." Ulian wiped his forehead with a beer-stained towel before turning and filling the first mug he saw from the keg beside him.

"I figured most everyone had left."

"Well, the soldiers stayed, 'course, and they've got coins to spend and—" Ulian paused, looking about, voice growing low. "And they're all feeling rather certain they won't be needing their chits any longer."

"Ah." Layla looked back down at the sword.

"I only wish some help were about. These legs of mine feel about as wobbly as the seaweed in Port of Gibyal. That is to say, very wobbly. But no matter now. *You* are here!" He dropped the filled mug before her, waving for her to stop as she moved towards the money pouch in her pack. "On the house! No, don't argue, I insist."

Layla took the mug, bowing her head in thanks. Ale wasn't what she needed, of course, but she took a long pull anyway. "You're too kind," Layla said, wiping her mouth on her sleeve.

"Perhaps," Ulian said with a chuckle, scooping up discarded mugs and baskets from all around. "But I should reveal all my cards now, lest you think too highly of me."

"Oh? Is that your way of sayin' this mug ain't free?"

Ulian's cheeks flared red, and he ran a hand through his sweaty white hair. "Well, I shouldn't mean that, exactly, just that I thought, while you are here, perhaps you could enlighten me some. Well, with all the recent events going on."

"I don't know anythin', Ule."

"Of course, of course," Ulian said, nodding. "Just tell me, is it true?"

Layla looked up from the sword, eyebrow cocked. "Is what true?"

"The princess and your brother, obviously. Has he taken her *there*? To the Wood, I mean." Ulian's spectacles jiggled ever so slightly as he spoke, dancing atop the bridge of his nose. "I've heard rumors."

No one had said anything to Layla about the trip being a secret or even indicated the reasons behind the princess going to the Wood weren't common knowledge. And Windsun seemed to have been plenty aware, as well as the captain. She shrugged. "Aye, it's true. They left this mornin' before I was up. She's in a bit of a hurry, I guess." Layla said nothing of her mother.

"A hurry? Why is that?"

Layla waved a hand. "The attack. She'd probably rather not get skewered before doin' whatever she planned on doin'."

"Ah, I see," Ulian put a finger to his chin, then paused. "No, actually, I don't see. Why not stay and fight first? Why leave in a hurry, and in the dark? Why go into the Wood at all?"

"I, uh . . ."

"Yes, sorry." Ulian cut her off, waving his hand excitedly. "One question at a time, of course. Besides, I think I've pieced much of it together already, yes? Let me ask instead, why did she bring your brother? Why *Oli*?"

Why Oli? That *was* a good question, and Layla wasn't sure she knew the answer. After the previous night's talk with her mother and brother, she felt like she had at least a faint understanding of what was going on. At least, she understood the Wood had a "heart" of sorts, and she knew that in that place a being called "Staradovna" lived, if "lived" was the right word. And somehow it all meant the princess could stop Kātsracha from destroying the world, or something.

"I'm not sure," Layla said slowly. "I think it's because, well, Oli knows the place the princess wants to go. He's a guide, is all."

"And where does the princess want to go? The Tree?"

"Tree?" No one had mentioned a tree before. And besides, wasn't the Wood full of trees?

Ulian searched Layla's face, finger still tapping his chin. "No, not the Tree then. The Void?"

"I don't—"

"A barren stretch of ground, yes? With a pillar at its center?"

"Oy, Oli talked of somethin' like that."

Ulian's head bobbed excitedly, and Layla thought she could see his mind whirring about like a spinning top. "Ah, yes. They are after *her*, aren't they? Risky business, that is. I once tried to convince your father that the Tree, more formally known as *Lignum Vivi*, was far more potent than *Terra Vacua*. More dangerous, perhaps, but I feel—"

"Hold on, how did ya know my father?" Layla leaned forward, eyes narrowing. When had Ulian come to Watchful? Five years ago? Six? Her father had died eleven years ago, well before Ulian had bought the Downwind.

Ulian fidgeted with his spectacles, eyes suddenly interested in the bartop. "Oh, yes, perhaps that was something I should have mentioned."

"What's to mention, Ule?"

"Well, you see—"

Thunder, loud and deep, rumbled through the tavern. More than noise, the thunder *shook* the whole tavern. Tankards and plates rattled off tables and clattered onto the floor. A decorative lute above the fireplace shook loose, cracking onto the cobblestone and sending strings *twanging* free. Everyone stood now, the soldiers in the room unsheathing their swords, the farmhands backing up until they hit the bartop. Layla got to her feet and fumbled with the sword's handle, wanting to remove it but finding her hand shaking too much.

And then it stopped, all at once and without warning. Gone as fast as it had come. No one spoke, no one even dared breathe too loud. Only the crackling flames of the fire said anything for a long time. Lips moved in silent prayer, and Layla put a shaky hand over her heart. She meant to pray too, but no words came, only an empty quiet within her.

In the end, Ulian broke the silence. "That's it then. They're here."

TWENTY-EIGHT

L éonie ran through the Deep.

As she did, she tried to soak in every detail she passed. Everything here seemed odd, off. Mosquitoes buzzed, but their buzzing was not the continuous and sharp humming it should have been, but instead came at an odd rhythm: *hum, buzz, buzz*, pause, *hum*. And the pause lasted for *all* of them, a unison freefall for the dozen little mosquitoes flying about the group. Above, obscured by leaf laden branches, the birds sang something she could only describe as a dirge, and in the distance permeated a sound like the rushing of water intertwined with the growling of a rabid dog.

Her skin shivered with fear.

"Maker, it's hot," Victer said, pulling at his tunic's collar. He walked behind her, one of Fjord's arms over his shoulder.

"Don't think 'bout it," Oli called back.

Everything around them grew lush and green. The carpet of brown leaves was gone, and now her boots left prints in loose, black soil which released an aroma of earthy fertility. The trees around them loomed impossibly large, and with every step forward they seemed only to grow. Some were large enough Léonie could have hidden her whole carriage behind one, horses and all. And the tops of the trees grew well out of sight.

It occurred to Léonie that trees so tall should have been visible back in Watchful by simply looking out at the Wood from the hilltop. But that had not been the case, and this was yet another impossibility. It should have been black as pitch down on the forest floor, with the thick cover of branches layered above them. And yet, somehow enough light always found its way down through the boughs. Even when the sun set, the moon shined nearly as bright.

Yet the light did not shine everywhere, instead seeming to illuminate a winding path eastward: one that Oli sometimes followed, and sometimes ignored. Yet, even as eerie as it all was, it was also beautiful. The moonlight illuminated flies and dust motes while casting black shadows over wide swaths of brush and behind thick trunks. She wanted to paint it, to entomb this moment in a frame of permanence. She paused only long enough to commit it all to memory as best she could.

Oli proved true to his word. He ran and gave no sign of looking backward or waiting for the others. Even before Fjord had stepped into the Deep, the Woodsman had been moving as if a demon bit on his heels. Léonie kept up—for now—but she could already feel her lungs warming, her breath coming in less controlled gasps. Perhaps pride blinded her, but she viewed herself fit enough for war, like all Trevlarian nobility. She was no stranger to hard physical feats: long hikes in plated armor, hours on the practice field, days in the saddle. When she had been faced with the fiery blades of the Yelmes, she had been prepared, and she had held her own *for hours*.

And yet this seemed too brutal.

Pain stitched her side, her mouth grew dry, her head felt light.

A full day's march with no food or rest, followed by a sprint over several miles, was inhuman. Around her the rangers began to breathe uneasily, ragged even. Léonie glanced back and saw Fjord's cheeks flushed red, sweat drenching his face as he limped along at a frantic pace. Tâl's lips, usually thin and pressed tight, opened wide, her nose flaring.

How long could they keep this up?

And still, the Woodsman showed no signs of slowing. His steps were sure, his head up and active, his bow at the ready. He even jumped over tall roots or rocks. *Jumped.* He may as well have been a boy sprinting through a familiar stretch of countryside after a day indoors.

He has been holding back. Admitting that truth tasted like a sour medicinal, pungent and strong. A commoner was putting her and her best soldiers to shame.

Orelda was Léonie's only comfort. Besides Fjord, the woman struggled more than anyone else. Her cheeks had grown pale and sweaty, her breathing becoming uncontrolled. At this rate, Oli's mother would collapse, and then where would they be?

Oli looked behind him for a moment, eyes narrowing. "If we don't pick up the pace we'll be in trouble."

"Twit," Victer muttered.

Léonie's mind could not even begin to process what Oli had said. A maeifa scholar might as well have stepped into a nursery to discuss the complexities of naval engineering to toddling children, for all her mind could fathom his words. Léonie said nothing, unsure what she could say, and not wanting to waste a single bit of air.

Orelda called back, words bitten out between strained gasps. "Slow. Down."

Oli slowed and turned, though he bounced in place on his toes. "Oy, this is why ya should've *stayed at home.*"

"Shut it," Orelda said, letting out a gust of air and stumbling to a walk a few paces from Oli. "Ya don't . . . speak to me that . . . way."

Everyone else followed Orelda's lead, falling into a walk as they caught up to Oli. Léonie's head grew light, and her eyes and forehead seemed eerily cold. *Stay upright, stay upright.* Someone behind her coughed, then gagged, and vomit splattered the forest floor a moment later.

The Woodsman's nose flared and his fist clenched. His head kept twisting this way and that, as if waiting for something to pop out from the darkness beyond and swallow him whole. "We have to move. *Now.*"

Léonie raised a finger. "One minute."

"There isn't time. We move or we die."

Orelda coughed and shook her head, muttering, "I'm sorry."

Oli growled, but said nothing.

Tâl walked around the edge of the group, staring into the shadows around them, head cocking to one side. Listening.

"Sorry," Orelda muttered again and bent over, beads of sweat falling like raindrops.

Oli spat onto the dirt, then looked off in the same direction as Tâl.

"What?" Léonie asked, hands on her knees, chest heaving. Memories of vines were fresh enough that she kept fidgeting and turning about.

A howl pierced the night, cutting through the sounds of frantic breathing like razor to a taunt canvas. It dragged on loud and long, and when it ended, the echo lingered on the breeze.

"Wolves?" Victer asked, looking at Oli.

Fjord coughed, then nocked an arrow.

"We should go," Léonie said, already moving eastward.

"Too late. Running won't do no good." Oli did not bother to look her way. "Watch your feet for vines, but get ready for a fight."

"They're just wolves," Tâl said, readying an arrow. "They won't attack a group this large."

Oli snorted. "They'll be a lot of 'em, ya can hear it in the shake of the ground. And they're pissed, I think."

"Pissed?" Victer grunted, planting his feet.

"Aye. They might be holdin' a grudge."

No one bothered to ask. Léonie unsheathed her sword, the weight of it giving her confidence—if only a little. Whatever stalked out there, she could handle it. She was Léonie Baudelaire, Princess of Trevelar. She *owned* this land; she would not let it frighten her. A vine glided down from above, near Tâl. Léonie stepped forward and cleaved it clean through.

"Fjord," she said, gesturing to other vines writhing about. He nodded and pulled his sword free, hobbling about and cutting the vines before they got too close. Léonie tried not to look his way. He was a dead man, and they all knew it. She only hoped his sacrifice would gain her one more step towards Staradovna. *Remember the kingdom*, Léonie thought, tightening her grip on her sword.

"I don't like how quiet it is," Victer said.

Léonie realized it the moment he said it. There was no howling, no bird calls, no fluttering of insect wings. Only silence, with all the weight that brings.

Once, when she was only fourteen, she had been on a ship during a storm. She had been shooed below deck before the worst of it, but she could still remember watching the horizon as dark clouds rushed in. There had been a silence just like this, minutes before the winds and rains nearly capsized them.

She had never forgotten the silence, for it was the kind of silence that promised violence.

Oli muttered into that silence. His words unintelligible, the rhythm poetic. *That language,* she thought. She hungered to know more, to learn whatever secrets those words held. Whatever *magic* they held, for that is what it had to be—magic.

"There," Tâl said.

A ragged wolf, mouth covered in dried blood, stepped into a distant stretch of moonlight. *Wolf* proved a loose term. The size of a small pony with muscles squirming beneath matted fur, the wolf had a stench like tar and sulfur, and its eyes were wrong—slitted like a snake's.

"Oy, you all again?" Oli called out, pulling his bowstring back. The wolf dodged to the side, disappearing behind a large bough.

Fjord stepped beside Léonie, far enough away so she could swing her own sword, but close enough to protect her flank.

"Ain't right," Victer said, voice angry in the way that signaled his fear. "That ain't natural."

"We can handle one," Fjord said.

Then the howls sounded from everywhere. Two at first, then five or more: so loud the sound of them wormed its way into her ears. Even as the last of the howls died away, wolves dashed out from behind tree trunks and into the open, bearing down on them.

"Shoot!" Tâl called.

Victer's and Tâl's skill showed, and two wolves tumbled to the ground, arrows sticking from their eyes. But another half dozen more appeared in their place, and none of the group had time to loose a second arrow. Or, no one except Oli. His body became a blur, and he loosed *three* arrows in quick fashion, sidestepping to stand before his mother as he did. Two more wolves fell from his flurry, but then the rest fell upon them.

A wolf charged Léonie, leaping with its jaw toward her forehead. Léonie stepped to the side and swung her sword, her weight moving to her back foot as she dodged. The move took much of the power from her swing, but the blade's tip should have still easily bitten through an animal's hide.

Should have.

Léonie drew blood on the wolf as it flew by, but the blade's edge only made a shallow cut. The beast landed on its paws, twisted around, and then lashed out towards her with claws like small knives. Léonie stepped backward, praying nothing attacked from behind, and sliced upward in a parry. Each of her blocks left little cuts along the wolf's paws—once, twice, then three times. The wolf paused then, crouching low and growling.

Léonie did not wait for its next attack, but lunged forward. The wolf sidestepped, then lurched towards her throat. Léonie shifted

her weight onto her front foot mid-lunge, twisting and leaning backward, bringing her blade down in a wide arc. The speed and strength
of it cut into the wolf's neck, nearly severing it in two.

Léonie stumbled, then felt the weight of another wolf slam into
chest, sending her tumbling to the ground. Her backside hit the
ground for the third time that day, and for one instant Léonie felt
more annoyed than frightened. And then the wolf's jaws were snapping at her throat.

Instinct alone saved her.

She dropped her sword and brought her forearm up as the wolf
bit down. The chainmail sleeve protected her arm, but she felt
enough pressure to fear her bone may break. Humid, rotten air
poured from the wolf's mouth and warmed her face. She yelled and
grabbed at the knife on her hip, pulling it free and slamming it down
toward the wolf's face. The mangy beast reared back, the blade
lodged firmly in its eye. Léonie sucked in cool air as the beast skittered backward. Fjord stumbled into view, his blade coming down
hard on its back, ending its pained scream.

Léonie stumbled to her feet, grabbing her sword as she went. She
twisted her head about, looking around for the next attack, but none
came. The fighting had ended in the sudden way all fights did.

Blood covered the ground, glistening like the pools of water on
the street of Turris Regis after a rain. Wolves lay dead or dying all
around, their unnaturally large bodies strewn in odd contortions,
most still twitching in the throes of death. No one ever talked about
it, but swords and arrows rarely killed anything quickly. They
brought pain and blood loss—things that take time.

Tâl was safe, her face ashen. She stood above an arrow-ridden
wolf's corpse, beneath which a pair of boots stuck out, unmoving.

Victer.

And just like that, another one of her rangers was dead.

Rangers volunteered, Léonie reminded herself. They were not
conscripted, but they chose to serve. At some point, Victer had the
opportunity to say no, and he had not. Tâl covered her face with her

left hand and said a prayer, then walked toward Fjord. His face had grown pale, his breathing heavy, and he nursed a small gash on his neck.

Tâl put her arm around him and spoke something into his ear.

"Thank you," Fjord said, blood gushing from his neck as he spoke, his death looming so close Léonie could nearly touch it.

Léonie walked away.

Orelda and Oli had fared fine. Orelda's hands shook frantically, and her mouth parted in shock, but she lived. And though Oli's boots looked as if he had stomped through puddles of blood, and his quiver had been half emptied, his face looked as passive as ever.

"The vines are comin'," Oli said, reaching into the quiver on his mother's back and removing a few arrows. It looked as if she had not touched a single one. "We gotta go."

"Wait," Tâl said, turning to Oli. Fjord knelt, his breaths coming in slow rasps. "Just give us one—"

"Leave the dead," Oli said, then grabbed his mother's arm and made eastward.

Leave the dead. Léonie looked to Fjord, and when he looked back she met his bloodshot eyes as best she could. With a sigh, Léonie stepped over and knelt beside Fjord, placing her hand on the man's shoulder. She would never rid herself of this memory.

Fjord's eyes were losing focus, his face growing pale. Léonie brought his face up towards hers, waiting until his eyes focused for the briefest of moments. "*Me timí se stélno ston Parádeiso,*" she said. *With honor, I send you to Paradise.*

Fjord grasped her wrist, his mustache stained with blood and snot. He opened his mouth to speak, but nothing came out. Behind him, Léonie could see vines pushing their way across the ground, reaching for him.

"Come!" Oli called.

"Your Highness," Tâl said, eye dancing from Fjord, Léonie, and the Woodsman.

Léonie watched the vines, the memory of her own near-death still at hand. If she left him, Fjord would die alone.

The man could not speak, but his eyes pleaded with her. He knew what would come. Léonie pried her wrist free from Fjord's own, and whispered, "I will not let them have you."

"Your Highness," Tâl said, voice desperate. "We have to go."

Léonie said nothing, only stepped behind Fjord, and raised her blade. "Deōs take your soul, Fjord of the King's Spear."

CHAPTER

TWENTY-NINE

All the eyes in Watchful had turned southward where jagged strips of lightning ripped apart the sky. Layla stood on the dirt road, her hair whipping about her face in a cold and brutish wind. Thunder rolled over and over again, shaking the dirt beneath her feet. Doors rattled on their hinges, pots and pans shook loose from their shelves, and what few children were left began to cry out. The thin glass in the windows of the Downwind trembled in their frames. Then, one after the other, they exploded. Glass landed on the road beside Layla, but she didn't move.

The word *storm* didn't describe what she saw. A storm, even the worst of them, raged imprecise and indifferent. But this was focused, targeted—a hammer to the anvil. Layla couldn't look away. No one could. Ulian had removed his spectacles in reverent awe, his mouth hanging open.

"Deōs help us," someone muttered a prayer, but thunder drowned it out.

A bolt of lightning exploded at the bottom of the hill, and whatever trance had been on the dozens of onlookers in the street broke. Layla didn't see where the lightning had landed, but she screamed anyway. The air filled with the smell of burning leather and fresh spring rain. A tingle ran up Layla's arms and spine, standing her hairs upright.

They all turned and ran up the hill.

Layla's ears filled to bursting with the sounds of cracks and booms and screams behind her as she ran. Her mind tried to keep up, but her body ran ahead of her thoughts. She would pass a building and only register it a dozen steps later. The dirt of the street had turned to cobblestone before she realized the door to the sanctuary, now far behind, hung open. It was further still before her mind could comprehend that not everyone ran from the danger, but some ran *down* the hill. Men and women in dirty orange surcoats charged towards the chaos below. They held spears and shields, their faces hard, and the lightning in the sky reflected in their eyes.

Soldiers.

Ahead of her, people halted at the barricade near the upper half of the hill. One of those soldiers stood on a large crate, spear in one hand, the other cupped about her mouth. She yelled something down at the crowd forming about her, but Layla's mind didn't register the words at first.

"Turn 'round! Turn back 'round!"

Layla stopped beside a burly man with dark skin and a graying beard. She knew him. She knew that she knew him. But her mind couldn't recall his name. She could imagine him with a hoe in hand and a broad smile upon his face, surrounded by upturned soil and a wagon full of potatoes, but no name came to her mind. Now though, his jaw hung slack in horror and in his hands he gripped a naked sword.

Lightning flashed again, casting the whole scene in bright light for an instant.

"Turn 'round! Fight 'em low! Stop 'em low!" The woman's voice washed over them, but the effect was slow. Layla could see soldiers up ahead, shields butted up against one another, forming a wall which kept Layla and the others from retreating any further.

"Let us through!" someone called, their words punctuated by thunder and wind.

The woman shook her head. "Cowards! We have to fight them *now!*"

"I ain't fightin' nobody," the man beside Layla said, dropping his sword to the ground. It clanged against the cobblestones.

The crowd pressed forward, and the woman turned to the men with shields, face red. "Let the cowards through, this ain't worth it." The crowd ahead of Layla surged forward, bodies pressing frantically through the small path of the barricade now open.

Thunder shook the ground again.

Layla didn't move, didn't rush forward with the others. She wanted to, but her mind was catching up, her breath coming back. Where would they go? Up the hill where the cliff face rose too steep to climb down? They'd be trapped soon enough, dead later instead of dead now. Was that what the woman meant when she said they needed to fight them now? The woman with the spear leapt down from her platform and shoved past Layla as she ran downhill, the other soldiers close behind. Layla watched her go down the hill towards the lightning and noise.

Layla turned and looked down the hill, saw war for the first time.

Fires lit up the foot of the hill. Buildings that had been homes ignited like torches, their flames casting a smoky-red hue over the bloodshed below. Dark shapes, nothing more than shadows from where Layla stood, clashed against one another at the first barricade. Archers reigned arrows which disappeared behind the firelight and into the black. In return, the Yelmes—for Layla saw the Yelmes!— tossed lightning back towards the princess's soldiers.

And in the midst of it all, towering at the center of the barricade, loomed a silhouette twice the size of any man. It wielded a spear that lashed out like a blur, its tip catching the firelight as it skewered Yelmes fighters, one after another.

Anej.

Lightning struck near him over and over again, but his shield shunted away each blast as if made of magic and power instead of wood. The princess's soldiers gave him a wide berth, fighting the monsters clawing their way over the barricade of tables, dressers, and kegs.

The sight of the giant standing before the dark mass of the forces of Kātsracha, woke something deep from inside Layla. She felt the cool leather of the sword handle, still firm in her hand and carried all this way, her knuckles white from their hold on it.

She was a Ricker, whether she felt like one or not. Her heart fluttered and it became hard to breathe, but she clung to that thought: she was a Ricker. Her father, her brother, her mother, she suddenly felt as if they hadn't abandoned her as much as they'd only gone toward whatever danger they must. Layla had never felt that before: a danger she felt drawn to out of something like duty. Did Oli see the Wood this way? Was it how her mother felt when she chased after her son?

But Layla had always turned from the Wood, from danger.

Down the hill and toward the fighting was death, but what fate lay up the hill? If the line of soldiers down there broke, then Layla would die anyway. And worse, she would die without a fight.

She saw Windsun in her mind, saw his fingers like claws reaching out for her. And she saw the blood from his hand, blood she had drawn. She hadn't wanted to fight him, but *did*. When she had to, she could.

And there was Anej, standing in the midst of a battle for a town he owed nothing to. Layla felt certain, for reasons she could not explain to herself, that being next to him was both infinitely more dangerous and yet infinitely more safe than anywhere else in all the world.

She could go down there, she could stand beside Anej and be like her father, her mother, and her brother. But fear gripped her hard enough to force tears from her eyes and mumbled prayers from her lips. And still, with shaking hands, Layla pulled the sword free from its sheath and ran down the hill.

CHAPTER
THIRTY

Oli tried to keep his hands steady.

The problem with a bow was that even the slightest shaking would make the far tips of the bow move in wide arcs. Those wide arcs in the corner of Oli's vision were a constant reminder of his fear, a physical manifestation of his inward terror.

"Do you know where we're going?" Tâl said, running beside him. She had become even more stoic, closed off, since Fjord and Victer died. Oli didn't blame her. The Wood had a way of cauterizing the mind. It took away what you loved and made you keep moving.

"Aye," Oli said. Of course he knew where they were going. He could still remember this path, these tree roots, those shadows. He'd seen them night after night, in every nightmare, for years. He could still remember the smell of yew wood from his father's bow, the scent of these flowers, the salty sweat dripping from his forehead.

"Good," Tâl said. "But you'd best slow down, or you'll get there alone."

Oli blinked and turned. Léonie and his mother were a full bowshot back, their faces red and hot, glistening with sweat. Orelda especially looked ready to collapse, which only made Oli's fear worse. The only way she'd be making a return trip is if he carried her. They weren't far now, so maybe she'd make it *there*, but she'd never make it back out on her own feet. He'd see it done though, even if he had to carry her every step of the way back.

Oli didn't stop, but he did slow his pace. Tâl's eyes nearly bore a hole into the side of his face.

"What?" he asked.

Tâl wiped sweat from her forehead and sucked in a deep breath. "You ain't even tired, are ya?"

Oli snorted. Of course he was tired. He was tired of this Wood, of the princess, of death and fear. He was tired of worrying for his mother, his sister. He wasn't just tired, his soul was *exhausted*.

Tâl reached out and grabbed his shoulder, bringing his eyes back to her. "You aren't. How is that even possible?"

"What are you talkin' about? I'm tired."

"No, you aren't. That ain't natural."

"And what does that mean?"

"I've trained with the best soldiers in the king's ranks. A day like today would take a toll on any of them." She gestured to herself. "*I'm* barely makin' it. But you? You've hardly broken a sweat. It's wrong, *unnatural*. The Badaui would call that *syiyeog*."

"*Syiyeog?*"

Tâl nodded, but said nothing more as Léonie and Orelda stumbled closer.

Orelda gasped for breath as she slowed to a walk beside Oli. "Might be a bit outta shape, eh?" She looked as if she'd rolled about in a shallow stream, the sweat making her clothes cling to her skin. She fumbled for the waterskin on her hip with shaking hands, slopping the last bit of water into her mouth. Oli pulled her closer, handing her his own half-full waterskin.

Orelda didn't argue.

Léonie ran her hand through her hair, sticky with sweat. "How much further?" Her nose flared as she spoke, desperate for air but trying not to show it.

"An hour more," Oli said, steadying his mother as she swayed. She leaned into him, the top of her head resting beneath his chin.

Léonie closed her eyes, her fingers clenching and unclenching on the pommel of her sword. "Get us there quickly, Woodsman. And alive."

"Just keep up."

"You have said that before."

"I meant it before." Oli picked up the pace, half-dragging his mother along. They moved too slowly, and he felt at any moment another pack of wolves would come howling toward them. But as they jogged onward, his mother stumbling along beside him, he heard nothing. They passed over tree roots, beneath a ceiling of squirming vines, down through a small gulley, and around a trio of dark willows without incident. The only sounds were boots rustling dirt and the heavy gasping of breath from Orelda and Léonie.

It took nearly half an hour before Oli realized the birds had stopped singing. By then, it was too late, and he knew it. When the growling started, everyone else knew it too.

No, they didn't *know*. Not like Oli. He had heard that growling before, eleven years earlier. He knew what this was, what those guttural reverberations up ahead were. He'd made the same mistake his father had, and had led them right to its den. Like a fool, he'd been so caught up following the same path, he'd forgotten he would run into the same dangers.

"What is—" Tâl started, but stopped when Oli shoved Orelda right into her, sending both women stumbling back.

"Go south a hundred paces," he said, frantically readying his bow. "Then take 'em east. Keep the moon before you."

Tâl turned from Orelda to the direction of the sound. She must have seen it too. At first glance there was nothing but a wall of trees and shadows. But Oli could see it: a half-bowshot away there hid a stretch of strangely textured shadow, the leaves about its edges moving the opposite direction of the gentle breeze. Eyes hid there too, if you knew to look for them. And the low growling told Oli to look for them.

Léonie looked about, confused and as irritated as ever. She'd likely have asked a question or lobbed a demand his way, but blessedly her words cut off when the bear came roaring out of its hiding spot toward them, its patience gone.

"Go!" Oli yelled.

And they did, Tâl dragging Orelda away.

Léonie ran southward, which put Oli and the demon-bear to her left. She had only glimpsed the beast for an instant, but if she ever had the chance to paint the thing it would be the size of a small house with eyes of fire, fur like razor blades, and six pillar-thick legs.

We are in Damnation.

Léonie rarely fled a fight, but she was also well beyond arguing. If Oli wanted to fight on his own then she would not risk her and Tâl's lives if she did not have to. And besides, that beast had been otherworldly.

"Your Highness!" Tâl called, and Léonie twisted about to see the ranger and Orelda hobbling along behind her.

Léonie cursed and sprinted back. Orelda had one arm around Tâl's neck, and Léonie quickly grabbed Orelda's other arm and threw it over her own. Perhaps, if circumstances were different, she would have ordered Tâl to leave the woman. But if Oli found them without his mother then they would be as good as dead. She existed as the only guarantee the Woodsman would find them again.

It took another dozen paces before Léonie realized she assumed Oli would survive the fight with the demon-bear.

Oli loosed one last arrow before he turned and ran. The first two had glanced off the bear's hardened snout, leaving nothing but thin scratches. The third one missed the beast's head entirely but lodged itself into its shoulder, which didn't slow it at all.

Now Oli made his way north and west, running through dark patches of forest at a frightening pace, even for him. Trees became a blur of browns and blacks, with only the dirt path before him holding any focus at all. He didn't dare look back, certain the thing barreled along behind him. Based on the sounds of it, it demolished everything in its path. The sound of splintering and cracking wood became one constant, roaring noise.

The last time Oli had seen this creature, he had run around it with his father and four others, while two stayed back and kept it busy. They weren't supposed to die—just occupy it long enough for the others to get by and then run back to Watchful. When Oli had finally crawled out of the Wood, those two hadn't made it back, and they never showed up.

Now, Oli had returned to the same tactic eleven years later, and he was the bait.

He kept sprinting, doing everything he could to both watch his step and take in his surroundings. The last thing he needed was to escape a bear by falling into a sinkhole filled with deadly mice or get caught up in massive webs spun by dog-sized spiders.

The Wood, though, had other plans.

Oli noticed a curtain of green forming to his left. Vines, lowering themselves and forcing him eastward. He probably should've dipped beneath them before they got too low, but he'd sent his mother eastward, and so he took the bait. Oli turned right at the base of a large tree, then sprinted dead east. If he got lucky, the bear would be slow to make the same turn and he'd be able to lose it among the trees.

He wasn't lucky.

As if the bear had sensed the change coming, it made the same turn *before* the tree, bursting through thick brush to emerge beside Oli in a blur of slashing paws the size of kegs. Oli rolled beneath the attack with a yell, coming to his feet behind the bear who was already turning back around, all six legs a blur of motion. Oli nocked an arrow and shot it even as he ran. The arrow slammed into the side of the bear's snout as its head turned about, impaling it straight through so the bloody end of the arrow extruded out the other side like a morbid nose ring.

The bear roared in pain, charging toward Oli who was already twenty paces away.

The vines lowered themselves on his left and right, forming a long tunnel to whatever trap the Wood had laid for him. Their tips were down to his knees now, and Oli had to do something or see the trap through. His gut told him to get out, and with a grunt, Oli slid beneath the descending vines, using the heel of his boot and his momentum to get him back to his feet. He carved himself a random path, always moving south and east, hoping to ditch the bear and pick up his mother's trail.

If the vines slowed the beast at all, it wasn't apparent. Oli heard the *rip-pop* of vines yanked from the treetops as the bear passed through the vine-wall, and then the roar of crushed and cracked branches resumed. Oli's mind blurred in a cacophony of curses and frantic thoughts, his eyes scanning the world for something, *anything*, that would give him an edge. Nothing helped. It was all just squirming vines, massive trees and . . . birds? Perched in the branches above, watching Oli with all the cold interest of someone surveying a bland meal, sat a pack of vultures.

Dozens of them, or maybe more. Oli could hardly take his focus off the path before him, but he had seen their like before: massive and black, half-feathered with decaying eyes and chipped beaks. They smelled dinner.

Maker curse this place.

Oli dodged left, then back right, then over a fallen tree, a moss laden rock, and then back into the moonlight to go east. The bear never slowed.

Oli, however, struggled to keep up the pace. His legs moved as fast as ever, but the chase had been going on for far too long. If he didn't end it soon, he was bound to trip, run into a ditch, or fall into any other of the Wood's traps. Whatever happened, it wouldn't be good.

Oli nocked another arrow as he leapt over a knee-high rock. When he landed, he spotted the closest thing he'd get to a gift: a house sized boulder with moss-covered sides and a series of small rocks littered about it, all bathed in moonlight. Oli didn't think, just sprinted in that direction without a plan. Two heartbeats later, he leapt onto one of the nearest rocks and hurled himself towards the top of the boulder, throwing his bow and arrow onto the top as he did. Oli's fingertips fought for purchase as he tried to pull himself up and out of danger. Moss came off in clumps in his hand as he scrambled upward, catching sight of his bow and already working through the motions of shooting downward at the bear from the safety of—

A paw grabbed Oli's ankle. He had one heartbeat to realize what was happening, and then the bear yanked him downward.

For an eyeblink, Oli went airborne. And then he slammed into the dirt hard enough all the air rushed from his lungs and the world swam, black veils threatening unconsciousness at the corners of his vision. The bear roared in his face, the smell of death and rot getting Oli's mind and body moving. The beast didn't bother to maul him but instead brought its teeth to bare at Oli's neck.

The arrow Oli had shot earlier still stuck out through the bear's snout, the feather fletching all but gone, yet with the shaft still wholly intact. Oli grabbed the arrow below the tip, yanking it and leading the monster's muzzle away, like the bit merchants used to lead their horses. The bear growled and reared back. Oli brought his other hand up and grabbed the beast's fur above its eye, riding upward with the beast as it stood. Beneath his fingers, the bear's fur was sharp and rough, and his skin showed punctures everywhere he touched it, but he dared not let go. As he rose upward, Oli twisted the arrow, breaking the shaft off in the beast's snout so now he held a fist-sized length of wood with a razor-sharp arrowhead.

Oli plunged the arrowhead into the bear's eye.

The bear surged in anger, batting Oli away with one paw as it brought two others up towards its face, covering it in agony. Oli flew sideways, hitting the ground in an uncontrolled roll. The pain in his side kept him from sucking in air, and his left hand burned with a dozen splinter-like punctures from the bear's fur. But he had to move, to keep going. He stumbled to his feet, nearly drunk off pain, and twisted about, afraid of the next attack and desperate to avoid whatever the bear intended to do.

But the bear didn't bother him anymore. It stood on two legs, and all four of its other paws clawed at its face as it tried to rip the arrowhead free from its eye. It wasn't succeeding though, and instead it left long cuts along its muzzle and cheeks, until there was more blood than fur above its neck. The vultures hopped in the branches above, interest in Oli fading, eyes now fixed on the bear.

Oli didn't wait. He leapt high enough onto the side of the boulder to reach his bow and drag it downward, and then he ran southeast, hoping to find a hint of his mother's trail.

THIRTY-ONE

L éonie had slowed them to a walk. The Ricker woman was half-dead and could do little more, anyway. And Léonie struggled too, legs ready to collapse and chest heaving against her chainmail.

"We should move more quickly, Your Highness," Tâl said, eyes wide as she scanned the dark wood around them.

But Léonie could not. The Woodsman had driven them like cattle, worn them down beyond measure. Her lungs could hardly suck in enough air and her side felt like someone was playing with a knife in her ribs.

"We shall walk," Léonie said. "The Woodsman will need time to catch up and we shall catch our breath in the in between."

"As you wish," Tâl said, but she nocked an arrow. The ranger was flushed in the face and breathing hard, but she had not been running in chainmail.

Léonie scanned the trees and underbrush around them, following the moonlight eastward. Something about the Wood had changed, though she could not quite put a finger on it. The world seemed . . . lighter? More beautiful? More at peace? The colors a touch more vibrant, and she wondered if it was because she was slowing down for the first time since in the Timeless Depths. They walked in silence without any hindrance from beasts, vines, or traps. In fact, as far as Léonie could tell, the Wood grew steadily safer.

Which, now that she thought about it, made a sort of sense. Perhaps all this time it was Oli who had been the real danger. He had been dragging disasters upon them from the start. The *Vromia* only sought to repel him the way Léonie would fight an invader of her land. Yet Léonie had not come as an invader, but an envoy. She came here to make peace, to gain an ally, so why had she been traveling with a rogue? Perhaps, now that they had left him behind, all the ill will this place bore them would dissipate.

"Do you hear that?" Tâl said.

Léonie turned, reaching for her sword. "What?"

"Water."

They found it minutes later: a small brook, less than a hand's width deep, but flowing gently downhill over a bed of smooth stones.

"Praise Deōs," Léonie said, dropping to her knees in the moss-laden dirt beside the brook.

Tâl and Orelda fell beside her, each dipping in cupped hands and drinking greedily. They drank and drank, then splashed water onto their faces and necks. Léonie filled her waterskin, then sat back on her haunches. "Do we have food?"

Tâl shook her head. "Fjord . . ."

Léonie nodded and said no more. Fjord's satchel likely contained whatever stores they had, and that was gone now. She had gone longer without a meal than this, so in that regard, she would be fine. Still, her head felt light and she wanted nothing more than the briefest of rests. Orelda must have agreed, for she laid back and sighed. Tâl stood, however, offering her hand to Léonie to help her up as well.

Léonie dismissed her with a wave. "A moment. Five minutes rest, then we go on."

"But—"

"Sit, Tâl. For five minutes. Just . . . sit."

Tâl remained standing, which seemed like a strange and unfamiliar form of rebellion, though Léonie was too tired to mind. And besides, Léonie preferred her standing guard. The ranger shifted from foot to foot, then began pacing as Léonie's eyelids grew heavier, the world blurring until finally sleep overtook her.

Léonie never dreamed her way into the galleria of her mind. It was always an intentional thing, entering into those halls of art and memory. She should be dreaming, off in the unconscious without agency or purpose. Reliving Worchestern for the hundredth time.

Yet she walked through the galleria, the steps of her bare feet echoing off marble floor and white-stone walls, portraits and sculptures of her memories carefully manicured for her perusal. All was as it should be, and she seemed as in control of herself as ever.

So was this a dream?

She walked down a hall of abstract pieces where she stored memories of most of the Royal Court. Each was a portrait of a lord or lady, often contorted, and always surrounded by shapes and colors which told her more than abject realism would have.

Léonie paused to stare at a portrait of Lady Amandine. The least abstract of the bunch, and the only painting in this hall she had transcribed onto real-life parchment. The duchess's eyes looked into the horizon. Her son, twelve at the time, stood behind her, his hand on Amandine's shoulder. Yulif was his name. He had been sixteen when the Yelmes attacked. Just old enough to be mandated by Trevlarian law to carry a sword.

And now he was dead, like everyone else in Worchestern.

In so many ways, Amandine had become the most prominent thorn in Léonie's side. And yet she was also the only duchess in the kingdom Léonie did not fear would put a knife in her back. Loyalty, love even, held Léonie and Amandine together. It was a tight enough bond, for now.

Léonie pulled herself away and continued on. The hall branched off to the left and right. To the right was a candlelit room filled with busts of adolescent suitors, the left held a long hall with murals of her military campaigns.

She turned left.

Once upon a time, the murals hanging here had been of small battles fought against bandits, rebels, or marauders. Before that, it had been a series of canvases capturing images of duels or skirmishes which had never contained any real danger. Now though, every square inch of wall and ceiling were covered in images of Worchestern. Léonie had fought more during those days than in all the years before combined. She had been certain she and her brother would break the enemy siege. If nothing else, surely they would punish the Yelmes enough to force them to double back and regroup.

But instead, the forces of Kātsracha had broken the walls of Worchestern. Her walls in this room were dominated with dead Trevlarian men and women burned or stabbed upon a background of black smoke. This room existed as a reminder of her failure and of her purpose.

"Why am I here?" she muttered.

She moved into a hall she had never cared to name. Each piece here was a painting, but in each the subject was blurred. The focus of each was all wrong, the brush strokes untamed. Each was of her mother, a woman long since buried in both body and memory. Why Léonie had bothered to keep these, she could not be sure.

As she came to the end of the hall, a door slowly manifested in the wall before her. This was not wholly uncommon, she would often cause her mind's galleria to create shortcuts to rooms she wished to visit, or create new rooms entirely.

But she had not done this.

And this door did not lead into another room of art, but to a winding staircase leading downward into the near darkness. That seemed strange indeed. This place had no need of light sources; illuminated simply by virtue she ordained it. Here, she played god, and this world was hers to shape. Yet small black candles sat upon iron candle stands placed on every sixth stair, and the fickle light they provided barely illuminated the blood-orange runner carpeting the stairs.

Léonie dared not move for a long, long time.

"I am no fool," she said, loudly into the dark of the staircase. "I am not alone. Tell me, are you brave enough to show yourself?"

Though she did not manifest those reactions, Léonie was panicking. This place was supposed to be a sanctuary, an impenetrable fortress of solitude. And yet she had not come here of her own volition, and now there manifested before her a space she had not created. It should not have been possible.

Except, her body lay in the Timeless Depths. She vaguely remembered the stream and the water, and cursed. Had the Woodsman said something about water? Had that been one of his rules?

"I *am* a fool," she muttered.

The stairway still lay before her, emanating no voice in response to her previous goading. Nothing at all happened except the wavering of the candle flames, moving as if a gentle breeze brushed past them. There was, of course, no wind.

Well, she had no intention of marching down into a trap.

"Forsake this place, I am leaving." Léonie concentrated, and forced the eyes of her body to open, summoning her out of her mind. Or, she tried anyway. Except, she did not return to her conscious body, nor did the galleria disappear.

Nothing changed at all.

The black candles in the staircase taunted her.

"No." Léonie looked around as if just within hand's reach something would manifest to save her, to get her out of here. Nothing did. She was a prisoner, trapped in her own mind. She had not brought herself here, and she could not release herself either.

Léonie turned and ran, back down the hall of memories of her mother, back through memories of campaigns, and on through the hall of adolescent suitors, and beyond. She searched for her recent memories, the uncategorized trove of paintings and sculptures she had yet to sort through. Every turn she made, the alien door materialized beside her: a constant taunting, a reminder she had no control. It never blocked her, never closed off another path, but it always beckoned her.

Eventually, Léonie stumbled upon a cluttered room filled to the brim with paintings leaning against one another, sculptures scattered amongst them. A diorama of Fjord lay at the end, Léonie's sword poised above his head. The sight of it turned her stomach.

The room manifested itself as something like a large closet, dimly lit and filled with canvases leaning against the wall, one atop another. There were a few paintings off to one side of Watchful—of the sunrise, of Amandine at dinner, or the priest in his ramshackle Sanctuary. But everywhere else sat canvases of Oli and the Wood. Dozens and dozens of paintings brought the Woodsman to life, always with the Wood behind him and always with his features being highlighted just a little too much.

Her mind, it seemed, had been hard at work saving images of Oli, his tired eyes laden with fear, anger, and violence. She saw him fighting a wolf before his mother, an image she must have caught on the edge of her vision and not processed at the time. And there he stood in the dim light of the Wood surrounded by the colors made more vibrant when Léonie had nearly succumbed to the Call. Another had Léonie looking down the tip of an arrowhead pointed right at her face, though Oli's eyes had been painted into focus, and not the arrowhead.

"Bah," she snapped, grabbing the canvases by their edges and tossing them behind her. She had not come here to be sickened by her subconscious gawking. She looked for something specific. It took another few minutes of throwing around oil paintings of Oli before she found it. Léonie pulled free a small piece, vibrant in color and clarity: the moment before she had drifted off to sleep. Tâl was in focus, her Badaui eyes narrowed with concern, but her cheeks high and flush. But Léonie searched the background of the picture, the details *around* Tâl. She spotted nothing, at first. Trees, birds, sticks, leaves, and shadows. But as Léonie stared at the painting, as she studied it, two smooth orbs, like polished stone, slowly materialized in the shadows off to one side. Eyes. And not animal ones, but instead eyes that conveyed intelligence and intent.

"Staradovna," Léonie whispered.

The ground rumbled in response, then the floor beside Léonie shifted and widened. Paintings fell downward as a maw opened, stairs forming from nothingness, candlesticks growing from the ground, lighting themselves. The blood-orange runner materialized onto the stairway that no longer needed a door. It had brought its intent directly before Léonie, less "invitation" and more insistence.

"It is you, is it not?" No response. "And this is why I have come: to parlay with the Ancient One." She said the words aloud so as to bolster her own courage, but it did not work. She had so many questions, so little understanding, and yet no other options.

She stepped toward the staircase, kicking aside a picture which had fallen. She forced herself to remember her people, the Yelmes, the war. They needed help, aid from the same power that had defeated Kātsracha before. They needed Staradovna.

Carefully, she stepped onto the first stair.

CHAPTER
THIRTY-TWO

S moke had entombed the street of Watchful before Layla had
made it even halfway to Anej. Black and thick, it billowed up
the hill and pushed against her with hot, intangible fingers. Layla
faltered, thought to turn back, then shoved her nose and mouth into
her elbow and ran on. The image of Anej held fast in her mind,
pulling her on and towards the sounds of battle.

Screams barraged her first—screams of pain, fear, and hate. All
screams and yet each distinct and pained in its own unique way.
Most of the noises were recognizably human, but there were other,
heavier noises—more guttural. Those sounds of pain mixed with the
sounds of banging metal, cracking thunder, and breaking bones.

The sounds of nightmares.

"Archers, right flank!"

Layla looked up, blinking away tears from the smoke. It was the
voice of the captain.

"Release!"

The smoke had thinned and Layla could see him now, his
bloodied sword pointed to the right. As if by magic, a dozen arrows
appeared from all around, emerging from the smoke and flames like

flies and descending on a point merely a stone's throw away. Guttural screams followed a moment later.

A wall of soldiers moved back and forth like a breaking tide, spears and shields held before them. Anej stood in their center, terrible and glorious. The makeshift barricade of tables and chests and farm equipment rose up before them all, giving way in the center where Anej stood, filling the gap. Homes burned all around, and the nearest to Layla collapsed inward, supporting beams consumed in flames.

Before the barricade, revealed by the light of those burning homes, were the Yelmes. Layla saw them now, but they did not appear at all as she expected. They were not monsters on four legs and with hideous hides, they were . . . human. They wore dirty, brown and black armor, and carried glowing and hissing weapons: but still human.

It wasn't what she had expected, and she realized it wasn't what she *wanted*.

No one had ever described the Yelmes to her before. They had always been called monsters or demons, but that was all. Beasts of legend and nightmare. But instead, they looked like her neighbors.

Lightning flashed and there was a *crack pop* beside her, then everything became silence and darkness.

She had a vague feeling of being in the air, and then her shoulder hit dirt and she rolled along the ground, dropping her sword. Her body tingled, her shoulder hurt, and she couldn't breathe or see. Layla thought she might have been crying, but she couldn't hear her own voice.

Deōs help me. She had gotten to the battle a heartbeat ago, and she was already laid out flat, blind and helpless, ready to be skewered through the back like a fish. *If I'm not already dead.*

She kept blinking, praying her sight would return as she felt around on the ground about her. She touched only dirt and water, recent enough it hadn't yet formed into a good mud. Her sword lay nearby, and when her fingers touched the blade's fulcrum she felt her way down toward the hilt until she held it by the handle.

Should she stay still, pretend to be dead and pray she would be overlooked? She wasn't sure. She was terrified of death and—sound rushed back into her ears as suddenly as it had gone. Thibault called out, his voice loud and sure, "Fall back! Fall back!"

Layla lifted her head toward his voice, her vision going from black to gray. Layla stumbled to her feet, dragging the tip of the sword behind her as she cried, "Help!"

The outlines of buildings came into focus, superimposed onto the fading black curtain of her vision.

"Anej. Anej!"

She blinked again and finally she could see, though the images were blurry and warped. The world around her morphed into a collage of smoke, blood, and broken bodies. Like a moving mountain, Anej sprinted towards her with footfalls which shook the dirt beneath her feet. Behind him, the Yelmes ripped apart the barricade, scrambling over it, waving their swords, axes, and spears in defiance of the fleeing giant.

Anej saw her, and that saved her life. Without slowing, the giant flung his shield over his shoulder and with his free hand he yanked her from the ground by her armpit and tossed her to his shoulder. It hurt and knocked the air from her lungs, but she felt grateful all the same.

The ride only lasted a few dozen of the giant's paces, then they were behind the next barricade.

"Stay behind me, lass. Close behind." Anej dropped her to her feet.

"Close?" Layla asked, her voice trembling.

"Aye." Anej unslung his shield and turned to face the oncoming Yelmes. He looked back toward her and said, "Well, not *too* close. Back up a tad. That's good. Safer there."

"Safe?" Layla's heart pounded, and her breath came in short gasps.

"If I let one past, run 'em through."

Layla's eyes went wide. "Anej, I—"

The velk turned so fast, Layla's voice caught in her throat. "Lass, listen good. If one of them gets by me, you put that blade through their chest. There'll be an opening just beneath the breast where the armor overlaps. You'll see it."

"But—"

"If ya miss, we'll both be dead." Anej turned his back to her.

We'll both be dead. Layla hefted her sword and stood in Anej's shadow. She was breathing, she must have been, but she didn't feel like it. In this moment, Layla Ricker didn't understand who she was. There were so many of her, and yet so few of her at the same time. There was the Layla crying in frustration and helplessness, abandoned by her family. There was the Layla holding a kitchen knife with Windsun's blood dripping from it. There was the girl turning from the Wood's edge out of a mix of fear and obedience. Then there was the girl who'd charged down the hill moments ago.

"Archers, make ready!" Thibault called out, standing only paces away, his face black with soot and his knees and fingers dark with blood. He glanced at her, then dropped his sword and called, "Release!"

With Anej's bulk before her, Layla couldn't make out where the arrows went, but she heard the screams that followed. Anej bellowed in rage and lifted his shield. An instant later, scores of bright flashes lit the sky and dirt shot into the air as the strikes shattered the ground all around. Layla should have been blinded again, but she wasn't. The sound and light didn't overwhelm this time, but appeared muted—distant.

Safer there.

Layla tried to keep breathing. Whatever magic Anej or his shield had, it must've been covering her too somehow.

And then the Yelmes attacked. They hit the fortifications like a gust of torrential wind slamming shutters, and they must have hit Anej's lowered shield the same way, for the giant took a sudden step back and gave a growl. He stepped forward again with a heave, and Layla saw his shield fly outward and his spear thrust forward. The velk moved in a blur, his shield and spear moving too fast for Layla to see clearly, his feet shuffling carefully left and right. Every few moments he'd lash out with his spear, step backward, and lift the shield to the sky. How he knew when the lightning strikes were coming, Layla couldn't guess. However he did it, he redirected the blasts, and then he would shove forward, and it all would repeat again.

Anej fought on, the archers lobbed arrows, and the other soldiers used the spears to keep the enemy from coming over the barricades. It existed as an impossibly held tension, and Layla could feel the world hold its breath, waiting for something to break. Layla could only imagine skirmishes being fought elsewhere—the Yelmes must have been trying to push forward through and around the homes. But she couldn't see that. Her whole existence had narrowed to this fight and this moment.

Anej grunted, then yelled out, "Oy, lass!" And then he threw a Yelmes warrior back toward Layla. It was a woman in a tattered black cloak, her face painted with jagged red lines, her hair hanging down in long braids. She stumbled toward Layla with a small hatchet in her hands which flickered with blue light. She looked ready to collapse, her eyes blinking wildly, her knees weak.

It would have been easy for Layla to hold out the tip of her blade and impale her as she stumbled forward. The woman's momentum alone would've done the work. Instead, Layla stood wide-eyed as the woman fell at her feet.

Layla looked down, taking in the woman fully. What she'd mistaken for red paint wasn't that at all. The woman had a gash on her head, the blood smearing down her cheek like paint. She looked as if she'd die whether Layla did anything or not. The Yelmes woman heaved in a massive breath and looked up, her eyes meeting Layla's.

Layla saw then what made the Yelmes different: the eyes. One was nearly all black, with a white rim around the outside, and the other a pure-yellow, as bright as flame. The woman's lips curled in a smile, and she screamed. Layla stepped back as the woman got to her feet, the Yelmes woman stumbling left and right as she fought to stay upright. She stared at Layla as if weighing her on a scale of worthiness, then the woman turned to take in Anej: his unprotected back only paces away.

If ya miss, we'll both be dead.

The woman turned from Layla, disregarding her, and reared her arm back to throw her hatchet at Anej's back. Layla lurched forward on impulse, slashing her sword outward, aiming for the raised hatchet blade. She missed, her blade coming down not on the hatchet, but the woman's wrist. The woman screamed and then lurched for Layla with tears of pain rolling from her eyes. Layla stepped back and raised the point of her sword, then held on tight as she felt the force of the woman's body on the blade's tip. The woman threw herself on it, eyes wide in rage.

The screaming lasted only a moment, and then the light in her eyes faded.

When the woman collapsed, Layla kept ahold of the sword as the woman's weight slid from it. Layla couldn't see the body on the ground clearly, her eyes blocked by tears which distorted everything.

She's dead.

Shame and disgust welled up inside Layla. Saving Anej didn't make her feel better, cleaner. She didn't feel that she had saved a life, only that she had made an eternal trade.

A trade she had no right to make.

She retched, spewing the food from earlier onto the dirt and her boots. She coughed, cried, heaved. But when a hand grasped her shoulder, Layla twisted around and lashed out with her sword.

Thibault caught her wrist before she could cut him down, pulling her face close to his and shaking her slightly. "Get your head up, or you'll find it rolling in the mud! More are coming."

The captain shoved her gently in the direction of Anej, and then he marched down his line of soldiers, calling orders and swinging his sword towards attackers scrambling over boxes and kegs.

Layla coughed and spat, wiping tears and snot away with the back of her hand. Anej still moved, still fought. Still killed. She kept her eyes on his back and on his sides. She didn't look down, didn't want to see the woman there. Everything was complicated and wrong, but she couldn't think of that now.

The Yelmes were *people*, she couldn't un-see that. But they were people who would kill her and Anej and everyone else, and so they were monsters too.

And she could kill monsters.

CHAPTER

THIRTY-THREE

There was no need to breathe in the galleria of Léonie's own mind. It was not real, but only a mental construct she had carefully architected for years.

A literal figment of her imagination.

She had to keep reminding herself of this with every step down the staircase. Involuntarily, Léonie took a deep breath. She walked slowly, readying herself for a fight. Her fingers clenched around a sword that did not exist here, though she tried more than once to conjure it through focused thought.

In the end, she only had the next step, the next candlestick, the next turn to look forward to. It went on until she felt as though the stone walls were beginning to close in. She had nearly decided to retreat up the stairs, but before her courage could fully wane the stairs ended and she stood before another door.

A door that made Léonie want to turn and leave.

Made of onyx stone partly encased in ebony wood bark, the door looked like a solidified shadow threatening to swallow her whole. The dim candlelight hardly helped ease Léonie's dread. She grabbed the nearest candle and lifted it before the door like a standard, trying to discern any markings which would give her a clue as to what lay on the other side. She found nothing. Only blackness, shadow on shadow so deep it drank in the candlelight, refusing to reflect any of it back into the room.

"None of this is real," Léonie said aloud. "This is all in my mind." Her words echoed off the door and walls around her. Except, it *kept* echoing, over and over again, changing slowly each time so it sounded more and more manic. *None of this is real. All in my mind. None of it is real. It's all in my mind. It's not real. All in my mind—*

Léonie put her hands to her ears and looked around for something, anything, that would make it stop. A piece of ebony wood stuck out from the door as what appeared to be a handle. Léonie gritted her teeth and dropped her hands from her ears to reach for it.

Not real. All in your mind. Not in your mind!

She pulled on the handle and the door gave way with ease. Air rushed from the open door, blowing out the candles and, mercifully, ending the echoing noise as well. But with this new air came a reek of rot so strong Léonie gagged, stepping back in shock against the wall opposite the door. It was not only the smell, but the sensation of scent at all. There were no scents in the galleria.

Not real, she thought hastily. *None of this is real.*

"Oh, darling," a voice said, high and sweet. "Reality is something very much up for debate."

"Who are you?" Léonie pressed her back closer to the wall.

"Who are *you*?" It was not Léonie's words echoing this time, but this new voice repeating them back to her, slowly. "Come now, you already know."

Léonie did know, but she wanted to hear this voice say it anyway, to squeeze out an ounce of control. "How would I know who you are? Have we met?"

"Well, you have read all about me, haven't you? Oh yes, I have seen your memories, little princess. Hunched over scrolls and parchments in that high tower of yours."

"How—" Léonie's words cut off as the world erupted with light and color. Instantly, she appeared in a circular room with a domed ceiling covered in art of the realistic fashion: hyper-literal figures playing out scenes from holy scripture. Secret scenes. Scenes not read in the hearing of those outside of the Order of Deōs. Scenes Léonie had only ever seen once before.

She was in the High Thólos, the secret library of the Order. No windows let in light, only dozens of candles placed carefully around the room's perimeter. Low shelves, stuffed full of pristinely kept books, scrolls, and tombs lined the walls. A round table dominated the center of the room, its edges engraved in a language Léonie could not read. Upon it sat three more candles, a glass of wine, and several scrolls. Hunched over the table, brow furrowed, sat herself.

It was as if she stared at a self-portrait, but this one *moved*.

This other Léonie had one finger tracking along with the ancient script she deciphered, her other hand drumming on the tabletop.

"It is only a memory," she muttered to herself. Léonie's skin crawled, discomfort growing at watching *herself* sitting only feet away. In one sense, she had grown used to vivid memories relived inside this galleria, but those were always art she framed, that she posed. And Léonie never placed herself in the art.

This violated all the rules of this place, and the worst violation was that she had no control.

"Do you remember this day?" The woman's voice remained disembodied, coming from nowhere and everywhere.

Léonie did remember. She remembered it well, in fact.

It had happened hardly two months ago, just weeks after the battle of Worchestern. She had gained entrance to one of the Order's most secret chambers through a tireless week of bribery, threats, and murder. A reckless gamble which would not have worked if the Kātsracha invasion hadn't put the whole kingdom on edge and kept all eyes elsewhere. Still, her actions had been rash in the extreme. Even now, if the things she had done were ever brought to light, the consequences would be dire. Exile would be the most lenient punishment imaginable.

"How are you doing this?" Léonie said, the palm of her hand pressed firmly against that stone wall now. The wall had not changed, at least.

"Doing what?"

"This is my place. My mind. You have no control here." Léonie's heart beat quickly, her stomach tightening. "Get out."

"*Your* mind? Oh darling, you do not understand. You have flown too high. Can you not feel the heat of the sun? You are in my home, my garden, and there is nothing here beyond my reach."

"*I* am the Princess of Trevelar."

At the table in the room's center, Léonie stood. Or, not *Léonie*, but the memory of her. This memory-Léonie—dressed in a long, red dress—continued drumming her fingers along the table as she walked slowly in Léonie's direction. Léonie's stomach twisted. If she watched a memory right now, then it was all wrong. She had not moved for hours, not until her mole in the Order had given the signal.

And then memory-Léonie looked up, her eyes locked on Léonie's own. But they were not Léonie's eyes. They were two pits, one entirely white and the other entirely black. Léonie raised her fists and shifted into a defensive position on instinct. Whatever this thing was, it screamed of threat and danger. The smell of death and rot wafted everywhere once again as the twisted memory-Léonie opened its mouth to speak. The voice was not Léonie's, but the smooth voice of the mind-intruder. "Oh, I am aware of who you are, darling. Your memories are just filled to the brim with you throwing your weight around. Position, power, prestige—you have bathed in it daily your whole life."

"What are you talking about? What *are* you?"

"I'm talking about *you*. A palace brat who has had nothing but power, and yet dreams for more. You desire to wear the crown, no? I wonder, how do you plan to usurp your brother for the throne? Ah, never mind, one can guess." A knife emerged in the intruder's hand.

A familiar knife, long but thin. It would be a terrible weapon in a fight, but it had never been meant for a fight.

"A perfect blade to take a life from behind, yes?" The memory-Léonie said, lifting the blade and tapping the tip against her cheek. "You have been practicing for your big day, haven't you? You left quite the river of blood behind. Oh, don't think I'm not impressed. I am. A woman after my own heart, in a way."

"Who are you?" Léonie said again, balling a fist. Could she even fight here?

"Please, you know already. I want you to say it."

Léonie swallowed. "Why?"

"Why not? What's the harm? You know it, I know it. Now *say* it."

Léonie bent her knees and turned her body to the side. This memory-Léonie took another step forward, knife held carelessly in her hand. The name rose slowly to Léonie's mind. She tried to force it down, knowing she fought in some twisted power of the wills she dare not lose.

"There it is," the memory-Léonie said. "I can see it rising to the surface of your mind, aching to break free. Say it."

Léonie said it without thinking, as if pulled from her by an invisible line. "Staradovna."

"Ah, and there it is. That's a good girl. That's all I wanted. Was it really so bad?" She turned away from Léonie, waving the knife about as if conducting a symphony. "Now get going, we will speak again later."

The world shattered into a thousand shards of light flung wide, and then Léonie fell, the air pulled from her lungs as the world disappeared from beneath her. The world faded to black until there was nothing but the sense of falling and Staradovna's laughter from above.

CHAPTER
THIRTY-FOUR

Oli breathed in through his teeth.

He'd picked up his mother's trail and followed it to a small creek. From there, it had been far too easy to see what had happened. He knew the Wood baited him, wanted to lead him into a trap. Two draglines disturbed the soil like signposts to follow, and even small streaks of blood had been left for him to find . . . odd since the ground here drank blood nearly as fast as it spilt.

There were only two drag lines though, and Oli had found boot prints he thought may be Tâl's in the wet dirt near the stream, but he hadn't bothered to follow. Tâl wasn't his concern, his mother was. As he followed the tracks, the Wood didn't even bother to try and stop him. No vines, no wild animals, no trouble at all.

As if the Wood wanted him to press on, to survive until the end.

The trail led Oli to the one place he never wanted to be again, the same patch of dirt he'd stood on eleven years before. The Clearing stretched out before him, a vast run of scorched black land. At its center loomed a statue of black, about the size of a man and fixed upon a pedestal: Staradovna. It was here that Roi Ricker had dreamed of coming, and here that Léonie Baudelaire had demanded to go.

Oli existed in two places at once, or perhaps two times at once. He was certainly two different people at once.

He was Oliver Ricker, the boy, watching his father creep forward into the Clearing. He could see Roi turn, his beard filled with dirt. "Come on with me." But that boy had shook his head, his feet fastened to the ground as surely as if they'd been bound by cord or chain. Roi Ricker had faltered, looking from his boy to the statue just two bowshots away. Eventually he'd settled on, "I'll be right back. Keep watch."

Oli could feel that boy inside of him now, standing there, praying to Deōs his father wouldn't go, wouldn't die. There had been so much death that day, a trail of Stražar bodies littering the Wood, all so Oli's father could stand before this ancient being. Oli felt as if he had never moved since then, as if he had been standing here his whole life, waiting.

But he wasn't that boy anymore. Oliver Ricker died when he watched his father be cut down, when he had turned and ran. Every one of the days since had been dirt on that boy's grave, burying him deeper and deeper beneath a life of scrounging and fighting and wrestling to just survive.

But who had he become?

The Clearing looked as though it had never changed, which Oli supposed it hadn't. Black stumps encircling a black statue beneath a black sky. Red and purple vines lay dormant across the ground like veins, the only color or sign of life. Roi Ricker, man or corpse, was nowhere to be seen. Instead, in the place his bones should be, two figures knelt. They faced him, proffered up without subtlety or nuance.

Oli wanted to turn and run like he'd done before. It had kept him alive then.

But back then he had been a boy and his father had been dead, cut down without preamble or pause. Like an animal, Roi Ricker had been lured, trapped, and killed. That's not how things were now. Now, Oli's mother sobbed. The sound of it the only noise in all the world, devastating and broken. Perhaps it should have given Oli a slim hope: his mother still lived. But Oli was no fool. She would die, and he would die with her. The Wood had her and so it would have him too. The Wood had won.

It always won.

But though he knew that, he couldn't turn and leave. To escape now, with the echo of his mother's sobs fading behind him, would be too much to bear. He could not enter the Clearing and hope to live, but neither could he leave and hope to live with himself.

I'm dead already.

Anger, low and hot, burned in Oli's chest. It was wrong, so wrong, that he would work and work and still not win. Nothing he did mattered. He couldn't feed his family, couldn't outrun the nightmares, couldn't even keep his mother safe. His sister was alone now, and if the stories of the Yelmes were true then she'd be dead soon too. After everything Oli had done, had survived, after all the fighting and killing, he was still bound to this fate.

He squeezed the handle of his bow, the pain in his left hand igniting and stoking his anger. This was all *her* fault. Staradovna, and the power she represented, had lured his father here like a moth to flame. She *was* the Wood, the power drawing the animals deeper in and keeping Oli from feeding his family. That's why Oli's father wanted to get to her. He believed he could steal power somehow, had told all the Stražar he could make the Wood tame.

Every nightmare, every growl of his stomach, every tear held back, was *her fault*. And now she had drawn his mother in. Staradovna would kill Orelda the way she'd killed Oli's father, and Oli hated her for it.

"Woodsman."

Oli spun toward the sound behind him, yanking the string of his bow back and aiming it at—"Tâl?"

The ranger knelt a few steps away, cloaked in shadows and so close Oli had nearly tripped over her.

"I've been waiting for you." She looked haggard, bleeding from dozens of cuts over her body, a large bruise swelling above her left eye.

Oli looked into the Clearing again, feeling more than a little foolish. There were two figures in there: his mother and the princess. He should have known if Tâl wasn't dead, she would have followed Léonie. "What happened?"

"We found a stream. Your mother and Princess Léonie . . . wanted to stop and rest."

"Ya, that'll do it."

"I cut away at the vines for a time, but then there were spiders. I tried to fight them off, but—"

Oli spat to the side. He could imagine how things had gone from there. "How aren't you dead?"

"Why does it matter right now?"

Oli shrugged. It didn't matter right now, though something nagged at him that maybe it *did* matter. "Well, I'm goin' after her," he thrust a thumb toward his mother, still sobbing. "This is as good a time as any to turn back if you're gonna."

"I have a duty. We can go together."

Oli shrugged, "Then I guess we die together. C'mon." Oli breathed in and turned toward the Clearing. This was it, then. He would step forward and see what happened next. He figured he would die like his father, which seemed fitting.

His heart beat hard enough as to almost drown out the sound of his boot stepping onto the black dirt marking the border of the Clearing. Oli paused after the first step, waiting, though nothing happened. He moved on, Tâl coming up behind him. The statue didn't move as he drew near. From where Oli was, Staradovna hardly looked larger than a figurine you could hold in your hand.

Staradovna was a black cloaked figure of glistening onyx, and yet so much more. Her consciousness ran through the Wood, through the soil and the trees. Even above Orelda's crying, Oli knew she could hear his light steps. His father had talked of her with reverence, as though she were a god. He hadn't cared for Deōs, for the Order. He said there were older gods, wilder ones. Ones that could be harnessed.

"Oy, listen to me," Oli called out, eyes locked on the statue. "I'm coming for her, ya hear? I'm coming, and if ya hurt her then I'll drag your stony hide down to the grave."

Nothing happened.

"I know ya can hear me," Oli growled, stalking forward faster now. He wanted to say more, to use words with meaning, with power. He longed to know the name of everything his eyes could see, to recall their names like he had with the deer, with the stone. Words emerged in his mind unbidden, words Oli had never known before, yet the words each came to him with their meanings as well. Oli wielded each word like a weapon, flinging them towards Staradovna in a mad tirade. *"Lia iano kali urbich."*

I will be your death.

At those words, Oli felt the ground shudder and watched as the head of Staradovna turned toward him.

CHAPTER
THIRTY-FIVE

Léonie had been thrust from the galleria of her mind and back into reality with the blunt force of a battering ram. She was a prisoner: her body wrapped in vines which moved her about and propped her up like a doll. Everything about here was foreboding and dark, a treeless expanse of dead grass and burnt stumps. Even the sky pressed down upon her, and behind her . . . Léonie could sense Staradovna. A chill ran up her spine, fear so strong her heart beat out of rhythm.

I am not dead, she told herself over and over again.

She had been trained for capture, her father being paranoid in that way. She had been taught to keep herself calm, to hold her tongue, and to keep her wits about her. Of course, training only did so much. And nothing would have prepared her for a magical enchantress who could lull her to sleep in the middle of a forest and then entrap her in magical vines. Still, Léonie kept breathing, and took stock of her situation as best she could.

First, Léonie could not tell if Tâl was trapped as well, or if she had died protecting Léonie while she lay unconscious. Orelda cried off to her right, but Léonie could see no one to her left. Tâl's absence was unnerving, for Léonie had grown to rely on the ranger. At least Léonie's weapons were still with her: her sword sheathed and a few knives tucked in various places. But the vines held her tight, and she doubted she could reach them. Lastly, and perhaps most importantly, Staradovna wanted them alive for now.

Léonie knew she was bait, which was odd because if Staradovna had searched her memories, she would have understood Léonie's well-being would not lure the Woodsman into a trap. Unless there was another game Staradovna played at, or some other trap she had set. But what that could be, Léonie could not imagine.

Léonie had gotten only one glimpse of Staradovna before being spun about, but what she saw was terrifying. A statue with a cloak of black stone which absorbed, rather than reflected, the moonlight above. A woman made of blackened wood, still and foreboding.

Léonie thought about making a threat, perhaps shouting that her father would burn the Wood to ash unless she was released. But something inside Léonie was broken now, crippled. Staradovna had *seen inside her*, had commandeered the most secret place in Léonie's world. What could she possibly say to scare a being such as this?

Orelda cried beside her. Léonie could see vines slowly cutting through the woman's back and calves, torturing her, drawing out those cries. Léonie could do nothing for her, and it took all her effort to keep breathing and stay reasonably calm. Dropping her gaze, Léonie tried to look as pathetic as she felt while her mind scrambled for a plan. Meanwhile, she shifted her hands further down towards her boots and the knife she kept there. The vines tightened as she moved, but she felt her fingers get closer.

It was a desperate thing, thinking she could get a hold of her knife and then free herself. What would she do after cutting the vines holding her? Fight her way back to Watchful in time for a Yelmes invasion? Coming here, to this place, had been Léonie's desperate plan. To convince, or force, this power to rise up and destroy the forces of Kātsracha as it had once done.

"Please," Léonie said, trying to raise her voice above Orelda's cries. "Listen! The Dark Ones have returned, and my kingdom needs your help. Release me and come to our aid . . . ah!" Pain gripped Léonie's arms as the vines yanked tighter, thorns biting through her skin. Staradovna heard her, it seemed. And pain was her answer.

"Oliver!" Orelda screamed, her voice curling in pain.

Léonie looked up, blinking away tears. There he was, hood down and stalking toward them, his bow at the ready. *At least he knows it's a trap.* The sight of him filled Léonie with a pure, unadulterated elation. He was, very literally, her only hope.

Well, perhaps not her *only* hope. Tâl trailed him, looking the worse for wear. Whatever she had experienced since Léonie fell asleep by the stream had not been pleasant. Now though, she followed behind Oli with her bow likewise ready.

When the pair of them were two or three dozen feet away, Staradovna spoke. The sound of her voice was a carpenter's rasp riding across woodgrain, each syllable pushing its way into Léonie's skull.

"*Likoniaock, sian.*"

CHAPTER
THIRTY-SIX

A t last. *The son.*

The words and their meaning wormed their way into Oli's mind.

"Jiakal kali?" *You've been waiting?* Being here, in this place, awoke the Language of the Wild in Oli, and he found he wasn't struggling to find the right words. They appeared in his mind as if there all along.

The statue smiled. Whatever Oli had been expecting, Staradovna was not it. The cloak, all Oli had ever seen before, was made of a black stone that somehow shifted as Staradovna moved, animated like cloth. But Staradovna herself had skin made of ebony wood carved into the shape of a woman. The wood rippled and textured to show off muscle, bone, and sinew. But the smiling face was the most vexing.

"Iano lia ilpriava." *I have been preparing.* She—or it?—spoke through a lipless opening which shifted as a mouth should, but inside contained only a black void. Above the mouth-like opening were two diamond shaped holes for a nose, and above those were two eyes. One eye was entirely white, textured like a porous stone,

rolling around as it followed Oli. The other was not an eye at all, but a jagged pit in the black wood, the edges discolored and flesh-like, shifting subtly with each move of Staradovna's head.

"What is she saying?" Tâl asked, but Oli ignored her.

They were close now, under a bowshot away. With no breeze, he could likely put an arrow wherever he'd like, but it would be risky. The pedestal Staradovna stood on raised her up above the kneeling prisoners, but Oli dared not risk hitting his mother all the same.

His mother.

She sobbed hysterically, but also *screamed*. Her face was red, and there was a small pool of blood forming beneath her. Oli ground his teeth and walked more quickly.

"*Kali miet olopoto.*" You're hurting her.

"*Kilast kali preezt.*" I had to be sure you would come.

"*Lia fritolmny.*" I'm here.

"*Kion. Kali iano.*" Yes. You are.

"*Miet osa.*" Let her go.

"*Noik.*" No.

Oli didn't need to hear anything else. He hadn't come to parlay, to talk to this *thing*. He'd come to kill it or die trying. So Oli ran, rushing forward and closing the distance with terrible speed, putting himself in easy bowshot range in heartbeats. There were no roots to contend with, and the charred stumps were easy enough to avoid. The vines sat limp against the ground, lifeless as Oli ran over them.

Oli pulled back the bowstring, his side screaming in pain from the wound he'd taken from the bear. He loosed his first arrow, watching it slam into Staradovna's wooden chest, right where a heart should be, assuming she had one. She jerked back under the impact, body shifting though her feet stayed unmoving on the pedestal.

And then she laughed. A cackling, cracking sound, as if each pulse of laughter was the breaking of a tree branch.

"*Žiak,*" Oli screamed, nocking another arrow. *Silence.* Words continued to pour into his mind, as if this *was* his language and he had never known another.

Staradovna twisted her hands so her palms faced up, then raised both hands in unison. The princess and Oli's mother were lifted into the air, the vines ensnaring them around their torsos now raising them before Staradovna. She used them as shields.

Orelda screamed, tears flowing down her cheeks. "Run, Oli! Run!"

Oli did run, but not away. Not this time. He ran closer, now less than twenty paces away. His heart thudded, but he felt good in a wild sort of way. Focused.

Tâl loosed an arrow from behind, and it cut through one of the vines holding the princess aloft. It did little good though, for vines held Léonie at a dozen different points.

With one excruciating motion in which he thought his side may burst from pain, Oli pulled back his bowstring while at a dead sprint. He loosed the next arrow, screaming out "*žiak*" as though he could infuse the word into the arrow's shaft. Staradovna tried to shift Orelda's body in the way, but the vines were too slow. The arrow found its target, pummeling into Staradovna's open mouth and jerking her whole head backward, the sound of cracking wood ringing loud in the air, reminiscent of breaking bone.

Orelda and Léonie dropped, the vines holding them going limp.

Léonie rolled the moment she hit the ground, forgetting her knife and yanking her sword free. Pain riddled her whole body, but she was on her feet, breathing, and free. Tâl ran to her side, pulling her away before she even had her footing.

The ranger's eyes were bloodshot and scared. "Princess, come," she said, grabbing at her wrist.

But Léonie could not. She looked backwards, toward Staradovna, the thing of power and terror, stone and wood. All black and all otherworldly. Somehow more frightening than the Yelmes, able to penetrate minds and control beasts. Léonie had to stay, for what else could hope to challenge the Dark Ones but the power which had done it before?

"We need her," Léonie said, pulling away. It was why she had come.

"We'll die."

"Without this power my father cannot hope to—"

The ground beneath their feet cracked and shook, and thick vines jutted out from the dirt, thrashing wildly, cutting off Léonie's words and Tâl's arguments.

Oli had nearly made it to his mother. Tâl had charged in towards the princess, but Oli had gone wide, suspecting a trap. He couldn't possibly have killed her that easily, and he wasn't so stupid as to think he would actually win in the end.

He'd been right.

Staradovna had waited until his caution gave way, until he ran towards his crying mother. She lay on the ground, hand stretched toward him, tears of pain rolling down her cheeks. Her legs had been torn up too much for her to walk, eyes red, hair sticking to her face in sweat laden strands. "Oli!"

Their fingers had been a hair's breadth from one another.

The vines rose from the ground like the hands of the dead, enveloping Orelda instantly. Oli sidestepped, withdrawing his hand off reflex and running again. Vines swarmed around him and Staradovna laughed and laughed. She spoke no words, only twisted her hands about, controlling the vines as if through puppeteer strings. His mother flew into the air again, screaming as vines yanked her between Oli and Staradovna.

The vines moved faster than any he had ever seen before, thrusting themselves out like whips, aiming for his back, his throat, his head. Oli took it all in: the squirming vines, his mother's shifting form in the air, the glimpses of Staradovna and her smile, his arrow still protruding from her mouth like a feathered tongue.

His instincts took over.

Vines were unable to grab purchase on him as he moved, but over and again their outstretched thorns sliced through his calves, ankles, and thighs—dozens of little cuts poured forth droplets of blood. Oli yanked another arrow from his quiver, words running from his mouth as freely as the blood flowed from his open wounds. He spoke in the Language, drenching the arrow in the first words that came to his mind. They were the words he'd used his whole life to fight the pull of the Call.

"*Palmaditze bievly.*" *Remember who you are.*

It was less a call to remember who he was, and more a war cry to fight off the Call and the Wood and everything in it. A heel brought down to crush a vine or a snake, a way to say, "I will not go quietly." In a place that swam in forgetfulness and lies, those words were a pillar for the Stražar and their hounds to stay sane and alive.

A vine grabbed Oli's ankle and yanked him to the ground. He held his bow but dropped the arrow as he pulled his knife free, cutting the vines in one slash and fighting to stand. Vines swarmed all around, hungry and writhing. Some tried to wrap his legs, others snapped outward to cut and lacerate every inch of exposed skin. Oli yelled, his voice mixing with his mother's. There were no words, just the unintelligible, guttural calls of violence and anger. The vines came from everywhere, and in moments they would engulf him and bring him down to his father's grave. He would die, and his mother would watch.

Moonlight dimmed as vines canopied over him. His knife flashed outward in a forever whirlwind that left oozing stubs of the vines which were replaced by more vines. It was never enough, a struggle without point and with one sure end. His whole life boiled down into a single, pathetic, moment. And no amount of rage or hate could make any difference.

And then steel slashed through vines above and moonlight poured back in.

The princess roared as she cut through the forest of writhing vines, her face red with heat and sweat, her eyes narrowed. The princess's sword formed an opening between Oli and Staradovna. The vines held Orelda to the side, as if the ancient monster had wanted to watch Oli die with her own eyes and his mother had been blocking the view. But that meant there was a clear line of sight for him now. Oli dropped his knife and snatched the arrow from the ground. Vines grappled with his knees and waist, wrestling him down, but Oli pulled the bowstring back. His shoulder blades closed together, and pain from his side stole the breath from his lungs. But he refused to stop.

Oli released the arrow. He could feel it go forward, could feel part of himself fly away with the arrowhead, could feel it find its mark. And then Oli crumpled into the embrace of the vines: the tension leaving his muscles as thoroughly as it had left the bowstring.

Oli's arrow punctured Staradovna's eye, sending a dozen little white stone pieces flying into the air. And then . . . nothing. Léonie blinked as Staradovna appeared frozen in time, unmoving. The vines stopped moving too, not falling limp as before, just freezing. Léonie cut through the ones nearest her, and the disconnected tops fell away and thudded to the ground.

Orelda no longer sobbed, her body limp in the air where the vines held her, chin resting against her chest. The Woodsman made no sound either, trapped beneath a canopy of frozen vines. Léonie almost started cutting them away to free him, but she would just as likely cut into him. Tâl breathed unnaturally loud, the ranger saying nothing and yet begging Léonie to leave all the same.

The sound of wood cracking pierced the silence, and long cracks began to form along Staradovna's wooden skin. They started slowly at first, as if something inside was trying to hold the seams together, but eventually they quickened in their breaking. Something was coming, Léonie could feel it.

Staradovna began to pulse with light. No, that was not right. The dais she stood upon pulsed. A sickly green light formed a sort of language that grew bright then dimmed, then grew bright again. Léonie recognized the script, but she did not know how to read it. She had seen those same letters back on the table in the High Thólos.

The vines dropped then, going fully limp all around her like a few dozen stage actors all collapsing on cue. Orelda's body hit the ground with a crunch. Tâl ran up beside Léonie, and this time she let the ranger drag her away.

Oli crawled to his mother.

It was all he could do, all he had strength for. His body was cut and broken and whatever power had kept him moving beyond his limits had left him. He only wanted to see her, to hold his mother and feel her holding him back. To know that once, just once, he had saved someone.

But Orelda didn't cry any longer. She didn't move or make any sound at all. In the pulsing green light, Orelda lay still. The fall had been far, and she had already been weak. Before Oli had reached her, he knew what he would find. His tears drenched the soil as he crawled to her, his sobs drowned out by an ever-increasing *hum* emanating from Staradovna's now twitching form.

Oli didn't care about any of it.

When he got to his mother, he wrapped his arms carefully around her neck and dragged her close to him.

And Oli wept.

The green glow pulsed viciously, its pace quickening every moment. Like bubbles in a cauldron of water with a roaring flame below. First there were two or three flashes of light, then dozens of flashes every few seconds. Léonie could *feel* an explosion coming, could see it in the violence of the light, the shivering of Staradovna's body. Energy permeated the air and a low hum invaded every inch of space around her.

Léonie and Tâl stood at the edge of the Clearing, watching as Oli clutched his mother: the two of them turning into silhouettes in the light of the dais' pulsing. Léonie thought she could see Oli's shoulders shuddering, his head rocking.

Then everything exploded.

INTERLUDES

THE KING

King Adélard Baudelaire stood before a large window in one of his palace's hallways, gazing out at a dark horizon. Where night should have reigned in totality, there were instead distant glints of fires like ten thousand fallen stars resting eerily on the plain south of the capital. The armies of Kātsracha made their way from Worchestern to Eastgate unopposed.

Morning would arrive over Turris Regis within the hour. Soon the city would be awake and all the petty nobility would be nipping at his heels like undomesticated dogs. In the same way the sun would rise to blot out the distant fires of the Yelmes, so too would the lords and ladies of Trevelar block out his time and thoughts.

Years of work tumbling down atop me.

All of the planning, plotting, spying, and waiting, and the Dark Ones had unveiled themselves too soon. Far too soon.

King Baudelaire sighed and stepped forward, leaning onto the windowsill where the early morning breeze could run its fingers through his graying beard. The outer courtyard of the palace lay below him, the manicured plants and bushes of the garden now leafless. The crickets usually chittering away through the night had gone, and with them all color and signs of life. A familiar, if depressing, late-autumn drab which lasted only until the first snowfall ornamented the world with white powder.

Snow.

Adélard groaned. Of all the problems he had, the inevitability of being under siege during the winter was by far the worst. The Yelmes would be consumed with Eastgate for weeks or months, but not forever. Lord Hendrion was a shrewd man and would hold the city for as long as could be expected, but Adélard doubted they would hold for more than a month. But whether weeks or months, Eastgate would fall just as Worchestern had—and like Turris Regis would—if Prince Bastien did not return with aid from the Republic.

"Delroy," Adélard called out, not bothering to turn.

There was a shuffling of steps behind him, then the slow and intentional voice of Adélard's longtime advisor. "Yes, Your Majesty?"

"Any word from the prince?"

"There has not yet been word from the prince or princess."

"I asked only of my son."

"I assumed too much," Delroy said, his voice flat.

"Indeed. If my daughter cared for the welfare of this kingdom she'd be either here or at Eastgate, not tramping off into the south."

"Of course, Your Highness."

Adélard slammed an open palm against the stone sill of the window. "I'm done with her. We speak of it no more."

"As you command," Delroy said, his slow tempo dragging out the words the way a methodical seamstress might slip thread through the eye of a needle.

The king sighed, knowing they would, in fact, speak of it again. Posture as he might, it was no small feat to throw out a potential heir to the throne, especially during a time of war. "What of our rangers? What is the news at Eastgate?"

"The reports through the night have been few. It would appear the Yelmes know they have scattered our forces at Worchestern, but instead of pressing their advantage, they linger. They test their maiyea against the Eastgate walls, but no more."

"Maiyea." Adélard sneered the word. "They have all the power of the gods, and yet they toy with us. It makes no sense." Adélard turned away from the window.

Delroy stood straight, his dark skin and salted beard a stark contrast against the torchlit white stone behind him. His nose stood out boldly on his face, giving the spectacles alighted there a look of frailty. The creases around his eyes and near the base of his nose which showed his age as well as giving him a look of eternal gravitas.

The king stalked off down the hall and Delroy followed. Adélard's military boots thudded against the stone floor, muffling Delroy's pursuing steps. The king had been wearing them, along with his sword and chainmail, ever since Worchestern. He dressed for war each day, hoping the nobility would take heed and end the petty squabbles.

It hadn't worked.

"How do we fight *gods*, Delroy?"

"It is frustrating, Your Majesty," Delroy said as they walked. "Though perhaps 'gods' is a touch too heretical? The Yelmes are inhuman, surely. Defiled, even. But not gods."

"Don't toy with me."

"Hmm. Perhaps the first place to begin would be in attempting to understand what it is they want."

"We have had spies lurking at their borders for fifty years and still do not know what they want. I want to know more than just troop movements. I want to know *them*, and whatever weaknesses they have."

"I wholly agree," Delroy said.

"Take what we know, all our reports and all our findings, and put together a group of maeifa scholars." Adélard did not need to turn to see the crinkle of Delroy's ever suspicious eyes. "Yes, Delroy, the maeifa. Go to the University and bring every one of them that has studied Kātsracha with anything more than a passing glance. Bring them here, to share what we know." The king halted, then twisted about and pointed a finger which nearly impaled Delroy's eye. "*Everything*. We need answers, and we need answers today. This isn't the time for your damned conspiracies."

A pause stretched out between them as Delroy wrestled the inevitable words from his lips. "Yes, *Your Majesty*."

Adélard grunted, then turned and continued down the hall, passing beneath smooth stone archways adorned with ornate carvings of flowers budding on thorny vines. They approached a large set of oak doors flanked by silent guards. As the king marched forward, the guards reached out and pushed open the doors, the well-oiled hinges hardly making a sound.

The Throne Room was sparse, but somehow more extravagant in its scarcity. Tall pillars supported a distant ceiling and stained-glass windows consumed vast swaths of the outer wall. The colored glass remained dark in anticipation of the early morning sun. At the far end of the room stood two doors, the tops of which reached just shy of the ceiling. Once a week those were opened, allowing a small stream of common folk to petition the king. Or rather, that was how it was intended. More and more, Adélard found his time taken up with the nobility, marching in through the same set of side doors he had emerged from. They demanded his time, their money bags all but jingling before him.

The throne itself sat on a dais, fashioned from solid steel and meticulously carved cedar. Beside it stood two tall candelabras, the only source of light this early in the day. More and more the whole dais became like an anvil, beckoning him to sit and be bashed upon by the hammers of worry and plight.

Adélard blew air through clenched teeth.

"Your Majesty?"

"Yes?"

"We have a . . . visitor."

The king turned, eyes narrowing. He looked at Delroy, then followed the man's spectacled gaze toward the large set of doors at the end of the room. There, puffing a small pipe that flared red in the shadows, stood a man in the dark blue cloak of Adélard's rangers, the King's Spear.

"Caché," Adélard called out, giving a beckoning wave. "I am glad to have you. I'd begun to fear the worst."

Caché bowed low, his lit pipe held to the side.

"Arise, arise," Adélard said, waving his hand dismissively as he turned and approached the throne. He removed the sheath from his belt, leaning it beside the throne before turning and sitting heavily upon it. "I haven't the time nor patience."

"My liege and my lord," Caché said, putting out the pipe and placing it into a pocket of his cloak. "There is much news, and far too little time, I am afraid."

"I abhor cryptic words."

"My apologies. Eastgate stands, Lord Hendrion has prepared it well. They have food stores in plenty and the wells run deep within their city. They should not lack food nor water through the winter." After a small pause, he said. "I have seen these stores myself, Your Majesty."

Adélard nodded, envious of Hendrion. Turris Regis was without such stores. Still, they had the sea behind them, and the Yelmes had never shown much in the way of a navy. That, at least, was a blessing.

"What else is there? This is not a season for good tidings."

Caché nodded. "Lord Hendrion lacks much in the way of trained troops. He has armed every man and woman he can, until even the street urchins wield kitchen knives like swords, but the reinforcements from Folin and Southfern never arrived, and so the losses sustained at Worchestern have hardly been recouped."

Adélard's fingers turned white as he squeezed the arm of his throne. "And the call to arms? I sent the decree a month ago. Have my lords and ladies not had time to send aid?"

"Lady Intris has mustered more than a thousand in Southfern, equipping them with armor and spears, but they did not make their way to Eastgate, nor do they march for Turris Regis now." Caché let his words sit in the air between them.

Adélard felt his neck begin to flush red, but he waited for the ranger to continue, his body taut in the waiting. His daughter warned of this, which did nothing to lift his mood.

Caché coughed to the side, then said more quietly. "They linger within their city. The Dark Ones have sent sorties into the country-side, and these mustered troops would stand little chance in open warfare against them. So, Lady Intris keeps them back to protect her own walls. Other nobles are doing likewise. Lord Finron and Lord Grison, Lady June, Lady Thilonor . . . each have mustered troops but have yet to send them out for fear they will only perish along the way."

"The sorties!" Adélard roared. "Eastgate stands ready to fall, and next the capital, and they talk of sorties?"

Caché said nothing, only lowered his head.

"Insolent fools," the king sneered, slapping his hand upon the armrest. "They'll be the death of us all because of their pride. Spread apart, the Yelmes will eat us up. We'll be fish in a stream, they'll be the bear that plucks us from the water one by one."

"Your Majesty," Delroy said, his voice slow and even. "You speak truth. However, our nobles look out for their own lands also, for their people who are their charges. To send their soldiers through dangerous terrain to muster here and then leave their own lands defenseless . . ." He trailed off, leaving the rest unsaid.

"And so they will leave our whole land defenseless? Do not try to empathize with cowards. It is not becoming of you."

Silence settled in the room. Through the opened side door, the marching of patrolling guards could be heard, as well as a faint chat-tering of distant maids, but nothing else.

Finally, Caché let out another cough, bringing the king's eyes back towards him.

"There's more, then?" the king asked, his brow furrowed.

"My rangers have been following smaller Yelmes companies

throughout the south. I hoped as they reported on their movements, I would be more able to assemble a picture of our enemy."

"And?"

"And generally there is nothing to report. Forty or fifty troops on foot patrolling a few miles wide radius from the main body. Yet we have had one . . . anomaly. Two of these sorties coalesced near Glokin. We expected an attack on the town, but instead they headed further south. They moved with speed, Your Majesty, and such as we had not seen before."

Adélard scratched at his chin. "That would be too small a force to march on Southfern."

Caché looked about, as if suspicious of the walls. Delroy, sensing the mood, walked over to the open doors, and with a quick word to the guards, closed the doors with an echoing *thud*. The ranger turned back to the king, his voice a touch quieter than before. "I sent two of my men to follow. It was not until the Yelmes passed by Southfern and stormed through the forest that they understood." Caché swallowed. "My king, we believe they were in pursuit of the princess."

Adélard's breath became shallower. "That is not possible. She left in secrecy, with subterfuge on top of subterfuge. *I* had not known she was leaving. She could *not* have been followed."

Caché shook his head. "I know not how, my king. Her company should not have been on the main road until the Southfern Forest itself. By my honor, I do not know how word reached Kātsracha."

"How many?"

"Your Majesty?"

"How many of the Dark Ones follow her? How many days march are they behind her? How many days old is this news?" As he went on, he came to his feet, his voice rising with him.

"Perhaps a full hundred strong follow the Princess. We do not know how far they linger behind. Perhaps a day, or perhaps already they have overtaken her. And this news is long in coming. More than three days old since I've heard, and more days atop that."

Adélard's knuckles whitened. "Delroy, send a company of riders for the south towards . . . Where was it she's gone? I swear, that woman will bring me to the grave!"

Delroy did not move, but stood with his arms behind his back, his head bowed.

"Delroy . . ."

The older man looked up with a sigh. "Of course, Your Majesty, I can send riders for *Spectare* at your command. They will be weeks in arriving however, and not strong enough to fight a hundred or more Yelmes in open combat."

"Are you saying my daughter is not worth the effort?"

Delroy's eyes met Adélard's own eyes like a lance to a shield. "I am *saying* the princess is beyond our reach, as you had warned her she would be."

Adélard stared at Delroy, his teeth grinding loud enough to echo faintly off the walls of the room. Beads of sweat broke out on his forehead and his fingers grew sore as he squeezed them into his palm. "I should have thrown her into the dungeon."

"Princess Léonie is no fool, Your Majesty. She managed to leave with a company of your finest, so she is not defenseless. She may well return to you."

May. The word hung before Adélard like the blade of a guillotine.

The side doors to the throne room burst open, letting in light and noise from the hallway, as well as three old men in the fine white robes of the Order of Deōs. *Priests*. Adélard nearly pulled his sword free of its scabbard then and there.

"My king!" one of them called, running as fast as his decrepit legs would carry him. "We demand an audience."

Confused guards spilt into the room behind them, their spears wavering. A commoner, or perhaps even a noble, would have been skewered as they attempted to barge down the door to the throne room. But a Priest of the Order? Killing one of them meant eternal torment.

"Elatus?" Adélard said. "What is this?"

Elatus ran toward the king, the skin of his shaved head reflecting candlelight in beads of sweat. His eyes were wide, making his bushy gray brows chase up his forehead.

"The Order does not demand your attention lightly, King Baudelaire," Elatus called out, voice hoarse and breathless. "But Deōs has given a revelation to us this night, not an hour ago. We made haste first to your chambers, but you were not to be found there."

"I did not wish to be found at all." Adélard glanced from Elatus to the priests flanking him. He was required to deal with the High Priest on occasion, an unfortunate byproduct of ruling by Theía Entolí, or Divine Mandate. But priests other than Elatus? That was incredibly rare. "Speak quickly, Elatus, or your thin robes will not protect you from this offense."

An empty threat, but Elatus bristled at it all the same. "Take care Deōs' favor does not depart from your bloodline, King Baudelaire." Then, before Adélard could so much as grind his teeth, Elatus shook his head and said, "Bah, we have no time to spar words here. Our message is far too urgent."

"And that is?" Adélard said, a growing tickle of dread rising up in his mind now as he looked at Elatus, seeing the fear gnawing at the edges of the man's eyes.

Elatus turned to Delroy and Caché, flicking a hand in dismissal. "Leave."

Delroy's eyes grew a fraction wider, but neither he nor the ranger moved.

"Out," Adélard said. "Let the old bag speak in secret so this moment can pass." The two bowed and then left, the guards retreating alongside them. As the door clanged shut, Adélard said, "If this is one of your religious games . . ."

"It is no game. Many in our Order, myself included, have received revelations from Deōs this very night. There been a Great Awakening in the south, a darkness we thought would slumber forever has awoken."

The south . . . Adélard's thoughts went to Léonie, and he had to fight to keep his voice flat. "And what is this 'Great Awakening'?"

Elatus breathed in deep and brought a hand up to his temple. He looked every bit the prude he had been when he had tutored Adélard as a child. "What do you know of the Old War?"

"Do you think I do not know my own kingdom's history?" Adélard stood, hand moving to the sword leaning beside his throne.

Elatus hustled his words along. "There are tales we tell the common folk, and to the nobility as well. And then there are the . . . truer histories of Trevelar. Histories with details that may, uh, lead the flock astray, as it were."

"I am aware of your machinations, *High Priest*. Your schemes in the name of the divine are not as well protected as perhaps you think."

The old man pressed his lips together. "Well then, tell me, have you ever heard of the name Staradovna?"

THE STRAŽAR

Larz had moved out of Watchful proper years ago. He'd built himself a cabin to the north, far enough out so no one heard his nightly screams when he wrestled with the ghosts lingering in the soil of his imagination. He'd made a porch out front, facing the Wood, and he sat there now in a chair constructed of thick branches, roughly carved and assembled with rope and nails. It creaked as he shifted his weight, but he paid it no mind. He puffed small rings of smoke into the sky after every pull on his long pipe. The rain fell soft and nice, tapping rhythmically on the porch roof. It was almost morning, but he wouldn't be making his way eastward today.

Larz had decided to stay clear of the Wood until the princess and her people were long dead. He hadn't the slightest inkling how the Wood was gonna react to a dozen armed men and women plunging towards its heart with even more recklessness than Roi Ricker from years before, but it wouldn't be good.

Still, there lived a poetic justice in the Ricker boy going along with the princess. Finally, his blood would soak the soil beside his father's, like loose ends getting wrapped up all nice and neat.

And the Dark Ones? Larz had watched the whole town march on

out the day before. He'd nearly gone with them but, well, that wasn't for him. He'd thought about maybe joining the fight since that at least would be interesting. Too late though, since now he could see fires burning in Watchful. Most of the night he could hear the thunder, and now he knew why.

So Watchful was doomed, but Larz didn't think they'd come for him. Ain't no way some mystical army of monsters would go out of its way to find his little piece of ramshackle existence.

He'd survive. Always did.

So Larz sat, absently rubbing the scars on his neck, eyes glazed over as his mind wandered.

Until the world shook.

He blinked, pulling the pipe away. The ground around him stayed quiet and still, but he'd felt something. *Am I cracked for good now?* He'd go crazy eventually, it happened to all the Stražar who didn't die. Still, he hadn't expected madness to feel like the world was moving. Larz stood and stepped from his porch, eyes searching the ground, looking for signs of . . .

A green light lit up the early morning sky, stretching the shadows of the trees out towards him like grasping fingers. A heartbeat later Larz flew backwards, an invisible force having lifted and thrown him from his chair, his pipe gone from his hand as surely as the breath from his lungs. He hit the wooden planks of the porch floor and his vision swam with little green dots of light fluttering about like the fireflies. Larz tried to suck back in the air that had popped from his lungs, his ears ringing.

It took a moment, but the air came and his chest heaved as he sucked it in.

No, no, no.

Years of conversations flooded into Larz's memory. Roi Ricker hunched over maps and books convincing Larz and the others that if they could just go a little deeper, just a little further, they'd be able to break the curse on the land. They'd make the Wood safe and then food and pelts would be plenty, and gold would flow and strife would be over and blah, blah, blah.

It had all been a lie—a terrible, scorching lie meant to make Roi Ricker a little king amongst the Stražar. It had led to the death of everyone Larz ever loved, their bodies becoming breadcrumbs for Roi's boy to use to find his way home. And Larz's boy had been one of them breadcrumbs, taken in by lies and left to die.

And now Oli had done it.

That son of a motherless goat's little offspring had *actually done it*. And what now? Had Roi really known what would happen? Was it all just lies, or was Oli now something a whole lot more than just a piss-poor hunter playing at being a Stražar?

Still lying on the cold porch floor, Larz seethed. Whatever this was, it wasn't right, wasn't just. If Larz's son was dead, then Roi's should be too. He'd been thinking that for a long while now. Larz screamed and screamed, something in him vaguely aware that maybe he had finally cracked.

THE EXILE

A nej felt the tremor at the same time the Yelmes did.
It showed up first as a shifting in the Threads, the little lines of light weaving themselves through the living. Anej couldn't see those properly anymore, but he'd have to have been as blind as the humans to miss the way the world shimmered, distorting around the edges. To the Yelmes, the Threads must have twanged like lyre strings on the tip of a drunken bard's fingers. They had all stopped in unison, stepping back like a hive of ants.

Anej ran the closest one through before he also took a step back, nearly slipping on blood-soaked cobblestones. They stood near the top of the hill where the ground grew steep, and soon enough they'd be backed into one of the Wardens, hunkering down in those mansions of ancient stone where they'd die the same as those long-lost builders had.

The irony was wasted on the Trevlarians, who didn't know a lick of their own history.

"What's wrong?" Layla asked, still on Anej's heels. "Why are they backin' up?"

Before Anej could answer, the sky lit up. A green pillar rising up from the middle of the Wood like an obelisk erected to one of the Damned Divinity. Which, Anej figured, it sort of was.

"Twelve Hells," Anej said, his voice hoarse. Daylight had slipped over the horizon, lighting up the ruins of Watchful below and giving color to the night's horrors. Smoke hung like fog.

"Anej," Layla said, and he could feel her hand press against his back.

"Steady, lass." Anej shifted his feet, watching the Yelmes closely. They backed up, eyes wide and faces illuminated with green light.

"Hold the line," Thibault called out. If there'd been arrows left, he'd probably have ordered a volley.

Good man, Anej thought. He'd have made a good general if he weren't going to die on this hill. Miraculously, more Yelmes bodies littered the street below than Trevlarian soldiers, which was a feat in and of itself.

The Yelmes turned at Thibault's voice, but they looked uncertain now. Anej shifted the weight of his shield. He wasn't as young as he had once been, and his shoulders and knees cramped. It had been a long night, and one in which not a single command had been called out from a Yelmes commander. It seemed odd and the ongoing silence unsettled him. They hadn't flanked meaningfully, or fallen back to tempt the humans forward, or any strategy at all—only a brutal frontal assault sustained for hours. Now they looked like lost mutts realizing they'd been chasing the wrong meal.

"Ain't so simple anymore, eh?" Anej mumbled. His beard heavy with sweat and blood. He knew what they had wanted, and they'd just lost it.

"Anej," Layla sounded breathless, weak. "I—"

The ground shook, causing cobblestone to crack and homes to creak. Soldiers cursed as they tried to keep their feet, and Layla collapsed against his back. Anej didn't turn, even as he felt her slide down his calves and *thud* against the ground. Something tickled in the back of Anej's mind, a faint memory, but there was no time to consider it with the small army before him.

"Oy!" Anej called out, his words dragging a handful of Yelmes eyes toward him. "What now? Didn't find what you're lookin' for, eh?"

One of the demons stepped forward, the shape of a man with almond skin and sweat drenched hair. His arm bled freely, his hands crackled with energy. "*Olb oto ýlenie.*"

Anej spat to the side. "I don't speak *Pitch.*"

It bared its teeth, its Eye roaming up and down Anej as if wanting to pluck free his Threads. "You distracted us."

Anej glanced toward the Wood. The pillar of light vanished now, but he could imagine what he'd see if he walked into the Clearing. "It's done now," Anej said. "I'd run, if I was you."

"We don't flee."

"She'll be comin' this way. Lookin' for blood."

"She'll be weak." The demon breathed out from his nose, turning from Anej and running a hand through his hair. Then he looked at Anej again, but this time taking in the velk's eye. "How did a *Zanýom* end up among rats like these?"

"On vacation."

The demon snorted. "Stay out of our way and we shall forgive this transgression."

Anej nodded toward the Wood. "Go, I ain't stoppin' ya."

With a long whistle and a crackling hand raised into the air, the demon ran down the hill. One by one the others followed, until all two dozen formed a ragged black line running down the street of Watchful.

No one said a word for a long time, though that didn't mean the top of the hill was silent. Chainmail clinked, soldiers muffled sobs, the wounded and dying gasped out hoarse breaths. But no one spoke a word until the last of the Kātsracha force marched beyond the wreckage of the Downwind.

A woman's voice broke the silence. "They're gone?"

Like a spell, the tension in Anej's arms and shoulders gave out, his shield and spear falling to his sides.

"See to the wounded!" Thibault called. His sword sliding home into its sheath.

The wounded.

The word triggered Anej's memory, and he turned to see Layla sprawled out on the cobblestone behind him. Fatigue and something like grief brought Anej to his knees beside her. He picked up her wrist carefully, as if it were nothing but a soft marsh reed. He didn't expect a pulse. The girl had done good, if killing could be called that. She'd stayed in his shadow, followed him longer than she should've been able to. But battle was battle. There'd probably be a sword wound beneath the cloak. Blood flowed from beneath her, probably from that last one he'd sent her way before—

A pulse. Anej grunted, feeling again with his grimy thumb to be sure. It was there, and strong.

Anej shifted Layla's body, feeling around her torso and back. Around him, people moved in a hurry, running about with water and bandages. But Anej stayed there beside the girl, his mind still nagging him with distant memory as his hands tried to make sense of why Layla Ricker lay unconscious.

"Is she dead?" It was Ulian, his face covered with soot and grime, though his spectacles remained miraculously unbroken.

"Fainted," Anej grunted. "Where've you been?"

Ulian ignored him. "Same time?"

"What?"

"She fainted at the same time as the light?" Anej looked up at Ulian. The maeifa nodded, rubbing his chin as if studying jigsaw pieces. "That would be a 'yes' then. Fascinating, of course. I've read about this but, well, I suppose you've seen it before."

You've seen it before.

Anej fell backward as memories from decades past collided with the now. She'd fainted *at the same time* as the light.

"The light must mean she's been freed, yes?" Ulian chattered on. "And if she's freed, then we both know what that means."

"The princess . . ."

Ulian waved Anej's words away. "You people in Velik always give too much weight to fae tales. Do you really think it was the princess who did it? I think we both know the only one on that escapade who ever stood a chance."

"But if Roi couldn't—"

"Roi wasn't *of* the Wood!" Ulian's eyes widened with excitement, his braided mustache bouncing at his chest. "I was trying to tell the Ricker boy this. His father was an interloper, coming here just like, well, *me*! Curious, educated, eager . . . but still foreign. But not Oliver, he was *born* into the Wood. He is a true Stražar."

Anej looked at Layla, his mind grappling. "Then she—"

"Yes," Ulian nodded. "She's connected to him and which means she is also connected to . . ." He looked around for a moment, lowering his voice. "Praise the Maker those beasts didn't notice her faint, otherwise—"

"They'd have killed her."

"And Oli, by extension."

"This is bad, Ule." Anej stood. He grabbed his beard, pulling it hard and letting the pain keep him here, in the now. Layla was the *Kolut,* the Spool. Oli, was the *Retchen*, the Spindle. Two interconnected pieces of unimaginable power. And neither would understand any of it.

"It could be worse," Ulian said, shifting his glasses.

"How?" Anej growled, pulling his beard harder. He had to stay here, he couldn't let himself leave. He wanted to leave, wanted to run. But he *had* to stay.

"Well, at least the girl is with you. She'll follow you."

"Follow me *where*? To her slow death? Her life drained from her, bit by bit, while I sit back and watch?"

Ulian stood, breathing deep as he looked toward the Wood. *No,* Anej realized, *not the Wood. The mountains.* They were brilliant, their peeks bathed in warm morning light, white and perfect, while their feet still lay in the dark shadow of night.

"Beyond the Nevihta mountains and across the river. I've only

read about it, mind you, but I believe your people could save her."
Ulian smiled. "More than her, really. There's a power loose in the
world now, old friend." Ulian pointed towards Layla. "Protecting her
may mean protecting a great many others."

"Maybe. Could mean the opposite. It's . . . complicated." *Very
complicated.*

"True, but there are wells of wisdom in Velik. Giants older than
you, those who remember—"

"I know what lies in my homeland," Anej snarled, and he
stopped himself from touching his eye.

"Good!" Ulian said, clasping his hands together. "Then we are
agreed. I'll get my things and we'll be off."

Then Ulian left, his soot covered head bouncing down the hill
toward the remains of his inn. Anej stood there wishing he could
have argued with the barkeep, but there would be little point. He'd
known Ulian a long time, and he knew enough to listen when the
little creature was right. Beyond the mountains . . . maybe they
would know what to do. And if the elders didn't, then at least it
wouldn't be his problem anymore. He could give them the girl and
then leave.

"Velk."

Anej turned. Captain Thibault walked toward him, his eyes
rimmed black with fatigue. A woman marched alongside him, her
skin made darker by the scarlet dress she wore. She looked pristine,
like a fine teacup brought to sit beside dirty dishes.

Anej grunted.

"This is Lady Amandine, Duchess of Worchestern," the captain
said, gesturing a hand to the woman.

Anej knelt to pick up his shield. Whatever this was about to be,
he didn't want it.

The woman coughed lightly, then said, "We owe you our thanks,
and our lives, Master . . ."

"Anej," he said, slinging his shield over his back. "And I'm just
the tanner."

"Nonsense. I watched you, Master Anej. There is *Artem* in you."

"Is that what the Order calls it these days?" Anej picked up his spear.

Amandine gave a firm nod. "You are to be commended. When the princess returns—"

"I won't be here." With his free hand, he carefully picked up Layla from the ground, cradling her like a child in the crook of his arm.

Thibault stepped forward, eyes moving from Layla to Anej, "What are you—"

"Captain," Anej cut him off. "You did good, but this ain't over. You see them," Anej hefted the spear and pointed it toward the Yelmes, now a black line running towards the Wood like ship rats. "Soon they'll put things together and they'll start following her," Anej nodded down toward Layla. "And when they do, you won't want her anywhere near this town or your precious princess. Understand?"

Thibault sighed. He looked annoyed and more than a little uncertain. "No, I don't. But either way, I won't stop you. Go with my blessing and my thanks." Then he turned to Amandine. "My lady, with your leave, I'll see to my wounded."

Thibault left, walking toward the priest who had already begun chanting over the worst of the wounded. Anej thought he could feel the power from the old priest, faint as it was. A few lives would be saved because of him, which almost made Anej like the priest, if just for a moment.

Anej looked out at a broken and miserable Watchful. How long ago had he come here? He'd always planned to watch over this place, the last bastion of the Ancient One's prison. Now, in the end, he wasn't so sure he'd succeeded.

"Will you go across the mountains?" Amandine asked.

It had been a long time since he'd walked along those peaks, longer still since he'd crossed the river and walked beneath the falls.

"It's best I be on my way," Anej said, nodding to Lady Amandine.

"Maker guide you," she said, bowing her head low.

More than one retort came to Anej's mind, but he swallowed them back down. He'd learned to stop trampling over good intentions. So he turned and walked down the hill, the breeze picking up and running cold fingers over his sweat-soaked face. He'd need to stop by his cabin and grab something for the girl or she'd never survive the mountain winter. They were a week or more from Velik, and they'd be wading through mountain snow for much of it.

Perhaps it was the words of Lady Amandine or the growing feeling of desperation, but Anej found himself begin to mumble prayers. They were old ones, taught to him a millennia before, and not uttered by him for nearly a hundred years.

PART TWO

CHAPTER
THIRTY-SEVEN

L ayla opened her eyes to a black sky.

She'd collapsed. Her head had started to pound, thoughts drowned out by a terrible *thud, thud, thud*, then her knees had given out. She remembered leaning against Anej, feeling the cold of his sweat-soaked tunic, a green sky, and that was it.

Now, she looked at stars.

And . . . sand?

Layla sat up, hands grasping for her sword, for Anej. But there was nothing except a sea of sand rising and falling like hills. She scrambled to her feet, unsteady as the sand shifted beneath her boots. Turning, she tried to get her bearings, to find Watchful or the Nevihta mountains in the distance. There was nothing, only miles of sand beneath a night sky. There were no clouds, no trees, no moun-tains on the far horizon.

"I'm dead." She said the words with finality, certainty. It was the only explanation. "I'm dead," she said again, louder this time just so she could hear her own words. Utter silence. Not even the whistling of the wind.

It didn't help. With not even an echo, she only felt even more alone when her words faded into the sand dunes around her. Fear loomed over her shoulder, tangible in its weight. She wrapped her arms around herself to ward it off.

Some of these hills of sand rose higher than others, and some blocked her vision of parts of the horizon. Maybe if she climbed one she'd see a city, mountain, or something else. Maybe the afterlife had people and a civilization. Maybe she wasn't even dead.

She knew if she did nothing, her mind would eat her alive.

With a *humph* at no one in particular, Layla marched off toward the tallest of the sand hills, determined to scale it and find an ounce of hope. Getting up the sandy incline felt like playing in one of Watchful's small grain silos. For every five steps, she lost two. Worse than that, she got nowhere if she didn't crouch down and climb on all fours, sticking her hands up to their wrists into the hillside. Beneath the top layer of sand though, it was surprisingly firm. As she climbed, sand made its way into her boots, through the neck of her tunic, and into her mouth. It got everywhere and in everything. She had never seen so much of it before, hadn't known so much could exist.

Her mind wandered as she went, juggling around the idea this might actually be the afterlife. More than likely, she had gotten hit by a sword-slash or lightning strike so fast she couldn't even remember. Then her life had been snuffed out, as quick as a candle flame.

"Well," she said aloud, still craving sound. "Why did Damnation have to be a bloody desert," Layla muttered.

Bloody. Layla faltered. Memories swirled about her, and for a single moment those memories were more real to her than the sand she stared at as she climbed. They were terrible memories, ones she already wanted to forget. On impulse, she lifted one hand from the sand and looked at it intently for the first time since waking up. Blood had dried beneath the nails and in the grooves of her palm. The sand had worn some away, but she knew.

She was a killer now.

The top of the hill was but a thin line of sand and so standing proved hard: she had to place one foot on each side of the hill, adjusting every few moments due to the shifting sand. Eventually she managed a shaky equilibrium, and then she looked out to the horizon.

Starlight illuminated everything, which meant the world was pale and dark in an alluring way which made her want to walk on and on forever. She hadn't noticed until now, but the sky had no moon, only those numberless stars.

No city or mountains dotted the horizon, only sand. It rolled on and on as far as she could see, never broken. The weight of it brought Layla to her knees, pressed down as if by a millstone. The world turned and shifted as tears welled in her eyes. Her breathing grew husky and ragged, her mind rolling around one singular thought: *I am alone.*

Her tears wet her tunic and the sand beneath her. Snot filled her nostrils until her breathing became the gasps between sobs. Her body shook, and small ripples of sand fell down the hill beneath her, knocked loose by her own frantic rocking. Back and forth she moved rhythmically.

Oblivion would have been better: a true nothingness, a non-existence. But this? Alone, left to wander?

She let out a pain-filled scream, grabbing and hurling sand all around her. It was too much. She had killed to stay alive, but died anyway. And death was loneliness. Would it be for eternity, or could she die again?

She shoved her face into the sand, letting the grains fill her nose and form to every crevice and line. She would not breathe. She would force herself to die again and again until nothingness won out. She did not know what she deserved as an afterlife, but she knew she could not endure to be alone. Not forever.

Her body convulsed. It wanted air, her head and chest swelling with the desire. She would not give in. She would not stay here, in this world of sand and emptiness. It was oppressive, and she wanted out. She wanted to be gone, to be free and—

Her mouth opened and she sucked in sand and air.

Jerking backward, she gagged and coughed, air pulsing through her lungs in an angry and violent revolution. She kept crying, she had never stopped. She could not die and yet she could not live, and so she cried all the more.

An hour or more went by before the tears dried up and the rush of emotions ebbed away, leaving her numb. She looked to the stars, wiping her eyes. They were beautiful. Incredibly bright pinpoints of light that pulsed and moved.

Her head drifted downward, and eventually she looked back to the far horizon, and paused.

In the distance she saw a little shadow, faint but distinct. She squinted, and one last tear welled up in her eyes, the water magnifying her vision for just an instant.

A tree.

And then the tear ran from her eye and the tree disappeared, leaving nothing more than a distant black dot on the horizon. Layla staggered to her feet and began walking.

THIRTY-EIGHT

O li stood, ankle deep, in sand. He looked down at his hands, but his mother wasn't there. His mouth hung open. Slowly, he turned to look around, unsure he could believe his eyes. There was no black ground, no dais, no princess, no trees . . . no mother.

There had been an explosion, he remembered that. The world had pulsed green and then there had been a terrible *crack* and—had everything turned to sand? The night sky looked the same, though perhaps the stars had shifted. He couldn't be sure.

But his mother had to be here somewhere, she couldn't have just disappeared. Oli collapsed to his knees, shoveling dirt with his hands. At first it was slow, cautious. But moments later his movements became wild, his breathing harsh. He dug long, but beneath the sand lay more sand, compacted into a thick layer that tore at his fingernails as he scraped it aside.

Orelda Ricker wouldn't be under sand, Oli knew that. To think so wouldn't be sane. She had been dead before the explosion, dead before he'd even gotten to hold her. He hadn't saved her, he had gotten her killed. If he'd been stronger, or if he'd just run from the princess to begin with, she'd be alive. But he'd screwed up again. Failed again.

He sat in a hole now, shallow, but wide. All the sand he threw backward just ran down the hole's edges and collected around his boots and knees. And still he kept digging. The hole slowly deepened, and the walls of it absorbed his crying, his screaming, his cursing.

It was a long time before Oli bothered to stop.

His hands were scraped raw and his nails were bloody. He fell to the side, chest heaving and eyes burning. He couldn't see because of the tears.

His mother was gone, the Wood was gone, and he was gone too, though he didn't know where. Didn't care where. If he was dead, that was fine. Alone was fine. No one to expect anything, to need anything, to want anything. No one to hurt him, for him to hurt. He'd have preferred nothingness, but this would do.

He thought of Layla. Her face appeared in his mind without him trying. All at once he wanted to both push the image away and draw it closer. The last Ricker, the last bit of responsibility he had. Or used to have. Not anymore though. He could do nothing for her now. The Wood had won, had killed him like it had killed his parents.

The digging had worked out the grief and the tears, leaving only a numb ache. He could breathe normally again, and so he stood. Walking sounded good, and so he stumbled up the nearest sandy slope. He had no destination, no journey in mind. He just walked to walk.

He got to the top a quarter of an hour later, shoulders hunched. When he looked around he saw little more than sand. The air smelled nice though, fresh and clean. The Clearing had been rotten, like the scent of dead animals and burnt bread. Here, the entire world was washed by the sand, scrubbed fresh.

A small black mark sat on the far horizon, an imperfection on the starlit rolling hills. It was miles away. Might take a day or more to get to it. That didn't bother him. Death had found him and the afterlife he'd been sent to was far better than he'd expected.

With nothing else before him, Oli marched onward toward the silhouette on the horizon.

CHAPTER
THIRTY-NINE

Léonie had watched the pedestal explode into thousands of finger-size pieces, sending up a column of fire so bright the memory of it still floated in her vision. It had sounded like the crumpling of Worchestern's walls, long and unbearably loud. But after the fire and noise and light, the silence felt as though the world had forgotten how to breathe.

Tâl and Léonie stood at the edge of the Clearing, watching green-black smoke set in over the crater that had been Staradovna. Léonie still held her sword, the weight of it comforting, though her knuckles were white from her obsessive hold.

"Your Highness," Tâl said, voice gentle, quiet.

Léonie said nothing, only tilted her head a fraction.

"Perhaps we should leave?"

Leave. Léonie lips drew tight, her tongue moving against the back of her teeth. "This was our kingdom's only hope. We cannot leave without . . ." her voice trailed off. Without what? Answers? A weapon?

Léonie stepped back into the Clearing, both her steps and her resolve wavering. Tâl followed, the sound of her breathing both loud and comforting in this wasteland of death.

She had gotten less than a handful of steps forward before the smell of sulfur began to burn her nose, and the back of her throat began to burn as well. She considered turning around, but where would she go? To her father? Even if she could make it back to Turris Regis alive, she could not show her face again without a way to save her kingdom.

The smell of sulfur grew stronger, and she bent over as she began to heave. Tâl grabbed her hand and shoved a dirty linen into it which Léonie used to cover her mouth, breathing in the scent of earth and sweat.

Léonie never stopped to consider whether or not she *should* go back into the Clearing. These fumes could be noxious, there could be another explosion, or a new monstrosity could rise from these ashes. None of it mattered. She had come to this Maker-forsaken stretch of world for a reason, and this desolation was her last thread of hope. Without power to stand against the Yelmes, she had nothing to go back to.

Morning light filled the Clearing, sending rays of light through the smoky haze. On reflex, Léonie captured this image in her mind, stored for later when she could analyze it, paint it. Except, she doubted she would ever return to her mind's galleria again. She pushed the thoughts aside – they mattered little now. With the odds as they were, she may not live long enough for it to matter. Were there not Yelmes in Watchful by now?

She swatted away thick green wisps of smoke with her sword, still holding the rag over her face. The crater marred the ground only a few paces away, the ground cracking and dropping off into a hole six or seven feet deep. Charred vines crumpled beneath Léonie's boots like ash as she stepped closer, her eyes scanning the ground for any signs of the Ancient One. A small little flame of hope still burned inside her, tempting her to believe she may find an artifact that would make all of this worth it. Perhaps there would be scraps of paper with an incantation, or a metal bracelet holding infinite power, anything that could be used against the Yelmes.

But the body, the robes, all traces of Staradovna were gone, torn to bits with nothing left behind.

"No," Léonie said, picking away at chunks of charred wood and rock with the tip of her sword. "No, no, no."

She had been right, Staradovna had been *real*. There had been great power here, covered up by the Order and its machinations. But Léonie had failed to do anything more than watch the hope of her power slip from her fingers, gone in a flash of light and fire.

"My lady?"

Léonie cried. Tears rolled down her cheeks, finding their way to the corners of her mouth, the salty wetness of them awakening her thirst and hunger. "We have lost." She slammed the tip of her sword into a piece of black wood, holding it up to the morning light. "This is all that is left of what we came for."

Tâl looked from the wood to the princess, and back again once more.

Léonie screamed. She pushed every ounce of anger and violence and shame and fear into that one sound, forcing it out through her throat. Let the world hear Léonie Baudelaire, Princess of Trevelar, failure of the kingdom. Léonie lifted her sword and heaved it, sending it spinning into the distance.

She screamed again and again, but it was not enough.

Her mind filled with images of Turris Regis aflame, smoke billowing into the streets, children crying and bloodied corpses strewn about for the crows to eat. The throne would be smashed, her father beheaded, her brother hung from the walls. The water in the harbor would run red, the ships would sink. The Kingdom of Trevelar would fall because the only power which could have defeated the Yelmes had shattered to pieces before her.

"Your Highness."

Léonie looked up, her vision blurred by tears. "What?"

Tâl gestured to the ground a dozen paces away. There, two bodies lay, black with soot and half covered in rubble.

The Woodsman and his mother.

Léonie shook her head. "Leave the dead."

"But he's not dead." Tâl's voice rang with solemnity and reverence.

"That is not possible." Even as Léonie said it, the two of them walked towards the soot covered forms. Orelda lay broken, her face contorted and still. She was dead, as surely as her son should have been.

Should have been.

Impossibly, Oli's chest rose and fell, small bits of debris shifting around on his tunic as he did. He did not look broken, even the cuts all around his body had stopped flowing blood. He looked dirty and worn, but almost restful, as if he merely slept.

"He should be dead," Léonie said. He had been mere feet from the explosion, and he looked unburned.

Tâl shook her head, palms splayed outward.

He had killed Staradovna: Trevelar's one hope, their greatest defense, and he *killed* her. Léonie bent down and grabbed Oli by the tunic, dragging him away from his dead mother. Breath came in short gasps for her now, her brow drenched in sweat. Where had the rag gone? The sulfur tempted her to gag again.

"Your Highness?"

"He killed her," Léonie spat. "He killed her and now we will all die." Léonie dumped Oli back to the ground a dozen paces away. He moaned and the sound infuriated her. She pulled her dagger free and knelt beside him.

"Princess, you can't!" Tâl fell to her knees on the other side of Oli, her face close enough to almost touch Léonie's.

"Who are you to tell me I *can't*?" The last word came out as a sneer.

"M'lady, please, listen. Oli *destroyed* the Ancient One. That shouldn't be possible."

"I know," Léonie said, the sound of her grinding teeth loud in her ears. Oli had killed Staradovna. An illiterate peasant blew up the most powerful being in all of La'Azurus. It scared her.

"But, princess, that makes him . . ." Tâl looked about, as if trying to find her next word. "The last link, the last connection to her and her power. If he could defeat the power of Staradovna, then maybe—"

Hope, fragile and timid, kindled inside of her. "Then maybe . . . what?"

"Then maybe he can fight the Yelmes too."

Léonie dropped Oli and leaned back, her eyes looking the ranger up and down. Dried blood smeared her forehead and caked in loose strands of her hair. "Who told you?"

"M'lady?"

"Who told you of the Ancient One? Who briefed you on our mission, on Staradovna?"

Tâl's eyes darted about. "You were not discreet around myself nor the captain—"

"Thibault briefed you?"

Tâl paused, licking her lips. "No, Your Highness."

"I did not divulge the entirety of our mission to you, did I?"

"No, Your Highness." Tâl's voice became cold, distant.

"Perhaps I have not been overly cautious within the confines of the Wood, but neither have I been exhaustive." Léonie stood, acutely aware her sword was somewhere in the distance. "But you speak as if you know far more than you should."

"M'lady, I—"

Léonie stepped forward as Tâl stood, sending the ranger scrambling back. "And you did not succumb to the Call, did you? And you traveled the Wood as safely as the Woodsman, yes?"

"Princess, I—"

Léonie stepped forward again. "And you were wounded while standing guard over me, yes? And yet *I* was taken captive and you are not dead, rather curious."

Tâl's fingers twitched near her dagger. "Please, let me explain, I—"

"And now you have stayed my hand," Léonie stepped forward again. "Speaking of power, of connections, of the Ancient One as if you *understand*."

Tâl shifted her feet, moving one foot subtly forward.

Léonie waved her hand as if swatting away a fly. "Please, ranger, if I wanted to fight I would not have lectured you first. I would have slit your throat and been done with it. No, you are still my ranger and I am still your princess. You will tell me everything, *now*."

Tâl licked her lips again, looking from Léonie to Oli and back.

Léonie narrowed her eyes. "Everything."

Tâl relaxed some, then breathed in deep. "I am Badaui."

"I can see that. Your father must have been Trevlarian though."

"Yes, Your Highness. I am Trevlarian," Tâl said. Citizenship ran through the father's blood. "But though my father was of the kingdom, I never met him. I was raised dockside beneath my mother's wing."

"In one of the Badaui communes? I have heard of them. Illegal." *A whore's daughter,* Léonie thought.

"I was a teen when the Order purged our community."

The Badaui worshiped their god in small Jegja Jumun temples set up in little homes in the ethnic communities famously found dockside, often beneath brothels and gambling dens. The Order's constant push to purge them proved a source of diplomatic pain for the crown. The Badaui Republic was open to alliance only under conditions of immunity from religious purges from the Order of Deōs. And though her father needed that alliance, he would lose his crown if he made such a compromise.

Politics and religion.

Léonie puffed air through her nose. "And what is this to me?"

"I was raised on stories of the Jegja Jumun, Your Highness, and they tell of the true histories of La'Azurus, far more than what the priests of the Order would dare utter."

Léonie rubbed her temples. It felt both defeating and deeply ironic that a prostitute's daughter from the docks would know more about the secrets of the Order than she had. "The Jegja Jumun is secretive in the extreme, no?"

"We know how to hold our tongue, Your Highness."

Léonie snorted. "Better than most priests, clearly. So, you are telling me that in some dank, dockside basement you were taught of Staradovna as a little girl?"

Tâl's nostrils flared. "Indeed. Or some of it, at least. We had scrolls, or letters, really. Teachings snuck across the border in crates and barrels from the Republic. When the priests came, my mother sent me away." Tâl looked away, eyes glazing over.

"With the letters?" Possession of those would have Tâl burning at the stake.

"They're gone now. Burned. I would never have been able to hide them forever. But first, I . . . I read them. Over and over again, every night for months."

"And the Ancient One?"

"It taught of a demon, caged beneath the shadow of the Nevihta. There were prophecies, talks of monsters and beasts, of men with fire for eyes and women giving birth to gods. I understood little of it. I was young."

Léonie shook her head, stepping back over to Oli. He groaned again. "This does not tell me how you have stayed alive in this Wood. How you have been unaffected."

Tâl swallowed. "The letters spoke of rituals to ward off the powers of the demon. They are the rites all Badaui children go through when they come of age. My mother would have led me through them, if—"

"Rites?"

Tâl shook her head. "Your Highness, please. There are things not meant for outsiders to know."

Anger flared inside Léonie. "Do you withdraw your pledge from the crown?"

"I would lay my life down for the crown." Tâl clenched her fist. "But you already know enough to consider me a heretic, do you truly need more? My life is already forfeit."

"Heresy means little to me now," Léonie said, voice going quiet. "Fine, keep your Jegja Jumun for now. But you must swear that if need arises, you will tell me this rite."

Tâl breathed out, nodding.

It was not enough. "Swear it," Léonie said. "Swear it on the grave of your mother and on your god."

"Your Highness, I—"

Léonie lifted the knife in her hand. "If you hold allegiance to the crown, you will swear it *now*."

Tâl's hands shook, but she met Léonie's eyes. "I swear upon my mother's grave and upon my god, I will confide in you the secret rites of the Jegja Jumun should it prove vital for the safety of the crown."

Silence stretched out between the two women for a long time.

Strangely, Léonie felt as though she had just violated Tâl, stolen something deep and sacred. But the feeling did her no good, and so she pushed it away. "That shall do, for now. And I suppose we have both shown ourselves heretics now. Perhaps we shall hang together when this is done." She looked toward Oli. "What do your sacred texts say of him?"

"I'm not sure. When he fought, he spoke in that language of his."

"You called it something before, when we were at the Wall."

Tâl nodded. "Yidumetcha. It means 'Namer' or even 'He who names the world'. Once, long ago, people had the power to give names to all that is in La'Azurus. And in those names was power."

"So, the Woodsman . . ."

Tâl shook her head. "If he could speak the names of things, then that power would be older than even Staradovna. But I am unsure, Your Highness. I still understand so little."

Léonie looked toward the crater and frowned. "Magic has no rules. I hate it. Who could understand what has happened here? I feel like a child who is trying to understand how birds fly."

"I think it has rules, though perhaps only the Maker understands them."

Léonie ran a hand through her hair. "Well, rules or no, we have need to find out whether Oli Ricker can kill the Yelmes. He appears to be all we have left."

Léonie stood over the Woodsman, hands on her hips. She still wanted to drive her knife into his heart. Yet Tâl had given her a pinch of hope: just enough to stay her hand. She *had* to bring a weapon back for this war, and perhaps this man—this insolent and angry fool of a man—was all she had left.

"Fine then," Léonie said. "Try to wake him. I want my sword." Léonie stalked off in the direction she had thrown her blade. It was not hard to spot—it was the only thing gleaming in the morning light. The blade was dulled and dirty, but she shoved it into her sheath anyhow. It would be her armorer's problem to clean it, assuming her armorer was still alive.

And then Oli screamed.

CHAPTER
FORTY

W hatever Layla had expected to find at the end of her hours-long march over the sandy sea, this wasn't it. She stood at the trunk of a tree nearly a dozen paces wide and with its head in the stars. Its roots were like trees themselves, and they spread so far out and around the tree that she had first encountered one sticking out of the ground three bowshots back.

And yet, somehow, it wasn't the size of the tree which proved the strangest part. It was that the tree was ever-changing.

Depending on the angle from which Layla looked, it shifted and changed. She saw every tree along the edge of the Wood, and a hundred others she couldn't have ever begun to imagine. This one tree was every tree, and yet none of them at all. For Maker knows how long, Layla walked around it, eyes scrunched up and mouth hanging open. With each step, the bark shifted—moving from smooth to rough, from dark and then to light. The leaves changed as well, one moment large and green with finger-like extrusions, the next moment they morphed to shapes like raindrops and colored in a multitude of browns and oranges. There were fruits sometimes, and they changed just as much—berries of all sizes and colors, apples and things which looked like apples but with a fuzzy outer layer that reminded her of poor Tuck, purple and blue hiwaya fruits, and a dozen others she couldn't name.

Layla paused her march and ran her fingers through her hair, turning to look out at the endless sea of sand once more. The tree cast no shadow. In fact, she hadn't seen any shadow at all since she'd been here, including her own. The only sources of light were the stars above, and yet Layla felt as though she could see as clearly as though it were day.

She hadn't seen another soul. No towns, no people, no lights on the horizon. Nothing. She must have walked miles and hadn't caught a hint of life. In fact, walking had only raised more strange questions. The going had been long and tough, and yet she wasn't tired or thirsty.

Layla bit her lip. It was just her and this tree in this strange place, though she supposed having the tree was better than nothing. At least it was interesting.

She was a handful of paces away from the trunk. From this angle, the bark of the tree appeared smooth and orange fruits the size of cauldrons dangled from thorny branches above. She longed to taste one of them and could feel saliva pooling in her mouth at the thought of it. She stepped closer to the tree, keeping the same angle as best she could, though still the tree shimmered and morphed into a willow with long, mossy, leaves with tiny berries growing in thick patches. One of those bunches dangled close enough to touch.

She raised her hand, reaching for just one of those small little fruits—and stopped.

Her hand had changed. No, not changed, exactly. It was the blood beneath her fingernails: it had turned black and moldy, spreading down her knuckles and to the back of her hand. Like a plague, the color worked its way over her body. She wanted to retch.

The tree forgotten, she twisted around looking for somewhere, anywhere, to wash the blood free before it spread further. Layla's heart pounded in her ears, a deafening *thud, thud, thud* making her vision blur at the edges with each beat. She felt certain this plague would spread, would cover her whole body. She had to do something, had to find something to help, had to—

"Layla?"

A voice? Not just *a* voice, but one she knew. Layla looked up and saw her brother walking toward her, dressed as he'd been the night before. Or had it been two nights before? His eyes looked more sunken than usual, though they were wider now than Layla had ever seen them. He was covered in blood too, and soot, and he smelled like a campfire that had been smoking rotten meat.

But he was *here*.

She ran toward him, already crying and falling, but scrambling toward him because now she wasn't alone.

"Stay back," Oli said, raising his hand, palm outstretched as though to shove her away.

Layla skidded to a stop in the stupefied obedience that comes with shock. "What?"

"I know a trick when I see it."

"A trick? Oliver Ricker, I'm your sister!" She choked on the last word, falling to her knees. The beating in her ears had gotten louder. "And I'm scared."

Oli hesitated, looking around and flexing his fingers. "Where are we? And what is that?"

Layla had forgotten about the tree, though she could see the reflection of it in Oli's eyes.

Layla shook her head, sobs shaking her chest. "I—don't—know."

She hated herself for crying, but she couldn't stop. Soon, Oli would see her hands and he'd know she was a monster. He wouldn't want to touch her, to talk to her. Suddenly, Layla felt certain Oli would leave the moment he knew. She leaned forward and shoved her hands into the sand, hiding them up to her wrists.

There was a sigh and Layla could feel, more than hear, Oli approach.

"Is it really you?" He stood above her and she could hear the sand shift as he crouched beside her.

Layla didn't say a word, only shook her head. She was so confused, so lost. Seeing Oli should have been salvation, but instead her head pounded and a thousand thoughts impaled her mind between each loud *thud*. She remembered Oli leaving. *Thud*. Mother waking her up, leaving her too. *Thud*. Lightning and fire, death and swords. *Thud*. The blood on her hands . . . she had killed. *Thud*.

Oli was speaking. Had he stopped? "Look, we'll figure this out, right? It's a lot, but we'll be . . . okay."

Oli shifted again, and Layla felt his hand touch her shoulder. It was warm and kind, the feeling of awkward love between brother and sister. This was Oli, and he loved her and would protect her. But that love and warmth was fleeting, there and then gone, for just as Layla was leaning into his embrace, pain ripped through her body.

Layla screamed, jerking away and grabbing her shoulder, feeling for a knife or hot poker which must have been stabbed there. Oli screamed too, but his screams quickly faded, pulled away into the far distance.

The world changed. The sand and tree disappeared, replaced by a thousand flashing images. She understood none of them, all pictures of places she had never seen with people and beasts that looked unfamiliar and dressed strangely. But the pain never abated, only growing stronger as Oli's voice faded from existence. The pain grew until every inch of her body seemed to be trying to rip itself apart. She watched as her fingernails ripped away, as the bones in her hand snapped, all to a backdrop of images of an ever-changing people and world.

And then, like the lid of a coffin snapping shut, there was darkness.

CHAPTER
FORTY-ONE

Oli yanked his hand away, flailing backward as Layla's body burned with light.

And then she disappeared, leaving him alone and feeling as though he had just clenched his fist around a burning coal. No, the pain hurt more than that, going through his palm and deeper inside him. It was like watching his father ripped apart, like holding his dead mother. Pain in the depths of whatever thing he called a soul.

Layla's screaming hadn't gone the moment she had, but it hung in the air for a breath. It left the world feeling eerie and cold, and even more lonely. It had been a trick, of course. His sister had never been here, and the thing he'd seen had only been an illusion.

A trap, and he had fallen for it.

Now he lay on the sand where he'd fallen in his scramble to get away from the Layla-illusion, waiting for the pain to subside. Above him were the same sea of stars he'd been walking beneath for hours, but that wasn't all. He could also see the eaves of a roof, the top of the massive house.

He'd been watching the house take shape for miles, a tall building which dwarfed the Wardens back in Watchful. Layla, or the illusion of Layla, had been staring at it when he'd approached. The windows were all black, the door a solid metal, and the siding constructed of a thousand timbers of knotted wood. There seemed to be no foundation other than the sand that shifted around its base.

When the pain became bearable, Oli stood. He rubbed away the pain in his hand as he made for the door. Nearly an hour ago he had decided he'd try to get into the place once he got here, and seeing Layla hadn't changed that. There was nowhere else to go.

He hadn't expected to see an image of Layla though. She had been scared, pained, and—Oli shook his head. He needed to keep going, Layla hadn't been real. He spat on the sand then trudged over to the door. A large bronze handle protruded off to one side. He nearly knocked, but thought better of it and pulled the handle. He braced for pain.

None came. There was only the cool touch of the bronze, then an ounce of resistance before the door swung open. A hallway stretched out before him, its floor lined with flat stone and the walls draped in banners of reds and greens. The ceiling rose high, and from it hung black chandeliers every half-dozen paces, each with a handful of wax candles. The candles burned with small flames that did little to illuminate the hallway, leaving long shadows in the corners.

It was almost certainly another illusion and another trap. But Oli could hardly help but step forward, kicking the door shut behind him. Whatever trap lay ahead, Oli didn't want to run from it. He felt too tired and too angry. Whatever lay before him, he just wanted to see it and be done.

There were three doors: one to the right, another to the left, and a last at the end of the hall. The one to the left and at the end of the hall were closed, but the door to the right hung open. From it, light poured forth onto the stones of the hallway.

Oli walked toward the open door.

The room beyond was as large as the dining room in the Tote mansion, yet had been so stuffed with shelves, tables, and books it appeared cramped and small. No wall could be seen behind the bookcases for each ran from the floor to the ceiling high above, their shelves piled high with thick tomes and nonsensical baubles. It was as though the cluttered bookcase in his home, filled with his father's books, maps, and nicknacks, had been repeated a thousand times over. A table dominated the center of the room—like the one in the Tote home, but instead of food it lay covered in even more books and the occasional empty plate or cup.

Beyond the table, between two leather chairs, was something like a hearth. It was a metal ball, open on one side to reveal a crackling fire lighting up much of the room. But it did not lie on the floor but *floated*. Oli couldn't take his eyes off it as it bobbed in mid-air around the height of his chest. It gave off no smoke and no flue had been attached to the top.

Magic.

"Well, that entrance was rather delayed, I think."

Oli looked up, searching for the source of the voice.

The ceiling went up nearly a bowshot, but a small landing protruded from the wall halfway up, complete with another table and piles more books. The voice, feminine and low, had come from there though Oli saw no one. He considered replying, thinking he might draw the speaker out into the open, but his eyes had caught sight of the ceiling.

And it mesmerized him.

It was less of a ceiling and more a domed window to the sky, but a sky like nothing Oli could have ever imagined. There appeared blackness and stars, but far more too. Streaks of oranges and blues, like slowly flickering candle flames, shot out across the black expanse. There were two lights across from each other: the sun and the moon. The moon shone brighter than Oli had ever seen, a brilliant pale blue whose skin looked as smooth as pearl. The sun though, burned dim and appeared far away. Where there should have been blinding light, Oli could stare right at its center and see the small silhouette of a man.

"Over here, darling."

A woman had appeared at the edge of the landing, leaning on the railing and eyeing him over the edge of a black book. Her hair dangled in curls around her shoulders, her thin lips smiling carefully. As attractive as her voice was sweet, in another place and time Oli may have looked at her with longing. But her eyes told Oli all he needed to know. One was milky white. The other was a vacant hole.

Staradovna.

Oli clenched his fist, his heart quickening. "I killed you."

She cocked an eyebrow. "Child, you haven't the faintest idea how to kill me."

"I put an arrow through your face." He began looking around, keeping one eye on Staradovna while the other tried to find a weapon.

"Ah, yes." Staradovna closed the book with a *thud* and tossed it onto the table beside her. "Thank you for that, by the way."

Oli could feel himself shaking. He needed a ladder or a set of stairs, a way to get up to her. He walked forward now, unsure where exactly he went, but determined to do something, anything. "I saw you die."

"Really? What did you see *exactly*? Oh, wait!" She held up a finger, face beaming. "Don't tell me, I want to see for myself." She flung one hand into the air and the world around Oli shifted.

He stood in the Clearing again, holding his bow with an arrow aimed at the twisted statue of Staradovna. Vines rose, engulfing him. He had no control of his body, and everything moved slowly and strangely fluid. There was no sound other than the soft laughter of Staradovna from above him.

It was not real: a vision just as Layla had been. And yet, Oli still wanted to scream. In moments he'd be engulfed and he would drown beneath these vines, dead while Staradovna and his mother watched.

His mother! She dangled in the air to his left, alive and trapped in a tangle of vines. No, not alive, just a vision. It was only a vision, and yet Oli felt a surge of energy for he needed to save her, to stop this madness. He released the arrow and—

Everything changed and morphed, colors and shapes distorting for an instant, and then he stood once more in the room with the books, the table, the floating hearth.

His mother was still dead.

"Ah, you see, *there* it was," Staradovna said from the balcony above. "That little trick you played with your little pointy sticks and your words? You did this." Staradovna lifted her hands, gesturing about her. "I couldn't have planned it all so cleanly myself. Well, if you could call this neat." She whipped a finger across the banister and held it aloft.

"What are you talkin' 'bout?" Oli stepped back, looking around for something, anything, he could use as a weapon. "You died. That arrow killed you. The whole pedestal was destroyed."

Staradovna laughed, sweet notes echoing off the walls. "No, darling, you did not kill me. In fact, I think we may consider the opposite true. Truly, I am feeling much more alive."

A poker stuck up from a metal pot near the floating hearth. His best option, Oli marched towards it, kicking books and chairs aside.

Staradovna laughed. "The key was the words though, and it was brilliant the way you imbued them onto the arrow. Where did you learn that, I wonder?"

Oli scooped up the poker, feeling the smooth wood of the handle in his palm. It seemed heavy enough, and the tip was sharp. He looked around for some way to the landing above.

"Gods, you do get fixated don't you?" Staradovna said, leaning over the railing to look down at him. "Well, if you plan to stab me with your little stick, you best use the stairs. Look behind the bookcase over there."

Between two bookcases, Oli glimpsed a small opening he had missed before. He quickly stepped between the bookcases and into an alcove with a winding staircase. The steps appeared to be of dark wood and the railing made of polished bronze. Oli began to climb.

Staradovna continued, her voice bored. "Darling, you really need to learn to slow down. Have you even stopped to consider this place? One would think it rather familiar; though, by the state of things when I arrived, it seems you hadn't visited in ages. Curious."

Oli stepped onto the landing, poker readied in his hand. Staradovna smiled.

"Oy," Oli muttered. "I'll kill ya again."

"Come now," she said, holding her arms to the side. "We could do far more together, if only you would leave this pettiness behind."

Oli didn't bother to retort, to remind her she had killed his father and mother. In three strides he had closed the distance between them, and then he thrust outward with the poker, aiming the tip right for the woman's abdomen. She did not try to stop him. She merely watched as the poker shoved through her dress, into her stomach, and then punctured through the back. Like pushing a needle through fabric: Oli felt a little resistance at first, then the poker went through to the other side with ease.

All the while, Staradovna never stopped smiling.

"What?" Oli blinked, looking up into Staradovna's white eye.

"If it makes you feel any better, this goes both ways." In a blur, she pushed Oli back, ripped the poker from her belly, and shoved it through Oli's own chest. Oli felt a jolt as the poker hit him, and then nothing. No pain, no sensation of any kind.

"Am I dead?" It would make so much sense.

"No, thankfully. You are very much alive, and I would like to keep it that way for now." She patted Oli on his cheek. "Life will be so much more entertaining."

"But . . ." Oli's voice trailed off. He couldn't think, his mind looping in circles around itself. The poker still stuck from his chest.

"Oh, come now, don't you understand anything, little Stražar? You would think you would recognize this place. Come, read this." She grabbed a book from the table, holding the crimson cover before him. "Do you see that?"

Oli saw nothing in particular. There were golden lines around the edges, letters in the middle which meant nothing to him.

Staradovna waited, as though expecting understanding to dawn upon Oli. None came. She appeared confused for a moment, then looked at the book cover as though she had forgotten something.

A moment later, she laughed, loud and vibrant. "Oh darling, you can't read, can you? Oh, that is too rich. Look at me, set free by an illiterate. Never in a thousand years would I have thought!"

Oli stepped back and pulled the poker free from his chest, feeling a similar sensation to when it had pierced him at first. His ears rang with a rhythmic *thud, thud, thud* and the edges of his vision darkened. "Oy, and what does reading have to do with it?"

"Everything, darling. Everything." She stepped toward him, and Oli stepped back again, checking behind him to ensure he didn't fall down the stairs. "But I shall need to spoon feed you for now, I suppose. This place," she turned, throwing her arms out to encompass the room. "This is *your mind*. And the two of us will be spending a lot of time here together. So, it may be best you get used to me."

"My . . . my mind?" Oli couldn't breathe, couldn't think. He understood nothing she said, and yet somewhere inside him he knew it was true.

Staradovna paused, looking to the side just as Oli's head thudded again. Then she shrugged and said, "Well, we are already out of time. Truly, you took far too long to arrive."

"I—"

"Shush," Staradovna snapped her fingers and Oli's body went rigid, face looking upward into her own. "We're running out of time, but there is one thing you must know. It is *very* important. You *must* kill the Dark Ones. The Yelmes will be hunting you now, so you must kill them first. Be ruthless and be quick. If you die, then we're both dead, and I won't have that. Do you understand? *Kill them*, Oli."

She snapped her fingers again and Oli was free, though the suddenness of it made him fall forward. "Screw you," Oli said, mind racing to take in all she had said. If he died, then she would too. He wouldn't mind the trade. "I'll let 'em kill me."

The thudding came again, but it wasn't just in his head any longer. Each *thud, thud, thud* shook the house, knocking books and baubles off the wall and rattling cups and plates against one another.

"Charming," Staradovna said flatly. "But you understand far too little to play games with me. Think of your sister, Oli."

"Layla?"

"She is your link, the source of your power. Didn't you feel it when you touched her? I was in here and even *I* felt it. Powerful bond, it seems."

"What are you talking about?"

The house shook again. "There is too little time. Understand this, little Stražar: your sister *is* your power, as such your lives are linked now and forever. If you die, she dies. If she dies, you die. It's inconvenient, but power always has its drawbacks. The Yelmes will be hunting her, too, but she will be a dim light compared to you." She laughed. "Right now, you will be like a gods-forsaken lighthouse to them."

"What power? What are you talking about?"

"Oh, you look so adorably lost. All will become clear in time. For now, kill the Yelmes and don't die. But fear not, only think of me and I'll worm myself into your ear. You shall not be alone." Staradovna stepped forward as the house shook again. "Now, let's speed this up, shall we?" She placed a hand on Oli's chest, then shoved him, *hard*. He flew backward and into the wall, then the house disappeared.

FORTY-TWO

Léonie turned at the sound of Oli's scream.

He thrashed on the ground, not far from Tâl. The ranger backed away as Oli clawed at the ground, tossing soot and dirt into the air in a desperate attempt to grab at something only he could see.

"What is wrong with him?" Léonie snapped as she ran back towards them. "I told you to wake him up."

Tâl shook her head, then pulled her sword free. "I hadn't even tried to wake him yet."

Léonie stood over Oli as he thrashed, unsheathing her sword and leveling the tip toward him. His eyes were still closed, and he paid her no heed. His twisting and scratching began to slow however, calming down like someone waking from night terrors. Léonie understood then this may be the last time she would be able to take the Woodsman's life with ease. If she allowed him to come back, to return to consciousness, who knew what would happen? But Tâl's words echoed in her mind. For better or worse, Oli was the only potential weapon she had against the Yelmes.

But she had to learn to wield him.

Oli quieted now, still on the floor with eyes fluttering, though not fully open.

"Get up," Léonie said, barely restraining herself from kicking him as well.

He began to comply, sitting up slowly. But before he got to his feet, he began to retch and heave. He went to all fours and Léonie stepped backward in disgust as he vomited. It was a moment later before he stopped, breathing heavy and deep.

"I told you to rise," Léonie said.

Oli took one more deep breath, then spat on the ground. "Shut it."

Léonie clenched her fists, hissing air through her teeth as Oli stood up, his back to her. "I should end your pathetic life right now, but I have chosen mercy. Do you even realize what you have done? The Ancient One is dead. *Dead.* As is our hope of saving this kingdom."

Oli said nothing, though he did go still as Léonie spoke, head cocked to the side as though listening. After a while, Oli broke the silence with one, simple, question. "Where is she?"

It took Léonie a full three heartbeats to understand who he meant by "she". When she did understand, Léonie's blade faltered and she went silent. Neither she nor Tâl said a word.

Oli's head turned until he spotted the broken form of his mother. When he made his way towards her, Léonie finally looked away.

The sun was higher now and the ominous mystery of the Clearing lessened, replaced instead by the horror of black soil, hacked vines, and a few dozen dried bones Léonie had not noticed in the dimmer light of night. Suddenly, the wisps of green smoke that still lingered felt as if they may be the spirits of the dead. She turned when she heard Oli speaking, though his voice stayed too low for her to make out any words. On his knees, he cradled his mother, rocking back and forth like one of the time-telling pendulums back in the city.

"He will turn on us," Léonie said, her voice quiet. The hilt of her sword felt cold.

Tâl shook her head, eyes rimmed in black and the cut on her head purpling in a bruise. "I don't think he will."

Léonie prayed Tâl was right. If Oli blamed her for his mother's death, she doubted she and Tâl could kill him. It should be possible, the two of them against a mere hunter, but Oli had proved to be anything other than a mere hunter. He seemed incapable of dying, as though death itself would not take him. Even now as she watched, Léonie saw his clothes were a patchwork of holes, beneath which his skin should have contained hundreds of lacerations. But though the explosion had shredded his cloak and tunic, his body remained untouched by anything except old scars.

Léonie feared him.

Oli laid his mother down carefully, positioning her arms above her head with palms facing the sky, then gently closing her eyes—burial preparation. Then he pulled the cowl of his hood over his head and turned toward them. Tears glistened on his beard, but he did not look back at his mother as he approached Léonie and Tâl.

Léonie cleared her throat. "You have destroyed Trevelar's last hope of repelling the invasion from Kātsracha, Oli Ricker. Without the power of Staradovna, we are at the mercy of our enemy."

Oli said nothing, only stood, unmoving. She had expected a retort or an angry tirade. An attack, even.

She swallowed, then continued, "As payment for your crime, I command you to serve the crown in the fight against—"

"Have they attacked?" he asked, cutting her off.

Léonie paused. "What?"

"Have the Dark Ones attacked Watchful?"

Tâl spared her the need to reply. "Last night was the earliest we expected an attack. It's impossible to be sure, but it is likely."

Oli nodded. "Then I'm going back."

Léonie and Tâl shared a glance. "To fight the Yelmes?" Léonie asked.

"To find my sister."

Oli turned westward, but Tâl stepped forward, and grabbed for his shoulder. "Wait, Oli, we can—"

"Off me," Oli snapped, twisting from her grip. As he did, his cowl dropped back revealing his eyes.

Those eyes.

Tâl gasped and stumbled backward, raising her sword, but Léonie only stared.

"Maker help us," Tâl muttered. Then, louder, she said, "It's the sign of maiyea, Your Highness. He's possessed."

The Woodsman turned around as if looking to see if Tâl spoke to someone else. Then he looked back to Tâl. "Oy, what in the Twelve Hells ya talkin' about?"

Opportunity appeared like a flash before Léonie. It was faint, but she thought she saw a path forward, a way of pulling the Woodsman's strings just right. She stepped forward, sword low. "It is your eyes, Oli. They have changed." Oli snorted, but Léonie continued. "Take my blade and see your reflection for yourself." She held out the sword, offering him the handle. It was a reckless gamble, to give up her weapon, but Léonie's mind raced ahead, putting pieces —and a plan—together.

Maiyea, magic, was marked in a man by the change in their eyes. One eye would become vibrant, like yellow of the Yelmes, the other would become white and black. Centuries before, it had made purging the kingdom of magic a simple matter, if a bloody one. She did not know how, but in killing Staradovna Oli had inadvertently become imbued with maiyea.

Perhaps a magic so powerful it could defeat the Yelmes.

Léonie only needed to wield him in order to wield his power. Right now he would be confused, upset by the death of his mother and shocked by the change he had undergone somehow. He would never be more pliable than right now.

Oli stared at the proffered sword, looking as though he feared a trick. Eventually, slowly, he reached out his hand and took the handle of the blade.

CHAPTER

FORTY-THREE

E ver since Oli had woken up, the world had looked strange. Colored lines danced in his vision, bright and in focus. Everything else though looked dim in comparison, like looking through a muddied glass. Léonie and Tâl looked strange as well. They were themselves, but *more*, their bodies made up of lines of yellow and white light. Oli didn't look directly at them, unsure of what was going on and more than a little scared and confused.

And his mother—he couldn't think of her now.

The princess held her sword out towards him. Oli reached out and took the handle of the blade, its weight heavy and awkward. He'd never held a sword before, and he wasn't sure what to expect. He used his free hand to support the metal of the blade itself, holding the flat of it up towards his face like a mirror. It took a moment of twisting and turning the blade so he could see his reflection, but eventually his smudge-laden face came into focus. And on his face were set two terrible eyes that were not his own. He'd seen these eyes before, but they belonged to the tanner back home.

One was the green of a leaf with a flame burning behind it. The other was milky white, a small black dot in its center.

Anej's eyes, on Oli's face.

Or, not exactly like the velk's eyes, Oli realized. Anej's white had more black in it, like cracks shooting out from the center. And he had a blue eye, didn't he?

"Green, not yellow," Tâl muttered.

"What?" Oli looked up, suddenly hungry for whatever the ranger mumbled.

Tâl ignored him, turning to the princess. "The Yelmes carry the yellow eye."

"And the velk carry the blue." Léonie said. "Then what, in La'Azurus, does *his* mean?"

"Only that he has power, though *what* power, I cannot say."

Léonie snorted. "Oh, I think we can guess that, no?" She turned to the heart of the Clearing, then looked back at Oli. He'd dropped her sword, stepping back and shaking his head.

He had hoped it had all been a dream. The sand, Layla, the house, Staradovna—he had hoped none of it had been real. But it was, and the realization pressed down on him.

Léonie stepped forward and picked up her sword. "Woodsman, tell me what you see. Does the world appear . . . different?"

Oli focused on her. The yellow lines of light inside her bright and pulsing, outlining her whole body from toes to head. "I see lines. Swirls in the air. What's wrong with me?"

Léonie smiled. The creases of her lips were subtle, but impossible for Oli not to see. "I have only read of this, of course. But you can now see that which holds the universe together. The *Nema*, or Threads. Oh, to see what you do now . . ."

Oli hardly heard her, his mind racing through the last words Staradovna had said. The Yelmes would be looking for him. And worse, for Layla. "I have to get her out, I have to find her."

"Who, Oli?" Léonie said, voice softer than Oli had ever heard it.

"Layla. My sister. They . . . they'll be looking for her."

Léonie shook her head. "No, Oli, you do not need to get her out of Watchful."

Oli stepped back. "What do you know?"

Léonie raised a hand as though to calm a wild beast. "Your sister does need you, but not so that you can sweep her away. She needs you to return to the town and to fight. To *fight*, Oli. The Yelmes will kill her unless you destroy them."

It made sense, didn't it? If all the Yelmes were dead, then Layla would be safe. And hadn't Staradovna said something similar?

Léonie wasn't done. She pressed in, voice urgent and needy. "They want to kill her and every other person in this kingdom, Oli. They will never stop until all are dead. If you love your sister, if you want to save her, then you must kill the Dark Ones."

Oli laughed. The sound coming out bitter, leaving a foul taste in his mouth. He couldn't save his father, couldn't save his mother, he couldn't save anyone.

And yet, what else was there but to try? If he didn't save his sister, he had nothing. If he died trying, then at least that would be a mercy. Except, hadn't Staradovna said something about Oli and Layla being connected somehow.

Oli shook his head and breathed in deeply. "Where's my bow?"

CHAPTER
FORTY-FOUR

L ayla was screaming when she woke. Her skin must have been on fire, her whole body dipped in a furnace.

"Put her down, you oaf! Give her space."

The air around her shifted, and Layla felt the pain ebb away on her back as she was laid on something soft. But that didn't help her hands, her feet, or her face. She made to scream again, but this time it caught in her throat and she coughed.

"Calm down, lass. *Dihitcha. Meera.*" The voice rested on her like a blanket and a salve.

"It hurts," Layla said, wrestling her voice to try and calm it down. The pain ebbed some, but was still there. She feared it would flare up.

"Aye, but only for a little longer. You're over the worst of it." She knew that voice, it was Anej.

Knowing the velk hovered over her was a relief, her shoulders releasing their tension. It was still a long time before she opened her eyes, though. And when she did, she shut them again. The world had too much light, too much color.

"Ah, Miss Ricker! It's good to have you among the living. You know, I've read not everyone survives the connection."

"Ulian?" Layla squinted her eyes open a touch to see the bartender standing over her, pushing his spectacles further up his nose.

"It is! And I'm dreadfully glad to be on this adventure with you, I assure you."

"Uh-huh," Layla said, feeling like she understood Ulian about as well as usual. "Anej, where are we?"

Anej stood a couple paces back, scratching his chin. He looked up, touching a high branch with the tip of his blood-laden spear. "Oy, lass, tell me you don't know."

Layla sat up and looked around, her body shivering in pain and cold. They were on a rocky slope in the early morning light. Except a hundred leafless branches filtered and dimmed the sunlight. And on those branches scurried small creatures with soft bellies and hard, pointed mouths. Their arms looked like little fans, and they jumped —no, *flew*, from branch to branch. There were little brown critters too, scampering up tree trunks with swishing tails. And then there were a hundred other beasts as small as the nail on Layla's pinky, swarming everywhere, and coming in different shapes and colors: some red and dotted with black, a few were black and bulbous look-ing, others a sickly brown with a dried looking shell.

Animals. Bugs. Birds. Critters. Creatures. Beasts.

Words Layla had heard, but never understood. All of those things didn't exist inside Watchful. They existed only in the Wood, the place she was never to go. It was a dangerous place, a place of death.

"Oh, she looks sick. Do something, Anej!"

Anej dropped to one knee, face not far from Layla's. "Look at me. C'mon, eyes over here. That's a good lass."

Layla's lips had gone dry. "I want to go home."

Anej sighed, shaking his head. "You don't have a home no more, I'm afraid."

"Watchful didn't . . ."

"No, not that. Well, maybe that. The town's in shambles, but that ain't what I mean."

"Then what—"

Ulian clapped his hands together with excitement as though he were a child watching a puppet show. "You're being hunted! It's all rather exciting, though I imagine also rather disorienting."

Anej turned to the maeifa and growled, "Shut it, Ulian. Ya ain't helpin'." Then he looked back to Layla, eyes apologetic. "Oy, we ain't got much time. We best be gettin—"

"Tell me what's happening." Layla worked her way to her feet, knees giving way so she had to catch herself on a tree. The bark felt so thick and deep, she thought it may be able to cut her hand.

"This really ain't the time," Anej said. "But soon if—"

"Oy, it's the time if I say it is," Layla mumbled, looking Anej in those strange eyes of his.

He snorted. "You've got your mother's fire, when you want it." That caught Layla off guard, but Anej continued on without noticing. "Look, the Yelmes will catch your scent soon enough, and when they do I want us to be as close to the Roz as possible."

"Wait, the Razdelnice?" Layla's mind scrambled, trying to conjure up an image of one of her father's maps. How many times had she sat on his lap, watching his finger as it slid along old parchment, listening to the names of those places she could only dream of, would never see?

"Aye. It's on the other side of the West Nevihta. We'll need to cross it, and it's best to do it before—"

"My scent?"

"Huh?"

"You said they'd catch my scent?"

"Oy, I did. The thing is lass, your brother he—"

Ulian waved his hand, stepping forward eagerly, bouncing on his toes. "He has somehow absorbed the incredible powers of the Ancient One! Which is remarkable; though, rather unfortunate for you, of course." Anej's glare made Ulian take a handful of steps backward.

Layla shrugged. "I didn't understand a word of that. But you're talking 'bout Oli? I saw him . . . did you say he killed Starmoda?"

"Staradovna," Anej said, gently placing a hand on her shoulder. "And oy, do I wish that Oli had killed her, but that wasn't ever in the cards. No, lass, he released her."

"Released? Like, she was trapped?"

"For near a thousand years, and until your brother did what your father wanted to. Though, I don't think he understands a bit of it. And here's the thing, somethin' like the Ancient One needs a, well, a home. And your brother, knowin' it or not, just became that."

Ulian coughed. "Some may call it a sort of possession."

Anej nodded. "And . . . that ain't all." Layla said nothing, just tried to stay upright as the world shifted. Anej continued on. "Where the Ancient One goes, so does her power."

"Power?" she asked, the word coming out numb and slow. Memories of the desert, the tree, and Oli began to come back to her like an ugly dream. Oli had scared her, and then he'd burned her. Her skin still tingled.

"Aye. More than you could fathom, right now."

"Ain't this what the princess wanted?"

"Well, I doubt the princess had this in mind, exactly," Anej said. "And things aren't ever simple, lass. Your brother can wield an ungodly amount of maiyea now, but all magic is ruthless. Costly. And you never really know the price when you get started." Anej leaned closer, his breath smelling of pipe weed, his eyes squinting like the words he spoke pained him. "Your brother has become a Spindle, able to weave the disparate Threads of life into concrete and chaotic powers. And you are his Connection, his link to life, and his last source of power."

"And what's that supposed to mean? I'm his source of power?"

Anej breathed through his nose, flaring his nostrils. "All life is made up of Threads, impossible to see for most. A Spindle can take the energy around them and spin it into what they want it to be. The Yelmes use this to make lightning and fire. But the power to wield those Threads to make lightning must come from somewhere. A strong Spindle can pull it from the plants or lives around him, but it always starts with a Connection. A person connected by blood who —" he paused, breathing slow for a moment. "A person who will be their first and last source of life."

"Ya make me sound like a ball of yarn," Layla said. "Like I'm just these Threads my brother is gonna pull on to work magic."

"Too close to it, I'm afraid."

"So your sayin' Oli will, what? Unravel my life Threads?" The words felt strange in Layla's mouth. "That don't make no sense."

Ulian stepped forward. "It's *your* life he is tethered to, Miss Ricker. When in need, he will pull your life force away and turn it into energy. A miraculous process still without any academically agreed upon scientific basis. It's truly incredible that—" Ulian caught Anej's gaze and stepped back again. "Actually, there isn't really time for this, is there?"

Anej grunted. "Here's why this matters now, lass. The Yelmes will figure out you're Oli's Connection. They'll sense it soon enough. When they do, they'll figure that killin' you is the easiest way to killin' him. You're linked now."

Layla shook her head. "Oli would never hurt me. He'd never drain my whatever you called it."

Anej lifted a hand up to touch his eye. Not the blue one, but the white and broken one. "I don't think any of us knows what we will and won't do, in the end. But either way, we should get you to safety. That's what your brother would want."

"And how is runnin' through the Wood *safe*?"

Ulian smiled wide. "Oh, it isn't the journey that is safe. We may not survive, actually. But the destination, Miss Ricker. We're off to Velik!"

CHAPTER
FORTY-FIVE

Oli had escaped the Wood along this same path once before. But back then, he had run *from*, and now he ran *to*.

Eleven years before, he had run from danger, terror, and death—the image of his mangled father chasing him all the way. None of that had changed, all this time later. He was still afraid and still leaving the dead behind. But it wasn't fear for his own life that he ran now. He ran to his sister, and the slim hope that maybe—just maybe—he could finally save someone.

It was this new power giving him this hope. The evidence of it manifested everywhere, for the Wood did not appear the same as it had been for him hours ago. Before, he had been an interloper, understanding the warning signs and paths only enough to stay barely ahead of the Wood and its traps. But now, he could *feel* everything all around him, all at once.

Or maybe "sense" was a better word for it.

It was the feeling of someone familiar walking up behind him. Even if he couldn't see them, an awareness of their presence would be palpable in the familiar smell, the sound of their steps, the rhythm of their breathing, the way their shadow shifted in the corner of his vision. Familiar even if unseen.

That's how the Wood was now. It wasn't a seeing exactly, but a deeper knowing.

He could sense moles and badgers burrowing in holes nearby, giant cats prowling in the treetops, a fox fleeing, and a whole colony of spiders skittering about wildly. He could sense the trees too, and their roots tunneled beneath dirt and soil.

An entire world laid bare for him to sift through with only a mere thought.

But though he could sense the Wood, only the vines noticed him in return. He could feel them constantly leaning towards him, their presence thick upon the forest. But it wasn't antagonistic like before —they didn't want to trap him. Instead, they *bowed* to him. No longer did they reach out and try to trip or ensnare him, but they made a path before him with their tips pointed downward in submission. And they looked different now, too. Still green and thorny, still pulsing with purple blood, but now the vines swirled with red lines of light, vibrant and beautiful against the dark canopy above. Like the light he had seen in Léonie and Tâl, but red and pulsing.

Still, despite those changes, the sight of the vines made his skin crawl and itch. He gave them a wide berth whenever he could.

Oli made it to the Wall while still at a dead sprint. He felt good, energized and strong. Nothing had gotten in his way, nothing had even tried to stop him. He scrambled up a low, broken part of the Wall and leapt down. Frigid wind pushed against him, reminding him the world outside of the Deep was still on the edge of winter.

He almost began running again, but paused.

His sense of the Deep had left him, as if the Wall were a divider of more than just stone. All the beasts and vines he had felt moments before, had suddenly disappeared. In their place was a whole host of new sensations stretched out before him. It disoriented him and he fell to one knee as his mind tried to take it all in.

Like a finger tracing a map, his mind traced the world spread out before him, sensing and cataloguing what he found. The vines appeared weaker here, thinner and less active. In fact, there was less life in general, compared to what he'd sensed in the Deep. But his senses also stretched further, and he could feel the awareness taper away into the distance. It seemed like standing on a hilltop, watching the world fade into the horizon.

Oli stood and tried to keep moving, but he made it only two steps before his head pounded with a new awareness. Something approached from ahead, something he had no name for, yet he felt as though he should know. When he focused his mind on that presence, his imagination conjured up images of rot and maggots, but he also felt the same pulse of vibrance as he had in the vines.

"What in Damnation are those," Oli muttered, his breath misting before him.

The Yelmes, of course.

The thought was not his, but came from elsewhere, as though someone had planted the words in his imagination. He knew who it was, and at the thought his mind reeled with anger. Staradovna, it seemed, could speak.

Oli hissed. "*You.*"

Oh, darling, don't be angry, this is harder than you think.

"Get out."

Easier said than done. And besides, you will need me.

Oli wanted to argue, to threaten and rage. But Layla was back in Watchful and ancient monsters stood between him and her.

And maybe, just maybe, he really did need Staradovna in order to save his sister.

With a grunt, Oli took off westward, chasing that foreboding sense in the distance.

The smell of ozone filled the air, and Oli could faintly hear the crackling of lightning. It felt like walking into a storm, though minus the wind and rain. He ran faster, perhaps faster than he had ever before. His whole body teemed with energy and life without end. It was intoxicating and comforting, and he felt his confidence surge.

Who could stop him?

A few moments later, he caught sight of one of the Yelmes for the first time.

In one regard, they looked like mere humans in poor clothing and weathered cloaks. Except they were clearly more than just *mere* humans. Their hands and swords crackled with energy, and the lines of light flowed through their bodies. They each had one eye that burned bright yellow, gleaming beneath the shadow of their cowls, just as Tâl had said.

He could see two of them running toward him, weaving around trees, but he sensed more in the distance. Four, maybe? He wasn't certain.

Just get close, darling.

Oli nocked an arrow.

He had no intention of getting anywhere close to someone with a sword, no matter what Staradovna said. Still running, Oli would be close enough to shoot an arrow in moments. But before he got the chance, one of the two Yelmes lifted a horn to her lips and blew. The sound reverberated through the trees and birds scattered from the branches high above, chirping and cawing as they went.

Oli could see the lines of light in the Yelmes better now. It was similar to the lines he had seen in Tâl and the princess: each made up of a complex web of white and yellow lights, except for their hands and weapons. Those were covered in lights of bright red, like those in the vines.

Get close, Staradovna said, the words pushy and urgent.

Oli loosed his first arrow. He'd aimed it at the one with the horn, right at the base of her throat. She sidestepped it easily, dropping her horn back to her side. The other Dark One, a broad-shouldered man with thick braids in his hair, charged. As he ran, he swiped his free arm forward and a streak of lightning seared the air and shattered a tree a half dozen paces to Oli's right. There was a *pop-crack* and the world became light and noise.

"Ah!" Oli cried, stumbling backward.

He couldn't see, everything was white and blurred, as though he'd been staring into the sun. Blind, he'd be cut to pieces and he wouldn't even be able to fight back. He blinked over and over trying to clear his vision, but nothing more than vague shapes formed before him.

The Threads are still bright, little Stražar. Use them!

Oli blinked and looked again. The world still appeared all blurred and pale, but Staradovna had been right. The lines of light inside the Yelmes stayed clearly visible, easy to make out in the vines in the treetops and forest floor and in the moving shape running toward him. Off to the side, dissipating fast from the lightning strike, floated a thousand little black lines.

Reach out and snap their Threads. They're close and unguarded. Fools, they have sent children after us.

Her words didn't make sense. Oli hadn't the slightest clue what it meant to snap a Thread, all he knew now was he could at least make out the enemy. He backed up, nocking another arrow. He couldn't see his bow well, but he let instinct guide him and loosed at the Yelmes charging him. The lines of light flinched, and Oli thought he even saw a small white one break. But the figure kept coming, new red lights swirling into existence.

Stop waiting. Reach out and snap its Threads!

"I don't know *how.*"

If you can see them, you can break them.

The Yelmes closed in and Oli's vision had cleared enough to see it as a black blob bearing down on him. With a cry, Oli tossed aside his bow, pulled his knife free, and dug the toe of his boots into the dirt to brace himself. Oli could make out the man's sword hefted into the air, ready to strike. Oli leapt forward, thrusting his shoulder into its midsection before it could bring its blade to bear. He couldn't win a sword fight with a knife, but Oli could bring the fight to the ground where his knife would work to his advantage. Oli grabbed and twisted the man about until his feet lost balance, then Oli shifted his weight and slammed him to the ground, sliding his knife up towards his throat. The Yelmes grabbed Oli's wrists, keeping the knife at bay as Oli leaned his weight into the handle, driving it slowly downward.

Oli's vision had mostly returned, and he could see the Yelmes' eyes now. They were not unlike Anej's, except the bright blue had been swapped for a fiery yellow. And there was fear there, the kind of fear that came from seeing death. Oli had expected a monster, a beast like the wolves and bears of the Wood.

He hadn't expected the Yelmes to be so much like *him*.

Snap his Threads, you fool.

Oli could see the lines of light more closely now. They truly were as thin as thread, though the brilliance of their light made them look larger at first. They moved of their own accord, and they were incredibly long. What Oli had mistaken for many little Threads was actually a complex weaving of one or two long Threads. The white twisted and twirled around the man's midsection, the yellow more around his face, arms, and legs. Oli could feel the power of the red Thread hovering around the man's hands like heat from a fire. It seemed to have substance, like it was more than just light.

The tip of Oli's blade closed in on the man's throat, slowly breaking skin. In a moment his muscles would give and—

Oli leapt backward as a sword slashed through the air where his head had been. He rolled on the ground and stood, the woman with the horn bearing down on him with another strike. Oli dodged to the side and then tried to tackle her like he'd done with the man, but she dodged and sliced him along the shoulder, forcing him to spin away.

Cut their Threads before they tear you to pieces!

"How?"

The woman sidestepped around Oli, forcing him to put his back to either her or the man stumbling to his feet. And that wasn't even the worst of it. Oli could sense the other four closing in on them, moments away.

Look at your hand.

Oli dropped his gaze. Around his fingers floated a small red streamer of light. It wasn't much, but it danced with power.

Use it.

Realization dawned as Oli saw the red light. He wasn't sure if it had always been there, or if he'd somehow taken it from the Yelmes when he'd had him pinned. But it was there now, and it quickly formed itself into the shape of a knife without any command or impulse from Oli.

The woman shifted her feet, readying for a lunge. As fast as he could manage, Oli flung his arm forward, throwing the Thread-knife toward the mass of white light at the woman's center. The Thread-knife jolted forward, faster than any arrow Oli had ever shot, and ripped apart the mass of white Threads in the Yelmes.

Layla screamed, clutching at her head as pain leapt through her.

"What's wrong with her?" Ulian's asked, voice distant.

"The Spindle is spinning," Anej grunted, lifting her into the air, cradling her like a child. "We have to keep moving."

"Her nose is bleeding. Is that normal?"

"Aye. It's her first time."

"Will she die?"

"No. Not yet."

"How much of this can she take?"

"Forget it, Ulian, just keep moving."

The Yelmes woman's eyes went wide and her mouth slack as she crumpled. The lightning around her palms faded, and the red Threads dispersed into the air.

Grab them.

Oli reached out for one of those red lights and it shot toward him, wrapping itself around his hand.

The other Yelmes scrambled to his feet, the broken shaft of an arrow sticking out from his chest. Red Threads spun around the wound, filling in the broken gaps of yellow and white lines. Oli had just started to turn toward him when the man let out a savage cry and threw his sword toward Oli, who stumbled backward as the blade spun wildly by. The Yelmes didn't let Oli recover, but spun his hands in a complex maneuver, sending lightning and red lines shooting out towards Oli.

Without thinking, Oli dropped to the ground and covered his ears and closed his eyes as the world exploded in light and sound. He could hear a tree shatter, and Oli opened his eyes to see a tree fall between him and the man, spraying Oli in chips of wood. Everything smelt of smoke, fire, and ozone.

The Yelmes leapt over the tree trunk before it had fully settled, his hands stretched out towards Oli. Throwing his hands out, Oli screamed and shot the red Threads around his hand outward. This time, he didn't send a sharp, knife-like set of Threads, but a haphazard ball of force which knocked the man into a tree a few paces away. Oli didn't wait but scrambled over to the Yelmes before he could recover, driving his knife downward and ending the Yelmes's life.

Oli stood back up, heart racing and hands covered in red light and blood.

He looked around, sensing the four others before he saw them a bowshot away. They approached cautiously, giving Oli wide berth as they spread out, working to surround him. Two had almost killed him more than once; he doubted he'd survive fighting all four.

Take power from within. You have it to spare.

Oli clenched his fists and looked down. More red lines appeared around his fists, summoned from thin air. He felt as if he pulled them from a distant place, tugging them slightly until they pulled free and flowed around him.

The four Yelmes charged in unison, coming from all sides with lightning and swords.

Oli shaped the Threads into daggers and threw them out as before. It felt easy, almost effortless. All four of the Dark Ones collapsed moments later, their white and yellow Threads snapped, leaving only the red Threads behind to squirm in the air like worms.

In a moment, a heartbeat, they were all dead.

Their Threads are your boon. Take. It is the Cycle.

And Oli did. As simple as breathing, he held out a hand and pointed to each corpse, one after another, collecting the red wisps as they began to fade. When he finished, his hands and arms swirled with power, latent energy filling his bones. It thrilled him in a way nothing ever had before.

He could save Layla with this. He could fight these monsters and princesses and anything else that threatened them. He could snap anyone's Threads and leave them lifeless with nothing but a thought and the flick of his wrist.

For the first time in his life, Oli had power.

CHAPTER

FORTY-SIX

Léonie and Tâl marched in silence. Whatever evil havoc the Wood usually wreaked, it did none of it now. No wolves, bears, or vines hindered their way, though Léonie and Tâl stayed cautious enough to follow carefully behind the Woodsman's footsteps. It was not difficult; he had run with little care for the trail he made.

Léonie and Tâl also took little care, for their fatigue dragged at their steps and pulled them down. If the Woodsman's path had taken them into any form of danger, whether beast or trap, they would have died.

Gurgling water sounded nearby, and though their waterskins hung empty at their sides, they gave the stream a wide berth. Léonie's lips were parched, her throat dry, and her stomach ached. Every step was pain and she repeatedly tripped because she did not pick up the toes of her boots far enough to avoid rocks and roots. They passed the place where Victer and Fjord died. The ground laid bare, stripped of any evidence of their fight or their companions.

When they finally reached the Wall, Léonie leaned against it and did her best to catch her breath.

"M'lady?" Tâl said, leaning close. "Are you alright?"

"We have miles to go yet," Léonie said, the words heavy as she spoke them. "I must lighten my load if I intend to make it." There was little for her to lighten other than her sword and chainmail, and she refused to part with her sword. It took a few awkward moments, but eventually she peeled away the scraps of cloth that had formed her outer tunic so she could lift the chainmail from her shoulders. She dumped it to the ground where it curled itself into a flat, ball-like shape. Then she removed the gambeson, the padded shirt she'd worn beneath the chainmail.

She stood there in nothing more than a thin, white shirt, made nearly see-through because of her sweat.

Tâl put a hand on one of the stones of the wall and used it to stretch her back. "This forest is different now. It's more . . ." she trailed off.

"Normal."

"Yes, but I wonder why."

"The number of questions I have is growing," Léonie said. "But I have a distinct feeling there shall be little in the way of answers."

"Perhaps," Tâl said. "But we are halfway there, so we shall soon find out." She moved toward a section of wall rising just barely above their heads. They would need to climb upward to make it out of the Deep. It should be a small matter, but Léonie dreaded it.

"And what will we find when we arrive in Watchful, I wonder," Léonie mused. "Captain Thibault standing upon a pile of Yelmes corpses, or will we find a burned village and an angry woodsman?"

"Perhaps just Yelmes," the ranger said.

"And that would be a swift death."

They worked their way over the crumpled section of Wall, and as Léonie landed on the other side she felt the full force of the winter breeze. "Of course it would be freezing," she muttered, wrapping her arms around herself and rubbing for warmth.

"Here, m'lady." Tâl removed her cloak and held it to Léonie.

Léonie almost waved it away, but then she nodded and took it. The warmth it provided was minimal, but better than nothing. "I had nearly forgotten it was winter. Snow will fall soon."

"I can smell it on the air," Tâl said. "We have days, perhaps."

Léonie nodded. She could smell it too. "Snowfall is the last thing we need."

"The road back to Turris Regis will be terrifying enough, but snow may make it a death march, Your Highness."

Léonie sighed. "Let us be off, ranger. One death march at a time."

"Deōs help us." Tâl had walked ahead, eyes fixed on something behind a large tree.

"What?" Léonie asked, not bothering to quicken her pace.

Tâl shook her head. "Yelmes, Your Highness. Dead ones."

Birds chirped harmlessly in the treetops above as Léonie approached, her hand wrapped around the hilt of her sword involuntarily. A Dark One in the form of a man lay on its back, eyes lifeless, mouth agape. There was no blood, though. No wound Léonie could see at all. With her boot, Léonie rolled the corpse over with a kick, checking the back.

"Died of shock?" Léonie wondered aloud.

"Not unless they all did," Tâl said.

Léonie looked up and saw a handful of other dead Yelmes littering the ground around them. At least one bore a bloody wound —an arrow in his chest—but the rest appeared to have simply lain down and died. A tree had cracked and fallen in the midst of all of them, blackened and fried at the break.

"Did Oli do this?" Tâl asked. "These are his tracks, and the way the leaves are disturbed shows a struggle. And the tree, of course."

Léonie shook her head. "Perhaps Deōs has not forsaken us after all."

"I wonder if it is right to attribute Oli's power to the Maker," Tâl said. Then she put her fingers to her forehead in prayer and mumbled to herself in Badaui.

"Come," Léonie said. "Deōs or not, our Woodsman has power. And that power is a little hope, at least."

CHAPTER
FORTY-SEVEN

Layla marched alongside Anej, rubbing her arms to fight off the cold. Her sword jostled alongside her. She wasn't sure if she should be grateful or disgusted Anej had thought to bring it.

It had been a few hours since she had collapsed in pain. It had come suddenly, an immobilizing throbbing in her head that brought her to her knees and had blood running from her nose and ears. Her hands had gone warm as though they'd been shoved near the heat of a fire. A coppery taste still hung in her mouth from where she'd bitten her tongue.

"It's your brother," Anej had said when she could walk again. "He's spinning power."

"What does that mean?"

"It means he's takin' life from you. Slowly. You have more to give than you think, though I'm not sure that's good news."

"He wouldn't do that to me."

"He's just as lost as you, lass. Bet he doesn't have the slightest clue what he's done."

"We should find him, then. Tell him."

"No."

And the conversation had ended there. If Layla had known where to go, how to find her brother, she would have. But she didn't even know where she was. All she knew is she trudged somewhere in the Wood, east of her home and far from safety. And besides, Anej may be the only one who could keep her safe from the Yelmes.

She had always expected the Wood to be an exciting, if dangerous, place: filled to the brim with creatures, bird songs, and something trying to kill you. That's what her father had told her and what she had believed. But after a couple hours of walking, of the never-ending onslaught of trees, and the chirping of birds above, the world seemed to grow irritating and oppressive.

"You know," Ulian said, seeming to read her thoughts. "I'd have thought with all the drama built up around the Vromia, things would be more . . ."

"Dangerous?" Layla said. "Less boring?"

Ulian gave a "humph" and nodded. His spectacles jostled on his face as he walked, legs moving twice as fast as Layla's in order to keep up. Anej walked out front a dozen paces, a pack on his back so large it looked like a load that could have weighed down a wheelbarrow. He'd pulled a thick fur coat from it sometime ago, draping it over Layla's shoulders. It hung like a weight on her and the hem dragged along the ground, but it kept her plenty warm even as the air grew colder.

"It isn't the Wood that's the danger now," Anej said from over his shoulder.

"Oy, how's that?" Layla asked.

Ulian clicked his tongue. "Vergrinch had hypothesized the displays of maiyea that demonstrated themselves as enchanted flora and fauna within the Vromia were rooted in the presence of one single entity. He thought if you removed said entity, such displays would also be removed."

"You don't know how to speak plain, do ya?" Layla asked, narrowing her eyes.

"All I mean is, the power of the Wood was bound up in a single entity. A being, as it were."

"Staradovna."

"Yes, and if that bright green light has told us anything, it is that Staradovna's power is no longer reaching its fingers out through the Wood. It is safe now, in a way."

Layla nodded. Anej had told her about the light and her fainting. He'd put two and two together then, and swooped her off eastward. "There is one thing that don't make sense about all this," Layla said. "Why is Oli connected to me? If it's about blood ties, why not my ma? Ain't she just as close?"

Anej faltered. "Connections aren't always predictable. Nothing about magic is, really."

Layla nodded, though the way Ulian chewed on the inside of his mouth told her there was more they weren't saying. She wasn't stupid though. The moment her mother had gone into the Wood, Layla had figured she wouldn't come back. If she had died, then Layla would grieve later.

"Hmm," Ulian said from beside her. "I think our giant friend is acting rather odd."

Anej stood a few paces ahead of them, motionless, his head cocked to the side. Layla opened her mouth to ask him if everything was alright, when he dropped his pack and lay on the ground. He turned to them, grunting, "Get down."

Layla threw herself onto the ground, forearms lost in the thick leaves. They had been climbing up a gentle incline, flat rocks sticking out from the ground here and there. The trees crowded one another, and Layla couldn't see anything beyond a dozen paces.

They lay there, Layla's breath shifting the mound of leaves before her. Ulian muffled a cough and suffered a glare from Anej, but otherwise the moment passed without event.

Eventually, Anej sighed and stood. "Oy, right then, I guess it was nothing. C'mon, let's—"

A *crack* split the air and a light exploded around them. Anej spun, flinging his shield around and battering away a bolt of lightning, reflecting it upward so it split the top of a walnut and sent a massive chunk of the bough to the forest floor. Everything became a riot of sounds and flashes of light that drowned out every other sound and color in the world.

"Dark Ones," Ulian hissed, pressing himself further into the ground as though to crawl beneath the leaves.

Two Yelmes leapt from the cover of a patch of brush, charging Anej. Their swords blurred, forcing the velk backward as the blows hammered his shield. He tried to jab at them with his spear, but they came on relentlessly.

Layla scrambled to her feet, the fur cloak dropping from her shoulders. Her heart raced as she tried to pull the sword free from its sheath. It took a terribly long moment for her hand to stop shaking enough to grab it. It stuck from the cold, but after a pair of rough yanks, Layla got the sword free.

And there she was, standing just nine paces away from the three fighters, her sword in her hand. She did not move, could not fathom what she should do now. Standing and fighting had felt right, but this was not like back in Watchful. Layla knew she should help, but what could she do? And if Anej died now, where would she be?

Anej roared, thrusting his shield forward and pushing one of the Yelmes back, but the other flanked wider around to the side and Anej had to step back or become surrounded. He moved downhill, back towards Layla and Ulian.

For the briefest of moments, Layla thought to turn and run. Anej was buying her time, and she could flee north like she had planned. But if Anej was right, and she did not doubt him, then the Yelmes would hunt her down. She needed Anej to survive.

And Anej needed her.

Unsure what else to do, Layla ran up to the giant and placed the palm of her hand firm on his back. "I'm here," she yelled, voice cracking.

Anej didn't respond. Instead, he waited until the Yelmes on his right, a pale man with a patchwork beard, stepped in for a blow. Then Anej dropped his spear and grabbed the fighter by the elbow in one motion. The man yelped as Anej yanked him, forcing him to stumble toward Layla, eyes wide in surprise. Layla was already swinging her sword, her blade coming down hard and fast, stopping only when it hit bone. She didn't look at what she'd done, only kept herself behind Anej who turned toward the second fighter. Anej put a hand behind his back, pulling his dagger free. The last Yelmes stood little chance after that. With only one enemy, Anej's barrage became merciless. His shield turned into a club, battering down until his blade found an opening.

The man screamed, then silence followed.

"Ya did good, lass," Anej said, wiping the blood from his knife onto his pant leg. "Here, give me that, or the blood will freeze in the sheath." He took Layla's sword and carefully did the same, wiping the blood clean.

She stood, crying, but did her best to ignore the tears. How she felt didn't matter, only that they were all right. And right now, they were all right.

"Brilliant," Ulian said, holding the heavy cloak out to Layla. "Both of you, brilliant!"

"Just shut it," Layla mumbled, putting her sword away. She took the cloak from Ulian and handed it back to Anej for now. She didn't want to feel warm or comfortable or good. She wanted the pain of the cold, for the wind to nip and bite and hurt.

Anej took the cloak and sighed. "There'll be more after this. They sense the Connection. We better make haste."

"How much further do you think?" Ulian asked, stumbling ahead of the others.

Anej shrugged. "We'll march through the night, but by sundown tomorrow we'll have to make camp. If the Maker is with us, we should get to the mountain pass the day after."

"Make camp with the Yelmes after us?" Layla asked.

"Oy, even a velk can only go so long without sleep. Now, Ulian, climb on up here. We'll make better time if your stubby legs aren't holdin' us back."

FORTY-EIGHT

Oli encountered more Yelmes in groups of threes and fours. He had slung his bow over his back, no longer bothering with it. He had a new weapon—one which made him almost heady with power.

Like smoke on the breeze, Oli could smell out the Yelmes now. They were strange and distinct compared to everything else he could sense. Whenever he felt a group of them, he charged in their direction, falling upon them at a sprint and ripping through their Threads with hardly any effort. More red strands would waft up from their bodies, and he'd take those and keep on.

He did this again and again.

Of all the encounters, only one Yelmes fighter had escaped. A thin-framed thing with her hair in a bun and a song on her lips. Oli cut down her companion, but when he'd sent a blast of power at her she'd dodged away and ran off. If Oli hadn't known better, he thought she'd *deflected* his Thread-knife.

Maybe she had. What was possible with this power?

Oli knew enough to know he knew less than nothing. He didn't understand what he did or even what he was. He knew only that, for years, he had trudged in and out of a maddeningly evil Wood, barely surviving day-to-day. He'd never understood that either. If he were honest, he had only ever been following his father.

He hadn't bothered to chase the woman. She wasn't between him and Layla and so she didn't matter.

Faster than he could have thought possible, Oli neared the tree-line as the sun began its afternoon descent.

And he laughed. He wasn't sure why, but it felt right to be happy. Something had finally, in all his years, gone *right*. He'd flown out of the Wood in good time, unhindered even by the demons of Kātsracha. Who could stop him? Finally, after all this time, he would *save* someone. He would find Layla, and then he could protect her and take care of them both.

But as Oli stepped out of the Wood and onto wheat-colored grass, he stopped laughing.

Fires burned in small patches through the potato fields, and what wasn't currently on fire had been scorched black. The large buildings, which had once corralled manic animals, were largely destroyed as well: cows, donkeys, chickens, and goats roamed free and aimless. *That* was odd. Each of them should have been in the Wood by now, drawn by the Call. And stranger still, Oli could hear birdsongs *outside* the Wood. Birds danced in the sky, far above in the thin clouds.

Oli hadn't known they could fly so high.

But down on the ground, the lowest stretches of Watchful smoldered with black smoke rising like incense. He had gotten there too late, though he should have known. He wouldn't have encountered Yelmes in the Wood if they hadn't destroyed Watchful first.

Except, Watchful wasn't burnt to the ground entirely. The three Wardens stood, untouched. The mansions looked down upon the wreckage below them with the same disinterest as the Hilltoppers themselves might. And it wasn't just the Wardens, but most of the homes further up the hill still stood.

But there *had* been fighting, which meant there had been dying. And Layla was in there somewhere.

Oli made the trek into town quickly, ignoring the stares from haggard soldiers. Everyone looked worse for the wear, covered in soot or blood, or both. Most of the homes at the bottom of the hill were gone entirely, nothing more than a few blackened beams. It got slightly better as he followed the road upward, but even that was still bad. Yelmes bodies had been haphazardly stacked in piles to the side, debris lay everywhere, and men and women carried buckets of water from the wells in a daze, dumping them on the remaining flames throughout town. They let the fields burn.

Oli could see everyone twice: once with his eyes and again with this new sense. He could still feel the presence of others further away, but outside the Wood his power felt dimmer, as if his sense was muddied or muffled. Though he tried, he couldn't seem to sense Layla, though he had no reason to think he would be able to tell her apart from any other person.

Still, his heart raced faster the further up he went, his gut twisting at the thought that he wouldn't find her among the living.

He began shouting her name.

The Downwind rested in ashes, but his home remained miraculously intact. Oli sprinted for the door, pushing through a gaggle of people who cursed in his wake. He didn't care.

The door hung ajar, but he slammed it open the rest of the way so hard a hinge broke.

"Layla!"

Darkness greeted him.

Oli panted, looking around the home, ready to begin toppling furniture as if he'd find his sister hiding beneath the cot or table, but it looked as if someone had already done that. The table lay sideways, sheets were scattered, the contents of the bookshelf mostly on the floor. A bloody knife lay near the fireplace beside a red blanket in a lump.

Oli stopped.

There were white Threads—faint but visible—coming from within the blanket on the floor.

"Fool," Oli said, tears already filling his eyes. He knew who it was. "Tuck, I'm such a bloody fool!"

He approached slowly, kneeling beside Tuck as carefully as he could. The pup's eyes opened, but there was little life left in him. When was the last time he'd even considered the dog? The bandage Anej had given him looked redder than his fur, and much of him was covered in the soot and ash from the burning outside. His nose had dried and cracked; his tongue lolled from his mouth.

"I'm so sorry." Oli lifted Tuck into his lap, running his fingers through the fur on his head, scratching behind his ears. The white Threads weren't merely faint, they were broken, snapped entirely in a dozen places. "I'm a fool."

Oli had forgotten about him. He hadn't meant to, but he had. His life had been shaken upside down, and his sister had consumed his thoughts so much he'd spared none wondering where Tuck was or *how* he was.

Anej was supposed to take care of Tuck, though Oli wasn't sure why he'd trusted the tanner. The velk had probably bolted when the Yelmes arrived, stopping only long enough to ensure Tuck didn't die inside his cabin. The thought of Anej dumping Tuck here to die angered him, and that anger only widened and grew. Anej wasn't the only one at fault. The princess had dragged him away and, ultimately, gotten his mother killed. None of it would have happened if his father had been here, but he'd been too stupid and too ambitious, and he'd gotten himself killed.

None of it was fair and none of it was right.

And Oli was no better than any of them. The self-loathing appeared right there, easy for Oli to grab and wield against himself. He was as much an idiot as his father, had gotten his mother killed as much as the princess had, and he had treated Tuck far worse than Anej. He deserved to watch his friend die.

He deserved worse.

It was Tuck who'd done nothing wrong. And Layla too. The two of them were the victims in the end.

Oli squeezed Tuck hard, gritting his teeth to keep back the rest of the tears. Tuck wriggled in his grasp, squirming and pushing at Oli's chest, but Oli held harder and harder.

Tuck barked.

The sound was so loud Oli jumped and nearly threw Tuck as he did. But the moment he eased his hold on Tuck, the dog twisted in his lap and licked Oli's face, scouring his neck, chin, and cheek with his coarse tongue.

"What? Tuck, how?" But Oli didn't care. He cried in earnest now, letting Tuck lick him and paw at his chest. Through the tears he could see Tuck's Threads and understood, if only a little, what had happened. In all the places where Tuck's white Threads had snapped, red Threads had been grafted in to connect the bonds. He had seen that Yelmes do it to himself after the arrow wound, and somehow he had done it for Tuck.

All the red Threads which had been floating around his hand moments before were gone.

I healed him. Oli stared at those Threads inside Tuck even as the dog continued to lick and scratch at his chest, begging for his attention. *I healed.*

Is this what the priests did? Is this how their miracles worked?

A shadow fell over Oli from the doorway. He turned to see Captain Thibault standing there, sword in hand. Blood had caked along the toes of his boots and his surcoat was torn in a dozen places. Soot smeared across his face and his eyes looked bloodshot.

"Welcome home," Thibault said. "Now, where is Princess Baudelaire?"

CHAPTER
FORTY-NINE

"She's in the Wood," Oli said, flinging his cowl low over his head as he stood. No one had noticed his eyes yet, and Oli wasn't sure he wanted them to, especially since the captain looked all too ready for a fight.

Thibault stepped forward, his boot thunking on the wooden floorboard. The captain's eyes looked wild, his hands dirty, the hair of his beard flaked with grime. Oli spied Lady Amandine behind him, still looking as pristine as ever. "If she's in the Wood then you should be with her."

"I took her where she wanted to go." Oli said. "Now I'm back for my sister."

Thibault's face twitched and the tip of his sword rose slightly. The blade was badly dinged, but it had been cleaned and looked sharp. "Your sister is alive."

"You've seen her?" Oli stepped forward and Thibault's sword shifted. "Where is she?"

The captain narrowed his eyes on Oli. "I'll say no more until I see the princess alive and well."

Oli gritted his teeth, hand dancing near the knife on his hip. His new power was gone now, the red Threads used up to heal Tuck. He had conjured them from nothing before, but he had no idea how to do it again. Tuck growled dangerously, crouching beside Oli. Thibault stepped backward, nearly stepping on Amandine's feet.

"Your princess is in the Wood," Oli said. "She was alive when I left her. Go get her, if you want."

Before Thibault could reply, Lady Amandine grabbed his shoulder, the rings on her fingers clinking against the exposed chainmail. "Oli," she said. "Please forgive us, but the princess's well-being is vital for Trevelar. And, as you can imagine, we are all rattled from the battle. Perhaps, as a loyal subject of the crown, you could provide the captain with more details?"

Loyal subject. Even Oli understood the threat in those words. He spat on the floorboards between them, catching sight of Tuck. He almost felt he could see Thibault through the hound's eyes, smell Amandine's perfume through his nose.

"I'm as loyal to the crown as it is to me," Oli said. "Besides, I told you what I know. I led your princess to where she wanted to go."

"And then what happened?" Amandine said, eyes moving between Oli and Tuck, who continued growling.

What happened? *Yeolasi was let loose. My mother died. I became something else.* "You'll have to ask your princess when she gets back."

"So she *is* alive."

"I said that already. When I left her, she and Tâl were fine, not that you all care none about the others."

Thibault shifted uncomfortably. "The rangers . . ."

"Dead. All except Tâl, anyway."

Amandine raised a hand to her lips. "Deōs, help us."

"Wouldn't bet on his help." Oli nodded to the town behind them. "And how many of my people are left, eh?"

Thibault cursed and placed a palm against the door frame. "Most left before the battle, following the magistrate south. It's impossible to know whether they got away safely, or if the Yelmes cut them down along the way."

"Did my sister leave with them?"

Thibault shook his head. "No."

"But she's alive?"

"When I saw her last, she was."

"And where was that?"

"I'll tell you when Princess Léonie returns, and not a moment before."

Oli could have stabbed him right then, and he nearly did. But Evanvalt darkened the doorway, his bald head barely visible behind Amandine and the captain. "Captain, you are needed up the hill."

Thibault nodded, then looked at Oli. "Her Highness better return soon, Woodsman, or I swear by Deōs I'll string you up." Then he stalked out, Lady Amandine trailing him. Oli didn't bother to call out after him. He would find Layla without the captain. If Thibault knew where she was or where she'd gone, then surely someone else did too.

He would have left, but the priest still stood in the doorway, his eyes grave and heavy as he took Oli in. But it wasn't his eyes that drew Oli, but his Threads: they glowed a brilliant, almost angry gold. Not yellow, but *gold*. It appeared so bright Oli nearly looked away.

"It is done, then." Evanvalt said, voice low. "Your father's vision has been fulfilled through his son."

Oli's throat went dry. "What are you goin' on 'bout?"

"Roi Ricker wanted that power, the one now flowing through your veins. He died to have it. I thought you understood that."

Leave. Staradovna spoke again, the first word she had said in hours.

"You don't know what you're talkin' 'bout," Oli said, though he suspected Evanvalt knew exactly what he talked about. It made Oli uncomfortable. Afraid.

"Don't I?"

"Nothin' happened. I just want to find my sister." He stepped forward prepared to push past the man.

The priest nodded. "Well then, if nothing happened, you surely won't mind this." He moved quickly for an old man, hand reaching up and ripping back Oli's cowl. In the same motion, Evanvalt's hand grabbed the curls of Oli's hair, yanking his head forward so their eyes met at hardly a hand's width apart.

"*Uay losten mi leris Deōs,*" he said, voice sending wafts of garlic up Oli's nose.

As the last syllable faded, Oli's body burned the same way it had when he had touched Layla in the desert. It was fire, starting at his eyes, then burning through his body. Thousands of images flashed through his mind: all of trees, each unique and each beautiful. But the images, popping into his mind and then out again, combined with the pain brought him to his knees.

Tuck barked but stayed beside him, his fur pressed against Oli's side.

And deep within the depths of his mind, Oli could hear Staradovna scream.

FIFTY

Léonie refused to collapse.

She was not her mother. She was not weak. She would keep marching. She would not stumble. Would not fall.

The shadows had grown long on the leaf-ridden forest floor. Léonie watched those shadows, trying to take her mind off her aching knees. She wiped snot from her nose and ignored her knuckles, which had cracked from the cold.

They followed the path left by Oli: footprints, broken sticks, trampled leaves, and Yelmes corpses. She shivered relentlessly, her undershirt sticking to her skin and amplifying the bitter wind.

The Wood had become merely a wood, that much seemed clear. If it still had its power then they likely would have been dead hours before. Nothing at all bothered them or paid them any heed. In fact, Léonie had the sense she and Tâl were only one small part of a greater exodus. Animals skittered about, moving west like water flowing downhill. Or maybe they were refugees. Or escaped prisoners.

Whatever it was, the spell of the Vromia was no more.

"We're nearly there, Your Highness."

"How can you tell?" Léonie asked, looking around. The forest all looked the same.

"I smell smoke."

Smoke. Which meant fires, and the work of the Yelmes.

A few minutes later they saw their first bits of ash falling from the sky. "Let us pray the captain held out."

Tâl nodded, tripping over a stone and nearly tumbling. "Perhaps the Woodsman arrived in time."

Léonie doubted it. She and Tâl had not been traveling quickly, but the signs of Oli's passing were not old either. If her people had survived, if Thibault and Amandine still lived, it would mean they had done it on their own. And that would have meant a miracle.

"They did it," Tâl said, awestruck. "They're alive."

"Let us pray that is true," Léonie said as she stepped out of the treeline. The sun had just set, the stars bright against the early night sky. And Watchful smoldered. That was the word for it. Though she saw no open flames, patches of red embers dotted the lower portion of the town and the fields beyond, columns of smoke rising up from the ground in dozens of places.

They marched slowly through clouds of smoke which wafted in the breeze, the heat a momentary relief from the brutal chill. More than once she inhaled enough smoke to get her coughing, which evoked memories of the Clearing she wished to push aside.

There must have been watchers posted, for Léonie and Tâl were still over a hundred yards away from the main road when Thibault and a half-dozen others marched towards them—their orange surcoats ravaged to the point of being unrecognizable, their faces so darkened with soot the whites of their eyes stood out in the night.

"My lady, I cannot say enough how glad I am to see you." Thibault fell to one knee and bowed his head. Every soldier with him followed suit, leaving only Lady Amandine and a pair of Léonie's maids standing at a curtsy behind them.

"Rise," Léonie said, ashamed by how weak she sounded. The edges of her vision darkened, but she bit the inside of her cheek and kept standing. She became vaguely aware of that Tâl's cloak did little to cover her undershirt. "You have done well, Captain. I had feared the worst."

"My lady," Amandine pushed past the captain and quickly pulled Tâl's cloak aside and then tossed a heavy wool one over Léonie's shoulders, wrapping the front of it closed. It was, Léonie realized, *Amandine's* cloak. It sat upon her shoulders heavy, warm, and wonderful. And yet, it was also too much of all those things.

Her legs were tired and her eyes heavy; it had been the bitter cold and the pain keeping her going. Now, more than ever, she was tempted to collapse. But she had questions which needed answering and now was not the time for rest. She stepped forward, preparing a barrage of questions for the captain.

How had they repelled the Yelmes? What was the state of her forces? And, most importantly, where was Oli? She could not let the Woodsman escape, she needed him near.

"M'lady?" Was that Tâl or Amandine? Léonie could not tell, the voice was fading away. "Your Highness, are you—"

"Catch her!"

CHAPTER

FIFTY-ONE

Layla's nose would bleed sometimes. Anej said it was because Oli was using his power, but Layla still didn't understand what that meant. All she knew is she had seen her brother near that tree in the desert and something had happened when he'd touched her. If Ulian and Anej were right, that had been the moment Oli had connected with her, binding her life to his.

Anej had kept them marching until sunset, Ulian perched on his shoulder so they were limited only by the reach of Layla's stride and her own dwindling energy. The march had been brutal at first, but eventually the stitch in her side had subsided and her feet went from sore to numb. She had pushed through the pain until it had subsided, as if her body had given up telling her how exhausted she was.

The birds had been the only thing that brought her anything even hinting at joy. They were strange and gentle looking, with arms as soft as dishrags. Wings is what Ulian called them. And by some magic that Ulian swore wasn't magic, they skittered about *in the air*. They stayed aloft like fire smoke, their movements a blur as they whirred about among the treetops.

Eventually though, as the hours drew on and the sun began to set, the birds had gone and the little joy they brought had gone, too. The miles took their toll on Layla's chest, knees, and feet. The air grew colder and dryer.

"Are you certain we should not camp?" Ulian asked, his voice low.

"Tomorrow." Anej grunted. "We'll be in the mountains then, and I know a place or two."

"It's cold," Layla said. Her cracked lips leaked blood into her mouth and her whole face was unfeeling. If not for the cloak Anej had given her, she'd have spent half her energy shivering her way through the Wood.

"It shouldn't snow 'til we're in the mountains," Anej said. "We're makin' good time, lass."

Layla didn't think she could push on until tomorrow night. They trudged uphill almost constantly, and it would only get worse as they got closer to the foothills of the mountain. She would never make it. And despite his words, Layla knew she slowed the velk down, distorting the way he calculated time and distance as he tried to compensate for her shorter gait. He tried not to show it, but he was growing restless moving so slowly, often doubling back to Layla when he'd gone too far – or sometimes pausing and pretending to investigate the forest around them.

Ulian, still perched on Anej's shoulder, adjusted his spectacles. "Going around is taking quite some time, but perhaps if we go *through—*"

"No," Anej said. "If I even glimpse the Wall, then we've gotten too close. We go around."

"It would be more direct. And warmer, too."

"Aye, and unstable. Without the witch as a focal point, it'll be volatile, manic."

"Conjecture. It may just slowly slip back into time and space, becoming harmless."

"Whatever it'll be, it won't be harmless," Anej snorted.

"What are you two goin' on about?" Layla called, trying to catch up with Anej, who had the habit of walking faster when he got distracted. And the dark wasn't helping matters. Layla kept tripping over roots and stubbing her boot on the ever-increasing collection of sharp rocks sticking up from the dirt. And moreover, the elevation kept changing: they'd go uphill for a time, then stumble down a slope which stretched on for a few dozen paces, then back up again.

Ulian twisted to look at her. "Our guide is taking us the long way around."

"Oy?" Layla said. "If there's a shorter way, shouldn't we—"

Anej spat to the side, the weight of saliva heavy enough to hit the ground with a loud *splat*. "It ain't shorter if it gets ya killed. And Ule shouldn't believe everything he reads."

Layla said nothing. She wanted to offer her thoughts, to be able to say "we should do this" or "we should do that", but she found she only had questions. Questions she felt too afraid to voice, to give life too because she might get answers that scared her more than not knowing. She felt like the same girl standing before the treeline, terrified of what lay beyond.

A branch snapped in the distance.

Anej stopped and Layla walked into him, her head banging on the bottom of his pack. "Ow!"

"Shh."

Layla could hear the rustling of Anej's pack hitting the ground, Ulian's boots landing on leaves beside it.

"Anej—" Layla started, but he thrust his hand before her, blocking out faint starlight like a basket dropped over her head. She got the message and stayed quiet.

A moment later the starlight reappeared and Anej moved away, leaving Ulian and Layla crouching in the open between a scattering of trees like black pillars. Her skin crawled and her spine tingled, as if at any moment a beast or knife, would be upon her. Anej moved with a kind of quiet that was impressive for his size but still wasn't truly silent. There was no hiding the two dozen leaves and occasional stick which crunched beneath every step of his trunk-sized boots.

Layla tried to keep her breathing calm, but her hand shook as it held onto the handle of her sword. It wasn't any easier now that she knew what a fight felt like. If anything, it was harder. She blinked away a tear before it could fall, sucked in a breath, and forced herself to steady. Ulian shuffled, pressing his back into Layla's shoulder. He wasn't crouched like her, but stood as tall as he could, his head swiveling about, his breathing heavy. He still smelled of the Downwind—of a good hearth fire and fruit-infused ale.

"Do you think he sees something?" Ulian whispered.

"I'm just prayin' there's nothin' to see."

"Wisely said."

Layla breathed out into her hands, trying to warm them up, to loosen her fingers. If there were Yelmes around, Layla didn't expect to see them. They were called the Dark Ones for a reason, and if they had finally caught up to them then luck alone had given them a warning. The Yelmes must have been careless to break a stick so loud Layla and the others could hear it over their own rushed flight. That was, if the sound had even been caused by a Yelmes at all. It could have been one of the animals, perhaps some large—what had Ulian called it?—squirrel.

Anej crept away toward the direction of the sound, the tip of his spear reflecting the starlight, his silhouette distinct among the trees. Layla had the sense he knew he was too loud, that maybe he was trying to lead any enemies away.

Layla squinted harder, trying to force her eyes to see more in the pitch of night. How Anej saw anything at all, how he had been able to guide them, she couldn't imagine. No moon had emerged and the dim glow of stars couldn't penetrate the heavy ceiling of branches above. It was all black upon black, a game of shades and not colors.

Movement caught Layla's eye. It seemed strange, but out of the corner of her vision she thought she saw something like an ember floating in the air a few paces behind Anej: a red light swirled for an instant. Gone now: only blackness remaining where she'd seen it. Though, now that she looked, the blackness shifted. It moved slowly, but—

Layla stood and cried out, "Anej!"

He twisted as lightning crackled and flashed. Layla covered her eyes to block out the burst of light and thunder that boomed in her ears. Wood let out a screaming *crack* and when Layla looked up she saw a massive tree falling slowly downward toward the velk, its trunk alight in unnatural white flame. Anej blocked a sword blow with his shield and then threw himself out of the way as the tree slammed onto the ground. The leaves on the forest floor proved themselves as kindling and a roaring fire sprang up, throwing light and shadow, heat and smoke, in every direction.

"Maker, help us." Ulian stood with a knife in hand, his jaw hanging slack and his skin pale in the firelight. What the fire had revealed, Layla wished would have stayed unseen.

They were surrounded.

Two dozen Yelmes stood around them in a wide circle, their cowls low. They each held a blade in hand, but they did not move and did not attack. The one who had almost taken Anej in the back held a defensive stance as the giant brought himself back to his feet.

Layla shed the cloak and ran toward Anej, Ulian close behind. She couldn't hide behind him now, not like before. The Yelmes fanned out all around, encircling them, penning them in.

"Your sword, lass," Anej said, rolling his shoulders.

Layla's hand shook so hard she struggled to get a firm enough grip to wrench her sword free of the sheath, though once she held the blade her nerves steeled a little. The weight of it made her feel more in control, if only slightly.

The Yelmes nearest Anej pulled his cowl back to reveal a complexion not unlike Layla's own, his hair weaved into thick braids, the brim of his nose wide and flat. His voice flowed like oil over smooth rocks. "Hand over the *Cievka*."

"What did I tell you about pitch?" Anej snarled. "I don't speak it."

"We can smell the girl."

The girl. Layla had believed Ulian and Anej when they'd told her the Yelmes would be after her, but hearing one of them say it made her shiver.

Anej snorted. "Ain't a chance in all the Hells."

The man cocked his head to one side, tapping the flat of his blade against his thigh thoughtfully. The fire behind him kept spreading, but far slower than Layla thought it should. Nothing about that fire appeared natural: it was too bright, too controlled. It wasn't like any fire she had seen before. This felt wrong, more . . . threatening.

"I can make a deal, velk," the Dark One said. His voice sounded so soft, so easy to listen to. "I have that authority. You may say I have the *Hecúved's* ear."

"Save it," Anej said, but Layla's mind reeled. Why did the Yelmes talk to them? And what was this about a deal? And whose ear?

The Yelmes pointed his sword toward Ulian. "I'll spare you and the little one."

"Little one?" Ulian said, shifting his knife. "Well, I—"

Anej shifted his spear and said, "After I gut ya, remind me to tell ya the story of the last time I made a deal with a demon."

"Ah," the Yelmes chuckled. "Is that how it happened then?" He pointed to Anej, then gestured to his own eye. "After just one little deal, they cut you off? Just like that?"

Anej said nothing.

"Do you miss it? The sight, I mean." He lifted his hand and the fire behind him shot up a dozen feet. "I would miss this. Those old artifacts you carry aren't the same. Your little shield just reminds you, teases you. It just makes you want it *more.*"

Layla shifted. "Anej, what's he talkin' 'bout?"

Anej shook his head. "Just forked tongues and lies. Best ignore 'em, or you'll end up burned."

"Anej, is it?" The Dark One stepped forward casually, nearly close enough for his sword to reach Anej. "I can make you a god again,

Anej. I can give you your power back and then I can give you more. It won't be hard, the *Hecúved* has done greater things. It would be easy, merely a simple—"

Anej stabbed out with his spear and caught the man beneath the chin, running him straight through his throat. Anej yanked his spear backward, and the man collapsed to his knees, the color fading from his eyes like a star winking out in the sky.

"Run!" Anej yelled as he stormed forward, Layla and Ulian on his heels.

The fire roared to their left, a pair of Yelmes right in front of them. But the enemy had been caught off guard, moving just a touch too slow.

Every step Layla took, something changed.

She leapt over the dead Yelmes, and that seemed to trigger every other Dark One around her—urging them to charge forward, their hands cackling with blue energy and that strange red light. Her hair stood on end, her skin crawled with goosebumps, as the whole Wood filled with energy and the promise of lightning.

Her next step was nearly into flames. The fire spread like someone had poured cooking oil by the buckets onto the forest floor. The Yelmes Anej had killed had been controlling it, keeping it at bay. But with his death, it broke loose.

By Layla's third step, Anej had stabbed another Yelmes and thrown him like a doll into the fire. A woman off to Layla's right ran toward her, trying to cut her off from Anej. Her skin looked gray in the brilliant light of the fire, her yellow eyes burning bright. Red lights danced excitedly over her free hand, which she pulled back the way they did before shooting lightning out.

There was no fourth step, for Ulian dragged Layla down into the dirt as Anej's shield sailed over their heads. Screams of pain erupted from behind her where the shield must have ripped through the enemy. Then Anej stood over them, cutting off the charging woman, clashing spear to sword.

"Up!" Anej called. "Now!"

Ulian grabbed Layla's hand and pulled her up and forward. A stretch of ground lay before them, free of Yelmes. The fire worsened to their left, so hot it began to burn the side of Layla's face. Anej stayed behind them, fighting with a spear in one hand and a knife in the other. By the time Layla had gone three more paces and looked backward, a pair of Yelmes were already dead.

But the enemy pressed Anej back toward the fire.

"Come on!" Layla screamed. "Anej, run!"

But it was too late, he couldn't run. He had been surrounded: fire to his back and Yelmes stretched out before him. Somehow, he moved his weapons with such speed he blocked blows even as four or five pushed in on him at once. But hope had gone now, even Layla could see that. Anej stepped back again towards the spreading flames, unable to do anything more than block the incoming blows.

"Miss Ricker," Ulian yanked at her arm. "They're coming!"

Four had broken off from the rest, ignoring Anej to come for her. *Her.*

Who was she that Anej would fight for her? Would die for her? She knew there was more going on, that she was connected to a power she couldn't understand. And still, she could not ignore that everyone she had loved had abandoned her. Her father, her mother, and her brother had all gone and left her behind, whether they meant to or not.

But not the tanner.

"Layla!" Ulian cried out, trying to pull her along. She looked at the bartender, saw herself reflected in his eyes.

She could be like her family, and she could turn and run, right now. Or . . . a word appeared in her mind, demanding her attention, forcing her to see every Layla she could be.

"Palmaditze." It was the Language of the Wild, of Woodspeak. A word her brother had taught her. A word with power.

A word that forced her to remember who she could be, and not just who she was.

Layla pulled her hand free from Ulian and raised her sword up before the oncoming Yelmes. She would die, she was certain of it.

But she wouldn't abandon Anej.

FIFTY-TWO

O li sat in a wingback chair beside the floating hearth. Staradovna was lounging on a plush looking sofa a few paces away. The sofa wasn't there the last time Oli had been in this room, when he had tried stabbing Staradovna just to find out she couldn't die. Most everything else appeared the same: the high bookshelves, the long table, the incredible glass ceiling opening up to the strangeness of stars, moon, and sun.

If Staradovna could be believed, and he wasn't sure she could be, then this room existed as a place in his own mind. Or more specifically, she had called it, "a quasi-physical representation of the immaterial space of the mind". Which Oli figured just meant it was a place in his mind.

Whatever it was though, he didn't want to be here. He wasn't even sure how he had gotten here in the first place. The priest had mumbled something and then looked right at him in an eerie way that had been more than just a look. He had felt the same pain as when he had touched Layla, and then he had woken up here, sprawled out on the floor like a drunk.

Evanvalt's words still rang in ears, and he mulled them over as he stared at the sky above. *It is done, then. Your father's vision has been fulfilled through his son.*

Oli understood what the priest had said better than he would have liked. He had what his father had wanted, what the princess wanted. He had *power*, the kind capable of snapping the life-strings of anyone he wanted. And not just that. He'd saved Tuck, hadn't he? He had sewn the dog's life strings back together and pulled Tuck back from the cusp of death. It was easy to see why Léonie wanted to wield this power, easy to see how even waves of Yelmes soldiers wouldn't be able to stand against him now.

But Oli didn't understand why his father had wanted this.

"Do you plan on just sitting here, moping about?" Staradovna said, not bothering to look up from the book she read, its cover a complex pattern of gold upon black. "You could use your time for so much more, you know."

Oli stared at her. The ground around her littered with broken glass and shredded rope—his last two attempts to end her life. She had merely been amused.

This was the price of his power. *Her.*

"And what else would I do, eh?"

"You could tidy up, for starters. You will never find anything around here if you leave it like this."

"Oy, and what am I tryin' to find around here?"

"Memories are usually the most productive, but you could work through other musings. I would begin as far back as you can go, then work up from there. This is your mind, after all, so begin where you'd like."

Oli shook his head. "How is this *my* mind? It ain't anything like what I think about. I don't even know what this is." He said, shoving a thumb in the direction of the floating hearth.

Staradovna lowered the book. She smiled wistfully, looking over at the metal ball floating near Oli. "I've made additions, of course. That's an antique stove, you know. Just like the one my grandmother forged herself." Then she frowned, looking toward Oli. "Odd, though. As I've been perusing your memories it would seem the world has regressed noticeably."

Oli leaned forward and pulled at his hair. Every time she spoke he only became more confused. "What do you mean you've been perusing my memories?"

Staradovna watched him for a long moment, silence stretching out awkwardly between them. Then she closed the book so suddenly it sent a gust of air upward, rustling her hair. "You really have no understanding at all, do you?"

Oli crossed his arms and sat back.

Staradovna rubbed at her temple. "It's strange. You are of the Stražar, and yet you comprehend so little. Once upon a time, your people understood all this rather thoroughly. *Too* thoroughly, if you ask me. And yet time, it seems, has been rather cruel to this world."

"Is it always riddles with you?"

"These aren't riddles. These are the ramblings of someone who has woken from a thousand-year slumber."

"You plannin' on explaining any of your ramblings?"

"In time, perhaps. Maybe when you are not so aggressive." She kicked a piece of glass with the toe of her shoe.

Oli stood and spat on the carpet in front of her.

"Delightful," she muttered.

"How do I leave?"

"In this case? You wait." She opened her book again. "It will happen rather suddenly."

"What happens?"

"You wake up. It will be a bit different when you learn to come here on your own. When you are forced here not of your own will, the rules are a little different. Someone will need to wake you. The longer it takes, the harder it will be." She frowned. "Ask me how I know."

Oli didn't.

Staradovna turned a page in her book while she continued

speaking. "Don't worry though, little Stražar, you're missing far less than you think. Time is rather fickle here. Fluid, some have called it."

Oli began pacing around the table. "I can't leave? So I'm a prisoner then?"

"Darling, you're the prison warden. *I'm* the prisoner."

"You sayin' you can't leave?"

Staradovna laughed high and long. "Oh, do I wish. But there are boundaries at play. To live on the mortal plane one must have a mortal body. And I," she gestured down at herself, "am without."

Oli thought for a moment, picking up a strange metal cylinder from the table. A hundred letters had been etched around the outside, a purple stone inset on the top. The lid appeared to twist on and off, but when Oli tried to open it, it refused to budge. He put it down, then looked over at Staradovna. "Did you ever have a body?"

"Oh yes, a long time ago. But there were . . . complications in the political and religious environment of the day. It resulted in my imprisonment. Over time, my prison and my body became indistinguishable from one another."

"The Wood was your prison, then?"

"That was the prison grounds, I suppose. The pedestal you found me upon was my cell. A cell whose door, I should add, you so eloquently destroyed."

"You mean when I killed you."

"When you released my soul onto the mortal plane. Since I was without a body, I took the only option available to me."

Oli paused, his mind assembling the disparate pieces together. "So when I shot you and you," he gestured with his hands.

"Blew up?"

"Sure. After that you . . . what? Possessed me?"

"That's a rude way to put it. Your words and your arrow formed a nice connection between you and I, and that connection was the only one offered to me. Be honored, little Stražar, it's not everyday one gets to house one of the Divine."

So, he had done this to himself. By trying to kill Staradovna he had freed his parents' murderer. Even when he succeeded, he failed. Oli grabbed the metal cylinder from the table and threw it at Staradovna's head. He missed, sending it ricocheting off the bookshelf behind her.

"Don't be so rude, darling," she said with a smile. "It's not all bad. Now you have the power to save your little kingdom. It's rather heroic, really. Together we will bury all the warriors from Kātsracha and you will have all the glory. Maybe they'll make you a duke, in the end. If you're shrewd, perhaps you can even marry that princess you're fond of."

Oli shook his head. "Let Trevelar burn, for all I care."

"Ah yes, that is the thing about you I keep seeming to forget. You are a rather focused man."

"I just want to find my sister."

She nodded thoughtfully. "That is a poor idea, which is a pattern with you."

"Oy, and what do ya mean by that?"

"It means you have poor ideas and subsequently make bad decisions."

"Oh screw off. I meant about my sister. Why is finding her a bad idea?"

Staradovna stood and stretched. "Because it is the quickest way to get you both killed."

Oli thought about grabbing the poker and stabbing her again. "How?"

"Because, little Stražar, you are both beacons of power. Think about how you can sense the Yelmes. You can *feel* them, can't you? It's because they have this same power, or a lesser form of it anyway. Have you noticed how much harder it is to sense mortals?"

She was right, of course. The people of the town had been like silhouettes compared to the Yelmes, able to be sensed but barely.

Staradovna pressed on. "If you can sense the Yelmes, then you should assume they can sense you. But where they are torches in the night, you are a bonfire, and your sister isn't much smaller. Together the Dark Ones could sense you from across the kingdom. And if they can sense you, they will hunt you."

"So I'll kill them."

Staradovna laughed. "You have been playing with children, Oli. There are beings in Kātsracha that you cannot fathom, and they will come after you. They have felt this power before, the last time they were shoved into the depths of the earth. They will stop at nothing to make sure it does not happen again."

"I don't believe you," Oli said, shaking his head. "You just don't want me to find Layla."

"Actually, I would very much like to find your sister. Her safety is important if we are to stay alive. But I fear there is more at play here. I sense . . . another with her. An old one."

"What does that mean?"

"It means finding her is not in our best interest, not unless you enjoyed the run in with that priest and would like something even worse. And it means she is safe enough, for now."

Oli clenched his fist. Staradovna knew more than she said, and she clearly picked her words to be as vague as possible. She had the power here, where death could not find them. She had knowledge, and she could wield it without consequence. It angered him, kindled his hatred for her into a raging fire. "Stop the riddles. Tell me where my sister is or I'll—ah!" Oli stepped backward clutching his arm. He felt as if he'd been stabbed, as though a knife had been pushed into his arm below the elbow. "What are you doing?"

"Well, perhaps I was wrong about her being safe." Staradovna said as she stepped forward. "And this isn't me."

Oli breathed heavily, working hard to swallow the pain. "Then what's happening?"

"You're connected. This is your sister's pain."

Layla. If this is what she felt then she was in danger. He needed to get to her. "I have to get out. I have to get to her."

"It's too late. Sit down."

"I—"

"I can save her," Staradovna said, pushing away his objections. "But you must sit down. *Now*."

Oli bit his lip and walked back to the chair, sitting and staring up at her. He wanted nothing to do with Staradovna, but if anything she said was true then he had no choice but to listen.

Staradovna stood over him now, hand stretched out above his head.

"What are you doin'?" he asked.

"Connections are powerful—" Oli screamed as pain ripped through his leg. "—and painful. We are lucky. Both of you are ignorant, and she'll be defenseless to our tampering. If we are careful, we should be able to interfere quite nicely."

Oli gritted his teeth as he rode out the next wave of pain. He didn't understand anything she said, and he didn't care at the moment. "Just save her."

"My pleasure."

Oli wanted to wretch as Staradovna placed her cold hand upon his head. It was the touch of a corpse, chilled and lifeless. Her nails were long, and they pressed into his skull with five precise stabs of pain. Slowly the room faded away into a black blur, replaced by the familiar sights and sounds of the Wood.

FIFTY-THREE

Layla slashed out wildly with her sword and backed away from the Yelmes, her vision confused by the hundreds of shadows cast by the light of the raging fire. Every shadow melded into a Dark One, lurching forward and backward, cutting at her thigh, her side, her forearm, and each cut sliced deeper than the last.

They toyed with her.

She protected her stomach and face with her feral swings, but it would only be a matter of time before one of them chose to end the fight.

Pain erupted in her back and she twisted to swing at the moving shadow. Her blade hit nothing, but the momentum of her swing forced her to step forward, and the toe of her boot caught on a root. She stumbled, trying desperately to stay on her feet. Light flashed as lightning struck in the distance, illuminating a man before her just as he brought down his blade. She raised her sword in time, but blocking the blow exposed the rest of her body. Pain erupted in her calf and she screamed, throwing herself backward onto the ground. But they were fighting on a hill, and when she hit the ground she began to roll downward uncontrollably.

Seconds later, the trunk of a tree stopped her. Her head cracked against its trunk and the world went black all around the edges of her vision. But whether by some mercy or some evil, she stayed awake.

She had rolled a bowshot from the white fire burning out of control, the bitter air especially cold against her blood-soaked skin. Anej was alive, miraculously, a silhouette before the light of the flames. Poor Ulian . . . he'd be dead by now. She hadn't seen the maeifa since the fight began, except for one glimpse of him charging the Yelmes, knife in hand.

Four Yelmes approached her now, moving cautiously down the steep hill. They flanked outwards and approached with far more caution than needed. They acted as though they feared her.

She wanted to stand and keep fighting, but nothing was left in her. Whatever strength she once possessed had been drained, poured out into the pool of blood she could feel running down her back and beneath her. Feeling ebbed from her fingers and toes.

So she watched the Yelmes approach, four shadows descending toward her. If not for the red lights around their hands, Layla doubted she would have kept track of them. They would kill her, but she had known that when she had chosen to stay and fight. At least she hadn't abandoned Anej.

She had given to him what he'd given to her. A life for life.

Maybe Deōs would call her brave. Maybe he would let her enter through the doors of Peradisos. Would she see her father again? Would she find her mother already there?

The Yelmes were close now. The lights in their hands burned brighter—more vibrant and alive than before. And she thought now she could make out lights of yellow moving through their bodies. They looked majestic, holy. They looked like gods.

Layla wanted to say something, to ask them why they glowed. But her mouth wouldn't work. In fact, nothing worked. She didn't hurt anymore, but neither did her hands or legs respond to her mind's commands. She accepted that. It would make receiving death that much easier.

But then, when the Yelmes were nearly close enough to strike, her hand moved of its own volition. It jerked upward, her fingers contorting so they spread unnaturally wide.

The Yelmes paused for a heartbeat, then one charged forward with his sword raised.

Layla watched her hand close into a fist and then move downward as though pulling a heavy rope. All the yellow lights before her went out, and the four Yelmes collapsed as though they had been merely black sacks of cloth.

Mind reeling, Layla wasn't sure what to do. Didn't know what she *could* do. Her body still would not respond to her and it seemed as though it were not finished. Her other hand raised, one finger pointing up the hill towards the fire and to the swarm of Yelmes around the velk.

Her hand repeated the motion again, fingers spreading wide, then clenching to a fist which yanked downward. And all the Yelmes collapsed. To Layla, it looked like faint stars going out in the distance.

She watched Anej go still and saw his shoulder shift from side to side as he tried to understand what had happened. Her hand fell limp to her side and Layla felt blood pooling in her mouth.

Anej screamed her name for a while before he found her. Layla had listened and watched as he'd searched by the firelight, but she'd been unable to wave or even say a word, drained of all but even the faintest thoughts. It was a miracle sleep hadn't come. Or a curse. She wasn't sure which.

Vaguely, she understood she had stopped bleeding, which shouldn't have been possible. But nothing should have been possible anymore, and yet everything seemed to happen anyway.

Eventually, Anej spotted her. He snapped branches as he closed the distance to her.

"Layla! Are ya alive, lass?" Anej knelt beside her, his rough hands feeling her head and cheek, carefully looking over her wounds. She could feel his hands, which felt like a good sign. But still, she could not move or answer.

"We gotta go. I can lift ya, but Ule is up there too and—can ya hear me?" Anej leaned closer, feeling at her forehead and looking into her eyes. A moment later, his blue eye widened. "Oy, I should've seen this comin'. Oh, ya poor thing. Your brother saved us, I'd guess. But he possessed you to do it. And that's hard to shake. Ya ain't gonna be movin' for a bit." Anej looked around, taking in the dead Yelmes and then looking up at the spreading flames.

"Alright then, let me get the barkeep."

CHAPTER
FIFTY-FOUR

Through the thin glass of the window in Magistrate Tote's office, Léonie watched daylight break over the mountains. Black smoke billowed in the Wood to the southeast, and Léonie could only guess at what that could be. The hearth raged behind her, stoked nearly to the point of foolishness, but she still felt cold. Sleep had rested her body some, but her mind had found no solace. She had questions that needed answers, plans that needed making, and people that needed dealing with.

And she was so cold.

Léonie turned from the window and pulled her cloak tighter around her shoulders. A plate of fruit and cheese had been laid out upon the desk, and she forced herself to pluck a grape and eat. She had no appetite, but skipping meals would do little to help with her waning energy. So she would eat, whether she liked it or not. Beside the bowl of fruit, her naked sword had been carefully propped up, not yet cleaned or sharpened.

She dare not yet be separated from it.

"Where is he?" Léonie asked.

Amandine turned, her hand still holding the spine of a book she had halfway freed from its spot on the shelf. "He should be here shortly, I would imagine. I am unsure if he was awake when you called for him."

Léonie had heard of Oli's foray into the town looking for his sister, and his confrontation with the captain. Oddly though, the priest said he had watched Oli collapse shortly after. Evanvalt had Oli taken to an impromptu infirmary and kept in isolation there. The captain had added a pair of guards.

If anything, the princess imagined the Woodsman, with his newly formed powers, would have been off in search of his sister immediately. And that would have been bad for her, indeed.

"Perhaps I should go to him," Léonie said, carefully choosing another grape from the plate.

"Perhaps you should remember you are still a princess. You do not seek out commoners, they come to you." Amandine had chosen a book now and had walked to the window, carefully turning its pages.

Léonie tapped her fingers against the desk. "Oli Ricker may not be a commoner any longer."

"Whatever unholy power he now has, it has not changed his birth. A commoner is a commoner, no matter how great the blaspheme."

"This blaspheme may yet save our kingdom."

"*Deōs* will save our kingdom, and he shall do it without heresy."

"And where was Deōs at Worchestern?"

Amandine slammed the book closed, her eyes growing dark. "Not all of us question God like petulant children, Your Highness."

Léonie leaned back, her lips thinning. The urge to throw something grew incredibly strong. "Perhaps it is only petulant children who contain the courage needed to take desperate gambles. Perhaps it is on the other side of questioning, on the other side of *heresy*, where a regime of corrupt old men can finally be unmasked."

"You go too far!" Amandine turned to her, for once her eyes showed wrinkles of anger and age all around them, her porcelain mask cracked.

"I shall go only as far as I need to save my kingdom." Léonie stood, flinging the chair backward. "The Order of Deōs would choose to let the people of this kingdom burn, their corpses picked by crows, rather than to reach out and take the only power which could have saved them. And why? Because that power will threaten their hold on this kingdom."

"Heresy and lies. Deōs will—"

"God will not save this kingdom, Duchess Amandine. *I* will. *Me.* And I will burn to ashes anyone or anything that stands in my way, even the Order, do you not yet understand?"

Amandine stepped back, hand rising to her lips. Léonie held her sword, though she was unsure when that had happened. Finally, as though with great effort, Amandine shook her head, rattling the beads in her carefully braided hair. And then she left.

Léonie fumed for a moment longer after the door closed, then weariness took her. Stumbling towards the hearth, the tip of her sword dragging along the wooden floorboard, Léonie sat in a chair by the fire. She wanted wine, but lacked the energy to call for any.

It was impossible for her to tell how long she sat like that, but long enough for the fire to warm her toes and comfort her, if only a little.

"M'lady?"

She did not bother to turn at the sound of the captain's voice. "Yes?"

"I have brought Oli Ricker to see you, as you have requested."

Léonie turned. The captain stood just inside the room, his face pale. She had tried to warn him, to brace him for what he would see, but it had hardly mattered. Say what she might, Oli Ricker looked unnerving, and even more so in the daylight. His cheeks were gaunt, his beard disheveled, and he had not bathed. His clothes and every inch of visible skin had been coated in soot, dirt, and long-dried blood. But his eyes . . . the sight of them made her tighten her grip on her sword.

He looked so much like the Yelmes.

Perhaps his only redeeming feature, the only thing which still made him look truly human, was the dog at his heels.

She tried to smile. It would do no good if he hated her. "Our hero awakens, it seems."

Oli frowned as he stepped into the room, Tuck padding along beside him.

Hero? She mocked him, surely. It would have angered him, but he found he hardly cared. It was hot enough in the study that sweat broke out along his forehead. Could books catch fire from heat alone? He wasn't sure, but he thought it may be possible here. Tuck whimpered and made for the window, propping himself up onto the sill and nuzzling the cool glass. Oli thought maybe he could also feel the cool touch of glass on his own nose and cheek, though he still stood by the door.

He turned his attention back to the princess. "You owe me," he said.

"Do I?" Léonie dropped the smile she'd been wearing.

"Four hundred and ninety-nine gold nũmuns." Oli walked toward the princess, listening as Thibault's chainmail shifted. He almost wanted the captain to attack. To give him a reason to be angry, to fight, to summon power.

Léonie cursed.

"You were never gonna pay me, were you?" Oli said, fists clenching. Tuck dropped from the windowsill and turned back toward them.

"No."

Oli blinked. Whatever he'd expected the princess to say, it wasn't the truth.

Then Léonie looked at him. *Really* looked at him. Her eyes searched him up and down, and when she met his own eyes she didn't flinch or look away. "It is time," she said slowly, placing her sword gently on the floorboards. "For us to parlay as equals."

The words tasted strange in Léonie's mouth, but she meant them. Oli was more than she had ever imagined, though she still hated him. But hating him did not mean he was not worthy of her respect. In the last two days he had saved her life numerous times, fought terrible beasts, and then killed dozens of Yelmes warriors.

And he had killed Staradovna.

"What do you mean, 'parlay'?" Oli shifted on his feet, eyes roaming about the room.

"It means come and sit," she gestured to the chair near the hearth beside her. "And let us see how to work together."

"I don't want to work with you," Oli said, but he sat in the chair across from her all the same, his dog lying at his feet, panting.

"The feeling is mutual," Léonie said, rubbing her eyes. "But wanted is not the same as needed. And we need each other."

"Why do you think I need you?"

"I have information about your sister, for starters."

Oli stayed silent, eyes narrowing. "What information?"

"The captain told me where she was off to and with whom she left. I would be glad to exchange such information, provided there was reciprocal benefit."

Oli waved a hand. "She's gone toward the mountains with Anej. My tanner."

Léonie sat back, glancing at Thibault. But he only raised an eyebrow. "Well, it appears I am rather shy on leverage then." Her mouth grew dry, and she gestured to Thibault for the glass on the desk. After a sip, she said, "It is gold you want then?"

Oli said nothing for a long time.

In his mind, he could still see the white flames and feel the wounds on his body. *Layla's* body. Staradovna had said she had healed the damage done to Layla before she surrendered control, though Oli had no way of knowing if she told the truth.

Still, Layla was with Anej, which had to be good.

He had only been awake for a quarter of an hour, but there had been several hours in the room with Staradovna before they'd woken him. Plenty of time to think. If he wanted to, he thought he could find Layla. Anej would leave a trail easy enough to follow, and Oli could move faster than they could.

But he believed Staradovna when she said that together, Oli and Layla would be a beacon for the Yelmes. If she were going west toward Velik, then maybe he would keep her safer if he drew attention eastward, and brought the fight to the Yelmes. That's what Staradovna thought would keep Layla safe, and Oli had watched her save Layla's life. The Ancient One had a vested interest in keeping Layla safe, so Oli felt inclined to believe her that going eastward made the most sense.

If you kill all the Yelmes, darling, Staradovna had said. *Who would be left to threaten your sister?*

So Anej could keep Layla safe for now, but Oli could keep her safe forever. He only had to bring the fight to the Dark Ones.

"I don't have four hundred and ninety-nine gold nūmuns," Léonie said, the princess shifted in her chair, knuckles going white on the sword she held. "I . . . I am sorry I lied."

Oli snorted. "I doubt that." Léonie made to say something else, but Oli leaned forward, cutting her off. "Look, it ain't gold I want now. Or not yet anyway. I'll go ahead and fight your war, but it won't be for free."

Léonie took a deep breath. "I am listening."

Oli smiled, realizing this was another form of power, and one he had never had before. What had Léonie called it? Leverage? Léonie needed him, and Oli planned to hold that out before her as long as he could.

CHAPTER

FIFTY-FIVE

A nej carried Ulian in one arm and Layla in the other. His spear and pack were gone, but Layla saw his shield slung over his back, bobbing as he moved through the forest with terrible speed. His breathing grew erratic, filled with false starts and gulps of air.

He's afraid, Layla thought.

If she hadn't already been stupefied from complete horror, that would have terrified her all the more. They had been going like this for an hour or more, and all the while she couldn't move, couldn't even speak. She was a puppet without strings to pull, helpless. But Ulian was worse: his right hand gone at the wrist and his skin had become moon-pale. Anej had taken a blade from the flames, and Layla had listened to Ulian's screams as the wound was cauterized. When they had finished, the smell of burnt flesh filled the air. Now Ule's eyes were closed and mouth open, his clothes drenched in blood. Layla wasn't sure if he'd passed out or died.

Anej gulped air, grunting as a tree limb smacked against his face.

Layla tried to speak and managed a moan.

Anej looked down at her and nodded. "Good. You're comin'

back." Then he looked over his shoulder as a horn blew in the distance. "We'll be at the Wall soon, lass."

"Uh?" Layla moaned again.

Anej nodded as though he understood her. "It's the only way now. Best hope Ulian's right."

Layla vaguely understood that Anej felt desperate, that he was carrying them somewhere he had wanted to avoid. But beyond that, she was as confused as ever.

"W—why?" she managed. Feeling slowly coming back into her mouth now, though a headache grew as it did.

"Straightest shot to the pass," Anej said. "And if we get to the pass, I can hide us."

If.

"Oy," Anej said a moment later. "There it is."

Layla could shift her head slightly, awakening latent pain in her neck. But ahead, approaching at a terrifying pace, Layla saw a long wall, pale beneath the moonlight from above. And then, before she could barely register the broken bricks and murky world beyond, they sailed over it.

"Aw, hells," Anej said as his feet hit the dirt on the other side. "This ain't good."

Whatever Layla saw, she didn't believe it could have been real.

They were in a forest, but it wasn't anything like the one they had just left. Everything moved and shifted and changed. Trees were there one moment, then gone the next. Leaves on the ground appeared then disappeared. Animals of a thousand different shapes and sizes faded in and out of existence, only the sounds of their cries and growls echoing and creating a constant barrage of sound.

And the distant horizon appeared the same.

The Nevihta Mountains no longer dominated the horizon, but instead creatures whose heads disappeared into the sky above marched in the far distance. But those creatures shifted and changed as well: one moment a lavender thing with a dozen legs and tail catapulting trees into the air, the next moment something orange with no legs at all seemed to destroy the world as it squirmed. But always the heads of those beasts rose too high to see, hidden by clouds which themselves morphed.

Even the stars were all wrong, having stretched themselves out to become wild and wide lines of light emanating with energy. They illuminated everything so that, though it was night, nothing stayed hidden from Layla's sight.

"It's like the sand and the tree," Layla mumbled, though she felt unsure why she said it aloud.

Anej ran again and the chaotic world around them became a blur. Somehow, the giant avoided running into whatever would materialize before him, though he had to constantly weave left and right as he ran. "It ain't that different," Anej said, lips barely moving beneath his beard.

Layla looked at him. "Oy, you know it? It was real?"

"'Real' is one of them funny words. All I know is that it *is*."

"What—" she paused, working to loosen her jaw. Her fingers moved now too, and she gestured slowly as she spoke. "What is it?"

Anej kept quiet, and Layla wasn't sure he heard her. The velk dodged beneath a branch, but another materialized before his forehead. He slammed into it, snapping it at its base. But the branch, the trees, and the splinters all disappeared a moment later.

Anej groaned. "It's everything, I guess. Or it's the center of everything."

"Everything what?"

"Of, well, everything. All the stuff that's ever been and ever gonna be. Humans called it *Lignum Vivi* once. *Žhiofy* is how it's called over the mountain. Guess there's a name for it in Pitch too."

That didn't make sense to Layla. Anej spoke like people had known about that place, like it was somewhere others had gone. But it felt so lonely, so much like death and whatever came after. "Why haven't I heard 'bout it?"

Anej blew air from his nose, flaring his nostrils. "Complicated, lass. A thousand years of people tryin' to purge magic, mostly. But it comes back 'round. Always does."

"So it's about magic?"

"The *Žhiofy* is where all the Threads of life flow. You're connected to it now, on one end of a short piece of twine wrapped about the base of the Tree you saw. The other end is your brother. Some would say he got the better side of things."

Layla said nothing else. Every time she asked questions, she only ever got answers which dug up more questions. She was confused, and every bit of feeling that came back to her body made her hurt more and more. But Anej held her close as he ran, the smell of his sweat and the faint whiff of pipe weed filled her nose as she turned into him.

It reminded her vaguely of her father.

Eventually, she drifted to sleep.

CHAPTER
FIFTY-SIX

Léonie stepped out onto the sun-soaked street and smiled. Things were, amazingly, working out quite well. Oli would fight for her, and she hardly had to give anything away at all. For now, it was all just promises. And promises could always be broken, if need be.

A half-dozen horses were being groomed in the courtyard at the top of the hill. They were all that had been recovered from the battle. The horses had been sedated not long after they had arrived, kept in barns at the bottom of the hill and under guard. Only one barn had been left standing. Still, days of sedation had not been kind to the beasts: their flanks appeared gaunt, and their eyes bulged slightly.

But they still had horses—another miracle.

Tâl stood alone near the road leading from the courtyard and into the ruined town. She was the last of the King's Spear on this journey, and Léonie had not spoken to her since they had returned the night before. As Léonie approached the ranger, Tâl turned and knelt on one knee.

"Your Highness."

"Rise," Léonie said. "You have done well."

"Only my duty, Your Highness."

"Perhaps."

They stood in silence, Léonie squinting in the sunlight. Vultures dotted the sky, looping in wide circles above the town. Below, along the street, two dozen animals roasted above spits. Deer and boar had roamed out of the treeline and her soldiers had taken the liberty of building up their stores of meat. It would almost all become jerky for the long walk home.

"The Woodsman will fight for us," Léonie said.

"Of course, Your Highness. You have commanded it."

"Let us not pretend my words have sway over him. For now, it appears our goals are aligned. However, ours is a tenuous arrangement. One day, before this is all over, it shall not be so."

Tâl nodded, but said nothing.

Léonie looked at her, trying to see the woman with fresh eyes. She looked pretty in her way. Tough, mysterious, determined. She alone had been capable of keeping up with Oli. Something about her was kinsman to him, though Léonie could not tell what. As far as she knew, Oli had no Badaui in him.

"I have need of you," Léonie said.

"Anything, Your Highness."

Léonie frowned. "It is not a task I ask lightly. You may find it . . . disturbing."

Tâl said nothing, only shifted slightly on her feet.

Léonie continued. "You must grow close to the Woodsman. Get to know his inner thoughts, become his confidant."

Tâl tilted her head. "I think I understand."

"You *must* understand, Tâl. The survival of our kingdom teeters on the edge of a knife whose name is Oli Ricker. We must be certain this balance stays firmly in place. But the Woodsman will not grow to trust me, I fear. You must become his confidant, his friend. Let him grow to trust you, to seek your counsel."

Tâl stared at her, mouth working slowly. She could not say "no" to Léonie, of course, but she searched for some form of escape.

Léonie leaned closer. "You and he are not unalike, you must see that. Only spend time with him, share meals with him, confide in him. Make him trust you. If needed . . ."

"Share a bed with him, Your Highness?" Tâl's cheeks did not flush, though her lips thinned.

"If it comes to that," Léonie said, looking away. "I must know his wants and his fears. What drives him? We must understand him and find a way to put a leash around his neck, or eventually he will turn and bite us. And when he does, I fear we shall have no way to muzzle him."

Tâl said nothing for a long time, her breathing shallow. But eventually, she came to the only place afforded her as someone who has bent a knee to the crown. "Of course, Your Highness. What you will shall be done."

FIFTY-SEVEN

Oli stood in the doorway of Anej's cabin, Tuck at his heels. He wasn't sure why he had come, except that it was one of the few buildings surrounding Watchful which hadn't been burned down to mere cinder. It had been looted, though. Every pelt or scrap of meat was gone from the lawn outside, and inside the place had clearly been ransacked. All that remained was the velk's bed and chair, and even the chair had been toppled so someone could remove the rug beneath it.

The Yelmes would likely have just torched the place, so Oli figured it had probably been Léonie's soldiers that had stripped it bare. He couldn't blame them. They prepared for a snow-laden journey and would need all the supplies they could gather.

And Oli would be going with them. For the first time in his life, he would travel further than Riona, the small fishing town on Lake Folin. And he would do it in the company of a royal caravan. It wasn't something he had ever thought possible. He had long since settled on the fact that one day he would die in the Wood, a Stražar to the end.

He stepped over the threshold of the cabin and into the dark.

This was the last place he had been before Tâl had found him and his everything had changed. He wished Anej had never opened that door, but what was done was done. The door had opened, he had met with Léonie, had taken her to the Clearing, had watched his mother die, and had become . . . something else.

Oli stepped over to one of the windows and opened the shutter, letting light pour in and illuminate the dust in the air. Beyond the window, Oli could see the Wood and the distant Nevihta mountains beyond. Velik lay over there, past those mountains. It occurred to Oli that Anej would've looked out toward the horizon everyday, always facing his home. Was that where he took Layla: home?

Oli stirred, sensing something unfamiliar at the edge of his new senses. Tuck barked and ran outside, Oli close behind.

"You! I'll bloody kill you!" Coming up the hill towards the cabin was a one-eyed Stražar, furious and red-faced.

"Larz? What are ya doin' here?"

"Ya little arse, I'm gonna end your miserable existence." Larz pulled his knife free, though he was still half a bowshot away. The knife and the rage didn't bother Oli. This was about as Larz as Larz could get. Except, now Oli could see Larz on another, deeper level. He could see the man's Threads, and they weren't like everyone else's. He had that familiar white bunch in his center, but around the edges was a dim green which made Oli think of forest dew and rich soil.

"Huh," Oli muttered. Oli's eye, the one that wasn't black on white, had turned green when he'd woken in the clearing. A green eerily similar to the Threads running through Larz.

The old Stražar came closer now, and he clearly wasn't bluffing about killing Oli. With a roll of his shoulder, Oli brought out his own knife. "Oy," he called to Larz. "I'd not come any closer unless you mean what ya say."

"They all died 'cuz of you and your dirtbag father!" Larz picked up his pace, flipping his knife so the point was down. "And you went and did it anyway. You went and did it anyway!"

Tuck bared his teeth, but Oli tutted to calm him. "He's mine, boy. This'll be quick."

Larz never stopped moving. When he closed in on Oli, he threw out a wild swing with his off hand, then followed it up with a quick knife strike. Oli backed up to dodge the blows, then lurched forward with his own barrage. There was hardly much in the way of blocking or parrying blades. Within a handful of moments both men had cuts along their forearms and bruises along their eyes and cheeks. Oli stepped aside from a kick, then caught Larz's wrist before the older man's knife could slice into his ribs.

Oli shifted his weight and pulled Larz forward, keeping his hands firmly on Larz's knife-hand. Larz swung his fist, pounding into the side of Oli's head. But Oli ignored it, jamming his knife into Larz's gut as he pulled him closer. It felt almost intimate, the way they stood: holding one another tight like brothers, Larz's blood running down Oli's fingers.

Larz grunted as Oli pushed him away, leaving his knife in the man's stomach.

Oli spit blood onto the ground. "Oy, what were ya sayin' about my pa?"

"I was sayin'" Larz paused, staring at the knife handle in his gut. "That he's got as much blood on his hands as you."

Oli shook his head. "I don't know what your problem is with me, Larz. What did ya think I had to do with anything? I was a bloody *kid*! You think I had a choice? I was the only one without a choice! Every other Stražar chose whether or not they wanted in, *except me!*" Oli screamed down at Larz who'd fallen to his knees, holding his belly around the knife blade. Blood ran between his fingers.

Red lights danced in Oli's vision, swirling around his clenched fist.

"Ya should've died too," Larz said, coughing. "At least then things would've been even."

Oli snorted. "Oy, is that it then? The son pays for the sins of the father?"

"Didn't my son die? His should too."

Oli dropped to a knee beside Larz, leaning forward so they were face to face. "Ya see this?" Oli pointed to his eye, the one which was white and black. "I'm payin' the price, Larz. You have no idea the price I'm payin'. And you—" Oli reached forward and ripped his blade from Larz's stomach. Larz coughed and groaned, doubling over onto the ground. "You're gonna hang around and pay the price with me. A failure of a son and a failure of a father."

The white and green Threads in Larz's body were broken where the knife had cut through, but Oli had the red Threads of power again. He tried with Larz what he had done without thinking with Tuck. He threw the red cords into Larz's mess of tangled life strings. He had little understanding of what happened, but he watched the red knit themselves into the broken sections of white and green. Larz gasped for air and lurched on the ground.

And the blood stopped pouring out of his stomach, leaving only an angry, red, scar.

Oli spat on the ground beside Larz. "Pack up whatever it is you're bringin' and be ready to march. We're leavin' this place for good, and you're comin' with."

Oli marched off back towards Watchful, letting Larz cough and curse behind him. Oli wasn't sure how, but he knew Larz would follow. He had guessed it with Tuck. Ever since Oli healed him, Oli had been able to faintly sense whatever Tuck could. But it was more than that: Oli didn't need the old commands any longer. A deeper connection had formed, one tied to those red Threads.

And Oli bet it would work with Larz too.

You are a natural, darling.

Oli didn't bother with a reply to Staradovna. He was stuck with her in his mind—the price he paid for this power. But he wouldn't be her puppet. He would use this power to bury every Yelmes in Trevelar and then he would find a way to kill her too. Afterwards, he would find his sister and they would go somewhere, anywhere, and have peace.

But he had to fight a war first.

CHAPTER
FIFTY-EIGHT

Layla walked beneath the light of the morning sun, her body back under her own control. Everything hurt, but outwardly every wound she had endured had healed, leaving behind only red scars beneath the rips in her clothing. She didn't understand how that could be, especially when she looked at the frail and fading form of Ulian, still in Anej's arms.

But she understood nothing anymore.

Sometime during the night, Anej had gotten them to the other side of that strange world they had delved into. They were now on the foothills of the Nevihta mountains. If the Yelmes had followed them, there was no sign of them now.

Since waking, the true impact of what happened to her had sunk in. She had lost control of herself, had *been controlled*. Now, atop of every other growing fear and anxiety, loomed the knowledge that she could be possessed at any moment.

Would it happen again? Would there be a moment when something else takes control of her and waves her hand, like before, suddenly ending life? Next time, would it be more Yelmes who die, or Anej? When she had asked the velk, he had said they were safe. He had said Oli had done it, and probably in order to protect her. But Layla wouldn't believe him. She couldn't stomach the thought that Oli, of all people, would do that to her.

Layla's boots crunched against a thin layer of snow. It was growing colder with every step they took. She pulled her cloak tighter and stepped into the footprints of Anej, where he had packed the snow tight so dried grass and dirt poked through.

It didn't escape her mind that their trail would be easy enough for even a child to follow. If the Dark Ones still pursued them, they'd know where to go for certain. Anej wasn't even bothering to hide their destination with zig zags or false trails. He aimed directly at the looming maw between two mountain peaks—what Anej called Ũzky Pass.

"He's still alive," Anej said, turning to her as he shifted Ulian in his arms.

"That's good," Layla said, unsure if she meant it. She wanted Ule to live, but she wasn't sure it would be a mercy to the poor bartender to try and drag him over the mountains like this. Layla saw little chance he'd make it, and death now might be a mercy. But Layla wouldn't say that aloud.

Why the velk tried so hard, Layla couldn't fathom. Her, Ulian, Watchful . . . he seemed a slave to keeping everyone else alive. It made no sense. He should've left by himself and just gone home, letting her and the world burn. Instead, he pounded the snow before her and made her steps that much easier.

"Ow," Layla said, grabbing at her head. She felt like someone had just punched her in the chin.

Anej turned around, narrowing his eyes. "Your brother, I'd guess."

"What?"

"Someone's hurt him. The pain goes both ways now."

"Oy, great," Layla muttered. She prayed to Deōs for Oli, but it was more because of reflex than belief. If a Maker existed, he didn't seem to be one who answered prayers.

"We'll stop soon and give ya rest," Anej said. "I remember a cave up ahead somewhere. Camped there before."

"When you were on your way to Watchful?"

Anej shook his head. "I never meant to go to Watchful. That was always a mistake. One in a long line."

Layla swallowed her questions and wiped her nose with the back of her hand. It came away bloody. A faint headache formed behind her eyes, and she had a feeling she knew what that meant: Oli was pulling power from her. Had it been Ulian who'd first asked how much of this she could take? She wished she had an answer to that question. Would it grow worse? Would the nose bleed become a river one day, draining her dry of her lifeblood? And if Oli were fighting right now and died . . . would her life be snuffed out? Was she just steps away from collapsing, dead?

Anej stopped and turned. His steps had grown slower by the hour, and finally he looked as if he may be unable to go further. The velk had bundled Ulian up beneath his coat like an infant. Flakes of newly fallen snow dusted Anej's coat and settled in his beard.

"If you get far enough away, it almost looks peaceful," Anej said, looking beyond her.

Layla turned and her spine shivered in wonder. The barren tree-tops of the Wood stretched on for miles, and beyond she could see the hills surrounding her home. Watchful was a series of black and brown dots obscured by the smoke rising from the forest below.

The fire set by the Yelmes Anej had killed.

"Will the fire burn forever?" Layla asked.

"Just until snowfall. Though, I suspect much of the forest will be gone by then. A fitting end."

"What do you mean?"

"Nothing," Anej said with a sigh. "We better keep movin'. Oh, and grab what sticks ya can along the way, eh? Won't be any trees up in the pass and we'll need a fire."

Layla nodded, turning to follow Anej as he began moving again. "Anej," she said. "Will they catch us again?"

"Aye," the velk said after a moment. "They know where we're off to. This stretch of land will be their last chance, and they'll claw like desperate rats to take it."

"Last chance to kill me?"

Anej nodded. "Your brother will only grow more powerful. Killing you now is the easiest path forward for them. End your life and they end his."

Layla didn't bother saying anything else. She knew now that Anej wouldn't always be able to defend her. Even he could be outnumbered, outmatched. She only prayed he was right, and that if they could get across the mountains and the river they'd be safe.

Her hand fell to her sword, but clutched only air. She'd dropped it when she had tumbled down the hill, and Anej hadn't thought to grab it. It didn't matter though. It had hardly helped her the last time. She may have been able to chop down dazed and wounded enemies Anej sent her way, but she was less than capable in a true fight.

"Why?" Layla said, voice quiet, almost hoping Anej wouldn't hear.

"Why what?"

She swallowed, thinking maybe she shouldn't say anything, just let the moment pass. But she wanted to know, wanted to understand. "Why are you doing this? Why are you tryin' to save me? Why not just . . . just go home and leave me. They won't fight you if you aren't with me."

Anej slowed and turned, eyes searching Layla's. "Is that what you want?"

"No, but why does that matter? What I want, I mean."

"Maybe it doesn't."

"What do *you* want? You don't want to fight, I can see that. You don't like it."

"I don't. But . . ." he sighed. "Look, askin' what I want just isn't the right question."

"Then what is?"

Anej's shoulders slumped. "I used to think I knew. Now, I've stopped asking questions altogether. I don't know why I'm helpin' you, lass. And that's the truth of it. I just know I should and so I am."

Layla put a hand on Anej's arm. Even through the heavy wool he wore, she could feel the warmth of his body. She thought maybe she could see the hundreds of miles he'd traveled, the lifetimes he'd lived, and it felt right to say nothing at all.

Anej snorted, air steaming from his nostrils in the cold. "We better keep movin' and get Ule near a fire."

Layla nodded, then fell in behind Anej, trudging up the mountains and following in his steps.

EPILOGUE

THE PRINCE

Prince Bastien sat back in his chair, the velvet fabric of the seat's cushion rustling softly against his shoulders. In front of him stood a side table made of ornately carved wood and embossed with gold leaf around its edges. In fact, every piece of furniture within the spacious room had been handcrafted with meticulous detail, from the windswept sails carved into the marble of the fireplace mantle to the subtle clouds painted on the domed ceiling above. Even the four posts of the bed had been carved to give the impression of being reeds swayed in an invisible wind.

The prince noticed none of it.

He had focused all of his attention on the simple wooden board made of square spaces in a ten by ten pattern and filled with dozens of figurines.

It was Pado, a traditional game of strategy amongst the Badaui. The board was broken up into four sections, each five squares by five squares. Those four sections represented the four seas, and within each section the two players' "ships"—represented by the game pieces—waged battle. Alongside the board lay a deck of aged cards. After each set of turns, a player took a card from the deck and laid beside a section of the board, representing the sailing condition for that sea and affecting the movement of pieces within the corresponding five by five section.

It had been described to him as simple to learn. Currently, he disagreed with that assessment. *This is*, he thought wryly, *rather much.*

He had always been drawn to games of strategy, and every culture had a predominant one. Here, in the Bada Republic, Pado was played as something like a rite of passage for school age children, a fact which did little to encourage the Trevlarian prince. Pado was like the culture that had created it: deceptively nuanced and complex.

Beside the deck of cards, a small cup of dark coffee steamed. After a long moment looking at the board, Bastien leaned forward and moved one of his smaller ships to an adjacent tile, then grabbed the coffee cup and sat back once more.

"Your turn, I believe," Bastien said, then gingerly took a sip. The coffee had been well made, a smoothness covering a small host of delightful flavors.

Across from him, Ambassador Susho sat with her hands gently holding her own cup of coffee, eyes looking through its wisps of steam to the board below. Bastien thought her attractive, by Badaui standards. Her skin was as dark as the coffee she sipped, without blemish or wrinkles despite being the prince's senior by a decade at least. She had weaved the strands of her hair into braids that fell around her narrow shoulders, adorning the braids with small threads of pure silver. Like all Badaui, she was thin and lithe, her every motion both quick and careful. The Badaui were not generally taller than someone from Trevelar, but their thin frames gave them that appearance.

Susho smiled before locking her eyes on Bastien and gently shaking her head. The way the points of her teeth gleamed in the early morning sunlight gave her a predatory look which both unnerved and allured Bastien. "One day," she said slowly, "you will learn to play with your eyes . . . open."

She leaned forward then and took a stubby little piece from the "North" quadrant of the board and moved it into the "East" quadrant, pinning Bastien's Flag Ship and spelling certain doom within a matter of moves.

"Well," Bastien said with a chuckle, waving a hand in acknowledged defeat. "I should not be surprised, ambassador. I doubt any of the king's house could best one of the Badaui with the smell of ocean air drifting in from the window."

"Hmm," Susho mused, taking a sip. "Perhaps next time, young prince. The day is early, and you await the Chancellor's call. Perhaps your mind is simply . . . preoccupied."

Bastien nodded in appreciation for the small extension of grace. Though the prince did not feel it necessary, Ambassador Susho was compelled to provide him ways to maintain his honor in the face of minor embarrassments, such as losing a game of Pado. It served as a sign of respect and kindness, though Prince Bastien would have instead preferred the Chancellor's commitment of troops and supplies.

One step at a time.

"Speaking of the Chancellor's summons, you do not happen to know when that will be?"

Susho frowned. "I do not. Exceptions abound for you, Prince of Trevelar. Three days, one after the other, the Chancellor has given you her first counsel of the day. I have not seen this before, and I am unsure if it will last."

"It *must* last," Bastien leaned forward and caught a gentle whiff of the ambassador's perfume, which threatened to make him as heady as a schoolboy. "Our meetings cannot end until Trevelar has what it needs to keep Turris Regis out of the hands of Kātsracha."

"Perhaps," Susho sighed.

"It is true," Bastien urged. "Imagine, ambassador, the borders of Kātsracha expanded and with access to the Great Harbor. How long will it be until they sail along the coast, burning as they go? By next winter they would be raining lightning and fire down onto your ships, setting your sails and hulls alight, tossing the stones of your great palace back into the sea." Bastien waved his hand about as he spoke, gesturing to the palace in which they now sat.

Susho nodded slowly, "Perhaps, prince, but it is not I who you need to convince."

"And that . . . is all too true." Bastien stood, pacing towards the windows on the other side of the room. "But the Chancellor is not an easy woman to persuade. It is all 'perhaps' and 'that could be' and on and on."

"She waits to see how the conditions are on the seas. She practices wisdom, Prince Bastien. It is what the Senate expects of her. It is what our people expect as well."

It is cowardice, Bastien thought, but kept those words to himself.

Out the northern facing window, he could see the familiar blue horizon of the sea. To the left, the early morning sun yawned its light over the city of Hanigu, the capital of Bada. Below, a city of white stone and golden domed rooftops stretched out far and wide, ending only where the foaming waves began. The Seraph Isles would be visible when the morning fog subsided.

This city will burn like Worchestern, Bastien thought, his memories of fire and ash transposing themselves onto the cityscape below.

Bastien half turned toward Susho, who still lingered in her chair across from the Pado board. "You have lived amongst our people for many years now, a liaison between your republic and our kingdom. Trade has been good, no? The gold has flowed, our people have been at peace, we reinforced your borders when tensions rose with Velik . . ." Bastien's voice trailed off. He scratched at his chin, feeling the freshly shaven skin there and picking lightly at a small scab.

Susho said nothing. She had set her coffee down and folded her hands in her lap, eyeing the prince with an expression that gave nothing away.

"Tell me," Bastien continued. "Do you think our people are worth saving?"

Susho cocked her head to the side, her eyes becoming distant. "I do think your people are worth saving," she said finally, nodding her head as she spoke. "I am simply unsure if they are capable of being saved."

Bastien's face flushed with anger and embarrassment, and he turned back to the sea with forced control so as not to give her the impression he was offended. Yet when he searched himself, he found he *was* offended—and deeply so. The ambassador's words struck a chord, insinuating weakness where there should be strength. Bastien worked through potential rebuttals in his mind, thinking through which ones he should try out on Susho in case the Chancellor said something similar.

A knock rattled the door of his chambers.

He turned towards the door as it was opened by one of his guards glancing into his chambers. In a world of thin and airy clothing, a pair of heavily armored guards in the royal orange looked clunky, odd, and reassuring.

"My lord," Captain Tinriel said, his voice sharp and alert despite the first rays of sunlight. "The Chancellor requests your presence with haste."

"With haste?" Bastien asked, looking at Susho who looked equally confused. "Did she say why?"

"No, my lord. Should I tell her messenger that—"

"We're coming, Captain. Tell the messenger to lead the way."

Bastien stepped into a large, dome-shaped room he had never seen. Perhaps twenty-five yards in diameter, it lay empty of any furnishings. The curved walls were painted carefully in dark blue and white, an imitation of the night sky. At the center of the ceiling was a window, the only source of light. Bastien imagined at noon the sun would shine down directly into the center of the room, though he was unsure why that would be important.

Around the edges of the room stood small clusters of strangely dressed Badaui. Instead of the tight-fitting clothing worn by most, these wore flowing robes of pure white which trailed behind them. Where most of the stations of government were dominated by women, these were all men. And strange ones at that. They bore thick beards and had unruly hair, a fashion unheard of amongst the Badaui politicians and commoners who preferred clean shaven faces and pristinely trimmed hairlines.

Bastien recognized them only from rumors. They were the *Seongiga*, the priests of the Jegja Jumun, the religious order of the republic. Outsiders were not allowed within the temple or the holy places of the Jegja Jumun. One of these priests knelt in the middle of the room, head bowed. Though he faced away from the prince, Bastien could see his back rising and falling slightly with ragged breaths.

Bastien turned to Susho as she came into the room behind him. "What is this?" he asked in a whisper.

Susho looked about quickly, then dropped her head in something like shame or reverence. She spoke as quietly as she could, so much so Bastien nearly missed her words. "This is a holy place, Prince Bastien. Bow your head, quick."

Bastien did so, dropping his gaze to the floor where his glossy black boots shone in the faint light of the room. He stayed like that for a long moment, totally unsure of himself and wondering if he was being made the fool.

And then Chancellor Jiah stepped into the room, her slippers hardly making a noise as she strode past Bastien saying, "Arise, prince."

Bastien raised his head and followed the Chancellor with his eyes as she strode through the room to stand next to the priest at its center. She was old, even by Badaui standards, her olive skin wrinkled with age and her eyes heavy with burdens. Still, she stood tall and confident, a dominating force in the room.

"Tell me, do you know where you are?" Her voice sounded like a song, gentle and rhythmic. She looked at Bastien, awaiting an answer.

"No, Chancellor Jiah, I do not."

Jiah nodded. "You stand in the center of the palace. It is a holy place, one where no outsider has ever stepped. This is an unprecedented moment, Prince Bastien, I want you to understand that."

Bastien nodded but kept his mouth firmly shut lest he open it and say something dreadfully stupid.

"Here kneels Dal, one of the priests of our order. Morning and night, at all hours of every day, one of the priests kneels in this very spot and prays to God on our behalf. Sometimes, when our god so chooses, he makes his ways known to our priests, often through the one who kneels here." She gestured to the center of the room. "Half of an hour ago, Dal was enraptured with a vision . . . or, so we believe."

Bastien said nothing. Every question he could think to ask felt wrong, as though any one of them could set off a whole slew of diplomatic problems. Silence often proved best in times like these.

"This vision, if true, changes everything we have understood about your war with Kātsracha." She stepped forward as she spoke, her eyes narrowed on Bastien. "It changes what is at stake, who is involved, and even the scope of the conflict."

Jiah let silence hang in the room as she slowly stepped closer to the prince. Bastien didn't mean to speak up, but before he could help it, he asked, "I do not understand, Chancellor. What is this vision you speak of? What new information has come to light?"

Jiah frowned. When she spoke, she closed her eyes as though to distance herself from the words. "The Ancient One is loosed on La'Azurus again, Prince Bastien. And that may spell doom for us all."

ACKNOWLEDGMENTS

Once upon a time, I thought writing was a solitary activity. Something one did with the aroma of coffee in the air, rain drizzling outside, and all was quiet in the house (or perhaps a perfect hum of noise from the background café). With the rise of independently published books and Generative AI, I'm sure this solitary practice is true for many.

It was not for me and this book.

More than a dozen people have come alongside me to bring *The Tragedy of Oli Ricker* to fruition. They have lent their time and attention, their skills and expertise, often for nothing in return but my deepest gratitude.

I do not, and have never, deserved such love and support. What follows is my best attempt to ensure the memory of their contribution lives on as long as this book does.

First, to my amazing editing team.

To Kaylee, who was the first person to ever read *Oli* with an editing eye. Without you we would have a far more simplistic book, free of the nuance and complexity these characters deserve. Thank you for creating space to dream together.

To Emily Whitten, thank you for coming alongside me and The Living Room Disciple as a whole. I didn't (embarrassingly) know an em dash apart from a hyphen before you came along. This book would have been a grammatical mess without you.

And to Leilah Wright, thank you for going the distance on this project, from early chapter reads in The End writer's group, to heading up Living Tome Publishing and bringing this to fruition. You have forced me deeper into intentionality with my words and have encouraged me every step along the way. We will be reviewing your debut soon (and I better appear on your Acknowledgments page).

And to all the others in The End writer's group: Kim, Charliy, and John. You have encouraged me more than I could ever possibly convey. Thank you.

To Emilie at EAH Creative, thank you for bringing our amazing cover to life. Taking a vague image that exists in the imagination of another human and bringing it onto the page is no simple thing, but you managed it beautifully.

To Austin, who not only read an early draft but has been an amazing friend for nearly two decades (we're getting old). Never have you stopped encouraging me, and I will never be able to convey just how grateful I have been for you.

And to Eric, who first said "I'll do it with you" when I threw out this crazy idea about The Living Room Disciple. You have stuck around through all its forms and shapes, and you have unfailingly supported this newest iteration. Thank you for being so excited for *Oli* and for what God has for us in the future.

But more than all the others, my wife and children have leaned in and pushed me forward in this journey.

To my boys, Henry, Caleb, Owen, and Luke, thank you. You four inspire me with your imaginations and push me to be a better man. Thank you, Luke for reading an early draft of *Oli* (without permission) and telling everyone your favorite book was "the one my dad wrote." And thank you to Owen, for sitting in my lap on those long days as I read (and re-read) drafts to myself aloud. And to each of you for starting a book fundraiser and being the first financial backers of this venue. The small coins you put into that paper bag had more eternal significance than you can ever have imagined.

And to Brittany. Without you there would be no *Oli* at all, for you alone read those earliest (awful) drafts and chided me for giving up. It is for you that I picked up Oli's tale again. Always, I write to you as my audience, hoping to make you fall in love with Oli, Layla, and Léonie. I cannot say how grateful I am that you have stayed with me through every adventure the Lord has sent us on. May we always dance through minefields together.

And to you, reader, for whom this book was written. Thank you for every word read and every page turned. I pray this story blesses you and finds its place as one drop in the river of your imagination.

ABOUT THE AUTHOR

Like all children at heart, Phillip Snyder loves stories. Also like all children at heart, he loves people. Phillip lives in the Nashville area and spends his days writing both fantastical stories as well as essays about the intersection of the imagination and spiritual formation. You can find his writing on Substack by searching "The Living Room Disciple". He is beyond blessed to live with his wonderful wife, Brittany, and their four amazing boys.